Slipping behind the door, he watched Antoinette's silhouette behind the clear plastic curtain and admired the way the steam billowed like clouds around her. Oh, yes, he was definitely in Heaven.

"I promised I'd wash your back," he said quietly, waiting for her permission to step into the tub. Her wide grin answered all of his unspoken questions, and he cautiously stepped in around her within the tiny confines.

She turned and stared at him, still smiling. Water flowed over her body and caressed her breasts, making her entire sheath of cinnamon coffee-colored skin shimmer. He touched her face and held her cheek as he watched the water turn what was once her ponytail into a cascade of rich dark-chocolate tendrils about her shoulders. The sight of her slowly lathering the soap between her palms made him draw his breath. "God.... you are absolutely beautiful..." Words escaped him as she began applying the suds in a rhythmic circular motion to his chest.

Indigo Sensuous Love Stories

Genesis Press, Inc.
315 Third Avenue North
Columbus, MS 39701

Still Waters Run Deep

ISBN: 1-58571-068-7
Manufactured in the United States of America

First Edition

Still Waters Run Deep

by

Leslie Esdaile

Genesis Press, Inc.

DEDICATION

Be gentle to one another... as we never know how deep another human being's waters run. We don't know where another person's scars are hidden, or how long they have been secreted away by what appears to be a still surface of calm

This book is thus dedicated to those people in my life who did not have to be told, or have things explained before lending compassion and assistance-they simply knew... and they loved me just the same, scars and all, and yet allowed me to preserve my personal dignity in the process.

To Father God, for loving me, healing me, and giving His angels charge to protect me, even when I didn't realize their blessings, or was blind to their Divine Intervention...

To my husband, Al, who always in the end, washed away the hurts...

To my daughter, Helena, who showed me the beauty of unconditional love...

To my mother, Helen L. T. Peterson, for giving me life, love, wisdom, and hope... and for showing me what steadfast Grace looks like.

Thank You All for Keeping The Faith, and Keeping Me in Your Light!

Chapter 1

The smell of bacon, sausage, and coffee filled Jerome Henderson's nose as he rolled over and stretched in the sun. It took a moment to orient himself in the massive king-size bed that had swallowed him whole during his sleep. Never in his life had he slept in such luxury, next to skin so soft, and on sheets so perfectly matched to the real purpose of a bed—sleep and love-making. His body hurt in a good way, and he hoisted himself up with help from the brass headboard. He could hear Toni moving about in the kitchen, and total satisfaction washed over him like the warm rays of sun that covered the spread. She'd even left a fresh set of towels on the foot of the bed for him. This was definitely the royal treatment, something he'd always envisioned sharing with her.

Swinging his legs over the side of the bed, he stood on wobbly limbs and bent over for a moment to let the blood flow back into his brain. His whole skeleton felt like it was made out of rubber.

"Six times in one night?" he chuckled as he grabbed the towel and washcloth and went into the bathroom. Never in his life. But thinking of the night before with Toni brought a new central ache to his frame. God, it had been fantastic. All he needed was a little water on his face, some toothpaste, and then he'd have to remind her not to get out of bed so soon—not when he was ready to salute her with a wake-up call.

Jerome peered down at himself and chuckled again as he flushed the toilet. Oh, yeah, Toni was going to kill him before he reached forty-five.

"Morning, baby," he murmured as he walked through the condo living room toward her in the kitchen, adjusting the towel around his waist. He could feel a big grin pushing it's way to his face as he looked at her dark, tousled hair and the way her tall, lush body swayed beneath her silk robe. Her heavy breasts offered a hypnotic focal point under the flimsy garment, rivaled only by the trance of her wide hips and high, round behind. God he loved the way she felt, and the way her beautiful cinnamon skin looked without makeup in the natural sunlight streaming through the picture windows. The way it made her rich brown eyes shimmer...

"Missed you," he whispered as he neared her and stole a kiss from her neck, inhaling her fragrance and closing his eyes to the sensory pleasure of it.

"Your coffee's ready."

Something was wrong. Definitely wrong. He knew Antoinette Reeves Wellington. His Toni was normally warmth personified. This morning, she was not. What had happened in the few hours between the mind-blowing, all-night lovemaking they'd shared, and this morning?

She had answered him without emotion, and hadn't responded to his kiss. Last night a mere kiss from him could elicit the kind of groan from her that made shivers go down his spine.

Jerome took the coffee mug from her and sat down at the kitchenette table. He watched her carefully. He'd been here before. A mysterious woman-temperature shift had occurred. Somewhere, somehow, during the night she had changed— and she had never answered his marriage proposal. This was obviously going to be a cold-light-of-day aftermath. Somehow, he knew it was coming.

"What's the matter?" he said after taking a steady sip. "It's all over your face. What did I do wrong?"

"You didn't do anything wrong, Jay," she said without looking at him. "How do you want your eggs?"

"It doesn't matter. I'm not hungry," he lied as the smell of bacon made his stomach growl.

"After last night?"

"Okay, I am a little hungry. But can't you just sit down for a minute and talk to me?"

"No. I can't sit down. I think better when I work. I got it from my Aunt Pearline," she muttered.

"Okay. Then, let's take it from the top," he said quietly, concern churning the coffee in his gut. "What happened from the time I had my last epileptic seizure in your arms and went comatose, three hours later until I woke up?

The fact that she offered a lopsided smile helped a lot, and he took another sip of the steaming brew. Maybe it was some hormonal thing? That would be the best case scenario. He didn't want to think about the worst-case possibilities.

"Do you remember what you asked me last night?" she said moving about at a dizzying pace in the kitchen. "Do you?"

Jerome relaxed and let out a deep breath. "Of course I do. Is that it? You think I forgot that I just asked you to marry me while in the throes?" He stood up and walked over to her, and took both of her hands in his. "Do you still have that ring I gave you a long time ago? The one with jade and little diamonds."

Seeming annoyed, she withdrew her hands from his and paced back and forth within the small confines of the kitchen. "Of course I do. I kept it for twenty years, Jay! I gave it to my sister to hold for me when I got married." Hot tears spilled from her eyes and she wiped her nose with the back of her hand and spun around toward the sink.

Antoinette immediately snatched a bowl and began cracking eggs, but wouldn't face him. "Go sit down. How do you want your eggs?"

Perplexed, he folded his arms over his chest and leaned against the wall. "I'll give you a diamond as soon as—"

"A diamond! A diamond? Are you crazy?" she whispered through her teeth, turning around quickly to face him.

He could only look at her. Toni's voice had become strident and her actions to beat the eggs into submission in the bowl fascinated him.

"Scrambled is fine," he said trying to lighten her mood and draw her out. Years of practice with his soon-to-be-ex-wife, Karen, had made him a pro at reading cryptograms.

"Good," she snapped, sloshing the eggs in the pan. "I'm glad you like them scrambled."

"Toni, you are not making any sense," he finally conceded as she buzzed by him to pull the biscuits out of the oven.

"Not making sense? Not making sense!"

"Baby, you're repeating yourself. Listen to you. What. Is. The. Matter?"

"You come back after twenty years, okay!" she exclaimed, waving a hot tray of biscuits, "then you don't want to just date, or find out if we even know each other—ooooooohhhh, noooo—you want to get married! Are you crazy?" Antoinette shook her head and her eyes held an expression of sheer panic.

"No. I'm crazy," she said with a hysterical laugh. "I was celibate for two years, trying to live the quiet life, trying to stay focused, reading all my girlfriends the riot act about the need for discipline and logic. Then I run into an old flame, and do a total melt down—and I'm making breakfast. I have lost my mind. A six-foot-plus, cinderblock-toting, construction working, no body fat having, half-Cherokee-half-African-American, testosterone sportin' man from my past, is standing in my kitchen with a towel on. He's graying at the temples in the most distinguished fashion, and saying, 'I missed you baby.'"

Her assessment of him burned his face and warmed him immensely. "What's my ethnic heritage got to do with it?" He chuckled. "We go way back, T. Dag. I didn't know you was like that."

Antoinette rolled her gaze up and sucked her teeth. "Man, shut up." Lord, I know what I'm supposed to do, but I keep looking at his chest, and his towel—like a junkie. I'm tryin' to make this make sense, even to myself. I'm looking at his mouth, and those intense, dark eyes set off by those high cheekbones I always loved, with burnished bronze skin that makes me want to jump outta mine. Here I am standing in my kitchen, with my child due home in a few hours, and I'm getting wet, tryin' to figure out what truck hit me last night. I am losing my damned mind here! "Jay, don't start no more mess. Go home."

"But, baby—"

"You have just left a wife a month ago—who threw you out for God only knows why—because I would have hung onto you with a grappling hook after what you did to me last night. But, while I'm out minding my own business, you bump into me and we rekindle this high school love affair.

Mind you, I just got divorced myself, by the way, and you have four kids, and I have a child, which makes five. Good thing none of them heard or saw any of this! So, we can't do this any more—and can't expect other people to watch them even if we wanted to concoct a reason to do this—but that's beside the point. I'm broke, and you're broke, and I loved you so much, and now you've got me hooked on you again, and all I wanted to do last night was go to the video store and rent a damned movie. But nooooo. I have to bump into you at the video store, and you had to be looking all fine, and whatnot, then you fall asleep, and I say to myself, 'good—God knows what He's doing. But nooooo, you can't just leave sleeping dogs lie! Then you come over here, and make love to me six times in one night—six times, Jay! Every hour, on the hour, like a madman—wilder than when we were in high school!" Antoinette paced away from him, waving her free hand.

He smiled as he watched her. "It was good, wasn't it, baby?"

"And, then, you politely ask me to marry you?" she raved, ignoring his comment, "And, I'm supposed to say nooo, but I want to say yes. I'm thirty-seven, and I'm supposed to know better than that crazy mess. Like love can solve all the problems we'd face! Are you crazy? My best girlfriend isn't even speaking to me, from before we did it—all because she thinks I'm home-wrecking, which I'm not. You left your wife before we hooked up, but that doesn't matter. But now...now we've really done it!"

"Done what?"

"Had sex!"

"Made love," he chuckled.

"You are splitting hairs, Jerome Henderson!" she shrieked.

"Oh, baby," he breathed, loving the way her voluptuous form swayed under the fabric and remembering the velvet feel of her skin, "you got out of bed too early."

"No, I didn't!" she snapped, her voice modulating between a laugh and true fussing. "I didn't get out of bed soon enough. I'm not trying to be a home wrecker. Had it done to me, and ain't trying to come between you and—"

"My home was already wrecked. You didn't do that. All you did was make love to the man that asked you to marry him twenty years ago, and who loves you to this day."

"Jerome Henderson, I slept with you last night—"

"—No, baby," he crooned with a chuckle. "You didn't sleep that much."

"And—and all I have as a raggedy excuse for

losing my mind at thirty-seven—when I'm supposed to know better—is a stupid dream that I had the day you first came by. Do you follow?"

She had cut him an evil glare in response to his teasing comment, then as she made her point, her eyes held a pleading quality to them. Her expression made him want to pull her next to him and kiss her, but he thought she might have a stroke if he did, given the way she was flinging one hand about and pacing.

"You had a dream about me? Wow," he murmured, "I thought it was just me having it bad for you. I used to have them all the time. C'mere, baby."

"Yes. No. It was a premonition. That's not what I'm talking about!"

It was all he could do not to laugh. She looked so beautifully crazy, wild in the eyes, and good enough to sop up with one of her biscuits. "I love you too, baby."

"Stop it!" she yelled, ignoring the ringing telephone and losing one of the biscuits from the tray. "We don't have anywhere to put five kids, any money to get married—we don't even know each other. Who am I, Jerome Henderson? You have no idea of what a trip I can be, and I don't know squat about you. Twenty years has gone by, and we're not in high school. We are not the same people any more!"

"Maybe we've had some experiences that might have changed us a little," he admitted, growing more serious. She did have a point. "You've always been used to better than I could provide. I guess I can't expect—"

"—See. You don't know me!" Antoinette paced over to the table and flung the biscuits in a basket. "You don't even know why we broke up, do you? Do you want jelly?"

"I want you to sit down," he said quietly, moving to the table and taking a seat.

Antoinette paced back over to the stove and flipped off the burner under the eggs then checked the breakfast meats. "Listen. My mother's sister married a man who was from the hood. He was tall, fine, and street smart. But he also had a propensity for the ladies and treated my aunt like dirt. She was seventeen when she ran off with him, and she and her father—my grandfather—fell out with each other till the end of time over it. My aunt died young, and left five little kids. Only the oldest girl and Nessa ever made it through, and that was with a lot of heartache and pain."

"But you and I never did get married at seventeen, baby. I'm not following what that has to do with now? We're grown."

"Hear me out, Jay," she murmured, using his pet name in a way that was hard for him to ignore."

"All right..."

Antoinette took a deep breath. "My father ran with those guys for a while until one by one they settled down. He saw them in you, and was afraid for me. He thought you'd dog me the way my mother's sister got dogged, and he couldn't trust that it wouldn't happen to me—history might repeat itself, in his mind. He wasn't willing to gamble on that when I was a teenager. Neither was I—not after hearing all of the stories told over and over again in the family, and seeing what one false move for love could do to generations."

"But we're grown now."

She didn't answer.

Pieces of an elaborate jigsaw puzzle began to shift in Jerome's mind, and he waited and watched and let Antoinette speak. He'd needed to hear this twenty years ago. He had needed to know that it wasn't about pedigree or college; it was about the streets he ran. But, better late than never, he figured. Then again, he wondered if she had known this then, and had never shared it? Or, was this simply a combination of age, new family information, and wisdom that provided Toni this insight now? He'd never know for sure, but would always wonder what would have happened if they both knew then what she was telling him now?

"My father was scared to death that I'd end up like Mom's sister, and her sister's girls," Antoinette finally murmured, picking at the edge of the sink with her fingernail. "So he wasn't willing to gamble on your integrity factor—like the way me and Mom were."

"Your Pop wasn't willing to bet the everything he loved, the maximum. I can understand that now, especially with daughter's of my own."

He could see her tearing again as she turned to slap the overdone eggs on a platter. "The bacon is burning," he said quietly, moving to help her take the pan from the flame. "Then why didn't you say yes, if you and your Mom had all of this belief in me?"

Again Antoinette brushed past him and she set the platter down on the table very precisely.

"Because, I was seventeen. And because, I couldn't tell which way you'd turn out either, and I was afraid to gamble at that age. I knew that as long as there was breath in my body, I could make sure my kids didn't live in squalor, no matter how many of them I had. But I couldn't take the other stuff—like the drinking, and gambling, and women." She stared at him and didn't blink. Her eyes held him in-state as she took him back in time. "Remember what I saw when I caught the bus down to Dover Air Force Base?"

He couldn't look at her and he went deeper into the kitchen and refreshed his coffee. Antoinette followed him, and it was his turn to avoid the conversation. He'd started it. Now she was obviously going to finish it. Perhaps he should have just let her fix him breakfast.

"Jerome," she said quietly, allowing her hand to rest on his back while he added sugar and half-n-half to his mug, "We had been apart for three months and I caught the bus down to Dover—thirteen hours from Ithaca, New York. While I was in school, I was surrounded by these nerdy, corny guys. I couldn't wait to see my baby... I was all excited, missed you so much... was horny as hell, and couldn't wait to be in your arms. It was all I could think about. Could hardly study."

He paced away from her and sipped his coffee as he walked back to the table. His insides churned at the memory of what youth, impatience, and his own foolishness for listening to the fellas had done to what they'd had. Hell, yeah, he remembered. It was a nightmare, not a good dream. His innocent Toni had gotten off the bus and waited for him, but he was in the throes of a craps game in the back of some off-base bar.

She'd taken a cab to the tavern he'd mentioned in his letters, hoping to find him, and had searched for him—but not before bumping into a sideline sister, a local who had helped him get through the lonely nights. And, she'd told his Toni everything. "That was a long time ago, baby—"

"—I had a real man," she went on, not letting him finish his statement, "not some little college boy." Her eyes were filled with the same hurt that had appeared in them twenty years prior. "Then, I finally got there, to The Base, and my real man was as drunk as Cooter-Brown, had this new crowd of people—who cussed, and fought, and drank worse than I'd ever seen. And he'd even had another woman," she said with a sigh, folding her arms over her bosom as she stared at him. "So, I saw my aunt's life flash before my eyes, and I turned-tail and ran back to school—crying all the way to campus for thirteen hours on the bus. That's why we really broke up, Jay. I loved you enough to give you anything—to go against family, my father, whatever... but I'd never give you my life. I wouldn't do that for any man, because if I gave up my life and what I believed in, I'd doom my children. That much I knew at seventeen. And, that's also why I left Brian. He loved the streets, too. Or, I guess I should say he grew fond of them once we got married."

What could he say? "I was young, stupid. Sweetheart, listen. I have learned from those days."

"Yeah," she murmured, sounding unconvinced. "I ran to what seemed safe. Figured maybe my Dad was right—go get an upstanding, college guy, from a solid family. We all learned from our youth, I suppose?"

The two stared at each other for a moment, silence standing between them like a specter in the room.

"After your lover sent me a dead blue-jay in the mail—that crazy heifer going so far as to try to root me, and after she called me a couple of times—leaving horrible details of your affair on my answering machine, I was done, Jerome. Pure and simple. Because the only way she could have gotten my address is if she'd had access to your bedroom, where you kept my letters and my personal belongings and your telephone book. Some women are treacherous. Hope you learned that, too."

"Yeah," he whispered, not sure of his voice.

"So, in truth, you did this, not my father. Guess we can both stop hiding behind that alibi, now. Brian was a reasonable alternative to the mess you created down in Dover."

"Did he treat you better than me, ever?"

"At one point, yes. But in the long run he damaged my soul—because I trusted him. That was enough of a reason to leave him. Just like I had to leave you back then."

"I always thought it was just your Pop, and about me not making it big," he said quietly. "You hated me so much that you wouldn't even tell me about your mother's funeral? I had to hear the shit in the street, four months after the woman died?" Incredulous, his voice found a new octave of sudden, unwarranted rage. "That wasn't fair, T. I loved her like she was my own! I know I screwed up, but damn." Emotion brought him to his feet and he walked out into the living room. "You held that over me like that for all those years? I was just a kid, and I loved you, girl! All right. I messed up. I'm sorry."

"I didn't tell you because I couldn't," she countered, walking toward him quickly and planting herself in front of him.

"Why not? Why couldn't you tell me, Toni, huh? Answer me that."

"Because I had married what I thought was a quiet, reserved, somewhat nerdy, safe guy—who found out after he was married that he had missed the high school and college party. My mother died six months after I got married. And during those six months, my new husband had tried and done it all."

"What the hell has that got to do with me?"

"Oh," she said with a shrug, turning away from him and going to fix herself a cup of coffee. "I had all of this pain bottled up inside of me—pain that I couldn't dare tell my aunts, my father, my baby sister or my mother, because Mom—the only one who could understand—was dying, then dead. I could only tell my girlfriends who couldn't understand how I could still love a man who'd been with another woman. We were all too young to fathom that. And, I was supposed to stand there in a church in front of four hundred mourners, people who had raised me—the minister, the old ladies— everybody, and watch you come into that church where I had just taken my vows? Then I was supposed to stand there, as you looked at me with your military blues on, and not run across that church crying and wailing into your arms?"

Her words pierced him, and he knew what she was saying was true. Guilt washed over him and nearly drowned him in remorse. What had he done? Yeah, it was twenty years ago, but it felt like yesterday, and there still wasn't enough of an explanation as to why he'd run on Toni. The worst part of it all was that now he had additional information. New, damning knowledge that wouldn't allow him to be the victim—the blue-collar lover cast to the side for the college sweetheart she chose over him. The girl, now woman, had her reasons. Valid, inarguable reasons not to call him and tell him her mother died.

"Damn," he whispered, keeping his gaze from hers as his mind turned the facts over and over again.

"I had to be strong, Jay—for my Dad, whose heart was broken when the love of his life died, and for my sister—who I had to raise. I couldn't run away, break camp, and do what I wanted to do. I had responsibilities—to everybody! Have you any idea the number of households that depended on my mother when she was alive?"

He could only shake his head no, because in truth, his family didn't function that way and he'd never thought about it. Looking at Antoinette now, he was beginning to see just what it meant to be a Kool-Aid Mom like Mom Reeves was.

"Yeah," she whispered, letting her breath out slowly. "You think about it, Jerome. Think about all the people who gathered at our house when we were kids. My dead aunts children, the older women in the family who were dying, or alone. When did you ever see my mother just sitting down and relaxing? Huh?"

Antoinette had obviously paused for dramatic

effect, and it was working. Images of her mother careened through his mind. It was the God's honest truth, Mrs. Reeves was always cooking for the church, sewing something on her lap, standing at the stove, bringing food from one room to the next. Poetry in motion. Poetry taken for granted. Because it wasn't until that moment that he wondered what really killed her—cancer, or too much motion.

"Right," Antoinette whispered, as though reading his thoughts. "She worried about the whole platoon of people that she loved, and when she passed, they came to me to replace that loss. I got the baton passed to me at twenty-three, okay. No bullshit."

"What would me being there at the funeral do to your responsibilities?" he said sullenly, trying to maintain his rage as an alternative to guilt. Walking in a circle as his mind tried to sort out her tainted female logic, he stopped short, and looked at her. "Tell me?"

Antoinette let her breath out hard. "I guess I wasn't supposed to bleed all over your uniform and beg you like a raving fool to take me back and save me from the hell I'd plunged in to—not while in church, anyway, right? And, I guess I was supposed to act like my husband, who wasn't around much at night to hear me cry for Mom while she was dying, was the man of my dreams? No. I wasn't supposed to sob on your shoulder and tell you that my Mom, who loved you like the son she never had..."

"Stop it. Okay. Please. I've heard enough."

"No. You wanted to know," she choked. "I was supposed to stand there and act respectable and give a brief, dignified, mourner's hug to the love of my life—then watch you walk out with your new wife and brand new baby? Are you crazy, Jay?" she whispered. "Have you lost your mind?"

Tears threatened his composure and he sat down on the sofa. His mind was too weary to confront the dead this morning. "Is that why you didn't come to my mother's funeral and just sent flowers?"

"Yes."

"I thought you hated me."

"No. I was losing my mind for you, Jay."

"I lost my mind too, when I thought I lost you." He looked down at the floor. Staring at Toni was impossible. "When I left Karen... my Pop told me that I wasn't a man. That I should have stayed—like he did. Like he stayed with my Mom, regardless of the fact that all the love had been wrung out between them. But I couldn't do it. He said that he was ashamed of me, T. That history was repeating itself—only I had made the wrong decision to leave." He issued a sad chuckle and shook his head. "Truth is, I got put out—all over a last ditch effort to save my marriage down in Atlantic City. Funny how things go. History."

"What are you talking about, Jay? What history?"

Chapter 2

Antoinette's soft question felt like a scalpel, carefully extricating a portion of his heart. He didn't have it in him to rake through his parents' marriage—or his own. Not this morning. Instead, he opted for heavy cover, and redirected her back toward the issue at hand.

"Toni, I thought that your family never believed I was good enough, so I went into The Service to scrape up enough money to go to school. I imagined all sorts of things—like the kind of rich guys who were up there with you... during the cold nights away from me. I started carrying on, drinking... and yeah, I got laid one time before you came to see me. Three months feels like three years when you're nineteen. It was wrong, and I know it. I'm not making that excuse. We know the deal. But then you parted the crowd in the backroom of that bar and like a princess, and I took one look into your eyes and knew—you still loved me. But the hurt in your expression, baby... it was like a nightmare, looking into your eyes, seeing it all over your face that you had been true. By then, it was too late—I hadn't been. My life went to shit at that point. I fucked up bad, baby."

"Wait," she whispered in a lethal tone. "Because I loved you and was faithful, I was the nightmare? Don't blame that on me, Jay. My ex-husband used to do that. He blamed everything that he wasn't, on me. And he resented the hell out of me for any achievement I ever made. It's not fair."

"I've always been proud of you, haven't I? So, I'm not blaming what I did on you," he murmured. "I did it to myself. I just never thought you'd stick around with somebody like me, anyway... that eventually, water would seek its own level—and I wasn't your level. So... hey. I don't know."

"Before I ever came to visit, and heard any tales of what you were doing while we were apart, why wouldn't you think I'd stick around?"

"I thought you'd go for a high-flyer college

man, and dump me as soon as you saw one with more potential. Male logic. Guess I was trying to brace myself for eventual impact."

"Flawed logic is more accurate. This chick was a plan B, in case I didn't stay in your life? That is so stupid."

"Yup."

For a moment they simply stared at each other until he looked away.

"My pop always told me you were too good for me, and one day, if I didn't get myself together, water would simply seek it's own level, like I said."

"When did what he said ever matter between us before, Jay? And why on earth would you think that, at a time when it was most important—when we were apart?" Her voice had softened and she moved over to the sofa and sat beside him. "Didn't you tell me I was the river of your soul... just like you were for me?"

"Face it, Toni," he whispered in a barely audible voice. "I was your first lover, and I knew it was only a matter of time until you looked around and saw how big the world really was. You were hundreds of miles from me, learning things I couldn't teach you—going to college. Maybe part of me just didn't want to see that look in your eyes that I knew was coming. That, 'I've outgrown you, and I have to move on for my own personal growth,' look. Guess I didn't want to witness the day when your well ran dry for me. So, I started doing crazy shit to numb the pain—it's like bracing yourself for sudden impact."

He could tell that she was studying his words even though he continued to study the floor. Although only moments had passed, it seemed like a long time had elapsed since sound had collided with the air in the form of sentences. He could feel her gaze boring into the top of his head as it hung down while his forearms tried to support his upper body as though to keep it from falling. How did one bury the dead when they were still living, he wondered? The person he was then was not who he was now. The old Jerome Henderson died the moment Antoinette Reeves looked away from him and cried into her hands twenty years ago.

"I didn't have the kind of family you did, T," he whispered. "Can't you understand that? My parents weren't full of 'I love yous', you know. I always wanted my kids to grow up with a lot of hugs, and kisses, and people telling them they were great. It makes a difference. When I lost you, I lost the only connection to something like that. Your Mom, your Pop... Pearline. Everybody. When I heard about your Mom, I cried like a baby."

"Oh, Jay..."

She reached over to him and he shrugged away. He didn't want her to see him like this. Not ever.

"Look," he said, standing up and walking over to the table. "The food's getting cold."

"I'll nuke it, but we have to talk."

"About what?"

"About the fact that there's a lot of miscommunication, and a lot of baggage between us. That, for starters."

"Yeah, I guess you're right," he said with resignation, turning over a cold biscuit and dropping it in the basket. "Me and Karen could never talk. Just like my Mom and Pop."

"I'll be honest, your family scared me, Jay. Nobody seemed to talk to each other, and they passed in the house like strangers," she murmured as she walked over to the table and sat across from him. "I married Brian as much for his warm family as for him. Even though he did a lot of hurtful things to me, I kept saying to myself, 'But his people are so nice, so regular. He'll change.' Truthfully, at that age, I couldn't make the separation. I needed them, 'cause my own family was dying away, getting small. We were tearing apart from all the funerals. I kept telling myself, 'the fruit don't fall too far from the tree,' you know? Brian will change. He won't be like my uncle."

Jerome turned his primary question and Antoinette's answers over and over in his brain. Taking a deep breath, he looked at her squarely. "So, when I came back for you, and begged you to change your mind—why didn't you leave him? It was like you left, immediately hooked up with somebody new, and it was so easy for you to move on."

"Brian had been trying to get me to go out with him since the moment I'd hit the campus," she admitted quietly. "I was younger than most of the other freshman, because I'd skipped a grade early on, so on that account you were right—a lot of guys thought I was young and dumb and pursued me. They thought I was an easy target because of my age—what they didn't know was that I had grown to deeply love someone. He was patient, though, Jay, unlike the others. I had repeatedly told him I had somebody I loved, and he hung in there being just a friend and hoping. That's what made me turn to him. I trusted him as a friend, then. Call it the boomerang effect, rebound, whatever, I went right to his dorm when I got off the bus."

"Oh. Deep." He'd asked for the information that now cut him to the bone. Some things were better left untold. He didn't need to know that, even though he'd requested it. Leave it to Antoinette to tell him the truth.

She flopped back on the couch and let her breath out hard. "When I came to Dover, and saw all of the carnage with you down there, I bolted for what I thought was safety. How many times do I have to say it?"

"You ignored my letters and telephone calls for two years, though. Once when I came to your dorm, you told everybody not to let me come in—and campus security hassled me like I was some stalker. The third year into that separation and campaign to get you back, I gave up."

"During those years, neither you nor I were monks, and we saw and slept with other people, so?"

"Yeah. True. But I always wanted you back. You wouldn't even talk to me."

"Yeah, well, it takes a while for a person to get past things. Me and Brian were both hurt, too. When I took up with Brian, who had seemed so wounded by the racism at school and the way his family expectations had trapped him, I thought of you. We all have baggage, Jay. You're in good company." Antoinette sighed and raked her fingers through her tussled hair. "Anyhow, midway through my senior year, your butt got married—

so I figured it was time for me to move on. Three years had come between me and you, plus a wife, and new baby was on the way for you, too. Married him almost soon as I graduated, eighteen months out, and I swore that I wouldn't leave him because of one indiscretion. At twenty-three years old you make grand promises to yourself."

"But your Mom died six months after y'all got married, from my memory. So, you mean to say the brother was with you for only six months as a husband before he started running? Y'all were technically still on your honeymoon!"

"Don't be the pot callin' the kettle black, Jay. You and I had been secretly engaged, promised to each other, when you ran. So?"

They both chuckled and he nodded.

"Difference was, you left me. Why'd he get a break?"

"Maybe because I was tired? Maybe because I felt like being married to a man, versus being almost married, made a difference to hang in? Maybe my Mom being sick made me unwilling to destabilize anything else in my life at the time? Who knows? All I'm sure of is that, emotionally, I couldn't handle a breakup and a death at the same time. So I stayed." Antoinette let her breath out hard.

His gaze searched her face as her line of vision

went off into the distance. He could tell that memories were washing against the present, battering her the way they were churning waves of guilt within him.

"I thought we could talk about it—communicate around it, like you and I never did," she whispered. "He was my husband, not my high school lover. That's why he got a break. But, as the indiscretions mounted to the point of the ridiculous, I had to finally say 'uncle', and give it up. Crazy, but I stayed with him because of you—I didn't want to throw away another possible love, and hurt someone like I had hurt you. One dead soldier was enough. It was never about the money, his college credentials, or whatever." She stood and walked over to the table and hesitated before she sat down across from him.

"Ain't that a bitch..." Jerome chuckled with sarcasm, picking at the eggs. "Here, all this time I thought it was about pedigree—Lady and the Tramp. So, what do I do? I go and marry a woman who is all about the money, who wouldn't know me if she tripped over me, and I hook up with a family that thinks I'm lower than dog shit because I don't make enough to put their daughter in a mansion. And, no matter how bad she treats me, I promise to never cheat on her... to never do what I did to you—in that one isolated incident at The Base—even if a few months goes by, and try to give her as much as I can financially. We were insane. Un. Be. Lievable!"

"And, what do I do?" she chuckled sadly with him, sipping her mug of coffee. "I run from what I think is a guy like all my father's worst nightmares—you—in order to find to find this wonderful family. So, I leave my street-wise ace for this nerdy guy, who transforms like damned Dracula over night—gets fly, because I dressed him. Gets hip, because I schooled him—teaching him everything you'd taught me! And he winds up leaving my ass, because I showed him the very streets of Philly that he couldn't get enough of. Meanwhile, my wild and crazy ace, you, Jay-bird, has gone cold turkey. What do I hear through the grapevine? That the love of my life is working a stable job, doesn't cheat on his wife, buys her a home and sets her up in Mount Airy—while I have to purchase my own home, because my new Lord of the Streets can't get any credit, or stay home long enough to care. Un. Be. Lievable!"

They both stared at each other for a long time, her smile soothing his soul as she seemed to drink him in with her eyes. Her silky voice seemed to apply balm to his wounded ego. Oh, yes, she was his river...

"Let the anger go, Jay. It'll kill the best part of

you," she sighed, slouching back in her chair. "You know, this whole thing was like that story of the husband and wife... The Gift of The Magi. He sells his watch to buy her an expensive comb, while at the same time, unbeknownst to him, she cuts her hair to sell it to buy him a gold chain for his watch. They're both in love, but without talking things over with each other, have given up their most prized possessions to make the other happy. Remember that old tale from Sunday school?"

"It was a goddamned soap opera, T. We wasted a lot of time—twenty years, girl."

"You ain't said a mumblin' word." She winked at him and lowered her eyes for a moment before she took a sip of coffee.

They both laughed and glanced at each other as they began to eat. Years of stress peeled away from his shoulders and he felt hungry again. He could tell a sudden mischief had crept back into her demeanor. It was in the way she glimpsed at him between tiny mouthfuls of bacon and eggs.

"And a lotta nights, you almost got me in trouble, girl," he finally admitted, watching her constantly for any signs of retreat. "Musta been callin' your name... been told I talk in my sleep, too."

Antoinette's hand flew over her mouth, and she laughed hard, her eyes growing wide in the process. "No! You didn't?"

"Not like that," he laughed, looking at her expression. "No. I didn't slip while in the throes. I always knew that I wasn't with you, baby—when I was awake. That situation wasn't no comparison to you."

Antoinette blushed and looked away, and he studied the rosy color that had risen in her warm-brown cheeks.

"No, I would get in trouble for just thinking and looking up at the stars. Karen would ask me what I was thinking about—and I'd tell her 'nothing,' then all hell would break loose. Your name was persona non-gratta... but I think it might've come up sometimes in my sleep. Maybe that's why I got banished to the sofa?"

"Oh, my God. For how long?"

"Seven months, or so, at a clip."

Antoinette stood up and collected the plates, shaking her head as she walked toward the microwave. "But you still made all those children. There had to be some good times?"

"Yeah, there were," he admitted begrudgingly, still watching her hard. "But, tell me, didn't you sleep with your husband—on occasion? How'd Lauren get here?"

"Yeah," she chuckled. "There were some good times. Like, twice a month."

"The way we roll, girl? That's like being in prison! Conjugal visits? Damn! How could he stay away from you like that?" Pure indignation arrested him. It didn't make sense. He looked at the lush body that had carried the food away from the table, and he scratched his jaw-line. "Girl... and you were both sleeping in the same bed—every night?"

"Yup. He didn't really like me, Jay. We were just co-dependent and both beat up and carrying luggage. That's the point. You can't make love when the person gets on your last nerve, can you? And I retaliated. I wasn't an angel, trust me on that. Look," she said on a heavy exhale, "when we first separated, I flung things in his face that should've never been flung. So, by that point I guess I wasn't his friend either. We both did irreparable damage to each other." Her voice trailed off, and became wistful. "Strange, but he's more my friend now than before. It's hard to explain. We started off leaning on each other during mutual hurt, got close, married, then began to hurt each other, got divorced, and are now just becoming distant friends again—even though there are times when he still pisses me off."

"But you all fought—had to, to not be sleeping with each other, right?"

"Yeah, but it's all relative. Early on in the separation and divorce, we fought like dogs—but that's sorta mellowed to a few feuds over child pick-up times and money, occasionally. He's not my pure enemy, though—can't be, we have a child between us. Maybe because he didn't dog me out in the divorce settlement and custody stuff, and I didn't do him, that's how we came to a civil true. Maybe? Who knows? All I can tell you is that we had a line that didn't get crossed, so hate isn't there; he never abandoned his child, and for that, I'm grateful."

He could relate to that, and could only hope that Karen would one day give him his due for loving his children despite whatever transpired between them. He nodded.

"When I came home," she murmured, "and had to pay for daycare, and his check was late and bounced, at first we fought, then I talked to him and found out the IRS had frozen his account and that he wasn't playing games, so some things came to light. He wasn't being a deadbeat dad. Dislike has even mellowed. Do you understand?"

"You still love him?" His own question tore at his insides.

"Yes. Like a brother, and I will always love his family dearly. They, and Brian, will always be a part of my life—and Lauren's life. You've got to understand that, too. I will not have a war over the child—or me. Nobody can afford that. I'm not looking for a replacement father for her—an addition, maybe, but not a replacement. I owe him that much. Understand?"

"He takes good care of her... and you let him see her... I mean, come over and visit and stuff?"

"Yes, Jay, he does. I don't get alimony, just child support—which goes directly to her school. I can take care of myself. Like I said, we talked—and more importantly, I talked to his Mom, who is like a second mother to me. He eventually gave me a check to give to May. Long story, but I had to go to my father and May to cover my first day-care bill, which wasn't fun. But, bottom line is, nobody was playing games financially, so what is there to still fight over?"

"Wait a minute... you said you were struggling... that you couldn't meet the bills..." He was stupefied by her statement. Outraged. He'd never heard of such. "Hold it. The judge did that to you, and he was the one who'd cheated first?"

"I filed No Fault. It wasn't the court's business what happened—not that I could have explained it if they'd asked. He only has to take care of the baby, not me. I'm grown. He has to have a life, will probably marry one day. Neither one of us needs to get financially raked over the coals to go bankrupt. That was my decision, not the judge's. It kept the peace—and him in her life. Plus, it made the divorce go through faster. Period. The cost to be the boss. Sometimes, you simply gotta walk on the past. The price of freedom is expensive. Yada, yada, yada. What can I say."

"But, weren't you angry, baby?" He stared at Antoinette for a long time. She wasn't his woman-child any longer, she was all woman. Her own woman. Antoinette's courage baffled him, and he wondered what she'd seen during their years apart that could make her walk without any support. He imagined it had to be pure hell. She seemed resigned as she let out a sigh.

"Sure I was angry, Jerome. But, even when we first separated, he would come and pick her up, stay sometimes and eat, and then cart her off for the weekend. When he brings her home now, sometimes he tucks her in bed and reads his child a story. We chat. The more peaceable I can remain, and the less rancor we have between us, the more comfortable he can feel in remaining a part of her life. I finally traded in my anger at the altar for my child and my sanity. Fighting over the money for years would have made a truce impossible. It's cleaner for the kid."

"I wish Karen felt that way," he admitted quietly, thinking of the violent episode of silence that had attacked him when he'd picked his children up and dropped them off at the front steps. "I can't even go into what used to be my own house. I don't think that's ever going to change. All she wants from me is a check."

"Then give it to her. She probably needs it." Antoinette folded her arms over her chest and stared at him.

"I do. I give her money when I see her to pick up the kids."

"Good," she said quietly, checking inside the microwave.

"But she still hasn't even begun to look for work. I pay for daycare too, and the oldest are in school all day. I'm not going to be able to support the whole thing forever. She even has a degree. And why do I have to pick up my kids from the steps?"

"That's because she's still angry," Antoinette countered in a gentle voice. "She needs time and fulfillment of her own to get past the rage. I was there. I used to be a wife, too. Now, I guess I'm soon be known as the other woman. Funny how life works."

"I can't imagine you being that way—a mean-spirited ex-wife. And you sure aren't the other woman."

"Huh," Antoinette laughed, issuing him a sardonic smile. "You don't know me, Jay. I was a real bitch, and put him through the wringer. He and I are even. I got my pound of flesh from his hide. Trust me. Women are wired that way. Sometimes, we just don't know when to stop for our own good. To quote Pearline, 'sometimes ya just gotta let go and let God.' Ooooohhhh... I was a trip."

"Sounds like he deserved it, though?"

"Maybe. Maybe, not. If he wasn't getting from me what he needed... and I wasn't getting from him what I needed... so, then really, who's to blame? Like, when I first found out that he had somebody new after we separated, I threw a hissey-fit. He was supposed to keep Lauren through New Year's Eve, and called to bring her home early. I was so angry, Jay, that I snapped a mental twig. I literally flipped. I screamed at him on the phone, threatened to call the police for having my baby out of state, and called the woman all sorts of names—none of which are in the dictionary," she laughed at herself as she shook her head.

"You did not," he chuckled, trying to picture it.

"And why?" she asked with a sad chuckle, looking away and toying with the salt-and-pepper shakers on the counter, not waiting for his response. "Because it was the first New Year's that I would spend alone, with only a baby to keep me company. Even though I was the one who'd filed for divorce, the reality hit me that I didn't have anyone of my own."

"But you wanted the divorce, right?"

"Wrong. I wanted my husband to love me, to be respectful and kind. I wanted him to change. After enough battling I realized that something had to give. I finally learned that you can't make a person change. You can only change yourself or your response to the old patterns you have with them. So, that's what I did. I changed by no longer being home to argue with him when he came in late, or he messed up money, or ran women. I was out of there. I changed. I filed. But still, all that notwithstanding, nobody wants to be divorced, Jay. Karen probably doesn't either."

"But, it was your choice," he pressed on, growing concerned over her acceptance of Karen, and feeling that, strangely, it would be so much easier if she didn't identify with Karen as much.

"A bitter one, too. Tell me, did you want your marriage to end in divorce, or would you have rather had a happy union for you and your kids—regardless of the circumstances that made you decide to marry?"

"I felt robbed, Toni." His quiet admission

made his heart slam against his lungs, and he swallowed hard to hold back a fresh torrent of tears. "I wanted it to work. I even tried one more time, but it didn't."

"So did we, Jay. I felt robbed. I was hurt, and angry, and insecure, and horny."

"Jesus..." He looked away and thought of Karen, and the way she'd had sex with him in Atlantic City that last time, even though she was furious with him during the act.

"Yes... I missed him that way too, Jay. But, I was hurt, and I had planned to polish off a cheap bottle of champagne and watch the ball drop by myself for New Years. That was stupid pride going before a fall, okay? And I couldn't even do that—not with Lauren in the house. There was no way I could bring in the New Year being sloppy drunk, crying, and getting myself off to keep from going crazy with a kid in my bed. It had been almost a year, then. So, I felt robbed of my one evening of peace without little eyes and ears to climb into bed with me. I coulda killed him," she laughed, shaking her head at the memory.

He looked at her then down at his plate and smiled, her admission oddly making his groin throb. He remembered too well having to lock the bathroom door to get that monkey off his back.

She returned his smile, as though having read

his thoughts, and took a slow sip of coffee before setting her cup down to speak.

"All the while, visions of Brian sinking into pleasure and having a romantic evening with a beautiful woman, and having his own space, with someone to laugh and talk with all night, tortured me. I went out of my mind with jealousy. The worst part was, the woman wasn't a she-wolf. Obviously, she had been sweet and kind to my baby, who'd spent the day after Christmas through New Year's—in my mother-in-law's house having the time of her life. I had been replaced. After my own mother died, his mother became my mother, and Lauren's only Nana. Jay, I wanted to slit my wrists over his happiness—and me and God fell out for a long time over that."

She chuckled and let out a breath. "For you, it's just starting, brother. If Karen finds out that you aren't paying penance, living in squalor and grieving over your loss of her, she'll hate you for it—until she finds something like this of her own. That's the reality, Jay. Do you understand?"

He did, and decided to let it rest. He didn't want to know how deep Antoinette's wrath could go, unless he'd incurred it. He didn't want to talk about Brian Wellington any more. They'd dredged the past enough for one breakfast. He also didn't feel like telling Toni about the way he would avoid

Karen by hanging out at the bar with the fellas. Nor did he want to investigate Antoinette's ambivalent affection toward a man who'd hurt her. It left too many loose ends in his mind. The past was the past, may it rest in peace, he told himself. They'd made too much progress this morning.

"Well," he finally said with a chuckle, then added a wink, "I guess I was just lucky when I made my kids. Suppose I wasn't shootin' any blanks, is all. But I didn't have much more frequency than you did, and that's the truth. Me and Karen were never really friends, I guess. An argument always cropped up. Got to the point where I would say anything, do anything, to avoid the bullshit—to get into the DMZ and get a little TLC, if'n, you know what I mean?"

"I know what you mean." She laughed and removed a plate of seconds from the microwave and brought it to him. "I was losing my mind. Some days, even when I was dead right, I would let stuff pass, just so I wouldn't miss my monthly installment—if'n you know what I mean. But I would wake up the next day with a serious attitude. Like I said, I wasn't an angel."

It still disturbed him, a little, to think that she had wanted sex as much as a man. It was honest, but it was hard to take. He knew it was a stupid thought, but it was hard to shake his original knowledge of her.

"Neither was I. I wasn't no angel—truth be told," he said, and chuckled after a moment, raising his hand as he waited for her to slap him five as she set down his second plate. Oh yeah, they were both definitely veterans. "But I never hit her, or ran. I paid the bills. Still do that. Like you said. There's a line."

"I don't know why she put you out, then—truth be told," Antoinette said laughing. "Seven months... sheeeit."

"Baby, you just don't know." He chuckled again, shaking his head as she lingered next to him for a moment. "I was getting a nervous tick." He looked up at her and nipped her side until she giggled. "But, Karen was all finance no romance. Always was about the money."

"Tell the truth, Jay. Did you run on her?"

"Nope—not while I was married to her," he said sheepishly, biting her side. "For real, for real. I did something worse."

She pushed his head back and stared at him. "What? What did you do to her to get put out?"

"I ignored her."

"That was worse, Jay. I've had it done to me."

Her voice had grown sad and distant. Guilt wrenched his insides and he needed to touch her to staunch the pain. In reflex, he covered her belly with his palm and looked at her seriously. "I can't ignore you, girl. Wouldn't. Never did."

He could feel the muscles in her body relax.

"Promise?"

He gave her a little wink and took her hand, pushing it down to his lap. "Evidence of my promise," he said with a chuckle that came from low in his throat.

"So, you gonna come around here more than once or twice a month?" she asked laughing, and then pushed his face away from her side while removing her hand from under his. "Or, am I eventually going on the dole, gettin' rations?"

"I can't ration you, suga." He laughed, pulling her onto his lap. "You can have the whole canteen. Damn, I can't get enough of you, girl."

She pushed him away with a smile and struggled against his hold to get up."

"I could get used to this, you know?" he admitted as he watched her saunter away from him.

"Don't." She grinned, setting the timer on the microwave unit. "This was special. Our first time. I hope you don't think I always do this?"

His spirits sagged a little as he sank his teeth into a tender, butter-filled biscuit. "For real?"

"For real," she said folding her arms over her chest as she waited for the microwave. "If I work late, I can't do this. Shouldn't have to. At this point, I just got my freedom papers. I like my personal space—sometimes."

"Not too much space, I hope?"

"I like the fact that the only child I have to pick up after is Lauren," she said with a smile, ignoring his question, "I'm not about to pick up after a forty-one year old adolescent. I'll do it for any and all the children, but not for a man-child. If I go in again, Jay, it's as partners. Even-Steven. And the first sign of high drama, I'm gone. Been there. Seen it. Done it. I want a friend, and a lover—not a big baby."

"Hey, girl," he countered, slurping his coffee, "I do laundry, change diapers, I can cook, I can braid hair and did it when I was married—"

"—You still are married—legally."

He waved his hand at the comment and shoveled a large heap of sausage into his mouth. "A technicality. Papers were served before you and I hooked up. Waiting on a signature, and she done took all I've got, so there's nothing left to squabble over. Can't get blood from a turnip, even a judge knows that. And, as far as me and you goes, I'm not home enough to make a mess, anyway. If you're working and I'm working, then whoever's home first should pitch in and get the job done. Plus, I take out the trash, 'cause I hate to smell it myself, and can even do a little bit of fixing-up and odd jobs too. That's how you met me again, right? Working."

She smiled and let her gaze rove over him. "We'll see. Time will tell. And a technicality, like waiting on papers, can cause a lot of problems. But it's hard to believe that you got put out, if you do all that you claim you do. 'Cause if you're telling it straight, Jay, I gotta say that the girl was outta her mind."

"Well, if you're tellin' it straight, girl, your ex was outta his mind. So, we'll have to see. Even-Steven, bet."

"All right, then. Time will tell."

Her smile was working on his reason, and he could sense that she knew how much.

"Then what did she want from you, Jay? Be serious," she said casually, adjusting herself against the sink.

"Aw, T... C'mon, let it be. I don't know, really? Never did know, I guess."

"Jerome, don't you think you should find out before we start this? I don't want to get burned."

He didn't like the way she'd used his formal name, or the serious tone that came with it. He liked Jay better. It was closer, more intimate, like when she'd whisper it in his ear. But, at the moment, she was going for distance again. He could feel it.

"It's over. Tried to get her to go to a counselor—she refused. Tried to get the minister involved—she went off. Tried to talk to her Mom and Pop—they didn't want to get involved. It's done. You won't get burned. I'm not going back." Jerome folded his arms across his chest and leaned back in his chair. He stared at Antoinette hard, trying to get her to understand that everything couldn't always be fixed. "Satisfied? Let it rest, girl. It's done."

"But, did you ever talk to her?"

"Your plate is ready," he said quietly. "Been done for five minutes."

"Didn't you try to make love one more time, to see if... Or, try to—"

"—So, are you going to marry me, or what, darlin'?"

"Jay!" She laughed, finally retrieving her plate.

"Well?"

"What about the kids?'

"We'll take them to the museum, or something—when you have yours and I have mine. They already want to play together. Next weekend. We'll spend the day, Saturday, then part as friends. We'll see how they take it—their Daddy and their Mommy dating someone new. We'll tell them the more permanent part later. Bet?" She was worse than he'd remembered, once a subject had her. "C'mon, T," he pleaded, "let it rest. Eat breakfast at the table with me—at least commit to that this morning."

"It's not that simple," she said with a smile, "and you know it. What if they hate me?"

"The lady who jumped double-dutch at the flea market fair with them when they first met you on a hummer? Impossible."

Antoinette laughed and picked at her plate while leaning against the sink. "But, if they do?"

"Then we'll stay lovers for life, and go at it like crazy on the weekends when they're away. I'll call you on the phone every night during the week and breathe heavy for ya, girl." He laughed as she walked toward the table slowly. "Then, when they're all finally over the age of eighteen, which will be when you and I are old and decrepit, we'll elope. Fair enough?"

Antoinette shook her head and smiled as she sat down. "This is very complicated, Jay. You've got an ex-wife who hasn't even signed the papers yet, and I know she's probably just angling for me—if you've been talking in your sleep. You've got a teenage daughter and another one getting ready to go through puberty, with all kinds of raging emotions ready to set on her plus one more girl, and a boy. I've got a little girl who loves the ground her father walks on—with bad asthma, who can't deal with smoke; and you must have your Marlboros—"

"I can get the patch and quit, but after all that lovin', and this meal, I could really use a smoke," he said with a wide grin, rubbing his belly for emphasis. God, he wanted her again.

"Be realistic, Jay-friend. Go ahead and light up while Lauren's not here. But—"

"Okay friend-lover... let's not ever forget the lover part, T. The word platonic gives me the hives around you, girl. I'ma be a pretty blue cat without that in my life. No lie. I'll pass on the smokes for a while to show good faith."

"And, I have a half a job," she went on, ignoring his reference to lovemaking, "with no medical bennies, that can barely meet the expenses here."

"I'm bottomed out, too—so, what it mean jelly bean?"

She laughed hard and slapped the table. "If you have four kids, and she doesn't work, and she's as angry as a wet hen—the judge is going to clean your clock, boy."

"Toni, do you love me?"

"That's beside the point. Did before, too early to tell now."

"Do you love me, woman?"

"Yes. So? What's love got to do with it?"

Antoinette laughed and closed her eyes, allowing her head to fall back. "Okay, okay, I'm mad, insane, ready to do the unspeakable with you. Yes. Satisfied?"

"Do you care that I left my wife a house with thirty-thousand dollars of equity in it, all the furniture I ever owned, and walked with only the clothes on my back? Or, that there's noting left for her to take; nothing left to fight about, except when I see the kids?"

"No. That was what you all built together. It's not my business."

She looked at him and her gaze edged away from his, but he knew he'd cornered her.

"Has the money ever been the issue, T?"

"No," she whispered, looking at him squarely.

"Will you eat rice and beans with me as long as we can laugh, and make love, and be friends?"

"Probably," she murmured, a wide smile gracing her face.

"You think we'll be able to laugh together, and cry together, and even though from time to time we might get on each other's nerves," he murmured, "still be able to drive each other nuts in bed?"

"Make your point, Jay." She chuckled.

"We are friends, right? Have been for a long time, right?"

"Yes," she said quietly, "I suppose we are friends."

"If I got hit by a bus, and was in a wheelchair, would you still love me?"

"Of course. What's your point, Jay?" She took a deep sip of her coffee, and he could tell that she was trying hard not to smile.

"Will you always tell me the truth, even if it takes an hour and a half of your crazy talk to get it said?"

"My crazy talk?" She set down her mug with mock indignation.

"Yes. Your crazy, turning-around-in-the-middle-of-the-kitchen-floor-rolling-at forty-miles-an-hour-while-spinning-three-pans-kinda-talk—first thing in the morning, isn't crazy?"

"Okay. It's crazy." She laughed easily. "I'm crazy."

"But you are honest," he admitted, growing more serious. "Even when I don't want to hear what you have to say—you tell me the truth, right? You'll promise to always do that, right?"

"You can count on one thing, I'm always gonna tell you that."

"Okay. So, when I become an old fool, will you walk on the boardwalk in Atlantic City with me, Toni, and help me feed the birds?"

"Yes." She giggled.

"And just because I get old and fart, and wear a dental bridge, will you still give me some nookie?"

"If I can get my arthritic knees to part by then." She laughed doubling over and wiping her eyes. "You are so crazy, boy!"

"If you love me now, but stop loving me somewhere along the way, will you tell me before you go to somebody else? I don't want to get burned either, especially not by your ex-husband."

This time she stopped and looked at him with a new tenderness. "Of course," she said, suddenly growing serious and touching his face across the table. "I never slept with another man while I lived under Brian's roof. I separated from him first. If I didn't do that to him, how could I ever do that to you, honey?"

"It's him that I'm worried about, T. You have a funny code of honor... and you still love him." He'd laid his suspicions bare, the vulnerable worry that he'd sworn to himself he'd never mention. Damn. This woman was like truth serum.

"He's like my brother, Jay. That's all."

"For real, for real?"

"For real, for real, Jay."

He studied her face and listened to the way she'd answered him. He needed to know, beyond a shadow of a doubt, that the man and family who'd stolen his prize once, would not be able to recapture her heart. He'd heard about people remarrying the ones they'd divorced. His own lack of paperwork, and his presence as a serious suitor, might make Brian reconsider tossing this gem out to the wind. Plus, Karen's venom, along with a potentially lengthy legal battle, might make Toni turn-tail and go back to what was safe. She'd done it to him once, with much less at stake. Now, there were babies to consider.

"I don't want my kids hurt, Toni. Before they meet you as the woman in my life, we have to be sure."

"I agree," she murmured sadly. "We cannot introduce children to something that might not last. They've already been traumatized enough. No more instability. Okay?"

He didn't like the way she'd spun his words around, making what they'd just rediscovered sound shaky at best. "Then, let's be sure."

"We have to be," she whispered. "That's how it has to be."

"Good," he finally said, settling for an uneasy truce and half promise from her. "Then, by my way of thinking, you just accepted me for richer, for poorer, in sickness and in health, to have and to hold, forsaking all others, to love, honor, and cherish. That's all I ever wanted, T," he said quietly, standing and moving to her side before going down on one knee. "And that's what I'll give you, too. No less than you'd give me. I am sure, baby. Say you'll marry me, even if we stay engaged for a long time while you decide, and while things sort out. We'll take the kids out on Saturday, okay?"

She lowered her face to kiss him, and he brushed her mouth quickly and held her back. "Nope. I did that to you last night to keep you from saying what I didn't want to hear."

"You know me, I'm busted." She chuckled. "I do love you, Jay. Always have."

"I have always loved you, baby. Marry me."

She let her hands trace his jaw and the sensation of her touch sent a shudder through him. "Okay... but, we take it slow... next week, no evidence of more than friendship when we all go out. Slow."

"Yeah, real slow," he said with a sly smile, kissing down her breast bone and finding her lap. "I have to make a run." He ignored the phone when it rang and held her firmly in the chair so she couldn't answer it. "Since I'm not shootin' blanks."

"Oh, my God! No. We have to cut this out, Jay. It's almost two o'clock—Lauren's due home at four. Brian might be calling to see if I'm in yet. I turned down the bedroom answering machine and the ringer while you were asleep, and by now the world is probably looking for me—"

"—So," he growled against her belly, "we have two hours. He'll have to wait."

"No we don't have two hours, and I'm not trying to fling this in his face, or piss him off. I have to get myself dressed, clean up the bedroom, and restore this place to some order before my child comes home. You have to get out of here! I can't have her coming home to some love den, with condom wrappers on the nightstand and her dolls flung in the bottom of my closet. C'mon, Jay... quit it." She giggled as his hand slid up her thigh.

Letting her go was totally out of the question—especially with Wellington coming back to her with her baby in his arms. He was no fool. Toni would take one look at her daughter, her heart would go soft, and she might even feel guilty. No way. His competitor would pick up his scent and stake a renewed claim. That was what a woman couldn't understand. It was never over between men—until they said so. He'd have to make her tremble again, hard, before he left her alone for a week—to ensure that she'd remember.

"I'll put away the food while you go find her dolls and hide the evidence," he said firmly, issuing more of a command than a request. "Then you can come to my place so you can relax. We won't be able to do this for a whole week—not with kids and work schedules, and all. That's a long time when you're forty-plus and have the woman of your dreams living around the corner. Think about it, baby, after none for twenty years..."

He was not going to lose her again. Not to Brian Wellington. Ever.

"Yeah.... okay, but you gotta stop." She laughed deep in her throat. "Let me clean up, take a shower, and grab some clothes."

"Uh, uh... I'll clean up the kitchen—fast. You clean up the bedroom—fast. I'll throw on my stuff—fast. You grab some clothes—fast. Nix the shower," he murmured against the thickness of her thigh. "I want to smell you in my sheets, and your perfume on my pillows... all week long, when I can't have you. Gimme something to go on, baby. C'mon, take the shower at my place. I'll wash your back."

The shiver that went through her sent a shudder through him. His competition was becoming moot as she stroked the top of his head. If she didn't remember, he would enough for the both of them.

"Okay, but we have to stop by Seven-Eleven on the way, Jay."

"No, we have to go to Rite Aide to get the big box," he murmured kissing back up her abdomen.

"And I have to get home by three-thirty."

"Hasn't he ever made you wait up for him, T?"

"Yes." She giggled as he clamped his lips over one of her hardening nipples.

"Then, isn't it time that he waited at least an hour or two for you—since you just got engaged?"

He continued to pay attention to her breast as she struggled against his attention to the taut skin beneath her silk robe. The look on her face was absolutely devastating... the way she responded to him...

"C'mon, baby... one more time. After twenty years, isn't it time that we did something we wanted to for a change?"

"Oh, yes...." she moaned, as his fingers teased the other breast. "It's definitely time."

Chapter 3

"Okay. On three," Jerome laughed as he pulled her almost through the doorway.

"Wait! I can't keep up, Jay. Wait, I have to set the alarm."

"C'mon. C'mon, girl." He chuckled slyly, tugging on Antoinette's waist as she tried to set the alarm and shut the door. "Times'a wasting. You remember the drill, don't you?"

Giggling as he half-dragged her down the steps, Antoinette held onto the rail to keep her balance. "I remember, boy. Stop pulling me."

"You know you like it," he said laughing, hurrying her across the street and into his car, "You know what's waiting for you too. Don't be slow, girl."

He slipped into the seat beside her, started the engine, and peeled away from the curb as she laughed and let out a squeal then covered her eyes. "Slow down, or you'll kill us both!" She slapped his elbow as he turned hard around the corner.

"Hey, T—'member how I used to wait for you after school? Mmmmm, mmmmm, mmmm—have mercy, girl! You used to sashay down the steps... looking all good with your tight, brick-house jeans on... trying to act like you were ignoring me—till you came right up on me."

"Yeah." She sighed, feeling a sentimental rush. "But, I wasn't ignoring you. How could I? 'Specially when you'd be standing there—already graduated, all tall, and fine, and whatnot, with this Sylvers afro—and mirror aviator sunglasses. Dag... I couldn't look at you too hard, or my girl-friends would have definitely known the deal."

Jerome drummed his fingers on the steering wheel as he waited for the light, giving her a sly sideways glance. "You remember me... down to the aviators?"

"Yup. Down to the bone. Couldn't let my girls know the deal, though."

"And, what was the deal?" he asked as his voice dropped a purposeful octave. "Tell me, baby."

"That as soon as I got into your car, you'd pull off and burn rubber to your sister's apartment."

He laughed, and hit the acceleration. "That was definitely the deal, baby. Good thing my sister had a day job, and I found the spare key, huh?"

"Good thing!" She tossed her ponytail over her shoulder and issued a sexy smile, suddenly feeling fifteen. "Those were some good days, Jay."

"Yeah," he agreed, "but the summers were hell!"

"Why?" Antoinette cocked her head to the side, which made him swipe her mouth with a quick kiss.

"'Cause, girl... we didn't have school as a cover. We didn't have from three o'clock when we got to Sissy's, till four or so—when I had to get you home, at the latest, before your Mom and Pop came in at five-thirty. We had to play hard and play fast. When summer came, I had to visit you at your house—or take your little sister with us or we had to be going somewhere in a group... all summer long, baby. That was the law. Now, that was rough!"

"I know..." she whispered against his neck, making him swallow hard. "But we made due. Remember, The Plateau. Remember, West River

Drive? I still love the park because of you, baby."

"You gonna make me hit somebody, T, cut it out." He chuckled low in his throat. "Damn, where is everybody going on a Sunday afternoon?"

"They're probably coming from church," she said with a laugh, "the same place we probably should've been coming from."

He slipped his hand up her thigh and she slapped it away. "Boy, stop."

"I just need some inspiration, baby, 'specially since I have to wait long enough to make a pit stop at the store first," he murmured as he pulled into a space at the Rite Aide lot, then shut off the ignition.

"Get out of the car, man, and go handle your business." She slapped his hand again as he stroked her knee.

"Oh, so now it's my business. Ain't you comin' in?"

She sat back in the seat and stared at him. "I know you are playing, Jay."

"C'mon with me, T, suga-girl."

"No." She laughed, doubling over and waving him away with her hand.

"Why not?"

"Because."

"Because why?" he asked, twisting his mouth then laughing hard. "C'mon, girl, where's your heart?"

"You treatin' me wrong, boy. I ain't buyin' no twelve box on a Sunday afternoon—not when I don't have to buy nothin' else. How'd that look? You must be crazy." She had to laugh, and his constant attempt to touch her legs while she slapped his hands made her giggle even harder.

"Ohhhh," he drawled as he laughed with her, wiping his eyes, "...so I'm the one who has to look bad, huh?"

"That's right. You're the man."

"You know that's wrong, girl."

"So. It's a law of nature. If the man wants nookie, he has to buy the condoms," she managed between fits of giggles as he tried to kiss her neck. "You're wasting time, cut it out, boy."

"See, you done confangled the laws of nature to your own benefit, woman—and you know that ain't right. But, because I want some so bad, I'ma let it go. I gotta let it go—and that's how y'all always win!" he quipped, jumping out of the car and giving her a wink as he shut the door. "At your side in five," he hollered through the glass, loud enough to make her blush and turn her head.

"Jerome Henderson, you are a trip!" she yelled back through the glass, blowing him a kiss.

She was in Heaven.

*

Blustery March winds pushed her up the steps and practically blew them into door as they laughed and giggled while he turned the locks to enter his apartment. She ran up the inside flight of stairs ahead of him and pressed herself against the wall, fending off his pinches and kisses, laughing even harder while he dropped the keys once before he turned the locks and dragged her through the doorway. They fell through the entrance, half holding each other, half holding onto the door, bright afternoon sunlight bathing their laughter.

"I gotta take a shower," she panted through bursts of giggles as he tried to pull her toward the bedroom. "For real, Jay. I'm all sticky. This doesn't make sense, carrying on like we're in high school."

"I gotta catch my breath." He chuckled, turning her loose and falling against the wall. "You're definitely gonna make me stop smoking. I can't keep this up. The steps did it. Twenty years has passed, I think. Gotta slow down sometime."

"Tell you what," she said between breaths, "let's slow down, honey. I'll take a shower, you catch your breath. Can't find us both dead and stuck together. How would that look at this age?"

They fell into an easy embrace and both laughed hard, their voices bouncing and reverberating off the walls to create a womb of echoes.

"For real." He kissed her neck slowly. "Now how would that look."

"I'm going to take a shower—before you get started again. Told you we have to slow down..."

"I'm already started, but you can feel free to use the shower," he murmured, growing more serious, "don't lock the door though. I'll be in to bring you a towel and to wash your back."

"Promise?" she whispered, inching away from him.

"Promise."

He was definitely in Heaven. Jerome paced, almost skipping, into the living room. All at once, he felt so light, so suddenly free. He dropped Antoinette's coat and his package on the sofa, and pulled off his jacket and cap. Leaving the coats in a pile on the couch, he paced over to his vintage album collection and rooted through the remnants of their era. Settling on the Isley Brothers, he found their Summer Breeze, put it on the turntable, and slowly cranked the volume. As the opening melody filled the room, the electric guitar ran through his veins just like Toni always had. Suddenly, he found a new appreciation for oldies, and wondered why he'd always hated them so? Jazz had its place, but there was nothing like an Isley Summer...

He could hear the shower go on and blend into the music. The combination was intoxicating. Who needed a drink? Ever. This was the way a woman should wash a man off of her, he thought, as he stripped away his sweater and T-shirt, kicking off his boots and jeans. This was the only way.

As he approached the bathroom door, he hesitated, and then turned the knob slowly. When the lock didn't catch, he let his breath out. Yes. This was the way it was supposed to be. Open.

Slipping behind the door, he watched Antoinette's silhouette behind the clear plastic curtain and admired the way the steam billowed like clouds around her. Oh, yes, he was definitely in Heaven.

"I promised I'd wash your back," he said quietly, waiting for her permission to step into the tub. Her wide grin answered all of his unspoken questions, and he cautiously stepped in around her within the tiny confines.

She turned and stared at him, still smiling. Water flowed over her body and caressed her breasts, making her entire sheath of cinnamon coffee-colored skin shimmer. He touched her face and held her cheek as he watched the water turn what was once her ponytail into a cascade of rich dark-chocolate tendrils about her shoulders. The sight of her slowly lathering the soap between her palms made him draw his breath. "God.... you are absolutely beautiful..." Words escaped him as she began applying the suds in a rhythmic circular motion to his chest.

"You make me feel beautiful, Jay," she whispered, trailing off and kissing his neck. As she wrapped her arms around him, she soaped his back and found his mouth for a deeper kiss.

Water fell on them like a hard rain, the soap slicking their skins and providing a new slippery surface between them. Their movements merged and swayed with the music as they danced and slid against their combined textures. He let his hands travel with the current of the water, re-exploring the curve of her breasts, her waist, and her hips as the memory of his palms glorified the past and reveled in the present.

"I always wanted to do this with you," he whispered, finding the small of her back and pressing her firmly to him. "Always dreamed of this."

She kissed his cheek and let out a low, sensuous chuckle. "Me too... but we need a bigger tub, and a bigger hot water tank."

He chuckled with her and kissed her deeply,

then drew back despite the urge to continue. "Yeah... the water is getting cold, isn't it?" he said with a smile. "I'll have to take you somewhere one day where it won't run out after five minutes."

"How about if you take me into the bedroom," she whispered. "We can pretend."

He caught her gaze and it burned him. There was something so open in the way she displayed her desire for him. It was more intense, yet oddly, it was also the same way she displayed ordinary affection for him. He drank it in now, in whatever measure she poured it.

"Yeah, let's rinse off, and I'll dry you," he breathed as her soapy hands slid down his abdomen and found their way home to his tension. "This is driving me crazy."

She didn't answer him, but continued to work with the lather and him in her hands. He closed his eyes and held onto the tile wall.

"For real, for real...." he murmured, catching his breath in his throat as a gasp traveled through his skeleton. "Let's go into the bedroom."

Again, she didn't answer, but stepped aside slightly to allow the water to hit him directly. The change in texture and temperature almost stunned him. Slightly disoriented, he let his breath out in a rush and held on more tightly to the tile.

"Turn around," she said in a low purr. "I have to get the soap off your back."

Beyond any resistance, he followed her instructions and waited while she caressed the soap away from his shoulders. Her hands slid down the center of his spine and over his buttocks and down his thighs. He could feel her breath heating the small of his back, and he almost flinched with over-anticipation when her tongue found the first vertebrae.

"The water's getting cold," he whispered, hoping to relocate her torture to the bedroom before it was too late.

"I'm done," she chuckled and brushed his shoulder with a wet kiss. "Let me dry you off."

Torn between wanting her to continue her water torture, and needing to be with her in the bedroom where he could end it, he stepped out of the shower and grabbed a towel.

"Uh, uh," she admonished with a smile. "Let me do that. I always wanted to do this for you, baby. When we were kids, we never had the time."

Another wave of anticipation coursed through him as he handed her the towel with only the steam providing a blanket of warmth between them. She turned him away from her with one finger, guiding the direction of his shoulder. He'd become putty, and he followed her unspoken instructions to the letter—heeding her wide, brown eyes and her slight body movements. When she covered his back with the terry-cloth fabric, she added her own body warmth behind it. Creating a seal over the towel, she dried her front with his back, with only the towel between them.

"Never in my life..." he murmured, as she refused to allow him to turn to embrace her. He let his head fall back and rest against her forehead as she brought the towel around to his chest.

"Turn around," she whispered, finding a deep chord of understanding inside his inner ear. "Let me do the front."

Expecting her to blanket him, he reached for her, only to have his hands returned to his sides gently.

"Uh, uh. Not yet."

She stood so close to him that he could almost feel the hairs on his skin brush hers. It was as though an electrical current had awakened every surface nerve ending, and he could feel her before she'd even touched him. But he waited, somehow knowing that it would be worth the excruciating time she took to dry him.

However, his intent to allow her to lead almost fractured when she followed the towel with a deep pant of hot breath. The difference in textures between the rough terry, her skin, then her breath behind it, flayed his nervous system.

"Am I dry yet," he groaned as her breath hit his navel.

"No,' she whispered into it. "Your legs are still wet."

A hard shudder quaked his body as she parted his legs and skipped over his groin and found the inside of his thigh. The sensation of her full breasts touching his leg, there, and her heated breath behind it, nearly took his equilibrium again. When she moved to his other leg, he held onto the towel rack to keep his balance and closed his eyes.

And she waited.

Millimeters away from where he desperately wanted her, she waited, and only breathed on the angry surface that had already burned dry on its own. His mind sent out a plea that she leisurely answered, drawing a whimper from inside his chest when she did. The slow dissolve of his sanity unraveled with her tongue, and was intermittently brought back by a graze of her teeth.

"I... seriously... baby... can't... guarantee..." he stammered and opened his eyes. When she looked up at him and took him again in agonizing slow increments, all he could do was pray.

"You're dry now," she whispered against his stomach, her breath lurching another spasm up from his spine. "Let's go lay down."

For a moment, he was immobilized. The thought of her touch leaving his skin, leaving the steamy enclosure of the bathroom, having to walk twenty-five feet down the hall, the way the cold would cut them... "Can't we stay here?" he breathed against her neck when she stood to embrace him. "I can barely walk."

She smiled and looked around the bathroom and slowly shook her head no. "You said you wanted to remember me in your sheets all week. Remember?"

He swallowed hard and again followed her lead as she cracked open the door and slipped around it. Her slow saunter in front of him was titillating, and he tried to regain his composure as he matched her stride. When she climbed into bed, he slipped in next to her, adjusting his nervous system to the crispness of the cool sheets and the warmth of her damp body. The March sun lit her face and throat, framing it with golden light that made her wet hair glisten. She smiled at him slowly and lowered her eyes. Never had he experienced such outright seduction in his life.

"Where's the box?" she chuckled as he pulled her beneath him.

All he could do was hang his head in pure frustration. Pain had whittled his common sense down to a nub.

"Tell me where it is, and I'll get it, honey," she said next to his ear, sending a burning shaft of want into it. "You're in no condition."

"On the sofa—or, maybe the coffee table," he groaned flopping onto his back. "Baby, I'm sorry..."

She was right. He was in no condition to move away from her, or think. As she slipped out of bed and went down the hall, he watched her form disappear. What if she hadn't asked? he wondered, trying to pull some faculty of reason back into his mind. The throb that answered him told him all he needed to know. Foolish as it was, he might have played roulette. She understood that, he was sure, as she returned with merciful speed. How did women know these things?

Without instruction or discussion, she opened the package and began tearing the foil. He studied her hard as she handled the thin latex, and his mind went to a dark region of his soul. She'd learned since they'd been apart. It was irrational, but it bothered him.

"I can do that," he said quietly, wanting to kick himself as the words fled his mouth. "What if a finger nail slits it?" he offered as a consolation to her sad expression and as a cover for his inappropriate jealousy.

"You're right," she said with an easy smile. "We have to be careful."

He relaxed a little as she accepted his flimsy excuse, wishing that her velvety hands could have applied the necessary protective layer between them. He was a fool... Next time, he'd let her do it.

"Lay back," he whispered into her neck, "it's your turn."

She smiled and followed his lead, closing her eyes as her head touched the pillow. What had he been thinking, to almost insult her while she was in the midst of giving him all that she had? Giving with all the tenderness and warmth that both his body and soul had craved. He had to let go of his demons, and he exorcised them as he paid sweet tribute to her skin. One by one, he threw out all reservations and inhibitions about where she'd been during her twenty years away from him. Landing slow kisses down her stomach, he begged her with his tongue to forgive all transgressions, until she arched her back and whimpered with exhaustion.

Returning slowly to cover her, he found the delicate curve of her neck and told her the truth. "I missed you, baby."

She had hungered for this kind of attention for so long. Someone to have and to hold, someone to trust and to love. Someone to laugh with and play with, someone to make her feel like a child, while appreciating that she was a woman. Oh, God, yes, she had needed this.

A gasp rippled through her abdomen and caught in her windpipe as she felt him enter her slowly. This was different than the night before. It wasn't rushed by passion, or consumed by unrelenting physical need. Nor was it dissipated by quantity. It was slow, and steady, and rhythmically constant, just like the lazy tick of the album that was done. Yet, the pace of his constancy wore on her desire, stoking the smoldering embers to a new level of heat.

"Please," she whispered, trying to rush his rhythm with her own movements, "enough."

"No," he murmured, holding her hips more firmly beneath him, "this has to last us for a week."

Again she closed her eyes as she felt him enter her by a fraction, then move away. Each time excavating a deeper moan from her as he explored a deeper terrain and retreated. Holding onto his shoulders tightly, she arched to every shallow stroke of motion that he offered. Tears ran from the corners of her eyes as he continued to pull shivers from her depths. Weak with anticipation, she bit into his neck and wrapped her legs around his waist to be rewarded by his full body weight and length. When he returned to her again, his own shudder connected with hers, and he enfolded her with his arms around her so tightly that her lungs competed for air.

No words were possible or necessary as his easy rhythm shifted and became a sudden acappella chant of mingled breath. In their world, the new place that they'd just created, time and space had no meaning. At once she was past, present, and future. She felt him go first, and followed him to slip behind the nourishment of the sun... eclipsed by completing desire, as they found another dimension under the moon.

Trembling in a damp pool of perspiration, she kissed his hot shoulder while he heaved in huge inhales. The now distant tick from the stereo became a metronome, coaxing her to delirium as the late afternoon sunbeams began a hypnotic dance of warmth across the spread. "I have to go home," she whispered reluctantly. "I have to, baby."

"I know," he groaned, seeming pained by her truth. "Maybe... can we just lay here like this for a little while. I want to stay like this forever."

"So do I," she murmured, as he rolled her over

to lie on his chest. She let her cheek find the spot that it had always remembered—right over his heart, where the thuds beat in her ear like a primal drum. She took a deep inhale through her nose and let his sweat after-scent conquer her. "Okay..." she whispered, drifting off to sleep, "since this has to last for a week."

Chapter 4

In the distance a dog barked in the alley, and she snuggled in closer to hear the steady drumbeat under her cheek. She was home. The dog was a summertime, Philly sound, she mused sleepily, as the unrelenting thud coming from within Jerome's chest matched her own. His breaths were deep and rooted in total contentment, like hers. Yes, summer would be here soon, she half-dreamed, as she drifted in and out of consciousness in sated splendor.

Slowly, her senses added other distant sounds as though composing music from her basic wonder of being fully alive. Sinking into Jerome's body heat, she yawned. The repetitive scratch coming from the finished album, the melodic echo of a child crying in the apartment below, the dog, all fusing with the constant drip of water in the bathroom tub. Traffic. Far-off student laughter. Urban symphony. His heart-beat. His breaths. Percussion, horns, strings, bells, bass. A child crying in the apartment below. A mother's soothing voice. Jay had once taught her how to really appreciate music...

A child crying!

Antoinette opened her eyes and sat up immediately. The sun was gone and the purple-gray haze of evening had replaced it. Panic constricted her breathing for a moment as she tried to orient herself to her environment. Guilt swept through her and propelled her out of bed, stinging her with a slap of reality. She was late! Seriously late. She'd missed her commitment. Her child was in the streets. Over a man. She must be losing her mind!

"Lauren—Jay, wake up! What time is it?" She gasped, answering her own question as the time on his clock radio punched her with the facts. "It's almost seven-thirty! Jay. Get up now!"

"Baby, what's the matter?" he asked in a semi-daze. "Where'you going?"

"Home!" she shouted, when he stirred too slowly and only yawned. Antoinette fled from the bedroom in search of her clothes in the bathroom, skidding on the small rug when her feet hit the tile floor in the process. She grabbed the towel rack to keep her balance, and righted herself as her gaze tore around the small space for her clothes. With one leg in her underpants, she hopped around in a circle till she got them on. "Shit!" she exclaimed as her own wetness dampened them. Tearing them down her legs, she kicked her panties away and turned on the shower, jumping in and nearly scalding herself, scooting away from the too-hot water and fumbling with the soap. "God forgive me, God forgive me for being late for my child," she murmured over and over as she lathered only the most necessary parts of herself, rinsed, and jumped out.

Almost bumping into the door as she opened it, she ran back to the bedroom leaving a trail of wet footprints down the hall. "C'mon, soldier! Look alive! This is not a drill!" she urged, trying to catch her breath as she flung a pile of now damp clothes that had been under her arm onto the bed. When Jerome moved in slow motion, she hop-ran down the hall and grabbed his clothes and scurried back to him, fighting against her own clothes as she tried to pull them on against her wet skin.

Hurling a bundle of jeans and his sweater at

him, she forced him to deflect the projectiles to keep them from hitting his face. "I. Said. Come. On! Jay." Her directive was clear. Her reasoning was painfully clear. She had to get out of there. She was a mother on a mission.

"Look." He chuckled, collecting the clothes and moving like molasses. "She's with her Daddy. No harm—"

"—No harm done?" Antoinette sputtered, finishing his statement and pulling her dripping hair into a knot. "My hair is wet," she nearly screamed, her eyes darting around for her shoes and socks. "I haven't been at the damned gym!" she shouted as she ran down the hallway and back into the bathroom.

Slightly relieved to see Jerome dressed when she got back to the bedroom, she placed her hand over her heart and began spinning in a circle. "Okay. Okay. Okay. Where was I? I was at the mall. No. I was, was at church. Oh... No.... that's sacrilege to lie like that. Where was I, Jerome—for three hours!" she panted as she spun to face him.

"With me," he said with a wide grin that grated her nerves.

"I was not laying up with a man for three hours—making myself late for my baby! Do you hear me?"

"You were taking care of some family business, then."

"Right, Jay," she puffed between shallow breaths, "Good answer. Family business—but, why didn't I call?"

"It was an emergency," he said, chuckled, and leisurely put on his watch. He shook his head and sat down to put on an alternate pair of sneakers that had been under the bed. "Should I take a shower first?"

"Are you crazy!" she squeaked, losing her voice at the suggestion. "Brian can't see you! Lauren can't think—no. Let me off at the corner. I'll walk down the block, just in case."

"You'll do no such thing," he countered, tying his sneakers slowly. Very slowly.

"Then, then... I'll run home, should only take five minutes. Ten, tops. Oh... hurry up!"

Jerome folded his arms over his chest and looked at her with a widening grin. "This definitely takes me back, baby."

"We don't have time for that yang right now!" she shrieked, running to get her coat. "Don't start. I have to go home."

"Why are you rushing for him? Who is he, your father? Thought he was your ex-husband, if I'm not mistaken?"

She stared at him with her jaw slack as she re-entered the room. It took a moment for his comment to catch up to her mind. "No. He's not my father. Just move like he's my father. He has my child in his possession," was all she could say. She steadied her breath and leveled her gaze at him when he chuckled again.

"All right, all right, Toni," he said with a grunt as he stood up. Smiling at her, he passed her in the hall and grabbed his cap and jacket.

She allowed the silence to envelop them on the way out of the building to the car, and she ignored the way he hummed and seemed to be in such a good mood as they got in and pulled off.

"You're losing all of your relaxation, baby," he whispered in a low, sexy tone. "And, after I worked so hard to help you find it."

She couldn't even address the comment or the undercurrent that went with it. All she could focus on was getting to Lauren, and trying to keep the peace with Brian. Why did everything have to be such a struggle? When Jerome turned the corner, the blood drained from her hands and they went icy. "He's parked in front of my unit," she whispered. "This is bad. Real bad."

"Want me to go around the block and drop you off at the corner?" Jerome asked in a too-casual tone that annoyed her to no end.

"No. Then where's my car?" she whispered as

he slowed down to pull into a space.

"In front of his. Only one on the block with out-of-state tags—good guess, huh?"

"Oh, shit! This is bad. It's bad... definitely not good."

"Well, at least—"

"—Don't say a word," she whispered, "I have to think."

"Can I have a kiss goodnight?"

"No!" she whispered through her teeth. "I fell in the Wissahickon. I jumped off the Ben Franklin Bridge. That's why my hair is wet, and my clothes are wet, and I'm late. Take me to the hospital and bring me home in an ambulance!" She laughed with a sudden burst of hysteria. "Jesus, Jay, this is raggedier than a bowl of yock!"

He stared at her for a moment then leaned his head on the steering wheel, letting out deep bellows of thunderous laughter in the process. "Now I'm a paramedic?" he heaved between breaths. "See, T, that's why I always thought up all the good lies for your folks back in the day. Yours are too dramatic, girl!" Jerome let his head fall back and he wiped his eyes with both palms. "Damn, my Pop was right—history's repeatin' itself. I can't escape the drill!"

"For real," she whispered, suddenly cutting off her release valve of laughter as quickly as she had turned it on. "What can I say?"

"How about, I'm sorry I'm late. It won't happen again. And I didn't mean to make you worry. No explanation, but throw your apology in the door on the way in. Works every time." He said still chuckling.

Antoinette went drop-dead serious. "Does it?" Something about the way the rehearsed phrase just rolled off his lips. It was too easy, and she'd heard it before.

"Now, what's wrong?" he asked, the mirth easing away from his face as he stared at her.

"Nothing. I'll talk to you later."

"Hey. Hold it," he said in a gentle tone. "You've gone schizo on me again. What just happened?"

"Nothing," she lied. "I'm upset because I have to get in the house to take care of my child. Call me later."

"Okay," he murmured, looking confused. "What time, baby? I know you have to put the little one to sleep, do some explaining, get ready for work—"

"—I'll let you know," she snapped and unlocked the door then jumped out. Straightening her carriage, she held her head high and slammed the door.

"Hold up," Jerome said in a firm voice, getting

out of his side of the car. "I want to talk to you."

"Not now."

"Oh, yes now," he said in a tone that stilled her. "There is nobody in Brian's car—which means what?"

"That he's probably in the house."

She began walking and he cleared the front of the Bronco and came to her side, holding her arm to stop her.

"What?"

"You heard me."

"You ex-husband has a key to your house?" Jerome paced in front of her and punched the hood of his car. "What the hell. I can't even find the words."

She folded her arms over her chest and looked at him hard. "Lauren has terrible asthma. Okay. She can't be out in extreme weather, for one. For two, I have all sorts of medicine for her in the house—Brian has to have access to that, in the event of an emergency—even though he has a duplicate set of medications at home. Just like my father and May have to have a key. But, so far, he's the only one that knows how to deal with her asthma. Don't even go there." She was resolute, and didn't want to hear his male bullshit.

"You got a key to his joint?" Jerome asked through his teeth, looking like he was ready to square off with her in the street. "Huh? What if he'd come in early this morning? Then she would have really gotten an education. No. You gotta rectify this, T. Pronto. I can't live with it. Never. It's not done."

"I don't have a key to his place in Jersey, because I don't need one. Think about it," she countered with her own version of logic. "Lauren is either with me here, or with him there. Let's say she has an asthma attack while she's with me in Philly. I then panic, and drive past my father's house, and twenty pharmacists, three area hospitals—I pass Mercy Douglas, University of Pennsylvania, Children's Hospital. I cross a damned bridge, Jay, the Ben Franklin Bridge, up the friggin' Black Horse Pike, to put a key in Brian's door? Pulleeeeese. Get over it. I'm going in the house."

"What if he came in unannounced?"

"He wouldn't. It's our agreement. I trust him. We talked about it... and he wouldn't have wanted to see this. Ever. Besides, he's probably getting married, anyway."

"What has his getting married got to do with him having a key to your door as an ex-husband? Antoinette, listen to yourself, and be real. No matter what happens with us—he shouldn't have a key to your door. His marital or relationship status shouldn't have jack to do with your personal independence."

"Jerome, look—"

"—No, woman. You look. This ain't just some jaded male logic—as y'all call it. I'm telling you the God's honest truth—straight up without a chaser. Now, either you deal with it, or you don't—but don't keep trying to tell me that everything between y'all is a groove after all he did to you. No. What it is is, you still love him, he still loves you, and you just walked to prove a point. Then, it got serious and papers went back and forth, and neither of you knows how to call a truce. Remember, I'm a vet, been in the service down at Dover Airforce Base, and I know a DMZ when I see it. Y'all ain't finished."

"Yes we are, because he told me that he wasn't trying to deal with this any more—just like I told him. We talked about it. So, it is what it is, whether you believe me or not."

Tense silence enveloped them, as both lovers stood deadlocked on the sidewalk. Antoinette could feel hot tears rising in her eyes, and his words had slapped her harder than he could have ever imagined. All the conversations with her girlfriends about peace and civility between ex-spouses came into focus and became moot. She wanted to wail as the internal conflict tore at her.

Yes, she loved Brian Wellington and his family with all her heart and soul. And yes, she still loved Jerome Henderson with all her heart and soul. And yes, she loved being married in the traditional sense, with all her heart and soul. And hell no, she'd never wanted to be divorced, to have a blended family, or a confusing list of last names living under the same roof. But, hell yes, she wanted to be happy, and in love, and married again to a man who loved, honored, and cherished her. But, dear God in Heaven, she was scared to death of taking that chance. One false step left, one false step right, could bring her out of the demilitarized zone, the DMZ, as Jay called it, and into enemy territory—the landmine strewn province of marital fights, power struggles, financial inequities and difficulties, and most of all, infidelity.

Antoinette could feel her heart beating a hole through her breastbone as though trying to escape her body. She couldn't go through another failed marriage, another divorce, and she damned sure couldn't take her daughter through it—not just for sex and companionship. Never. And, there was no kind way to say that to the man standing before her who'd just asked her to marry him for the second time in twenty years.

"Brian is cool. He said so," she repeated, looking at her hands, which were clasped before her. "I have to go."

Jerome's expression held a mixture of incredulous suspicion. "So... oh... then, I guess that's enough. You take a man that lied to you repeatedly at his word. Okay, T. Fine. Whatever you say. I was born yesterday. The day before yesterday, in fact. Cool. I can deal with it," he muttered, walking back to his car and hopping in. "Later."

She refused to dignify his position, which threatened her own. Antoinette turned on her heel and then suddenly stopped without looking back as she recognized her father's car. A sickening dread crawled through her belly.

What had happened to her baby?

Running across the street, she bounded for the building and fished out her keys. She managed the locks, took the flight of steps, and flung open the door so hard that it nicked the paint on the opposite wall. "What happened!" she gasped, searching the tribunal of worried faces that stared back at her. "Where's Lauren? What happened?"

"You were late, so I called your father," Brian said evenly, appraising her from head to toe. "I told him that I had a key, and could put Lauren to bed—if he and May could sit with her. She's in bed. Calm down."

“We were worried and ran down the list,” her father said quietly. “We called your girlfriend, Cookie, but got her machine. We called Val and Buddy, but they hadn’t seen you. We called Tracey, and her husband Scoop said you hadn’t been by. May called Vanessa, but I figured that you wouldn’t have been by to see your cousin Ness unless Lauren was over there. Then I called Adrienne, but your sister said she hadn’t heard from you—and none of us thought you’d hopped a plane to LA, but we thought if you were feeling depressed, you might have called your sister. I even tried calling your girlfriends Olivia and Francis, but nobody had heard hide nor hair from ya. That’s when I called my sister, Pearline, and she said to give it a coupla hours. So, we came here to wait to be sure you wasn’t dead in some alley, or in the morgue with a tag on your toe. This ain’t like you, Toni, baby.”

Horrified, Antoinette’s gaze tore from her father’s expression of concern to her stepmother May’s expression—that she couldn’t read. Jesus. Her first time out in two years on the other side of a divorce, and her business had been broadcast throughout Philadelphia like a police all points bulletin. All because her father, May, and even Brian didn’t think she could have a life beyond being a mother, or a teacher—since the divorce.

No, she was just a working-mother-drone with no life beyond that! Why, because she wasn't a high-powered sales executive any longer, after getting laid-off? Why, because she taught in a women's shelter now?

Why? All because they saw her as being slightly overweight, therefore, being unattractive for a suitor? Why, because being in an emotionally charred marriage made her eat for comfort? Oh, so she couldn't have been on a date? Therefore, if she wasn't helping someone, providing a service to someone, or running errands for someone, she had to be dead in the morgue—and it never dawned upon any of the people sitting in her borrowed living room that she might also have a private life! Oh. Because her mother was dead and gone, and she was the eldest daughter, she had to fill in the gap as Mrs. Dependable? Bull shit.

"If Adrienne was missing for a few hours," she whispered angrily, "would you have sent out a search party like this?" As soon as she'd asked the question, she regretted it, because she knew their truthful answer would confirm the deep gash of hurt.

"No," her father immediately replied, looking confused. "You know how Adrienne is, with her fly self. She'd probably be out on a date and getting into some trouble, if you know what I mean. Or, doing her artistic thing on a good gig somewhere. What's that got to do with where you been?"

Rage and indignation mingled with humiliation. Yet, self-doubt began to erode what was left of feeling pretty that she'd claimed in Jerome's arms. Something fragile snapped within her mind as she stared at them all in front of her and they stared back. No, she couldn't keep going to men like a junkie, seeking the elixir of approval in their eyes to give her the feeling of being pretty and worthy. That was something she had to give herself. She finally understood in that moment that this was what had been robbed from her, beginning with her father.

Brian's eyes had always seen her the way her father had, dependable and necessary. But as a woman just a little flawed, just a little imperfect. Whereas, Jerome had always seen her as a complete prize. That was the pivotal difference. One man's eyes dredged her soul, while the other man's replenished it. It took seeing her father's expression simultaneously with Brian's to truly grasp how deep this hurt went.

Defeat began to blanket the rage within her. Logic came to the fore in a reflex to block the pain. It would take days to clean up the carnage and to call all her girlfriends with some sort of explanation that didn't strip her privacy naked. Humiliation strangled the words in her throat, but one simple thought drilled its way out of her skull: why didn't men have to deal with this shit when they came out of a divorce? Why was it the woman's reputation that was always on trial?

May had smiled at her. But was it a smug smile of satisfaction, laden with the fact that May had finally caught her dead wrong? Or, was it something else? She couldn't trust herself to see the difference at this point. Tenderness, smugness, pity, were such thin lines from each other, and right now she felt too vulnerable to withstand any sort of attack. She was surrounded by the most important people in her life. These were also people who had always critically assessed her like she were a bug under a microscope. That was also the difference. Her mother didn't examine people like they were spectacles of life. Her mother listened and empathized, and offered balm through tender words, and sometimes with no words, but always in a way that allowed a person to retain their dignity. Inaudible Grace. That's what this situation required—her mother's special brand of inaudible Grace.

If she could have, in that moment, Antoinette would have died a quiet death standing in the middle of the living room floor... and would have gladly followed her mother's lead into the light—just to feel the warmest hug in the world again, besides Pearline's.

With that thought, humiliation edged away and emotional fatigue replaced it, as she twisted up her dripping braid of ponytail that had come loose.

She looked at Brian and gentled her voice. "I didn't mean to be late. Something came up. Next time I'll call."

Her parent's heads followed the discussion as though watching a tennis match, and for the first time in a long while, she wanted to talk to Brian without any peacekeeping forces present.

"Hey," he said in a more civil tone, then cast a sad gaze away from her towards the door. "I've been late for you before. If I didn't have an out-of-town meeting in the morning, I could have kept her. She was as good as gold," he nearly whispered. "I need to spend more time with her now, anyway."

"Did you guys have fun?" Antoinette asked quietly, this time really wanting to know.

His torment had suddenly become something she never wanted to witness again. In the past, she'd reveled in it, and would scavenge it from him at the least provocation. But this evening, in the way he'd glanced away and allowed her personal space and dignity without an argument, he'd become her once-ago friend. This wasn't a tit-for-tat, hurt-for-hurt lover she'd been with, and he seemed to sense that without her saying so. The lateness had been an accident, and this was real.

"We had a really good time, Nette," he said just above a whisper. "I took her to the movies, we went to the zoo because it was such a pretty day. I brought her some spring outfits, and she picked out something for you," he added quietly, producing a zoo token. "It has 'I love you, Mommy,' on it. It's a key chain."

He paused for a moment and looked down, pulling her key off his own ring and slipping it on the new one.

She covered her mouth with her hand and lowered her gaze to the little metallic gift that he placed in her palm. She couldn't look up, and she blinked back the tears as the words on it blurred. "Thank you," she whispered, "for everything."

Her comment seemed to hold him for a moment, and he looked away as she glanced up at him. Somehow she hoped that he could understand the volumes of truth in her simple statement. She was indeed sorry—for it all. Not just for being late this evening, but for all the hurts, the foul words, the contribution to the scarring of another human being's soul. They were once married, and they had both shared some dreams, and neither of their sets of dreams had been realized. From that perspective alone, the entire outcome was sad—regardless of who had more right or wrong on their side. Indeed, there had been a body count.

In that brief moment of time, she also remembered his early kindness, how they had laughed and dreamed together as kids. She remembered his keen intellect, and adolescent smile, and the way she'd admired his sense of what a father should be. She remembered his mother's Christmas turkey, and her ever-present hugs after her own mother had passed. She remembered their first dance, their first kiss, and his gentle loving of her when they were young. His pet name echoed in her mind when he'd used hers. Time was such an elusive, yet powerful, thing. It could expand and contract, and even make other people in a room disappear. It could haunt one like a ghost, and it could make a lateness reveal so much.

She now understood why her mother had once told her that forgiveness was Divine. She wondered how many hurts could have been spared if forgiveness had taken up residence in their home?

And how much of all of this could have been avoided if all the players in this tragedy had been able to see beyond their own hurts? Time. Yes, it was time to let it go.

Antoinette swallowed hard as her mind absorbed the last shreds of a distant life, one that had once held so much promise within its fragile shell. All of the communally reciprocated hurts peeled away and became unimportant as she looked at his stricken expression. There had been good times.

"I only want you to be happy, Nette. I'll always be here for you and Lauren. My people will too," he said softly, his eyes telling her that he'd also remembered the good times within the seconds that came between them. "I guess I can tell you now. I'm getting married," he whispered. "I hope you're happy with him."

As she stood staring at her ex-husband, no further words were necessary. She knew he knew where she'd been, and with whom, and that his decision to marry had been finalized in those waiting-for-her moments—no matter who the other woman was—his decision was carved all during the fragile hours he'd probably paced and waited for her to come home. Her lover had even sensed it—that the door to their marriage had remained open by a slim crack of hope on either side. It wasn't over, until now.

"It's Jerome," she murmured, offering the admission as a truce and to let Brian know that there was a good person who might share his daughter's life.

"It always has been," his whispered, then looked away from her towards the door. "I hope you're happy, Nette."

"I hope you are too, kiddo," she said quietly, using his pet name to let him know what she'd said was true. "You'll always be her Daddy. No stand-ins. Just don't replace her when the new babies come. Promise me."

Brian had swallowed hard and looked at her briefly when she'd used the term of endearment. "Her name is Crystal, and she won't hurt Lauren. I promise... on my mother's life. I'ma miss you, Nette."

"Im'a miss you too."

As though shaking off the memory, he nodded, then walked over to the chair to collect his coat. She resisted the urge to run over behind him and hug away his pain. Antoinette allowed her gaze to sweep her parent's confused expressions to help her remain resolved not to move. It was a decision made out of kindness, not malice. Somehow it would hurt them both too much to hug each other any more. Somehow, this exchange was different.

It wasn't about who was right, or who was wrong. It was about two people who had shared a life that was now finally over. It was about two old friends who were going their separate ways, creating a new path that even divorce papers couldn't have paved nor erased.

This evening, it was done. Finally. This was the real truce where she forgave, and forgot, and she could tell by the resignation in Brian's carriage that he had too. And it happened so suddenly, so quietly. All of the rage had left her soul, just as Pearline had promised her it would. She had spent the afternoon washed with happiness and baptized by hope, and somehow, her friend that now stood before her, had known.

Brian's knowledge hung between them and haunted her from his eyes. He knew that this time she hadn't slept with an empty suit, just some guy designed to inflict feminine revenge. The act hadn't been committed in a vacuous state of jealousy. Nor had she sought to inflict pain by coming home late. Rather, she had befriended someone new, had made love to someone from long ago. She had gone somewhere that he couldn't compete with, and the war was over. As simply as it had begun, it had ended. The last bit of passion that was always masked in rage and that had linked her to him faded. An unexpected melancholy took its place.

Antoinette closed her eyes briefly to let her tears recede. Without recrimination, or shouting, Brian had taken it like a man, and indeed, he had become her friend.

"If you need anything, Nette, let me know. Okay?" He pulled on his coat and took out his keys. "I know things are tight... been talking to your folks. Lauren's school bill won't be a problem any more. How's your car acting?" he said quietly, moving toward the door.

"It's a bomb," she whispered, "but, I'm all right. I appreciate your asking, though. You can't help with everything, that's not fair." She opened the door and let him out.

"If I can, I will—you know that... no matter what," he said softly, holding her gaze for a moment before he slipped out to the landing. "You were my best friend. Nothing can replace you, or Lauren. I am so sorry. You'll never know. Take care of yourself, honey."

"I will. Drive safe. Have a good trip—and, good luck on Monday. Go kill something," she murmured with a smile, wanting with all her heart to give him a transfusion of her sales ability, to give him back all of the dignity that she'd unwittingly robbed by her early successes and vicious words.

He smiled sadly and issued their old sales code thumbs-up and she returned it, then shut the door behind him. Antoinette let her breath out slowly and didn't bother wiping away the tears that had fallen. "It's over," she said quietly, staring at her parents.

"It's over?" Her father gave her a puzzled look as he'd asked the question curtly, then stood up as he glanced at his wife. "What the hell are you talkin' about, girl? Y'all been divorced for how long? Two years? Separatin' and gettin' back together like Liz Taylor, and what's his name... Brando. That's what y'all is like," he said shaking his head. "Where you been all day, anyway?"

"Shut up, Matt, and get your coat," May commanded with marked authority. "It's none of your business and it's late."

"But—" he protested, confusion settling in his expression as she held up her hand and cut him off with a black-woman-said-don't-argue flip of her wrist.

"She needs to be alone," May pressed on quietly as she walked over to Antoinette, giving her a hug. "And she needs to grieve. Get my coat and let's go home, old man."

Antoinette held on to May's embrace for a moment and swallowed a sob. She couldn't speak or thank May enough for hearing her without words. Somehow in that touch they both knew their war was coming to a conclusion, too. The older woman ran her hand down Antoinette's back then held her away to look into her eyes. May touched her wet cheek with her fingertips and then kissed her face. A fellow divorce veteran's understanding reflected back at Antoinette from May's wide brown eyes, and Antoinette closed her own as new moisture filled them. Something indefinable bound them as her father huffed and fussed about behind them.

May had finally become her mother-friend.

Chapter 5

Time. What she needed now that everyone had left the condo, was time—or at least four more bodies to fill the various competing roles in her life.

Antoinette looked down at her sleeping child and bent to kiss Lauren's cheek. Where had it all gone, she wondered as she left her daughter's room and went into her own?

She sat down with a heavy thud on the bed and stared at the answering machine counter. It had registered twenty-seven messages within the short pause in the universe when she had been gone.

Grabbing an unpaid bill from her nightstand,

she turned over the envelope and began jotting down the messages from the machine. Two from her sister with a blow-by-blow description of some new man. Four cryptic ones from Val, one elusive message from Fran. That's right, she had to call Fran! Nobody had really talked to her since they had all gone to the women's conference in the Poconos, not even Tracey, Fran's child's Godmother. But, then again, Fran was always busy. The thing that concerned her was that Fran did not look well at all the last time they'd seen each other. Antoinette made a mental note to connect with her before the week was out.

To be expected, her machine held the normal three calls from her father and May, but after the exchange she'd just had with May, those calls no longer grated her.

After those close friend and family calls, five more calls followed from her mother's elderly girlfriends—the women who just needed to see her mother, hear her mother's voice, and to look into her mother's eyes through Antoinette's face. She understood their pain, and appreciated their love, but her life had changed during the decade or more of service that she'd already rendered.

Reaching into her nightstand and taking out some note cards, she made herself a vow to stay in touch with them by mail—it was a compromise and a better way than tying up her evenings listening to who died, who was sick, and who was in the hospital. It was also much more efficient, provided contact through one-way communication, and she could write each of them a cheery little missive while sitting in a staff meeting. Maybe that's how her mother had multi-tasked all of those years?

Antoinette let out her breath and buzzed past their lengthy, guilt-generating pleas for her to come visit with Lauren, take them to the supermarket like she always had or to listen to the details of a funeral. Not tonight.

She didn't bother to write down those calls, and she flipped past two computerized collection agency calls. If they couldn't have enough courtesy to have a human being address her about her delinquency, she reasoned, then she wasn't going to give them the courtesy of an excuse, or a return phone call—and, they had called on a Sunday, no less! Wasn't Sunday still sacrosanct? Didn't people get one day off to not worry about what they had facing them all week?

Annoyed, she did jot down a reminder to call Consumer Credit Counseling Service. She'd remembered hearing about it while training for the counseling portion of her job. They'd told her that agency was above-board, free to the public, and would stop the late penalty and interest charges from accruing on her charge cards. She didn't even have to be on Welfare to be a part of the program. "One money order to CCCS," she mused as she wrote the note, "and you bastards will stop calling me. Should have done this a year ago."

When the phone rang again, she decided not to answer it, assuming that it was one of the girls. She needed to get the balance of the calls off the machine first, before she launched into a one-hour conversation with any of them. As she listened to her student calls, then two messages from the job about the monthly Monday staff meeting, she stopped and wound back the messages from her boss and one of her new co-worker friends. She played the tape again and slowed down her mind, but continued to riffle through her bills as she did so.

Doing three tasks at once, Antoinette pulled out a handwritten letter that had Pearline's distinctive signature on it, and set it aside while the messages played and she scribbled notes to herself. She'd enjoy Pearline's letter first—with a cup of tea. The bills could wait, she thought, as she tossed the invoices on the floor and listened more carefully to her job messages. "A four o'clock staff meeting?" she hissed as her boss' strident voice grated through the machine. "Why not first thing? Why not at two, so we can get the hell out and back to our kids!" she fumed, jotting down that message quickly. But the tone of her co-worker's voice in the next message froze her.

The information was cryptic, but the issue was implicit as the timid voice whispered through the speaker, "Be loaded for bear, when you come in tomorrow. A lot of changes are going on around here, girlfriend. Call me. We didn't get our grant from The Private Industry Council."

"Okay, so I'm probably jobless again," Antoinette said with resolution. "It was time." She was past the point of panic, and she found the edge of the vast border of being overwhelmed, which seemed to provide a circumference limiting her life. Tears of frustration welled in her eyes, and she blew past the messages that were left.

Okay, she would only call Francis back. They'd been playing a hellified game of phone tag for over three weeks, but Francis didn't stress her. Francis probably just wanted to say, "Hi," and that's when she could ask her how she was feeling. Francis was aware of her schedule, because she had one of her own. Francis didn't guilt trip her, or want her to take on any special role in her life. Francis could understand space and time and could just let life be. Even though they had grown less close over the years through time, space, and life in general, Francis was most likely the only non-judgmental one in the group. And, like her, Francis had fled Philly. Made sense.

All of a sudden, being home felt like it was suffocating her once more.

When the phone rang again, she refused to pick it up. The sound of the ringer clanged in her brain as though it were a steel mallet hitting an anvil. "Go to hell, Jerome." Tears coursed down her face as she waited for it to stop ringing, and she leaned her head back on the wall behind the bed. She'd only gotten to message number twenty-five and had two more to go, and they were still calling! "Mom, how did you do it?" she whispered into the empty room. "I can't do it. I just can't."

Fury replaced the tears as the phone rang again. She sat immobilized and slowly pulled her breaths in and let them out, then snatched the phone off the hook and slammed it down. "Look, I have laundry that hasn't been done," she argued to the noisy technology that refused to stop ringing.

When the sound stopped and immediately erupted again, she thought of throwing the telephone out of the window, or yanking the cord from the wall, but thought better of it. If she did, she'd be the one to have to buy another one for the tantrum.

Her mind raced through the list of to-dos: she had dinner to cook for the week that she hadn't started yet. It was already eight o'clock at night and she still had to lie out Lauren's clothes for tomorrow, and to pack her lunch. She had to get her own clothes for work ready, plus review her case files and update them for a meeting tomorrow. She had bills to pay—without any money. Lauren's school wanted another tray of brownies for the fundraiser. Plus she had to find time to buy and mail a belated birthday card to a cousin.

"Go to hell with your macho shit, Jerome," Antoinette whispered, thinking of all the things that had been left undone while she'd spent a night and a day in splendor. "Sunday is supposed to be a day of rest," she whispered bitterly, wondering when a woman got an opportunity to rest, then slammed down the receiver.

Lurching herself forward, she stared at the machine by her phone and took off the last two messages—one from Brian, and another from her father. At least the last two messages had been addressed in the flesh, she thought, her mood growing surlier as she tried to prioritize what she had to do. Jerome had some nerve just waltzing into her life and making demands. Everybody in her life had become time bandits.

When the phone rang, this time, she steadied herself, expecting Jerome's voice. But, when her sister's voice came through with her normal cheerful salutation, Antoinette's heart sank.

"Yo, guurrl, where you been?"

"I gotta lot of stuff to do, Adrienne," she said irritably, "and I gotta go."

"Oh, so you don't even have time for your sister, huh? Did you just hang up on me? I called and got disconnected."

"Did you have time for me when I needed some baby-sitting support so I could go to an important conference, in fact, have you ever made time for me when I really needed you to?" Antoinette seethed.

"Why do you have to always go back to that old guilt-trip. It's not healthy—"

"—Because I'm a mother, and tired of being yours. I need your help sometimes. So a breeze in celebrity visit, where you come and eat, crash, and pursue your own agenda is not helpful. Nor do I want to waste my time on the telephone with you at this juncture in my day. Like I said, I have things to do, too, and I'm prioritizing my life for once. Bye," Antoinette snapped and hung up.

For the first time in a long while, she felt liberated from an age-old promise. This was her new start, without a grown child or deathbed commitment to raise said grown child. Adrienne was an adult, her father was an adult, and anyone in her mother's sphere of influence would finally have to deal with the fact that the anchor was gone.

As the awareness congealed within her, Antoinette felt light, buoyant. After only having breakfast in her belly all day, for the first time in over a decade she also became aware that she wasn't hungry. She wouldn't call any family and friends tonight, or justify anything. She'd thank Jerome later for showing her how to do what she wanted, then beg for forgiveness later. But, she wasn't going to be indebted to him for that piece of wisdom. He, just like the rest of them, had to give her space.

After unsuccessfully trying to reach her new co-worker by phone, she went into the kitchen. No doubt Darlene was on the line with her own close-knit crew, Antoinette reasoned, and probably going over the options of a possible job lay-off. That was how it worked. Each woman had an inner circle, then a wider outer circle. The inner circle got the news flash, first, and resolutions were developed within the core before others got called. Others got called after all grieving, vulnerabilities, and options had been fully explored within the inner circle. It was the unspoken dynamic between women, and Antoinette took no offense as she hung up the phone and went to the refrigerator to prepare a week's worth of nukable dinners.

Dropping rice and frozen chicken wingettes—that she didn't have to clean—into a pan, she slathered on barbecue sauce and put the pan in the oven. They'd have to eat chicken all week. At least there was a starch to compliment it, she thought, trying to remember the nutritional basics. Maybe she could pinch-hit with McDonalds and, or, hot dogs for a meat—if Lauren got tired of what she'd made. Going against everything that she'd ever been taught, she opened up a bag of frozen mixed vegetables and plunked them in a pot. She added water and a smoked turkey butt to at least make it seem like she'd cooked for real. Flipping on the burner to low, she went back into the refrigerator and grabbed some pre-packaged juices, an apple, a Tasty Kake, a tiny box of raisins, and the bologna and cheese.

"Okay," she murmured to herself as she worked, "you can do this." Antoinette glanced up at the clock and put Lauren's lunch in her pail, then raced into the bedroom to begin sorting laundry.

She ignored the phone as it rang again. Her arms were elbow-deep in the washing machine, and she'd already attempted to return all of the most urgent requests of her time. Those she hadn't spoken to directly, knew from her messages that, she cared. That's all they needed to know, anyway, she reasoned, as she pushed funky little kid socks into the wash. At least Lauren's clothes would be done. She could scavenge something for herself for Monday. Hose. Damn! She'd forgotten to buy hose. That meant pants. Her big behind in pants? At work?

Antoinette left the laundry and began ripping through her closet, searching for a pair of good wool pants, and an acceptable over-blouse that would pass at the staff meeting. She prayed as she looked at the limited choices. How did her mother do this? Disgusted, she made a selection that added to her morose thoughts. She could remember her mother always getting dressed last, eating last, and buying herself something last. Now she knew why. Remorse filled her as she took down the items and thought of the once gorgeous woman that had been her mother, but who had simply worn out under motherhood and womanhood.

"I don't blame you, anymore, for dying under these conditions," Antoinette said aloud to the empty space while walking toward the kitchen to find the ironing board. "Who could blame you?"

She began ironing her shirt, ignoring the ringing phone. The peacefulness of her space enveloped her as she worked. She also now understood why her mother would find sanctuary in working spaces. She knew why the woman would shoo them out to play, or tell her father to go out with the fellas while she did chores. A deep appreciation for stillness settled in her bones as her hands smoothed the fabric, and the warmth of the stream iron seeped into the textures and patterns then back into her hands. She remembered her mother's struggle, and how she'd implored her to wait to get married—and understood. The dawning awareness propelled the iron across the wool. Her mother had wanted more for her than this. It was never about Jerome versus Brian; it was about her place in the world as a woman.

Antoinette allowed the quiet bubbling of the pot of vegetables to answer her thoughts. The smell from the oven added voice and harmony to the chorus of Amens in her mind. No mother wanted this for her girl-child; a life of juggling priorities, with no space for her own needs or wants. Why was everything such a struggle, even now, for women? How did the old girls do it, she wondered? How did they keep a smile on their faces, food bubbling in their pots, Jesus in their hearts, and their men satisfied?

Antoinette snatched her blouse from the ironing board and walked heavily into the bedroom to hang it up along side her pants.

For the first time, she understood why May didn't back down, flinch at her father's commands, or give way. It was about power, having one's own power, and viciously guarding one's own space. She wondered what her mother would have been if she had done the same in that era? She also wondered if her parents' marriage would have withstood such defiance, and therefore, wondered whether or not the entire thing was a sham based on one person's total sacrifice to the other's total power?

"They broke the mold," she whispered, still awed at how one could ever pay enough homage to a mother. Women allowed children to suck the life out of their bodies, make their titties droop, sacrificed to allow their children to wear the best clothes, while they sewed their own. Deep. A mere thank you didn't seem like it was enough to give to a person who'd stayed in a house that was too small, all because she wanted her children to go to school.

In that moment, she understood her best friend Valerie's rage. Val was in the same position as her mother had been—only Val wasn't taking it lying down. Did that make her best friend wrong?

Antoinette ran her fingers through her hair as the questions beat her conscience. How did her mother do it? Allowing her daughters to dress up for proms, while standing on the steps with her fluffy slippers and a tattered robe on, wishing the young well and waving good-bye and living on only memories. How did she ship people off to college, wanting to go so badly herself, and stay home waiting for stories of what it was like—while a husband took her for granted and bellowed for his supper in the background?

What did such a person get in return? Suddenly she wasn't sure if she could pull off that level of selflessness without feeling a twinge of resentment.

"Mom, forgive me, because you were right," Antoinette murmured with a sigh. "I couldn't understand until I had my own. There must be a better way."

She allowed tears of rage and remorse to run down her face, and let the dark emotions course through her and out of her. In that moment, she was determined to find a middle ground, one that kept some semblance of softness and nurturing, while preserving a space for herself. Lauren didn't need a martyr as a role model or a career shrew, like her girlfriend Cookie had become. Those were extremes. They, as mother and daughter, both needed a new paradigm. The question was how did one create it?

Remembering Pearline's letter, she went into the bedroom, retrieved it and moved back to the kitchen to fix herself a cup of tea. Antoinette glanced at the clock on the microwave. At eleven p.m., she reasoned that she could take a break and enjoy a bit of family news. Pearline's letters were always funny, warm, and wonderful. Carefully positioning herself at the dinette table, she opened Pearline's note as though it were a piece of Godiva chocolate and smiled.

Chapter 6

A bright floral border met her fingers, and two sticks of gum, a tea bag, a supermarket coupon, and a dollar bill for good luck fell out of the envelope. There was also another sealed envelope within the larger outer one she'd just opened, but she knew this was most likely one of Pearline's double letters—probably something to mail forward for Adrienne.

Antoinette chuckled as she pushed the treats to the side, slipped off her shoes, and fastened her attention to Pearline's words.

Hey, "Chile-of-mine"...

Just a quickie note to say hello. Been feeling under the weather, change of seasons—and all.

Where's my Lauren? Is she behaving? I put a dollar in here for you. Now you use it to buy something—just for you—NOBODY else! A woman's got to have something to claim as her own. Trust me. Praise Jesus! Anyway, have you talked to your sister? Can only get her machine—saw her a couple weeks ago when she breezed into town with her sexy self.

Now, you're like her mother, so you need to tell her to get a real job. I want to see her for Easter—even though she was just here. No excuses. I have to look in her eyes so I can see the truth while we're alone. My heart tells me that the girl is struggling and she's not as happy as she wants us all to believe—but, you know your father, my brother, can't see what I see, because he's a man. Anyway, in my mind, she's got to settle down, and get a real secure job with benefits—medical and dental, and a pension.

She won't be young and pretty forever—and needs to find a husband too. Share the gum with my baby, but the tea and the dollar is for you, love. You have to pace yourself, or you'll get sick. Can't get sick—cause you're a mother. Take some vitamins, so you don't fall out. I got a good recipe for baked chicken, see back of this page.

Did you read about the cows going crazy, Neicey? Mad cow disease, or something? Can't even eat red meat, now that don't make sense! People is crazy. Done messed up even the meat. We definitely in The Last Days and Times, honey chile.

Antoinette smiled and shook her head, hearing Pearlinc's authority jump from the pages. "A husband won't give her security, these days, Aunt Pearl. Neither will a job. Let her be, even though she gets on my last nerve," Antoinette chuckled. "Adrienne's got enough sense to follow her dreams, one of us did, anyway. That's why the cows went crazy." She laughed, reading on.

She allowed her eyes to greedily consume the rest of her Aunt's note. She loved the way it contained a recipe, a dash of advice, a bit of church wedged between a parable of common sense. She let her voice ring out with laughter at Pearline's commentary about a woman she hardly remembered, and smiled when she thought of how she'd editorialize her own girlfriend's antics one day for Lauren—when her daughter was old enough to hear kitchen-table gossip.

"I know you're probably turning fast and talking to yourself a mile a minute, Pearline," she mused with a chuckle out loud as she observed a sentence that was left dangling, and tried to make sense of another tangential thought scribbled in to take it's place. Reveling in the mental conversation, Antoinette took a sip of tea, and settled back to read the last page.

But, I won't be cooking—not this Easter, baby. This year I'm turning that over to you.

We all done taught you how, so it's time. You're the best one left, with young enough legs to stand over the stoves all day. If I can eat, I know it'll be good. Chicken prices are going down. There's a coupon in here for it. Call me and I'll help you with the menu. But, you have to also plan your desserts early. They take more time than the meats—and take up oven space. Can't put them in with the meats either, 'cause your cobbler will taste like ham, or chicken, whatever you make—but you know that already, so why am I telling you again? Must be getting senile (ha ha)! Don't think I have a cobbler left in me, Praise God. Well, got chores, so have to run.

*Love to your Pop, my wayward brother, for me. Kiss the baby and slow yourself down—turn that "D" answering machine on, for Sunday too. Folks can wait—even The Lord took a day to rest! See enclosure. I done spoke on it.Love, Aunt P

"Won't be cooking this Easter?" Antoinette held the letter in her hands and stared at it. "You, and Mom, and Aunt Marie, Marlene and Aunt Ruth... all of y'all always cooked?" She read the letter over again slowly. Something was wrong. Seriously wrong. Pearline wasn't even promising to bring a cobbler? A terror too horrible to imagine shot her out of the chair, and she went immediately for the telephone. Dialing her Aunt's number twice before she got it right, she waited as the phone rang ten times. Where was Pearline on a Sunday night!

"Hello?" a weak voice echoed through the receiver into Antoinette's ear.

It took a few moments for Antoinette to respond. Pearline's voice was different. Distant. It was too early for her to be asleep. Pearline was never in bed before eleven! "Aunt Pearl," Antoinette said slowly, trying to sound calm. "I got your letter. Is everything okay?"

"Oh, baby... that's good. I'm fine. Done made my peace. Now you do what I told you, and pace yourself. Start them desserts two weeks ahead'a time. Get some rest, and when I feel better, I'll call you about the menu."

"You're sick, aren't you?" Antoinette whispered, wrapping her arms around her waist for support. "It's more than a cold, has been for a while, hasn't it?"

"Well, baby... the Lord's been good to me. Kept

me here longer than any of my sisters, and your dear mother. You get some rest, baby. Done taught you all I know."

She resisted the urge to scream out. Antoinette paced in a circle and steadied her voice as she walked to and fro the length of the kitchen. "It's what Mom and Grandmom had, isn't it?"

"Now, baby, I kin hear you gittin' yo'self all worked up," the old voice drawled slowly, "Now, don't 'chu cry... yo'Aunt Pearline done lived a long life... things is da way they supposed to be."

Antoinette rocked as she walked. She didn't trust her voice yet, and couldn't speak. In such a short span of time, even Pearline's rhythm had changed. That's when she knew for sure.

Her Aunt breathed heavily as she spoke, and Pearline no longer lit upon subject after subject like a graceful butterfly, sucking the sweet nectar out of each conversation before moving on to the next, leaving you with a whisper of pollen to grow within yourself. And, yet, it was also like the tone of the porpoise. Not just butterfly-gentle, but splashing, laughing, with squeals and whoops.

Fear gripped Antoinette's insides as she wondered whether she'd ever hear their old dolphin speech pattern again? It was becoming a dying art form, spoken in quick rhythms and polyrhythms of partly telepathic clicks of the tongue, interspersed with hand motions, and high-pitched sonar squeals of delight. She could only wait as her heart became concave from despair. Where were the shaking hips, eyes that flashed fire or mirth with the same degree of intensity, the mouth that twisted dental-plates as the sonar-speed patois from Madagascar, the Caribbean, fused with Swahili of The Continent and The Queen's English of North America?

She had learned this mixed language as a child, made bilingual with formal education. The pace of retaining both forms of communication had been coded and staggering, yet, the patios of African American had always been what taught her to swim to safety with lightening synchronicity. Tonight, there was no speed in her Aunt's voice, and Antoinette knew the sound of eminent death in women's voices. She'd heard it all her life; her mother's echoing in her ears.

She also knew that the next time she laid eyes on Pearline, she'd see it—the way the ravages of time took sudden, overnight root... bending normally erect postures, placing lines on surfaces that had been once smooth ebony. That's the way they all went. Fast. At a predetermined time they'd established with God. Colon cancer.

Antoinette let out a slow sigh that matched her Aunt's. It was a last attempt to keep pace with the older woman's highly-stylized, evolved language of saying all by saying nothing—the language of black women.

"Beat the odds, though," Pearline finally said in a gentle tone. "Gave me six months. That was two years ago. Hmmph," Pearline chuckled, "my Jesus has his own timeframe. Ain't a decision of doctors, and man. Had to see my baby back home in Philly, first. Know that chu' was all right, and on yo' way. Now you is, and I done made my peace. Me and your Mom had a good conversation 'bout that. Did you open the envelope inside the big one?"

A sob broke through Antoinette's surface calm, and she stifled it immediately. She knew the baton had been passed—simply laid in her hand with a letter, and confirmed with a phone call. Now she was being asked to be strong. She had to be. The women in her family never cried over deaths, at least never in front of the dying. It just wasn't done. Those departing had to be lain to rest in peace. No spirits were to be troubled with worrying about the generations to follow. They had to be told that all of their work would continue. They needed to know that all the children would be fine, all husbands accounted for, all property settled, and that another woman-soldier would take the fallen's place.

"You and Mom settled it," Antoinette said, forcing the quaver from her throat. If her aunt and her mother had spiritually conferred... "Then let it be done. I'll handle whatever you need." She knew that it was beyond terminal, if her aunt had seen her dead sister-in-law, through either a vision or a dream. That was also how it went in her family. The women came for each other, picked a date, then it was over. Once that happened, time was short.

"You the one that cooks. You just like your mother. You the one that sews. You cleans, and you got good sense. You respectable and good wit money—'cause you was wit her longest, and she taught 'chu right. You got a sof' heart, and you lissens. You the family mother now. Pass it on, baby."

"All the holidays from here on out... all those that's left, I'll take care of," she whispered with newfound strength. "I promise. I'll take care of everything." Antoinette closed her eyes as her Aunt's words pinned her breast with a metal of honor. Indeed, she was the eldest. She was the first in a line of women cousins. She was the only one who had accepted the traditions and kept them alive. She held the history. She was the archivist. She knew all the rituals. She kept all the letters. She remembered all the parables.

She knew all the old faces of all their elderly friends. She kept the photo albums. She knew the recipes by heart, and, she too, was a dying breed. She had to accept the baton, Pearline's badge of honor, with certain courage. And she could not cry.

"You did your mother well," Pearline said in a faint whisper. "You made that same promise to her on her deathbed, and stood by your sister and your Daddy. Kept yo' word good. They been seen off now, though, baby. He got a new wife, and Adrienne got outta school witout a baby—got her education, jus' like you promised your mother. She seen to it herself, helped you, 'cause you was so young—angel that your mother is—she told me what you'd never speak on. Was even a baby yourself, being twenty-three when she passed on. That made her soul restless, to have her babies robbed so early—that wasn't supposed to be, chile. That wasn't God's will—was interference from The Devil. So, she's still watchin,' and won't rest till it's all solved. Even I couldn't fill 'er shoes, but Lord knows, you tried. Promise me, one thing that you'll do this time... owes it to yourself."

"Just tell me, Aunt Pearline, and I'll do it," Antoinette whispered, allowing hot tears to splash the telephone and drop onto the counter. "Anything for you."

"You missed being a young woman. We all got that, at least. We had our turn, and you didn't. You left your father's house with a sixteen year old chile, your sister... and a bran' new husband. Claim some peace for yourself, honey... before you leave this earth. That's all I want from ya, really. My girlfriends done all lived a full life—your mother's friends did too. My children went before me to glory, 'long wit my husband. Yo' sister's got her life in fronta her. Your baby, well, she'll git around to hers, soon enough. My brother got, and lived, his twice. He's a man—they gets theirs. But, your Momma got something for ya that's good, just 'round the corner. Call the man, baby. Let 'im give ya some joy... so I can rest wit yo' Momma. Open the picture I sent you. Kept it for your Momma, after she was gone."

Obeying her Aunt's request, Antoinette numbly opened the second envelope that was still stuck inside the first one. Gingerly, she took it out and broke the seal. Her fingers trembled as she looked at what it contained, and she briefly shut her eyes as Jerome Henderson's image in military uniform came into view.

"Turn it over, and read the back," her Aunt insisted, oddly seeming to know that Antoinette was just now getting to the task.

Antoinette again followed Pearline's instructions, and read the faded blue ink that made her swallow another sob.

"Read it out loud, so both me and your mother kin hear it."

"I can't," Antoinette whispered.

"Yes you kin, baby," Pearline soothed. "Character," the elderly woman stated flatly. "I remember that boy had character. Just like your father did. Could tell by the way he looked at'cha—like you was his entire world. And, that's how you used to look at him, when y'all thought us old folks wasn't payin' y'all no mind. Read what he said."

Steadying her voice, Antoinette drew in a deep, audible breath and whispered the unmistakable scrawl aloud for her Aunt.

"Dear Mom Reeves,

When I get out of the military, I'm going to use my money to go to school. Then I can come back right for Toni. Maybe I can re-enlist and learn to fly and show her the world... because, she really is my world. Just wanted you to have this so you'd know that I was serious about her. –Love, Jerome."

"I put that in the mail to you this Friday, and the very next day, your mother came to see me in a dream and tol' me she always liked that one in particular. I knew she wanted me to be sure you knew it too."

"Yesterday... she came to you? Last night?" Antoinette closed her eyes and hot liquid streamed down her cheeks.

"Last night. Probably when you was with him."

Antoinette stood still and didn't open her eyes. She didn't inquire about the mystery of how her Aunt had known about Jerome, but took her Aunt's subtle knowing on faith. "Mom brought him to you?" Her repeated question was spoken in awe and she had barely mouthed the words.

"Last night," her Aunt chuckled and coughed. "Now lissen... I'm gettin' tired. My voice is giving out. I'll stay till after Easter," she proclaimed, "Ain't gonna ruin no holiday. Also, when you come up in the next few weeks—"

"—I'll come tomorrow," Antoinette rushed in, feeling panicked by the urgency of her Aunt's certain demise. Time was short. Too short. Her Aunt had picked a due date, an appointment with The Lord. It was already established. She'd chosen a time! Just like all the women in the family, once they became ill, even God couldn't tell them to die on a holiday. But Easter was right around the corner!

"Naw, baby," Pearline began slowly. "First of all, you gotta work all week. Den, you got chores to do. You got a chile to play wit, and care for... and if you do like I tell you, a man will take up the rest of your time. Girlfriends you got to be keep-'in touch wit—theys the ones who stand by ya when yo' children die, ya gits widowed, when yo' money's funny... gotta keep the few good ones close, the circle tight—let the others go. Can't rush around for us old ladies, me and yo' Mom's girlfriends, no mo'—or you'll drop dead. They kids is responsible for 'em—and if they didn't teach 'em right, that ain't your bizness. It's a long road that has no turn. Me and your Mom tol' 'em so, too—long time ago, when they was young, out partying, and not teachin' they children, and not handling they bizness. You can't hold it all together no more, Antoinette. Lissen to me, and hear me good. I'ma go back to sleep, you come see me on a Sunday when you have time, and start taking things outta my house."

"Taking things outta your house?" Antoinette leaned against the wall, weak from shock.

"Yes, baby. You good wit numbers. Now lis-sen... ain't gonna have no fightin' in the family over my bones. Also, ain't gonna have the white man take all this silver and china your grand-mother polished all her life. Ifn' you don't get it 'fore I close my eyes, the tax man will eat it up—inheritance taxes, or gift taxes, somethin' like that. My Momma tol' me, cause the old white man she worked for, showed her—wit his own kids. They don't give nothin' to the tax man. Black folks best be gettin' realistic about death, and handlin' of they affairs before, not after, they go!"

"All right. All right, Aunt Pearline," Antoinette stammered as she began pacing again. She'd seen it done before. She'd handled enough funerals in the family to know how it went. She could do this. But this was Pearline! This was like her mother... How could God be so cruel?

"Now you thinkin', baby. Collect yo'self. When you come, I'll have names under everything. Nothin' written in no wills. Give it out to who I say, and make sure antiques—all that cherry mahogany—stays in the family. Properties too. But take yo' time gettin' up here. I done tol' The Lord my plans. I will not die before Easter. Hear?"

Somehow, through all of the pain, her Aunt's declaration made her smile and provided the security blanket of faith she needed at the moment. "You tell Him, Aunt Pearline," she chuckled, "we have too much to do."

"Darn right, baby. He done came once over Christmas, and I had to tell Him about Hisself then!"

Antoinette went still again, remembering her

Aunt's bad cold, and the way she'd picked at her food. It had to be intestinal cancer. It took all the women in her family.

"Ain't it jus' like a man, chile? To be worryin' you to death wit the trivial, when you got work to do? Hmmph, hmmph, hmmph," Pearline pressed on with a hoarse chuckle. "Got's plenty'a questions to ask when I get to glory. I can't wait to see my husband's face. He was probably the one rushin' God's hand in the matter, anyway!" she added with a snort. "Wonder how my boys been? Wonder if both of my sons even made it up there after what they had to do during the Vietnam war? Can't tell, gotta cogitate on that one. But, I'll be glad to see everybody, though. 'Specially my own Momma..."

"Yeah, they'll all be glad to see you," Antoinette whispered, repeating the facts over and over in her mind. Her Aunt was adamantly going to die a dignified, self-appointed time of death.

Antoinette knew that any tears shed were only to wash her own soul free. Pearline would be fine. She'd made her peace and now it was time for her to follow suit. Pearline had spoken of death with such a casual acceptance. There was no fear in her voice, no self-pity, and her Aunt seemed totally willing to slip beyond this life to join the ancestors. Pearline made dying sound like she was packing to go on a cruise. In that moment, she understood Pearline's lesson—live in a way so that you can die without regrets. Then go party with your family that proceeded you. What was to fear? This was a part of life, Antoinette told herself firmly. Everything will be fine.

"I guess another season has passed, huh, Aunt Pearline?" Her voice was resolute and the pain began to dissipate.

"That it has, baby," Pearline said with a happy sigh. "I'm done here. Did it all. Seen it all. Lived it all, honey. No regrets—save a few. That ain't bad for this life, is it?"

"Not at all," Antoinette whispered finding a weird mixture of peace amid the tragic news. "It's a long road that has no turn," she said, repeating one of her Aunt's favorite sayings to let the elderly woman know just how well she remembered all that had been taught.

"See, you even startin' to understand. Soon, you'll be able to read the signs witout dreams... be able to hear an angel speak to you witout gettin' scairt.... and know how to talk to The Lord. I'm proud of you, suga. You done learnt it all, jus' make sure you pass it on. Hear? If ya need any of us, we'll always be 'round. Call me when I'm gone. Talk to me, like I tol' ya to keep talkin' to yo' mother. Out loud, and witout shame. We answer. It'll just be in signs, not words, is all. Now, git off the phone, an' finish your work. Bye, suga-love. You'll always be my baby."

"Bye, Aunt Pearline. I love you, and always will."

"I know, suga. We all know that. Good night."

Antoinette hung up the telephone and stared into the open space. "One more's coming for you, Lord," she prayed out loud. "Make a special place for her. This was a good one... just like my mother."

Slowly, but surely, sobs replaced the calm, and she held onto the counter to let it all out—to get it all out, before she faced the family with the news. She'd go to each of them, one by one, over the course of the week. She'd hold their hands and wipe their tears and repeat what Pearline had said. She'd tell them about Pearline's acceptance, she'd let them wail. Then, she'd put Pearline's business in order—then they'd bury her after Easter. It had been decided, and as it had been written, so let it be done. Antoinette's body wracked with pain as she flushed the hurt out of her system. Pearline was right. It was time. But, God, how time flew by so fast when you loved someone. Years of love. Years of hugs and kisses... years of holidays... years of letters and cobblers, and the joy of a single voice. All of Pearline's decades suddenly felt like minutes, and there was no replacing that time.

When the phone rang again, it didn't startle her or make her angry. Antoinette wiped her face with both palms and let out a breath to steady her voice. Removing the receiver from the wall-mount, she slowly brought the telephone to her ear.

"Hello, Jerome," she said without needing to wait for his voice. "I'm sorry that I went off and wouldn't take your calls earlier."

He paused and let out a breath of annoyance. "I was worried about you, girl. I didn't like the way we parted in the streets. It felt wrong, like something serious was going on, so I kept calling, and calling. Hey, how'd you know it was me, anyway?"

"I'm learning to read the signs," she murmured, tending to the oven to check on her chicken then flipping off the burner under the pot of vegetables.

"What?"

"Listen," she said slowly, pulling the pan out of the oven to let it cool on the top of the stove, "I am extremely busy. Will be from now on—"

"—Just because we had one little fight?" His voice contained a plea laced with outrage.

"Hear me out, Jerome," she said calmly, walking toward the laundry area to toss Lauren's clothes in the dryer. "When I got here, Dad and May had provided a police escort to allow Brian to use his key to get in, " she said with a chuckle. "He called them, to be sure it was cool. I told you he wouldn't come in unannounced. He also gave me my key back."

"They let him in? So, you're going back to him?"

She could hear Jerome swallow hard and she shook her head as she tossed a load of wet clothes in the dryer. "No. I'm marrying you, if that's what you still want to do. If not, that's cool, too. Like I told you, he gave me my key back."

Silence built a wall between them and she walked into the bedroom and sat down.

"If you still want to get married, my answer remains yes," she said in a soft voice. "But, you have to deal with what's going on in my life. Are you ready to handle that? Because, my life is full, complex, and has a lot of responsibilities. I just got a few more tonight."

"I told you I love you, T," he said gently. "Whatever come what may. I know you're busy, handling things over there by yourself, and must have walked into a—"

"—Pearline is sick.... she'll pass probably after Easter. I have to cook. Do you understand?"

Jerome took the telephone up by its base and began walking with it. He'd heard what Antoinette had said, but he couldn't believe his ears. Pearline was sick. She had set a declaration date. He knew what that meant in Antoinette's family. His heart broke.

"Oh... baby..." he whispered, swallowing down the tears. "Tonight? You just found out tonight?"

"Yes," she murmured, "that's part of what took me so long to call you back."

Guilt arrested him. He'd been pacing like a cat, slamming doors, totally consumed by jealousy, and here his baby was losing her second mother. There were no words for his conduct, and he lacerated himself with that truth as he walked in a circle. "I'll be right over."

"No, I'm fine," she said firmly.

He couldn't imagine how she could be fine, yet, there was a gentle acceptance in her voice.

"Jay.... I'm so tired," she whispered. "I could just lay down and sleep forever. Pearline's made her peace. So be it. She lived a good life. Now, the baton has been passed, which means so many things. Do you understand?"

He hesitated and sat down. He didn't understand fully. She had spoken with a sigh so weary that it made his chest hurt for her.

"Baby," she went on after a long pause. "I'm

the next in line... the next female... and my house is out of order. I took too long."

"What do you mean... your house is out of order?" He asked slowly. Antoinette was speaking in some mystical female language again, with footnotes and references that he didn't comprehend.

"It means," she sighed with clear impatience, "that I do not have my fortress built. I will soon become the voice of reason, the one who dispenses remedies, and parables, and who is the epicenter for holidays. My home is supposed to be basecamp, like my mother's was, and her mother's before her was, and Pearline's was. The place where, if all else fails, younger family can rely on a roof over their heads, and a good pot to fill their bellies. I'm financially weak. I do not have a husband. I haven't learned all the stories. I can barely take care of myself. I've failed, when Pearline has counted on me most."

"You have not failed. Times have changed. Things are different," he countered, hating to hear the defeat in her voice. Something inside of her had broken, and he prayed to God that it wasn't her spirit.

"You see, Jerome," she said quietly, " there are no more family ports in the storm. No more old homes left. No more people who take in the weaker ones. No more people to keep traditions alive, and if I just got Pearline's baton, I'm not ready. I can't carry-on with a married man, and be like her, or like my mother. How can I be their baton bearer? I can't. I can't just pick up and leave a bunch of bills and go bankrupt. I have to secure a property, in case my sister ever has to come home. I need a place to not only store, but to also live amongst, my mother's, grandmother's, and Aunt's treasures—that's history. Those things that they scrubbed white people's floors for, and saved for nearly a hundred years—cannot slip through my hands because of debt, in one generation!"

Her voice had gone strident and he put on his jacket and cap.

"Do you hear me, Jay?" she nearly shrieked. "My mother is gone. My grandmother is gone. Nana Wellington is no longer my mother-in-law. Now, my Pearline is going! And none of my cousins, nor my sister, will be taking the weight," she sputtered. "I'm no role model! I don't even go to church on a regular basis. I had to do it for my sister," she sobbed. "I tried so hard. But now, they're all gone. None left but me! I'm supposed to be married, and settled, and in a home of my own. I'm supposed to have gotten my run out—long before now. I'm not supposed to want to look pretty. I'm not supposed to care that I can't date, or dance, or play. I'm supposed to be a mother—now. I have one child of my own, plus your proposed four to put before my needs and my dreams to start a business. I'll have to take care of you, too, in order to make it right.

"I'll have to get a property big enough to siphon five college education's out of, four weddings for the girls, five proms, grandbabies. I'm supposed to know it all, by now... to stand in church with you as my husband, not just my lover. Five school age children, an ex-wife to contend with, my own ex-husband to manage, my sister, and my friends. Time. There's no time. Not to get it all right before Easter! We don't even have time to make love, without something terrible happening, and I'm not supposed to want that anymore!

"Now that I'm a crone-mother, an ancient family wise-woman, I should be settled—and I'm not ready to fill those wife-mother-wise-one shoes! I don't know how they did it? Their homes were immaculate. Their children, obedient. Their husbands respectful. They catered to their men like they were kings. They never left the house without make-up. They did it with a smile. They even went to church every Sunday—and they worked! And they dropped dead in their tracks—working like Georgia mules pulling a too-heavy load. I just can't do it!"

Her long, agonizing, wail propelled him to the door. He didn't wait for a response as he dropped the telephone receiver, turned the locks, and headed for his car. He knew the sound of her cries. They'd been the same ones that were hidden inside his own heart, the ones that had tormented his own soul for so long. They were his cries—the cries of the eldest. The cries of the terrified, pressed into service too young. His mother had done it to him. His father had made him the man of the house, without any of the authority that went with it. And he'd given up his own childhood on the altar of expectations when he'd married Karen. He could not let his Toni take this on alone.

Jerome sped around the corner, and parked illegally in front of a hydrant, and left his flashers on. Racing down the street, he turned into Antoinette's complex, ran up the steps and rang her bell repeatedly until she opened the door. When he looked at her face, he just opened his arms, and she filled them. No words were necessary as he rocked her and stroked her back. Her sobs opened a deep fissure in his heart, and his tears soaked into her hair as he clutched her head to his chest.

"We'll make this official before Easter, baby,"

he whispered, leading her into her unit, and kicking the door closed behind them. He continued to rock her as her sobs abated, and he could feel her body slowly go limp against his.

Holding her back a bit so he could look at her, he wiped her tear-streaked face. "Listen, our relationship is unorthodox, and I have a lot of shit with me, granted. But, we'll make this work. Okay?"

She seemed too weary to resist, and as she nodded her head in agreement, then sought his shoulder again. "I don't know how we're going to pull this off, Jay," she murmured. "We're both broke. We don't know how the children are going to react. I don't know what I'm facing at work tomorrow. And I want something for myself out of life—a career and a good relationship."

"Shhhh," he murmured against her hair. "It'll be all right, baby. Don't worry."

Antoinette soaked in his words. She'd prayed for this for so long—someone to hold her when she was most afraid. Someone to tell her it would be all right, when all practical evidence told her otherwise. A strong shoulder that cared and wanted to make it better, even if he couldn't.

"What would Pearline tell you to do?" his asked softly, still stroking her back.

"She'd tell me to pray."

"Then, let's do that, baby. I don't know where the money will come from. I don't know how the kids will handle this. I don't know what tomorrow will bring. All I know is that I love you, I'll go with you to see Pearline, and I'll be there for you, this time."

She held onto him like she held onto his words—tightly—hoping against hope. Fatigue claimed her body and she swayed from the sheer emotional exhaustion.

"I'm going to tuck you in, and let myself out—so you can get a good night's sleep."

"I have to put away the food for the week, and pull out the laundry. There's so much to do."

Jerome glanced past her to the kitchen, and over to her briefcase on the coffee table, then to the opened mail on her dinette table. Renewed guilt flowed over him. She was a working woman. A single mother. She had a child to care for. Parents to deal with. She had a life, an agenda, things to do, with dreams that he could never finance. His temporary bout of territorial jealousy made him ashamed. Slowly an awareness of Karen permeated his thoughts as he stood with Antoinette in his arms.

What was his soon-to-be-ex coping with? She had four children and possibly quadruple the responsibilities. He'd tried to help her, and failed to the point where his wife didn't even want his assistance. His failure to help Karen realize any of her dreams had disgusted her until she couldn't stand his touch. Jerome closed his eyes and fought a sob down into his chest. He had to get it right this time. He had to be strong. Time was running out on his second chance. He held onto Antoinette more tightly and kissed the top of her head. "I'll put away the food, and finish the laundry. I won't let Lauren hear me. C'mon, let me tuck you in and I'll call you in the morning before I go to work to check on you. Okay?"

Her body gave in before her words were even spoken. He could feel her physically yield to his assistance as he took her by the hand and led her into the bedroom.

"Okay... "she finally whispered, as she slipped into the sheets with her clothes on. "I'm just so tired."

"I know, baby. It'll be all right."

If there was ever a prayer that he needed answered, it was the one he'd just submitted for God to make it all right.

Chapter 7

Jerome considered the grime beneath his fingernails as he took a last drag on his cigarette, and dropped it to the pavement. Crushing the butt beneath his work boot, he peered through the pristine glass window of the jewelry store and glanced at his watch. His gaze traveled to the well-dressed patrons happily moving about on Jewelers Row, then back to the window. As a police car slowed down and the officer looked in his direction, he thought about his presence on the white-collar strip. With dirty construction-work clothes on, an evening and half a day of stubble on his face, along with a baseball cap on his head, he knew he had to quickly make a decision—one way or the other. Standing there, looking in the window was now out of the question.

This was not how he'd planned it. He would have gotten dressed, taken Toni to a really special, top-shelf lunch, a place like Zanzibar Blue, and let her decide. But nothing in his life had gone to plan and time to handle things was short, he reasoned. Letting his breath out hard, he stepped inside of the shop with only a half hour left on his lunch break to spare, avoiding the suspicious stare of the policeman.

"May I help you?" an immaculately dressed black man asked as he entered.

The immediate courtesy annoyed him. Damn, even a brother probably thought he was in there to rob the place! Jerome cast his gaze around the establishment, noting how the other patrons had subtly stopped their transactions to watch him from their peripheral vision.

"I'm looking for a ring," he muttered, ignoring the others and trying to combat the feeling of uneasiness in his stomach,

"For yourself, or for someone special?"

Jerome relaxed as the man approached him. It was something in the man's tone that was hospitable, and not judgmental. He liked that.

"Someone very special," Jerome said quietly, then glanced around to see the reaction of the others. When they relaxed and went back to their transactions, he let out his breath. "I need an engagement ring."

"Well," the man helping him chuckled with a wide smile, "how much are you ready to be set back?"

The man's amusement made him smile. "Brother, I don't know... it's been years since I've done this."

"Ah, you want an anniversary band, then?"

"No, well... it's sort of an anniversary—but I want what I couldn't give her before," Jerome said in a low voice, trying to get a feel for the strange environment, and trying to guesstimate the prices that were hidden. "Something nice."

The older man leaned back on a wall case and folded his arms over his chest. "You look like a hard working man," he said with a smile, appraising Jerome thoroughly with a keen assessing gaze. "Now, if you were supposed to give your woman an engagement ring before, but didn't... How many kids do you have?"

"Huh?" Jerome stammered, taking in the view from the cases while trying to understand the tangent question.

"How many kids do you have?" The man repeated calmly.

"Four. Why?"

“Then, after all those years, you have to get her something nice.”

“Tell me about it,” Jerome murmured. “She waited for twenty years, and I have to get this right.”

“Whew,” his attendant whistled, “Yeah, you gotta go the whole nine yards...”

“But, it’s not for—never mind,” Jerome stammered, searching for the words. “Yeah. I gotta go the whole nine. Give her my best. Problem is, I’m not at my best these days... so... I don’t know.”

“Well, my name is Bullock,” the well-groomed man said with a smile. “I’m going to wait on you myself, since this is a delicate situation.” Mr. Bullock extended his manicured hand and Jerome immediately wiped his palms against his jacket.

“I’m Jerome,” he said feeling awkward and not extending his right hand for a shake. “Jerome Henderson. I should have changed. I’m all dirty—on my lunch hour. It’s okay, you don’t have to shake my hand.”

“Listen, there’s nothing wrong with hard work,” Bullock said loud enough for the other patrons to hear. “I always shake the hand of any client who comes into my shop. That’s my way.”

“This is your shop?” Jerome whispered in awe, looking around it as he shook the man’s hand. “I didn't know... I just picked this place because I saw you behind the counter."

"Yes," Mr. Bullock said proudly. "I'm the only African American jeweler on this row. Been here over twenty-five years—and, it wasn't easy to get, or stay here, believe me. Now, let's do business, brother. Have a seat."

Jerome let his breath out and relief poured over him. He sat down on a tiny velvet chair after receiving a nod of approval from Bullock. Vicarious pride filled him as he glanced around the well-stocked shop, and he didn't want to do anything that could cause the older black man to think less of him. This man had obviously paid his dues. An entrepreneur. He'd heard about this, but had never actually met one—a brother hooked up like this. Toni had talked of wanting to be able to own her own business, and now he understood why. There was a certain power and authority that came with the badge of honor. Deep. He didn't even want the dirt from his job to come off on Bullock's clean velvet cushions, and silently prayed that none would.

"Let's start with the basics," Mr. Bullock beamed, giving him a lesson as he removed velvet cases of pre-set diamond rings from behind the locked glass that separated Jerome from them. He carefully arranged three rows before Jerome on the counter and stood back. "First, let's pick a shape. Round, marquis, oval, pear, square-which is an emerald cut, and more expensive."

Jerome thought about Toni's hands and looked at the wide array of choices. "She has pretty hands. I sort of wanted to give her the same ring I gave her before, but with a diamond in the center instead of a jade."

"We can do that," Bullock said brightly. "How big was the stone?"

"About that big," Jerome noted, using his pinkie nail to demonstrate. "It was a diamond shape like that one, but bigger."

Mr. Bullock shook his head and chuckled. "A marquis that large would set you back a long way. That's a Princess Di-size diamond, son. And a marquis is also an expensive cut. No offense."

"Yeah, I figured," Jerome whispered, his hopes sagging. "You think she would like a round one? Are those bad, price-wise?"

Bullock smiled, leaned on the counter, and picked out a round stone. "No, a round can be very beautiful—if it's set right," he said with authority, handing Jerome a tiny ring. "Classic solitaire."

Shaking his head no, Jerome handed the ring back to him. "It's not big enough, sir."

"Now, you're talking weight. A carat stone

looks like this," the jeweler said calmly, offering Jerome a bigger ring.

"Yeah. Like that," Jerome agreed, feeling satisfied. "I could give her this... can you put three little diamonds on each side, about this big too?" Jerome said motioning to another ring as an example. "This way, it'll look something like what she had before."

"Son," Bullock sighed, "Now you're talking about a special setting design, plus about another half carat in weight for the baguettes. All together, we're now speaking of a carat and a half, plus the setting. I haven't even begun talking to you about clarity yet."

"Clarity?" Jerome asked with growing trepidation. His hopes were falling away rapidly, and his lunch-hour was running out.

"This showcase stone is extremely brilliant," Bullock said quietly, handing him a jewelers monocle. "See how it catches the light? You pay for that. Now, I'm going to put one up next to it that's not as brilliant. I want you to hold them side-by-side to see the difference. Then," he added, "I'm going to write the price differential down on this slip of paper... and I want you to pick a number in that range. Okay? Then, we'll try to find what you want somewhere in the middle. Fair enough?"

Jerome nodded his agreement and appraised each option. "God... this one looks like shit against the other one. No offense. But, it's all yellow and kinda cloudy... I couldn't give her that, after seeing how it looks."

Mr. Bullock let out a sigh and his eyes held a reflection of pity in them. Jerome looked down and studied the options in his hands carefully.

"Let me show you the difference on paper," Bullock said quietly, "we'll work something out."

As the jeweler slid a piece of paper with a set of numbers across the counter, Jerome stared at it, and stood up. His last bit of hope vanished and any prior confidence that Bullock had given him slinked away with his pride.

"I can barely afford the yellow one," he said quietly. "Sorry that I wasted your time, sir."

"Now, hold on, son," Bullock said with a chuckle. "You just got sticker-shock, that's all. Let's look at the between ranges, and you hold them up next to the best—then decide."

Jerome returned to his seat and sat down with a thud of resignation. "This is pointless."

"She's worth it, though. Right?" Bullock said, trying to encourage him.

"Yeah... that's not the question," Jerome muttered as defeat claimed him.

"We can finance it."

"My credit is going to hell fast, sir. I'm not a safe bet."

"You work every day, right?"

"Yeah, but—"

"—Then you should be able to get what you want. It's customary to spend at least a month's gross salary," Bullock said calmly. "We can work this out. Pick one, first—then, we'll go from there. Don't let anybody, not even me, rob you of your dreams. If you walk out of here and decide not to buy a thing, always remember that, brother."

Jerome let his gaze travel to several options, and settled on a large stone that was close to the one that he really wanted. "This is nice... large enough... sparkles a lot... you think she'd accept this one?"

"Sure, what woman wouldn't? It's a carat. It's brilliant—"

"—And probably expensive as hell, right?"

Bullock chuckled and wrote some figures down on a piece of paper again, then slid it over for Jerome's inspection.

"Jesus Christ in Heaven," Jerome whispered, shaking his head in awe as moisture began to creep into his palms. "It's a car note."

"If you can give me a thousand down on it, you can walk with it today. You own your own home, right?"

Rubbing his chin, Jerome stood up and paced before the counter. His mind fastened to the five-hundred and sixty dollars he had in his account. "Yeah, I do, but I wanna keep that separated from this. If I give you five hundred today, and another five on Friday—when I get paid... you think I can finance the balance?"

"If you fill out these papers, and take insurance on it, the ring is yours."

"I can't have anything go to the house," Jerome said warily, appraising the papers that Bullock had slid across to him. "No calls, no insurance docs—nothing about this."

"We won't spoil her surprise," Bullock laughed. "We're professionals. Give me some credit."

"The ring ain't for my wife."

Bullock looked at him hard, and Jerome stared back at him. A few moments passed before the older man could compose himself.

"Let me get this right," Mr. Bullock said quietly, moving to a seat opposite Jerome and sitting down slowly. "This is not for your wife?"

"No," Jerome said evenly, leaning in towards Bullock. "Do you understand?"

"I've been in this business a long time, and seen it all... but in the great State of Pennsylvania, son, bigamy is still illegal," he said with a chuckle. "Do you understand?"

"I know. I know," Jerome whispered, growing agitated. "But I have to give her something until everything is settled—and, before Easter."

"Ah," Bullock sighed, leaning back a ways. "Sort of like a bookmark, a place holder, so she doesn't change her mind and get away. Yeah. You need the big rock."

"That's my point," Jerome said quickly. "Plus, her Aunt is sick... and... and... I gotta do this to let Pearline know I'm not just jerkin' her niece around. I'm not. I gotta show her Pop, too.... Forget it. It's a long story. I just wanted to show her that I wasn't playing around with her."

"Like you did twenty years ago, right?"

"Well, not exactly, but I asked her before. She said no. Now she said yes, and I gotta get it right. Know what I mean?"

Bullock shook his head and let out a breath. "Can't she wait until you pay on it by layaway? What's the rush? Let the ink dry on the divorce," he whispered, "then make a decision."

"I can't. I love her too much, and—"

"—Son," Bullock said slowly, cutting him off, "if she loves you, she's not going anywhere. Are the four kids hers, or your wife's?" he asked in an amused tone.

"They're my wife's but—"

"—Do the kids know? Do they like this woman?"

"Yeah. No. I mean, they don't know the deal, but they like her—I think." Jerome pulled off his cap and ran his fingers through his hair.

"You are keeping up with your kids, aren't you? Taking care of them, I mean? And she likes them?"

"Oh, yeah, definitely. I wouldn't do this and not take care of them. Theirs comes off the top, first—and Toni loves kids. She likes them, I think."

"Hmmph, uhmph, uhmph," Bullock muttered, running his hands through his own hair as he peered down at the ring.

"She's the marrying kind, sir," Jerome said quietly. "I gotta do this, and do it right."

Bullock looked at him hard and a wry smile overcame his face. "She's a church-goer?"

"Yeah... Toni goes, listens to her gospel."

"And, you got it bad for her right? And she's a church-girl—now, I think I understand the rush. It's Spring... and been a long winter, right?"

Jerome looked away and smiled. The man sounded like Mr. Miles, his mentor.

"So, the ring is more than a bookmark, huh? Sort of like a liberty pass? She's got you on-hold, and making you lose your natural mind?" Bullock chuckled as he stood up. "Don't buy a ring out of passion or haste, let the decision fester a while, son. It's a serious investment."

Somewhat shocked, Jerome stood and shook his head quickly. "No, it's not like that. I'm not on hold, per se..."

"But, you don't want to go there, find yourself on-hold after a taste, or two. Like I said, I've been in this business a long time. Discretion is the better part of valor, son. It'll save you money."

"That's not why I'm giving her the ring right away, but, I gotta get it," Jerome said cautiously. "One day, anyway."

"I'm no shrink," Bullock said with a patient chuckle, "and no magician either. But, sit down," he sighed. "I must be out of my black mind. You shouldn't be at a jeweler, brother, you need to have your head examined—that's who you should have gone to see. A psychiatrist."

"I know I sound like I must be crazy." Jerome laughed, as the reality of what he was attempting sank in. "Mr. Bullock, here's the straight deal. I make good money, when I work overtime. But, I can't claim my house as collateral, or anything else I own. I've got a car note, car insurance, and child support to pay—and plenty of credit card bills that my wife ran up in my name. She doesn't work, so I gotta foot the whole bill. I can't show what I make on the side, because if it ever gets seen on paper, the judge might throw the book at me. Plus, I have to live in an apartment, and pay the bills there. But, I still love this woman—and want to give her what she deserves, for at least once in my life. At the same time, I want to be sure to take care of my responsibilities. Ain't tryin' to run from what's mine."

"And, now I'm supposed to be The Amazing Kreskin?" Bullock replied in a weary tone, letting his breath out in a rush as he sat down. "This new girl, from twenty years ago... how long you been running on your wife with her?"

"Wasn't like that," Jerome hedged defensively. "Met her first, she wouldn't marry me, hooked up with somebody I shouldn't have, but I did my time and didn't run on my wife. Me and the wife broke up, I found Toni again. So I'm gonna marry her this time, proper. That's how it happened, not that it makes a difference."

Bullock looked at Jerome hard for a moment, studying his face and eyes. "It makes a difference—at least in my book. Good. Integrity will help your credit rating. So you two must have been in high school, unless you age well, judging by your face?"

"Yeah, things got messed up, though. That's why I was in here dreamin'—more like acid tripping. Hey," Jerome said, standing up again, "thanks for the time. I gotta go back to work."

Bullock stood and extended his hand towards Jerome. Accepting Jerome's firm return shake, he issued a wink. "You move too fast," the older man said. "I told you to sit down, and we'd work something out. Had to do a credit check on you first. Had to see if you were legit."

Stunned, Jerome blinked and tried to comprehend Bullock's point. "I told you I didn't have any credit left. There's nothing to check. It always comes down to the money," he added quietly, "even if she doesn't think so. Doesn't it?"

"Is your word your bond?"

"Yeah, but that ain't worth jack in America."

"It is, in my shop," the old jeweler countered. "Fill out these papers with just your day job on it, and leave off the house. Just reference your landlord—how long have you been there at your apartment?"

"Less than a month..."

"Jesus! You are making me work, son. Are you sure about this?"

"I've been sure for twenty years. But look, I'm wasting your time if—"

"—Just fill out the top of the form. Christ Almighty..." the older man muttered as he walked away.

"What?" Confusion and excitement raced through Jerome's veins making his heart beat fast.

"Do like I said, and let me make a call." Bullock slipped into the back room and left the papers with Jerome, returning with a cordless phone and a small, brown, manila jeweler's envelope. "You know her size?"

"No... not since before, but she's gained a little..." Jerome stammered, trying to keep his focus on the papers and answer Bullock at the same time.

"Big as your pinkie, maybe?" Bullock asked, and before he could answer, went into a heated, whispering discussion on the phone.

Jerome watched the older man with appreciation as he initialed and scribbled on the papers.

"Yeah, yeah, David, I marked it. This one is special. Just call his job. Check his landlord. No extra crap. No, I know, yeah—he doesn't own a house. I got it covered," Bullock grumbled as he paced. "Yeah, he's family. Just put it through—with heavy insurance, cause it might get tossed in the Schukyll River, for all I know. Ummm hmmm, a real Days-of-Our-Lives case, buddy. Okay. Good. Thanks." Bullock turned to Jerome and stared at him hard. "You put five hundred on the table today, and bring me five more, plus one-twenty-five for insurance, Friday. I'll have it set and ready by then. If it doesn't fit her, bring her in for a sizing—and don't let her throw it in the river. Hmmph, the way your history goes with women... You got life insurance, son?"

"No." Amazement stopped any additional thoughts in his brain. He'd honestly never seen a black man wield power like that in his life—to be able to change someone's life with a phone call.

Bullock shook his head. "You need some life insurance, cause if your wife ever sees this beaut—"

"—She won't," Jerome cut in quickly, "But... I couldn't afford the payments on the last number you showed me—not without my lights going out. I can't "

"—Look at the number again," Bullock said sternly. "That's the best I can do without my lights going out. I have to pay my employees, and my lease, and run a shop, got grandkids to put through college—you know. But, I also want to see a good, young couple have a chance. I must be going senile—dealing with other people's business! Louise!" he yelled into the back room, "I'm going senile. Don't let me work the counters any more, honey. I'm losing my edge!"

An attractive, small brown woman peeped out of the back room and smiled.

"What do you think?" Bullock asked her, motioning with a nod in Jerome's direction.

She gave a little wink and chuckled as she slipped into the back room without a comment.

"Guess the wife likes you, she's the one with the intuition," Bullock grumbled as he watched his wife's form disappear behind the wall. "Pretty, ain't she?" he chuckled with appreciation in his voice, and returned his attention to Jerome. "Look at the number, son, and talk to me."

Jerome stared down at the paper and double-checked the figure, noticing that it was one third less than the original price quoted.

"Can you stand that?" Bullock asked, folding his arms over his chest, still seeming indignant until he smiled. "I am going senile, aren't I?" he said with a widening grin, "You better not make me a liar."

"I don't know what to say... except, thank you," Jerome said quietly. "I don't know how to repay you."

Bullock laughed and slapped his shoulder. "You repay me on the fifteenth of every month, cash on the barrel-head. And try not to get yourself killed between these two women before you pay my bill off. Okay? Then we'll call it even. Write me a check."

"You got it!" Jerome laughed, giving Bullock a

hardy handshake and reaching for his wallet. "But, I'd better get back to work. Now I really need my job," he added as he filled out a check.

"Yeah, that's right. Take all the overtime you can get too," Bullock chuckled, escorting him to the door. "Nice doing strange business with you. Good Luck. Hmmphm, hmmmph, hmmmph."

Jerome stood on the sidewalk for a moment and glanced back into the shop. The bright March sun and crisp near-Spring air provided a good day to work out-of-doors. He paced down the street and found the lot that housed his car. Each step made him feel closer to flight—like he could just catch a breeze and fly.

Chapter 8

Her eyes felt like someone had opened a salt-shaker and dumped its contents into them. Constantly watering from the granular feel each time she blinked, Antoinette dabbed at the corners of her eyes again and swallowed another yawn. Sleeping fitfully the night before, and still having to get up, get Lauren out, teach her class all day as though nothing was wrong, and now deal with a staff meeting was more than her nervous system could handle.

The strident sound of the Executive Director's voice was akin to fingernails carving out the slate of a blackboard.

"So, we need to get all reports inventoried and

a status of all placements immediately," Linda Kravats said sternly, looking around the meeting table. "All of our grants this year hang on the placement component. The rules have changed, as you are all aware."

Antoinette scanned the faces of her co-workers and then the Executive Director's expression, discretely tucking away her note cards. She wished she'd been able to catch-up with Darlene before the session, but it had been impossible. Addressing the director carefully, she chose her words with precision. "Linda," she began slowly, "how many lay-offs are necessary at this juncture?"

"At least two, possibly three. Although I might be able to save those positions if we all go on reduced hours until our funding hemorrhage has been repaired. The Career Placements will be key to restoring those funds, especially with the continued push to get people off of Welfare and into the job market. So, if you can permanently place all of your students, we'll have a great opportunity to show the progress of this agency. I've heard outstanding things about your class."

Antoinette cringed and looked around the table again at her female co-workers. Their expressions held thinly concealed anxiety, and she knew they were counting on her. Their immaculate suits, fine leather shoes, and stunning accessories couldn't hide their pure terror. Just like herself, they all had bills to pay, children to care for, and commitments to maintain.

Antoinette drew a breath and tried to weigh her options on which group to sacrifice. The grants called for blood—either her student's, or the agency's. The beast would be fed, and a pound of flesh would be extracted from one side or the other. She had to decide between women on the inside, or women on the outside. She had to decide whether to feed her own baby, or keep food stamps feeding her student's children...

"I can't sign off on my class," she said quietly. "They are all placed, but they don't have—"

"What! Don't tell me that!" Linda Kravats shrieked, causing the others at the table to hold their breaths. "You have them all in jobs, right? You've been sending in glowing reports on their progress—isn't that true?"

"Yes, and no," Antoinette said firmly, but in a quiet voice. "It's not that simple."

"It can't be both, which is it?" her director shouted, leaning in towards her across the table.

"On average, the women have approximately three to four children each. The jobs I've been able to find, are paying them off-the-record, and—"

"—Have you lost your mind?"

"And," Antoinette continued softly, "they are learning valuable business skills and regaining their self esteem. A job that I could find for them, even if it paid them an on-the-record salary, would not cover daycare, medical and dental for a family of four—or more, nor would they be able to still get subsidized housing, or food stamps. Five to eight dollars an hour won't do it—at the lowest, without benefits and before taxes, that's only two hundred a week. It wouldn't cover rent and food and utilities. They are not going to walk out of this program into a thirty thousand dollar a year job with benefits, Linda, even if they had college degrees. None of them even got out of high school. That's no less than they need to support themselves and their children, in this day and age. We have to be realistic."

"No. You have to be realistic," Linda Kravats countered. "Our agency has to meet its goals, or we lose existing funds. We didn't get expansion grants, or grants to cover some of the training we were projecting. So all new projects, which means your job, Darlene's job, and Inez's job will have to go. Which is it?"

Antoinette refused to look at her co-workers. She couldn't. Finally, she let her breath out slowly and folded her arms. "If you got in one grant, that would cover Inez and Darlene, right?"

"Possibly," her director seethed as she began pacing away from the table to the front of the room. Grabbing a felt-tipped marker, she flung over a clean page on the flipchart. "Do the math, Antoinette. You have an MBA. Here is where we are," she said in a barely controlled tone as she scribbled. "Here is the series of grants that we didn't get. Here is the staff reduction that will occur if we cannot prove that this new programmatic element is working. And the only way we can prove that it's working," she shouted, spinning around from the chart-pad to face Antoinette, "is to show valid placements. Five dollars an hour, fifty dollars an hour—I don't care. Place them!"

"The problem is," Antoinette said, standing up, "is that I care. Those women are from my neighborhood, and they trust me—we're all mothers in virtually the same situation, and trust is—"

"—Sit down, young lady! You work for us—not them. We trusted you when we hired you!"

Antoinette stared at the woman who was her same age. She mentally repeated the tone of the woman's voice until it rang in her ears. As she stared at Linda Kravats, and looked at her bleached-blonde hair and contact-lens-created blue eyes, something inside of Antoinette's soul gave way. It was the tone in which she'd been addressed—the way her boss had called her, young lady. It was in the way she'd arrogantly wielded authority, and assumed power over a person who was her same age—someone who had as much education, and many more life-times of experience. This double-income-no-children bitch was asking her to sell her soul for the price of silver.

"I trusted that this agency cared about its clients when I agreed to take this job," Antoinette said through her teeth. "But it's all about the numbers, isn't it?" she found herself yelling. "The money!"

"Sit down, Antoinette! This is stressful enough without—"

"—No! You sit down!" Antoinette screamed. "I'm not sending them out to starve to death—women and babies, because your damned agency has been built on a house of Welfare-to-Work hypocrisy cards! I won't do it. Not today! I've had enough," she said breathing hard as she slammed her briefcase closed. "I'm sorry, ladies," she said looking in her co-workers' direction, "You, I'll help place. Not them. They don't have a fighting chance, you do."

"Then, you're fired!" Linda screamed, pacing over to her. "Not laid-off, to draw unemployment on my agency's back! Never! This is rank insubordination! And yes, you will fill out those papers," she shrieked, invading Antoinette's personal space as their breasts nearly touched. Pointing her finger up towards Antoinette's face, she spoke through her teeth. "You don't have a choice."

"Get out of her swing range, Linda," Inez cautioned, "You're up in a black woman's face."

"What?" Linda bellowed, her gaze scanning the room quickly. "I'll sue her!"

"Get out of my face," Antoinette said in a voice that was too quiet. She resisted the urge to slap the petite woman who held a finger in her face. The bitch only had till the count of five....

Hearing the low growl that had come up from Antoinette's throat with her words, Linda Kravats backed-off, but not down. Stepping away from Antoinette, she motioned toward the door. "I expected more professionalism from you. Come into my office so we can terminate you officially. Now."

Antoinette stared at her boss' retreating form, closed her eyes, and counted to ten. Bright blue and yellow lights flickered behind her lids, and she could feel a hot, dizzying hum overtake her ears.

"C'mon, lady, you'll go to jail if you slap her.

You'll lose your job if you don't kiss her ass. It's not worth it," Darlene whispered.

"Sit down and take a breath before that wench gives you a stroke. Just give her the papers she wants, kiss her butt, and it'll be over," Inez pleaded, rubbing Antoinette's back and speaking in a conspiratorial burst of whispers. "She does this to all of her new trainers—gives them the suicide jobs in the community, then makes them deliver the noose around the people's necks. You'll get used to it. Then, you'll get promoted, and the new girl on the block will have to do it."

"Hey, lady, we all know the deal, but you gotta eat too. C'mon, Toni, go in there, let that short heifer kick your tail verbally, and keep your job. You made her lose face," Bernadette said sadly. "You know the deal. Don't know why you bucked her, anyway?"

"Girl, don't be losin' your job over no Welfare broads. Are you crazy?" A part-time temp, Yvonne, said with disgust. "After working in the system for a while, you'll be able to separate—they're just cases. Don't break your own heart, lady. You can't save them all," she said in a far-away tone. "It's her first class, y'all. Let her be. She came from corporate, and believed the hype. She hasn't gotten used to it yet, that's all."

"Now don't'chu be upsetting yourself no more,

chile," the oldest in the group named Beatrice said. "This is her agency, built with her parent's money, and you'll go before her. Don't get crazy—you've got a child to take care of. Now, it ain't pretty, but go in there and apologize for being foolish, out of control... you know how to kiss a white girl's butt by this age, darlin.' We all do. That's all she wants. You're the best trainer she's got, and the clients know how this goes too. It's a game."

"Okay," Antoinette said quietly, gathering her briefcase and coat. She smiled at her co-workers and accepted their hugs of support, then slipped down the hall. She, indeed, had forgotten herself. Forgotten her place. She was black. She was powerless. She was out of money and options. The elders in her family were dying. She had a child. But, as she opened the door to the Executive Director's office, something made her straighten her carriage and stand taller. If she was going to take a plantation whipping, at least she wouldn't cry out and beg for mercy in the process.

"Well, I'm glad to see that you have finally become rational, and have come to your senses," Linda said smugly. "I hope we won't have to go through an outburst like this again."

"No, we won't," Antoinette said in a calm tone

that sounded distant to her own ears. She opened her briefcase and scribbled a note and a signature on each file, then jotted a quick note on her yellow legal pad. She watched her boss sit back in her chair and smile as she handed over the stack of papers.

"This is my resignation," Antoinette said quietly. "And these files all say that each student is un-placeable."

"What?" Linda whispered, apparently too horrified to find her voice.

"If you place these students and terminate them from assistance, I will call every grant source and testify to your agency's fraud. These files require my signature, and only my signature, for student determination."

"The whole class.... can't you find a placement for even one?" Linda's gaze tore across the files, and she set them down slowly on her desk. "I can save your job... maybe we both went too far..." she pleaded without a direct apology. "Let's be rational here."

"I am," Antoinette said firmly, finding new strength in just saying no. "You know this isn't right, don't you? Can they make it on five dollars an hour, working as a cashier in a mini-mart somewhere? If so, I stand corrected."

Tears filled Linda Kravats' eyes and she looked

away. "I am not a bad person." Her voice quavered from repressed emotion and she folded her arms over her chest. "I have an agency to run, people to keep employed."

"A plantation to run," Antoinette said quietly, "and it's not your fault, and their lives are not your problem, right?"

"I help people through this agency. I've invested in it personally, and built it up over the years. We do good work here, Antoinette. I cannot believe your analogy to this being some sort of plantation. What has come over you? We do good work."

"Yes, you do." There was no malice in Antoinette's comment as she quietly closed her briefcase. She was simply out of energy, and her own fate loomed before her. There was nothing to really say or argue about. This was how it was.

"When I started out, I wanted to help people," Linda said quietly. "People who had been raped by the system. Women. I joined the movement, full throttle. I never wanted it to turn out this way."

"I know," Antoinette sighed in a tired voice. "None of us wanted to end up where we found ourselves. The clients didn't. Your staff didn't. You didn't, and I didn't." Antoinette shrugged as she looked around the executive office one last time. "You got trapped with the golden-handcuffs, Linda. You wound up like the budding young medical student who finds out about the bullshit in the hospital system. You wanted to heal, but found out that you have to push pills and suggest treatments that drive up costs when a good lineament would do. I know," she sighed with bitter resignation. "Or, you probably started off like the young law student, who wanted to fight for justice only to find out that justice can be bought, sold, and negotiated. You lost your ideals, because that's how the system is designed. How many other professions are like this, I wonder?"

Linda's eyes sparkled from the tears that she wouldn't allow to fall. "My hands are tied. I have to follow the grant requirements," she whispered. "The agencies that play the game, get the money. You have to understand that, can't you? It's not my fault. It's the way the system works. Why do you hate me for that?"

Antoinette stared at the woman before her and then shook her head. How could she tell her about the voices that raged in her skull? How could she make this person, who was so removed from her reality, understand that the selling of peoples' lives for personal gain had already been done before in this country, and this game was hardly one that she wanted to be a part of? And, yet, it was so ironic that even while holding all of the agency power, Linda Kravats sat there looking to Antoinette for a level of absolution that no human being could offer her. That was what Linda Kravats didn't understand—the pardon wasn't even Antoinette's to give.

"Do you understand my dilemma? My hands are tied, Antoinette. They just are," Linda pressed when Antoinette didn't respond immediately. "What am I supposed to do? You know how this works."

"I do," Antoinette murmured as she put on her coat. "Tell them that you got a bad class, and an even worse instructor. They expect a margin of failure. Parcel my job out to cover the women at risk on the inside. Don't lay anybody off, okay? That's the least you can do, is save the jobs of women who need it."

"You'll walk on this principle? Antoinette, all you have to do is—"

"—I have to be able to sleep at night, Linda. I can't have ten female ghosts from your shelter, with their forty tiny ghosts, haunting me for the rest of my life. Save Dar, and save Inez. I'm new and expendable. I'm not cut out for this, anyway."

"You could be fantastic, if you weren't so militant. You have this complex. I don't know what it is..."

A sardonic smile crept over Antoinette's face. "It's a Harriet Tubman thing, Linda—you wouldn't understand. You can hang me, but I'm not telling you where I've hidden Tianisha, or the others. Their children are tucked safely in the neighborhood swamp."

Linda dragged her fingers through her wiry, bleached hair and she let out her breath. "That's unfair. I marched during the sixties, I tried to right the wrongs, I care—"

"—And," Antoinette whispered, "when you got older, and were done with the passion and rhetoric, you had options. These women don't. I don't. You'll be telling this little episode over Chardonnay and Brie next week at your tennis club. Pulleeeese."

"Oh, that's bull, Toni," Linda exclaimed, using the abbreviated nickname that Antoinette's co-workers had adopted, but without Antoinette's permission. "You're educated, have a stellar track record and skills that any agency would love—if they could get their hands on you. Be honest. You have options, too, and that's why you can spew rhetoric. Sit down. Let's talk. You're a tough negotiator. I respect that in a woman."

Antoinette considered her boss' words and a chuckle erupted from her gut. The woman did not get it. But, she did have a point that had never dawned on Antoinette until now. Yes, she did have options—which made her not quite the victim she had perceived herself to be. That also meant she had some measure of power over her life. The dawning reality slowed her retreat and she stopped to listen to what else she might learn.

"That's better," her boss chuckled with her in obvious visible relief. "You scared me for a moment, Toni. How much?"

All Antoinette could do was shake her head. "You make four times what the highest paid, front-line, instructor makes. They work in the trenches, your entire staff is black, and all of the clients are black. This is—"

"—You're good, but, certainly you don't expect me to pay one of my instructors six figures?"

The look of outright shock made Antoinette almost lose her equilibrium. The woman didn't get it, and the bitter irony made her head spin. "No," she said quietly. "I want you to think about what comprises a plantation."

"Oh, really, Antoinette. Please, let's not—"

"—Hear me out. You want me to help rebuild Tara, right? And, you know I can do that."

Linda Kravats leaned in towards her and grinned. "I know you can. Okay, so we move you to executive staff....hmmm..." she said, thinking as she ruffled her hair with her fingers. "How can

I pull from the grants to cover a sizeable salary? Let me see... You'd be perfect in public relations... the students trust and love you... you can do the cocktail circuit... you're articulate—good for the cameras..."

"I'd be great window dressing," Antoinette purred, "I can talk the talk, and walk the walk—I'm bilingual. I speak street and I speak corporate... and I'm good with the numbers."

"Yes, indeed you can, and are," Linda murmured, "that's why I hired you. Because you're an invaluable asset, especially in this politically sensitive climate."

"So," Antoinette cooed, "all I have to do is tell you where the babies are hiding, so you can sell them, right? And then I get to sit in the big house. Not on your life," she said with a cold smile. "Never. That's not negotiable. That's the part of my history you'll never understand—and that's why a lot of us have trouble with buying into your version of the women's movement, because we remember. You don't. And you've never atoned for the indignity of sitting by and watching it happen or helping it to happen."

Her boss sat back as though she'd been slapped. Her expression held so much pain that somehow Antoinette could tell that a portion of what she'd said sank in.

"I need the numbers, Antoinette, and if you're not going to provide them, I have no alternative."

"I'm not giving you an alternative. I quit," Antoinette whispered. "I've had the fancy job, and watched my soul slip away in the process."

"Did you give them this much grief when you were there?" Linda asked, seeming honestly amazed, "or, did you save it all for me?"

"No," Antoinette chuckled as she stood, "I was quite well behaved. They were much bigger than me, and I was blind, then."

"Well, what's wrong with a great salary and a good career? You haven't gone communist, or anything—have you?" Linda ruffled her hair again and stared at Antoinette hard. "What, so is poverty in-vogue? Did I miss something?"

"No," Antoinette said calmly, masking her rage, "It's not in-vogue and it's not convenient, and I'm not a Communist. I'm becoming an entrepreneur, I suppose. I like nice things and good money. But, not at other people's expense. There has to be a way to do that. Remember the old eighties axiom of a win-win conflict management style?"

Antoinette glanced at her watch. It was five-forty, but emotional fatigue stifled her panic. "Look," she said with a weary tone, "You don't have a kid, I do. I'm going to be late, and will have to pay a dollar a minute after six. The rest of the gang has to go home too—so release your inmates and let those mother's pick up their kids."

"A dollar a minute after six-o'clock? Toni... you have got to be kidding me?"

"You ought to hang out in the field more. You'll learn something. Or, maybe you ought to go into daycare—it pays better."

"Are you really going to give up a good career in social services today? Sleep on it, take the files home tonight, correct them, and—"

"—I'm dully fired and I've already quit, so let's stop the conversation on a civil note."

"You were one of my best," Linda said softly, shaking her head and standing. "I knew you were trouble from the moment I laid eyes on your resume," she said with a chuckle and extending her hand for a shake. "I knew it would only be a matter of time. You were used to commanding too much power—and I wondered when the fallen sparrow I had scooped up would become an eagle and eat her young. You've got talent, lady. Talons too."

Antoinette shook her boss' hand and accepted the back-handed compliment with a smile that would have pleased her mother. Don't burn a bridge, she told herself, as she thought of an appropriate response to this woman's claim on her body. A fallen sparrow? Like there was some debt she owed for working at next to nothing in Hell's Kitchen! She hated pseudo-liberals, but continued to hold her indignation in check. "Good luck, Linda," was all she could manage, "I hope you get your grants."

"Look," Linda said cautiously, "I can't have the rest of my team think that it's all right to be insubordinate—that would result in chaos, but you and I understand one another. We're cut from the same cloth," she added, eyeing Antoinette. "How about if I lay you off and you just tell them I fired you? That way, I can sleep at night."

Antoinette didn't let her expression change. She had been given an offer by a benevolent mistress. All she had to do was not let the other's think she'd sassed the Missus and gotten away with it. It was a matter of honor. It was a very old ritual—one that all griots remembered. All her boss was asking was that, she let them think she'd been whipped till the skin bubbled and peeled from her back—whereas she had only been slapped.

Pearline's voice blended with a chorus of voices, ancient spirits, and ancestors unknown within her mind. Their wisdom and coping skills threaded around her anger and bound it with their elderly black hands. She heard them whisper that pride goeth before a fall, and remembered how the real game was played. Antoinette could feel them smile as her body lost its resistance against them. She had fifty-three dollars left to her name. She'd see her students in the Welfare line when her last check ran out. Reality shook her to her core and the ancient voices chanted within her brain. She had a baby to care for, and it could have been worse. They bade her to 'take the fatback, and add some greens—winter's coming.' They told her to take the small beating, and spare her life. They chanted their collective truth that, if she bucked the agency now, it would be bad on the one's she'd left behind.

"All right. That's fair," Antoinette finally whispered. "Thank you."

"See, I'm not that bad." Her boss smiled, her eyes searching Antoinette's face for approval.

Antoinette hesitated and returned the smile. "No, Ma'am. You're not that bad at all."

Chapter 9

"You did what?" Buddy coughed and nearly spit out his mouthful of beer. "Bought a ring? Don't tell me that, man! And you haven't even gone to a good lawyer? You just picked some guy out of the yellow pages, based on price, have him give Karen everything, and you think she'll sign? Are you crazy?"

"I really need a good lawyer now, too," Jerome muttered into his glass of Cutty, as he took a quick drag from his cigarette. "I've paid Karen every time I got paid. Now, she's taking me to court. Do you believe that crap? She acts like I'm gonna run away somewhere and forget about my kids. Why won't she just sign the papers, and we'd have an agreement without the need to garnish my wages? I don't understand this bull at all. I'm giving her everything."

"You dumb bastard," Buddy said with empathy in his voice. "You really don't get it, do you?"

"No," Jerome sighed. "I don't. Because every fight we had was about money. So, I'm giving her everything we bought and built together—no questions asked. So, what's the hold up? This should be a clean-cut, No Fault divorce, with liberal visitation terms, and no property to dispute, because I'm handin' over all property. No, brother. Make me understand."

"It was never about the money," Buddy sighed. "It never is."

Depression weighed heavier than anything he'd lifted all day and Jerome cast his attention into the dark liquid that filled his tumbler. He had gotten a summons. An order to appear in Family Court. His mind screamed out the reality as he sat quietly in the bar. Never in his life had he brushed up against the legal system, and the thought terrified him. Swallowing down another swig of Cutty, he looked at Buddy for reassurance. "Damned papers were waiting for me when I got home from work. I was all happy, ready to hook up with you, man... have a celebration. You know?"

"C'mon, man. It'll be all right. Listen," Buddy said carefully, looking around the dimly lit establishment, "you made a commitment to take the people at the jewelry store the money, right? Plus, you've got your own bills to pay, right? You gotta live, right? Have a life?"

"Yeah," Jerome grumbled without enthusiasm. For some reason the syncopated beat in the bar wore on his nerves. He didn't want to be in a dark place, getting totaled, trying to sort out his life. Tonight he needed fresh air. Clarity. Space. Quiet. He wanted Toni. She was good with contracts and legal stuff...

"Well, look," Buddy began again slowly, rubbing his chin, and chasing his drink with a sip of beer, "next time, when you pick up the kids, don't pay her."

Jerome looked at his friend hard. "What'do'ya mean, don't pay her? I have to pay Karen. I don't even want to start that, man. It might get good to me."

"Pay an attorney with what you were going to give her. She started the court action, so, let her wait until the court decides. I'm not saying stop all support, but if she's gonna garnish your wages, and embarrass you up on the job, then stop direct payments to her—pay your bills first, then when they say—"

"—No, man. As much as it'd serve her right, I can't. My kids will go without. Plus, she has the leverage of the kids, you know? I wanna take them this weekend, for the whole weekend. Why can't she just let go? I mean, Buddy, she don't want me, I don't want her, we both want what's right for the kids. Why can't we just go our separate ways, and be cool?"

His friend shook his head and put a hand on Jerome's shoulder. "Because, it ain't about being nice, or being cool. It's about being divorced. Revenge."

"It doesn't have to be like this, man," Jerome said quietly, dragging on his cigarette to help him think. "It really doesn't."

"Name me somebody who broke up that's still cool with the other side, and their used-to-be in-laws, who've become the out-laws?"

He stared at Buddy for a moment, noting his friend's appreciation for a woman who'd passed them. "Toni's still cool with her ex, and his people. It can be done."

His comment drew Buddy's full attention. His friend held his beer mid-sip and looked back at him squarely. "No shit? Damn. Well, you better hope and pray it works out like that for you. 'Cause if not, it's going to be eighteen to twenty years of armed conflict, man... till the last baby's gone. I admire your balls, brother. Me, I don't have the heart for it—truth be told. It's cheaper to keep her."

"Let me ask you something serious, man," Jerome asked quietly, rolling the tension out of his shoulders as he took a deep swig of his beer, then crushing out his cigarette. "Did you love Valerie from the beginning?"

"What kind of question is that?" Buddy scoffed defensively. "That's my baby. Of course... and it wasn't about nobody else. I had gotten my run out, bro."

"Do y'all talk? I mean, spend good times, even with all the kids?"

"Yeah," Buddy said in a serious tone. "Sometimes it gets hectic. Sometimes we fight—usually about money but, there's nothing in the world I wouldn't do for my wife. If anything ever happened to her, man, I don't know what I'd do."

"Then, you were lucky," Jerome said sadly, lighting another cigarette. "That's all I ever wanted, but I hadn't seen it done when I was growing up, you know what I mean? I didn't know how to get it right. I think I could have that with, Toni. That's why I'm gonna marry her."

"You really gonna give up the bachelor life after only a month out of marriage prison?" Buddy chuckled. "It's not all wine and roses being married, you know."

Jerome laughed and shook his head. "Okay, Poppa Joe, you gonna school me on a bad marriage, now? You sound like Mr. Miles."

Buddy slapped his back and chuckled with him. "Hey, all lovers change into wives once you marry 'em. Don't go into this blind. Valerie gets on my last nerve sometimes, and I honestly don't know how to make her happy. But, we manage. It's a day by day deal."

"The bachelor life ain't for me no more, man," Jerome muttered, finding himself pulled into deep thought again. He stared at the smoke coming up from the cigarette between his fingers and tapped it against the aluminum ashtray. "I like coming home to somebody, sometimes. I like waking up next to somebody and not having to play games. The thrill of the hunt is gone. We gettin' old, man."

Buddy chuckled. "Speak for yourself, brother. I'ma hunt till I need a support beam to hold me up."

"I thought you said you loved Valerie?" Jerome said in a quiet voice, staring at his friend.

"I do, man... but, you know... sometimes, you just wonder. I mean, I don't do nothin'—just talk a little b.s. in the bar, then go home."

"Talkin'll get you in trouble, man," Jerome

warned. "Trust me on that. Been there, and got in trouble—twice. Once with Toni, once with Karen."

"Damn, man, you battin' a thousand on bad luck. They didn't have to know, though," Buddy protested, "I don't intend—"

"—Just be mad, or lonely, or horny... sittin' around talkin' junk and feelin' sorry for yourself, drunk, tired, and let a pretty thing sits next to you, give you a rush. Next thing you know, trouble's found you, brother. I know what I'm talkin' about."

Buddy's confused gaze held him for a moment. Jerome looked down to his near-empty glass and motioned for the bartender to refill he and his friend's drinks. He took a long drag on his cigarette and watched the ember flare at the tip.

"Listen," Jerome said quietly. "They can tell when there's somebody else on your mind, even when you don't know that yourself. Heavy fantasy can get you in trouble, and all the money in the world can't fix it. Talk to her man, before it's too late."

"They can't tell, man. You and that Indian superstitious mess, boy." Buddy chuckled.

"Yes, they can," Jerome said quietly, and took a slow drag. "Did I ever explain to you how Toni found out?"

"Naw, man, I just thought you got cold-busted. Ain't that the only way you git caught? Boy, you startin' to sound like my old Aunties. Maybe you got a little West Island blood in yo' veins you don't know about," his friend joked, giving him a shot in his ribs.

"She had a dream about it before she came to visit me," Jerome said evenly, sipping his beer and watching the smoke rise from the end of the cigarette. "Had the girl's name, knew what she looked like. Walked up to her when she saw her in the bar, then when I tried to deny it, even pointed the girl out to me—but that was after they had talked, and before she found me in the back playing craps. I was all messed up, man. She was so dead-on-it, I had to confess to the Antoinette that she was right. Sobbed like a baby when she left. Damn. I ain't told nobody that before now. My shit was too raggedy."

"Git the hell out of here..." Buddy whispered, sitting back on his stool wide-eyed. "You never told me that shit, man. You shoulda told me about women and that kinda mess... my grandmother used to talk about it, but I thought it was just the old ladies talking junk. For real, for real,"

"They can tell, man," Jerome insisted staring at Buddy hard. "Karen found out too, just like Val will, if you go out like that. It ain't worth the risk. Trust me."

"Yeah, yeah, yeah... I hear you," Buddy muttered with resignation. "But, what if you weren't the one fantasizin'. I mean, what if she was the one who wanted somebody better, something better than you could give? How would you feel living with that all your life? Answer me that?"

Jerome pondered the question, knowing somehow that now was not the time to remind Buddy that indeed he'd been living with Karen all those years under the same circumstances. As memories barraged his mind, he swirled Buddy's question around in his glass before he took a sip, as though the answer would bubble to the surface of the dark liquid. Buddy's voice held such quiet pain... such shame... and it asked him to consider his own fate with Antoinette.

What if she wanted someone who could do more for her life? Would he end up like his friend, making love to a woman who wanted someone better? Jerome threw a large splash of alcohol to the back of his throat and swallowed hard. The substance burned the lining of his chest and stomach as it went down. Chasing it with a swig of beer, he looked at his friend and tried to reassure him with a hollow platitude that he wasn't sure was true.

"Val wants you, man. She's just distracted

with the kids and trying to manage the bills. Fact is, she loves you. Wouldn't a married you, if she didn't. She didn't have to. That's the difference between you and Valerie, and me and Karen—we had to get married, y'all didn't."

"You think so, man?" Buddy asked, his question holding onto Jerome's words as though they were a life raft.

"Yeah, man... C'mon," Jerome said with confidence, slapping his friend's shoulder with one hand and taking another swig of liquor with the other. "You just need to take her out, stop working so hard, and give her a little time and attention. That's all she's fantasizing about... the past, when it was real good between y'all."

"Yeah, man, I'm just trippin'. Maybe you're right. But, ever since this thing cropped up with you and Toni, she's been worse, Reds. Seriously."

Jerome shook his head, but continued to hold his friend by the shoulder. "She probably could feel you itchin' to make a run for the border. So, take her out, treat her nice, and talk to her. Maybe if I'd tried harder, earlier... who knows?" he said quietly, "Who knows?"

"We was goin' to go to counseling," Buddy whispered, "but then money got funny. Think we should go?"

"Is she willing to go?" Jerome asked, holding

Buddy in a truth stare. "Karen refused. But, I had found this sister who has her own center over in Cherry Hill. I still got her card," Jerome said in a low voice as he fished in his wallet. "Here," he added, handing the card to Buddy. "It's called The Generation Center."

"You went, man... checked it out?" Buddy whispered in awe. "Damn."

"I went over there one afternoon on my lunch hour. We was working a bridge job. Found out about her from a minister. The sister was sharp—low-key, professional, all about women's issues and wasn't text-book-cold. Has a family herself, pictures of her kids up and stuff. So, I got the bright idea to tell Karen, and almost got my face slapped for runnin' with a psychologist." He chuckled sadly. "I couldn't win, man. You got a shot; Val's not there yet. Don't let her go there, man. The more time lapses, the worse it'll get. Trust me, I learned somethin' out of this bullshit. Pay now, or really pay later. Fix it, man, and go home 'cause you love her. My situation was different."

"Didn't you ever love Karen?" Buddy asked quietly, tucking the dog-eared card into his pocket. "Don't you ever think about her?"

Jerome polished off his second drink and looked away with a new cigarette dangling between his fingers. "I loved her... but, I was never truly in love with her. There's a difference. She never forgave me for it, though. I guess I can't blame her for that. And, at the same time, I can't blame myself for not feeling what was never there. She thought that I had planned that other situation, you know that bullshit that went down after I broke up with Antoinette in Dover? Said, I had just done it to make her change her mind about getting married and keeping the baby. I could never get Karen to understand what that whole other woman thing was about, and that it didn't have anything to do with her."

"It was ugly, man," Buddy said confidentially. "I remember the babe... she went fatal. I also told you to never tell, K, didn't I?"

Jerome lit another Marlboro from the tip of the waning butt between his fingers. "Yup, that you did, brother."

The two men sat in companionable silence for a while, each far away from the other and absorbed in their own pasts. Memories of Karen filtered in between the lively discussions around them and mingled with the music. There were good times. Times after he'd broken up with Antoinette, times when he'd met Karen working a waitress job in a local restaurant on summer break from her studies at school. It was also his bachelor time, too, when his ex-interest from the bar told him things were cool, and Karen had said there'd be no strings attached.

He was single, and made no bones about it. It was a time to stop, drop, and roll. But, Karen had gotten pregnant, the other woman persisted in reenacting her fatal attraction methods—ultimately calling Karen to tell her everything about not just their relationship, but things he'd disclosed to her about Antoinette. And it was the timing of her waiting to tell all until he'd become engaged to Karen that was crazy.

"Women can be cold, man," Buddy murmured, as though he'd been inside of Jerome's head. "Complex."

"Don't ever cry in your beer to a woman who says she's your friend, then sleep with her." Jerome laughed. "Do not do it."

"Right." Buddy chuckled sadly. "We done learnt a lot the hard way for two old dogs, huh?"

"Yeah." Jerome sighed, the shook his head. "What went down with Antoinette and Karen was a separate issue, for different reasons, with unfortunately the same person in the middle of it. There I was, all lonely and messed up in the head, listening to a bunch of crap on a bar stool about what Antoinette is possibly doing with some college man. Next thing I know, I wind up taking somebody home that I shouldn't have. Somebody who says she's a friend, who listens to my long story and all the feel-sorry-for-myself-shit you talk when you're in The Service and away from home and they're kickin' your natural ass. Okay.

"Then, me and T break up, and I vow I ain't going down like that no more—but, I'm feeling so homesick for somebody steady in my life, and along comes Karen. We hook up, and whoops. My bad, her bad. Now, I've got a decision to make—and, where do I go, but back to my buddy to run it by her—and, I wind up where I shouldn't be. But, this time, because Karen is local, the other chick has a way to get to her. Not to mention, she uses my entire self-confessed history against me, and tells Karen what shouldn't have been repeated to her. Women don't understand that shit, man. Sometimes it's separate. They tie everything together."

"You been paying for that drama for fifteen years, brother," Buddy said shaking his head. "I don't know how you did it? A young run, and wasn't married yet, and it was just a run... Y'all wasn't even married, yet," Buddy repeated, as though trying to console Jerome's guilt.

"Doesn't matter," Jerome protested, pulling hard on his cigarette and blowing out the smoke even harder. "We was in a serious relationship, with a baby on the way. Same dif as bein' married. That's what I had to learn. It was the same thing Antoinette told me—married or not, a sacred trust had been established, and I blew it. Pure and simple. So don't be no old fool and mess up on Val, hear?"

Buddy slapped Jerome's back and took a swig of beer. "Let it go, man. You was young, dumb, and full of cum. That's all. But, you wasn't the kind to leave no woman at the altar—pregnant. And, you wasn't the kind to flaunt women in her face. Hell, you was tight-lipped about Toni all them years. What can I say? Let it go. It's over."

"Yeah," Jerome agreed, crushing out his half-smoked cigarette and lighting another. "It was like a cancer. Because I had lied, we couldn't talk. Because I felt guilty, I couldn't put my foot down when she would force me to do what I didn't want to do. I'd go along with her program, and then be pissed-off as shit, man. Then, I'd ignore her and go out for a drink. When I'd get home, the joint would be nuclear—so, I'd leave her again. Got so that all we did was hurt each other. She'd dig and I'd dig. When I couldn't physically get away, I'd mentally escape, and she would always get furious when I did that. She knew where I was—not with her. She knew because that other sister had told her just what Antoinette meant to me. So, we blamed each other for everything that went wrong; money, when the kids cut-up, jobs that didn't go right... You have no idea. So, that's why I'm telling you to do the right thing, while there's still some love left, man."

"I'ma call this lady, Reds. No offense, but... I can't go through that with Val."

"Good, man. I ain't gonna tell you no mess like Scoop would—to run on your lady, or hit her and shit. I'm still not speakin' to his ass," Jerome muttered, renewing his grudge against Scoop. "They think we're all like him, you know? Brothers like that make it bad on the one's who's tryin'."

"Word," Buddy said, raising his glass in Jerome's direction.

"Look, man," Jerome said as fatigue worked its way through his bones, "it's late, we've just finished the last two jobs were probably gonna get in a while. Let's call it a night."

"Yeah," Buddy agreed, standing up with effort. "We fixed everything the winter damaged. Gonna hit a dry spell, brother. Damned shame too, 'cause I know you need the bread now. And, me, I always need the bread," he said downing his drink. "Wish Val would take a little of this pressure off and help... just a little. Man, I'm so tired... my stomach's botherin' me. I just need some rest."

"C'mon, good brother. You still got a strong engine." Jerome chuckled. "But I hear you," he said standing and downing his drink. "But a man's gotta do what a man's gotta do. Right?"

Buddy weaved a little and wiped his brow. Jerome looked at his friend hard in the dim light and caught him under the elbow. "Yo, man," Jerome said cautiously, "you okay? We only had a couple."

"Yeah, I'm cool," Buddy said hoarsely, "Just gittin' old and need some air."

"How long a shift did you pull, man?" Jerome continued to stare at Buddy and watched his face with growing concern. In the dim light, it was hard to tell, but Buddy's color seemed off.

"An eighteen. Worked for Miles last night, a one-man job. Got up this morning and worked for twelve, and we just put in two more. I'm tired, that's all. Just need a good eight, and I'll be ready to roll in the morning."

"Okay, my brother." Still concerned, Jerome flanked Buddy as they went out toward the street.

But there was something wrong with his friend's gait. The way he'd opened the door with his arm that wasn't closest to it looked awkward. Jerome put his hand on Buddy's shoulder as a rush of cool air hit their faces. Turning him around slowly, he asked again, “Are you all right? Make a fist with both hands, man.”

“I’m cool,” Buddy puffed. “Air feels good.”

“Shake my hand then,” Jerome insisted. “Give me a high five with both hands.”

“I can’t, man,” Buddy whispered. “I’m really tired.”

Panic coursed through Jerome as they stood on the street. Buddy’s complexion was ashen beneath a sheen of unnecessary sweat. “I’m taking you to the hospital.”

“Man, I gotta go home. Gotta go to work. I have to—”

Buddy weaved again and Jerome caught his fall.

“You gotta go with me. I love you, man.”

Chapter 10

"Put him out!" Antoinette nearly screamed as she walked in a circle around Tracey. "Look at your face."

Antoinette almost wept as her friend balled up into a fetal position on her sofa. "I'm keeping the kids here with me, and you aren't going back over there till he's gone. That's final."

"But, I don't have a job good enough to support them alone," Tracey whispered past her swollen lip. "I don't have any real money of my own."

"Family," Antoinette said more gently, trying to stem her own hysteria in order to make her words reach Tracey. "What about your family? Can you and the kids go there?"

"My father used to do this. What would be different there? My people don't have the space, or the money." A large tear slipped down Tracey's cheek and Antoinette knelt down beside her to gently wipe it away.

"What happened, baby? What set him off this time?"

"I tried to go to Val's to get away, but she wasn't home," Tracey whispered and choked back a sob. "I couldn't have anybody else but you see me like this."

"But... why?" Antoinette whispered, "Why, Trace?"

Questions ricocheted off questions. Solutions tried to grow in her brain but were aborted. Antoinette stroked Tracey's hair and fought against her own tears witnessing the unforgivable destruction of her girlfriend's soul.

"Have you seen Francis since the conference?" Tracey said, closing her eyes.

"No, she's in Atlanta and coming home for Easter. She went to Chicago for another conference, but I haven't connected with her—except to trade answering machine messages. What has Francis got to do with this?"

Tracey let out her breath slowly, and Antoinette could tell that her ribs hurt by the way she carefully sipped in air.

"I'm her baby's Godmother. Francis' father is gone and her mother is nearly eighty. Francis was the youngest, and the only one left in her family who isn't crazy. I have to take that child in, T. I'm the only one, and the child's Daddy lives with some crazy woman who doesn't want her."

"What are you saying?" Antoinette placed her hand cautiously on Tracey's back and leaned closer to hear her friend's whisper. "Why do you have to take in Camille?" The strange information made her ask the question slowly, and her mind tore at what had been said. Something critical had obviously happened with Francis—something serious enough to make Tracey finally take the stand that they had all implored her to for years. But at this cost?

Tracey's gaze slid away from Antoinette's. "Because Francis won't be here much longer. She doesn't know how bad Scoop goes off, and when I looked in her face, I didn't have the heart to tell her no. She never went to Chicago, Toni. She came home to find me and you, and get her affairs in order. You weren't home this weekend, and I was."

Tracey paused and looked at Antoinette deeply, as though allowing enough time for the words to sink in.

"She's got spinal cancer, Toni. She's been on chemo for a year, and it's getting worse."

Antoinette's hand slid from Tracey's back and she clasped it with the other in her lap, as her gaze focused on the furthest corner of the room. Her friend had come looking for her over the weekend, and she was with Jerome. Her house was not in order, just like she'd tried to explain to him. There were no words.

"In six months, she's had three bad episodes, Toni. The girl is skin and bones and can barely stand up—"

"—But, we just saw her in The Poconos," Antoinette whispered, still finding the news hard to absorb. "Sure, she looked tired. But..."

"She came home to be with her Mom, and to be in a nearby hospital. She wants Camille to be around kids, to be in a loving household, one that she couldn't provide." Two big tears rolled down Tracey's nose from her eyes, and she didn't bother to wipe them away. "All these years, Francis was so successful, and I looked up to her. I couldn't tell her what was going on in my house. I had been fronting so hard, trying to keep up with her, and now when she needed me most..."

Antoinette allowed her knees to slide out from under her body and she sat back on the floor, trying to make her mind interpret what had just been said. "She's only thirty-eight..." Antoinette whispered, covering her mouth with her hand as her words trailed off. "Oh, God..."

Both women sat without speaking. Hearing of Francis' mortality, and Tracey having verbalized it, drove an immediate stake into their own. Sudden panic rippled through Antoinette, one that was different than hearing of Pearline's certain demise. Francis was a young woman. Francis had a young child. Francis' financial house was in order, unlike their own. The decision to act had to be now, because to be caught unprepared was not acceptable. Neither she nor Tracey could afford to let what had happened to her and Adrienne happen to their children, to be left without female support, because even Pearline would be gone.

An immediate, visceral awareness that there would be no female backbone gripped Antoinette and halted any comment she could conceive to utter. She knew Tracey felt the same icy panic as they gazed at each other and allowed the shock to pass through their skeletons.

"What am I going to do, Toni?" Tracey quietly asked, finally letting another sob to break through. "He went off... said he wasn't taking care of no orphans. Said that Camille probably had AIDS, and that Francis was lying about it being cancer. I stood my ground on that ignorant bastard, and he beat me up." She hid her face with her hands and wept. "But this time, I had to take a stand, and couldn't let him take my dignity—my ability to help my friend in need just because I was afraid of him. So I fought back."

Gingerly covering Tracey with her own body, Antoinette nuzzled her hair and allowed her own tears to fall. Rage mingled with unrelenting sorrow as she held Tracey and rocked against her.

"Help us, God,"she whispered, chanting the phrase over and over as her vision became totally obscured by tears and Tracey's hair. She kissed the back of her friend's head, and a new wave of fury washed over her as Tracey flinched from a concealed head wound. "It'll be all right," she whispered, "it has to be. We have to tell Francis the truth, and you can't go back to Scoop." Tracey threaded her arms through Antoinette's and clung to her like a child. Her friend's sobs were quiet and shame-filled, and all Antoinette could do was hold her.

"I've failed, Toni," Tracey whispered between deep breaths, "I was supposed to be there, have a place for the children and I can't even raise mine."

"Shhhh.... shhhh, now..." Antoinette whispered back as they rocked, "you didn't fail. This is not your guilt, and not your shame. I'll kill Scoop," she said quietly. "I'll have him seen by some of the brothers in the neighborhood. Their girlfriends are in my class. You will be able to live in your home. The courts take too long."

"No!" Finding enough strength to break their embrace, Tracey pushed herself up and tried to stand. "I told the officer that I just wanted to be left alone. I didn't want him hurt."

Antoinette sat back a little and stared at Tracey hard. "What officer? Did you file a report?"

Tracey looked away, and eased back against the sofa.

Antoinette stared at her hard and ignored the ringing telephone. "You have to protect yourself."

"That's what he said," Tracey whispered, "I thank God that he came by when he did. Scoop was dragging me down the steps by my hair. The kids were crying, but scared to get in-between it. He almost made my baby fall. This brother jumped in it. He's not Philly Five-O, he's a Penn bicycle cop—works night beat. He wouldn't call for back-up, just fucked Scoop up right there in the street."

Eerie satisfaction settled in Antoinette's bones, and she tried to hide it from Tracey as she spoke. "He didn't call for back-up, because he would have had to follow procedures. I hope you realize that he told you right. File a report at the hospital, then we'll call over to Fifty-fifth and Pine, or down to Family Court, and try to find out what you have to do to get a bench warrant established and get a peace bond, so he can't come within fifty yards of you—"

"I don't want to—"

"—You don't have a choice," Antoinette said through her teeth. "Think of your children. How long will it be before he goes after one of them? Or, what if you wind up like Francis, dead or dying at thirty-eight?" Her own words made her cringe. Francis was losing ground. A sense of failure swept through Antoinette. If only she had the resources she once had, if only she had a place—a safe place to offer her friend Tracey. If only Pearline wasn't dying. If only she had a good job...

New tears filled Antoinette's eyes and she let them fall without hiding them. "Who will watch the babies!" she asked just above a whisper, "Tell me, Trace. Triflin' ass Scoop, who killed you? Your folks, who you don't trust? Your crazy brother? Your drug-addict sister? Think, girl. This is serious. The brother on the bike told you right. We're going to the hospital."

"But who'll watch the kids at this time of

night?" Tracey's eyes held a combination of fear and need to believe.

"I'll call Cookie, or we'll try Val again," Antoinette said in a distant voice. "We can't hide this any more. We can't ignore it, and act like he'll stop one day. He won't."

"I don't want anybody else to know," Tracey said in a sharp whisper as her gaze darted to the ringing phone and toward Antoinette's bedroom where her children slept with Lauren. "Please."

"No. No more secrets. You have to act, we have to pull together, and we have to find a way to care for you, your brood, and Francis' child." She looked at Tracey hard and stood up, refusing to give-in to the plea in her friend's eyes. Secrecy was Scoop's weapon, along with his fists, and along with the humiliation and guilt that he'd somehow transferred to his wife.

"Anybody but them," Tracey said as she began to weep again. "Please, not Cookie."

Antoinette let her breath out in a hard rush. "I'll call May," she said quietly. "I have a lot of other stuff to go over with her anyway."

"But, it's eleven o'clock at night..."

"This is an emergency. She's my step-mom, now," Antoinette said aloud as though a prayer. "She'll understand."

"Okay," Tracey agreed quietly, "but, I don't

want to get you in trouble with her."

Antoinette waited for the phone to stop ringing before she picked it up to dial her father and May's number. On the third ring, May picked up, and Antoinette could tell that she'd awakened her.

Without formality, her message was brief, yet firm. "May," she said simply, "I have four children under ten years old in my house. Their mother, my girlfriend, was beaten by her husband. I have to go to the hospital. Can you come?"

May's return response was equally as immediate. "I'm on my way. Stay calm."

Antoinette hung up the telephone, paced to the refrigerator and grabbed out more ice to pack in a towel. She could feel Tracey watching her as she worked, but her mind became absorbed in her hands as they prepared a compress. How was she going to help Tracey? Was she really going to leave this time? What could she do for Francis and her poor elderly mother?

While crushing the ice, her mind lashed her own crumpling self-worth. She should have had her fortress secure by now, should have had it right—for eventualities such as these. She'd tried to explain this to Jerome—men didn't understand about being ready, just in case. Love didn't solve that, didn't put up canned goods in the cabinet, stores for a rainy day, or keep emergency money in a hidden account. What if this had been Adrienne laying on her sofa?

She had to call Adrienne—to look at her sister-child's face, just as Pearline had commanded. Despite their argument, it was time to see for herself where her sister was living in LA. It was time to always have one-way ticket money to bring that child in out of the rain, if necessary, and she had to always have long distance so she could check on those away from the nest. She also had to squash the drama with Valerie. This was a 911 situation that went beyond surface struggles. What if this were Lauren one day—or one of Val's kids, she thought, as new tears ran down her face. How could she save all of these women and children?

The chime of the bell stopped her, and she brought the new compress over to Tracey as she went to answer the door. May stepped in and gave her a brief hug, then quickly walked over to Tracey and lifted her chin with her finger.

"This is an outrage," May said through her teeth. "You will not go back," she commanded. "Ever. Not for love, or money, or misdirected guilt. You will not go back, do you hear me? You're worth more than this. Say it to me."

"Okay," Tracey said quietly.

"No!" May stormed, and Antoinette stood by

her side. "Say it like you mean it! I am worth more than this!"

Tracey shifted her chin away from May's hold and dropped her head. A sob swallowed her words, but May would no be put off. "Say. It. To. Me. Tell me—say it, Tracey. I. Am. Worth. More. Than. This!"

"Say it," Antoinette whispered, coming around to Tracey's other side and holding her shoulders firmly. "Say it like you mean it!" She yelled, looking at May. "Tell her."

"I'm worth more than this," Tracey wept into her hands, "so much more..."

May and Antoinette practically slumped from sudden release of tension that drained from their bodies. Each holding one of Tracey's hands so that she couldn't hide her face, they went down on their knees before her on the couch.

"That's right," May murmured, "nobody has the right to do this to you for any reason."

"Let it out," Antoinette whispered as Tracey's sobs escalated to wails. "It's going to be all right."

"You are filing a report," May said firmly, "so your son and daughters never have to have this happen to them. Right?"

"Yes," Tracey cried, "Not my babies."

"Not your babies—ever," Antoinette affirmed. "Ever. He's cancer, and has to be cut out now before it spreads." She looked at her friend hard but with compassion. "One day it would have come to this—regardless of what's going on with Francis. You understand that, right? It has to do with you finally just getting tired, and Francis was just a last straw... but anything could have been the last straw. It was time."

Tracey nodded her head slowly, and May and Antoinette exchanged a glance—each knowing that a tough love intervention was no guarantee of what would take place beyond the moment. May rubbed Antoinette's back, and Antoinette nodded her understanding of that reality toward the older woman. Without words, they both seemed to accept that Tracey could suddenly refuse to get into a car with Antoinette. She could get spooked by the bright lights of the emergency room and flee—never filing a report. And, ultimately, when the money got funny, or her husband came to her bedside with flowers, she might take him back.

The only glimmer of hope that they could hold onto was that because a friend's child was involved, maternal instinct would kick in and make Tracey stick to her guns, even though she hadn't found the strength to do that for her own until now. Antoinette silently prayed that her friend could finally see how much the children were at risk, and also prayed that that would be strong enough to end the struggle to stay with a crazy man once and for all. What Tracey did tomorrow was an open question.

But, none of that mattered as they sat in a three-way circle of hope. She and May continued to pray silently that Tracey would find strength, and hoped even harder that she could siphon a little of theirs as they encased her with their bodies, willing to give blood, or breath, or whatever it took to save her.

"I fought him this time," Tracey whispered, seeming to gain some life into her wilted soul. "I did it for Fran, you know... her baby, my Godchild. I couldn't let him take that from me, and that's why this time was so bad."

"What's wrong with Francis?" May said, growing alarmed, "What's wrong with her baby?"

"They found cancer in her spine, but it was untreated for so long," Tracey whispered, new tears brimming in her eyes. "She's dying."

May's hand flew over her mouth and her eyes filled immediately, then cleared. "Okay," she breathed out slowly, "And, you'll get custody?"

"Yes," Antoinette cut in, finding newfound respect for May's stewardship under pressure. "We have to get Tracey in a safe place, a place that she can stay without bills and without harassment for a while."

Silence fell over their circle and each woman stared off in the distance encased by her own thoughts.

"That's why we have to tell Francis," Antoinette finally said in a quiet voice.

"But—"

"—Hear me out," Antoinette commanded softly when Tracey tried to interrupt her. "That's also why you have to make this the last thing like this with Scoop."

Antoinette's gaze roved between May's no-nonsense expression to Tracey's look of dread. "Francis' mother is nearly eighty, but she gets around well, and has a four bed-room house. You're not working yet, but you drive—and her Mom is probably going out of her mind in that house alone. She can't watch the kids by herself, but she could for short stints with help."

Picking up the rhythm of Antoinette's thoughts, May led on with skill. "And, her mother will need help when Francis is too ill to move. Her child will be in familiar surroundings, your children will have a safe place—if her mother is in her eighties, the house is paid for."

They both banished the look of guilt that Tracey cast towards them, and she stifled her words.

"No. We have to be practical about this,"

Antoinette continued, leap-frogging May's comment. "I'll go to visit her mother and explain the situation, so you won't have to. I'll get Jerome and Buddy to help you move your clothes and sentimental items—leave the furniture. We'll take anything liquid, though—anything that can be sold for immediate cash, and we'll keep everything that makes your children feel at home. Also, by having her mother there, you have another adult on the premises for protection. Tell the cop where you're moving, so he can keep an eye out for you. Okay?"

"You think they'll have me? I mean, this is not what Francis expected. She wanted a family environment for her Camille, not this—"

"—She's getting a family," May said curtly, refusing to dignify Tracey's wavering response as a reinforcement mechanism. "Listen, in my generation, grandmothers, aunts, relatives all lived together. It kept a lot of this mess from going on. A man couldn't easily beat a woman with her mother, or his mother, still in the house. No. This makes sense. Toni's being realistic. Francis didn't expect to die either—nobody can expect life to go the way you want it to. So, you do your best with the hand you're dealt, and go on. Sometimes, life isn't fair—what's that anyway? Fair? It hasn't been for me. That's the way it goes, child. That's just the way it goes."

"I'm also going to talk to Francis about her will," Antoinette said quietly, holding up her hand to Tracey before she could disagree. "She has resources, baby. Resources you're going to need to take care of her child. She needs to get Scoop's name off of everything, because she'll cause us to kill him if she doesn't. Let the business part go, honey. That's my specialty, I'll handle it with her and her mother."

"But, all I left with are the clothes on my back.," Tracey said quietly. "I have to get—"

"—Give us the keys," May snapped. "You're not going back. Spend the night here, and in the morning we'll get this all solved over Francis' Mom's house. Right, Antoinette?"

"Right."

"Get her to the hospital, now. I'll sleep on the sofa till you get back," May said with a yawn, looking older from the sudden call-to-arms.

"Thanks, May," Antoinette whispered as she helped Tracey to her feet and bent to kiss May.

"Who's Jerome?" May asked with a wink, youth gradually reclaiming her face. "Tell me when you get back."

In that moment, May had just been promoted to the inner circle.

*

"It'll be all right," Antoinette said again as they crossed the expanse of Civic Center Boulevard and entered the Emergency Room of the hospital. Tracey squeezed Antoinette's hand, and she returned a tight grip to transmit safety. It will be all right, she said in her mind as the lights glared down on their tear-streaked faces. It has to be, Lord.

Grateful that it wasn't a weekend, Antoinette coaxed Tracey to the desk and began the sign-in process. She quickly glanced around the waiting area that was filled to capacity, and tried to will the nurse behind the desk to get her friend in fast. Gut instinct told her that Tracey couldn't take a long wait—where the time to think would give her friend a million justifications for going back to Scoop. They had to get Tracey's injuries on the record and get her home. Period.

"May I help you?" the nurse asked without looking up. "Nature of your injuries," she sighed still focused on the form. "I'll need your insurance card first."

Antoinette squeezed Tracey's hand and gave her a glance to be quiet. If they were going to avoid a five-hour wait, she knew she'd need a little theater to get Tracey seen fast—and free. So, she waited, using the silence to force the intake nurse to look at them. When the woman lifted her head and scowled, Antoinette leaned in to her. "She's been attacked," she whispered, "she came to my house in shock and traumatized."

"Has she been raped?" the nurse asked quickly in a soft voice.

Antoinette squeezed Tracey's hand hard and ignored her wide-eyed expression. "We don't know," Antoinette said clinically, fishing in her handbag for her brass business card holder. "Here's my agency's card. We deal with women in need of shelter. I'm a counselor there."

"Oh," the nurse said inspecting the card and standing. "We've heard of your agency, you have a location in West Philly, right?"

Antoinette nodded and watched in awe as the nurse's demeanor changed. In that moment, she understood what her oldest co-worker had been trying to tell her. Stay and redistribute the resources. Regret made her weak as the nurse motioned for them to follow her. Without formality, because they were on the inside of the system, things happened—no money down, a different set of rules, a double standard. She wasn't just another neighborhood native, she was an agent to a respected organization, and that conferred power to martial resources. And, this was the last time that she was going to be able to use them in any woman's behalf. She'd quit and was fired all in one day. But, if there was ever a time to scam for a good cause, it was now. Antoinette thrust up her chin and looked at the nurse hard.

"Unfortunately, we get a lot of admits from there," the nurse finally said, showing the card to a resident. "Has campus police made a report, or has the Eighteenth District been called?"

"What was the name of the officer who helped you," Antoinette said quietly, wiping a new tear away from Tracey's face. I'll handle your forms and call them while you get looked at. Okay? I'll be right outside the curtain."

"William Cooper," Tracey said quietly, "he was really nice."

"I'll handle the reports," Antoinette said with false authority to the nurse. "Do you have a phone and a clip-board? I need access to my office, and to call Campus Police."

"Sure thing, Ms. Wellington," the nurse efficiently piped, handing a clean gown to Tracey. "Here, honey, put on a drape and take everything off under it. The doctor will be right in."

Antoinette kissed Tracey and let the breath out of her body slowly when she accepted the gown from the nurse. Following behind the fast-moving woman, Antoinette kept stride with the nurse's brisk pace until they arrived at an interior desk station.

"Dial nine to get out, and on the wall is a list of emergency numbers. Campus Police is on that list, and I'll need you to fill out as much as you can on her forms. You can give us the rest of her information later—if she can gain access to her belongings, or tomorrow from your case files."

Antoinette couldn't look up as she accepted the paperwork and hospitality. While she dialed, her mind raced with a thousand questions. What if they had just tumbled in off the streets with no money, but in need? What if there was no official agency? What if Tracey was just a poor, jobless, minority woman in need of immediate assistance—in need of being treated with dignity and sensitivity? She now understood why her friend feared even trying, and wondered if she had attempted this before—facing the bright lights and hard stares with no money, alone? She wished Linda Kravats could be a fly on the wall to see the disparity in treatment, how to really use her power, and what a difference it could make. Maybe if Linda could have just seen this...

Antoinette huddled against the cubicle and made her report over the phone, and jotted down notes about the actions Tracey would have to take. Glad that they'd paged the officer her friend had trusted, she told him more details than he needed to know—it was insurance. She was talking to a good brother, a person on the inside, a 'spook who sat by the door', somebody who could make her friend's paperwork slide through the system. This was how it worked in Philly—ten years in Jersey hadn't been long enough for her to forget that fact.

"Toni?"

Her head snapped up from the forms on her lap at the sound of the familiar male voice. She looked at Jerome for a second and stood quickly.

"You heard? May called you?"

"I was there when it happened," he said slowly, "I still can't believe it."

"I hope y'all kicked Scoop's natural ass—"

"Scoop? He wasn't there."

She stared at Jerome's exhausted expression and noticed lines she hadn't seen before beginning to crease his forehead. "The cop put Scoop in his place, right? Tracey's being seen now by a doctor."

"What?" he nearly yelled, then checked himself as uniformed heads turned in their direction. "Val is back there with Buddy now," he whispered.

"Oh, my God. Did Buddy get in the middle of it?"

"Buddy had a mild heart attack," Jerome said

softly grabbing her by the shoulders. "When we left the bar. They're taking him up to a room. Val took the kids to her mother's. What happened to Scoop and Tracey, T? What's happening to all our friends? Our family?"

His voice sounded so pained and his eyes held a mist of fear. Touch was the only solution. She filled his arms and rested her forehead on his shoulder. "Scoop really hurt her this time, baby," she said rubbing his back. "Francis is really sick, and all Tracey wanted to do was take in the baby—he beat her, Jay. Like a dog in the street. She came to my house because she couldn't reach Val. I guess Val was here. Lord have mercy."

His grip became cement around her arms as he rocked and swayed against her. She could feel him fighting the urge to cry, and understood his need to be held while holding her. Their world was crumbling, people were dying in the line of duty, and nobody was well over forty. His hard swallows against her hairline asked questions that she couldn't answer. His quiet shudders asked, why now? Why this? Why good people? Why people with children? Why people who worked hard? Why people they loved?

"It'll be all right, baby," she whispered as she rubbed his back and rocked him.

"He's my boy—my best friend..." Jerome whispered thickly. "He worked like a dog with no appreciation, and dropped under the load. I don't want to end up like that, T... and now Tracey, and Francis?"

"It'll be all right," she whispered again as she continued to rock him. "All we can do is pray."

Chapter 11

"I'm calling in sick tomorrow, anyway, Trace. It's no problem. I can get your things out, and you won't have to worry about him putting his hands on you," Jerome said quietly as they stood on the front steps leading to Antoinette's unit.

"I can't let you two take a day off for me. I'll be fine, I can—"

"Gotta take a day off," Jerome reassured her. "After I move you, I have to go check on Buddy and to see if Val needs anything, you know? Maybe even pull some of Buddy's weight with Miles and send the check her way till they get his disability checks rollin'. The system moves slow, and can't have Val and the kids starvin' to death, or lose their house while they mess around with the papers downtown. Gotta tell Buddy not to worry, 'cause that'll give him a true coronary—worrying about his family while he's down in the bed."

"I never even thought about all of that," Tracey whispered, "but, you all have more important—"

"You're important," Jerome said firmly. "I said I'd be there tomorrow and I will."

"You stay here with May and the kids," Antoinette murmured, "while I'm over at Francis' Mom's. After me and Jerome get you settled—and you've had a chance to get some sleep, I'll take you down to fill out the paperwork at the police station."

"I'll give you my pager number, and my phone number. Give it to Francis' Mom, too," Jerome said while scribbling a note on the back of an old automated banking teller receipt that had been in his wallet. "If Scoop shows up, call me, then call the police. Give me a five minute jump on the cops."

Tracey wrapped her arms around her waist after she accepted the paper from Jerome, and looked down. "You guys have done so much... and Val's husband almost died... now Francis..." she whispered, shaking her head as though the reality was just hitting her. "I could have died, or one of the kids. Everything is in an uproar. Nothing's staying the way it used to be. Everything's changed."

"C'mon," Antoinette urged gently, "some changes are for the better—even though they hurt while you're making them. Just like the end of labor," she smiled, kissing Tracey's cheek. "Remember those last few seconds when you think you're gonna die—then out pops this beautiful baby, and you can't even remember the pain so much?"

Tracey smiled at her and gave her a hug, then looked at Jerome. "I was never angry with you, or thought anything was wrong about you two getting together. I know what living in hell is like. I was happy that you got out. But Scoop wouldn't let me call."

"I know, Buddy told me," Jerome remarked candidly, appearing not to care that his resentment of Scoop showed. "Actually, truth be told, it was Scoop. Said he didn't want you to be under the bad influence of Antoinette. I was done with him after that—and will kick his ass if he tries to hurt you. Okay? That's history. The old neighborhood crew is back together, minus one or two bad apples. We're family."

"Yes," Antoinette whispered, slipping an arm around Tracey, "We're family. C'mon, let's go inside."

As they stepped over the threshold, the smell of coffee greeted them. May was in the kitchen and Antoinette's father sat in the overstuffed chair with an old revolver on his lap. The sight was both comforting and alarming, and Antoinette could feel Tracey withdraw a little at the sight of Mr. Reeves.

"Knew you'd be here, son," he said with a nod in Jerome's direction. "May called me over to wait with her, in case there was any trouble at the door when you ladies came back. C'mere daughter," he said gently, opening his arms for Tracey to fill them. When she did, he gave her a very gentle bear hug and gingerly pushed her head against his shoulder, being careful of her wounds. "Shoulda told ya family, we coulda solved this a long time ago. You my other daughter—all you girls is."

Ignoring their embrace, Antoinette stared at the gun that rested on her coffee table. "Daddy... you brought a gun in the house... with all these children?"

Her father gave a little snort, and patted Tracey's face as he released her. "Been in Worl' War Two! Done kilt plenty enemies for my country—now, a man cain't protect his daughters? Must be crazy. See, the way I figure it is, I'm too ol' to be tanglin' in the streets wit some fired-up husband. Naw. That was a different era. An' Jerome here, he don' need to go to jail over no fool like Scoop. He gots his whole life in fronta him. Me, at my age, if I shoot some young, crazy, nigga that was beatin' on my daughter—worse I'll get is the rest of my life on parole." He chuckled and sat back down. "Humph, I'm retired anyway. Ain't got nothin' else to do but be black and die. So, what's a weekly visit downtown to a parole officer—it'd get me out the house, anyway."

Jerome chuckled and the two men winked at each other. May just shook her head, but Tracey seemed to relax as she basked under the protective extension of family. Antoinette stared at the gun and let out her breath.

"Take the bullets out and put it away, Daddy. We're not killing anybody today. All right?" she pleaded, looking at May for support.

"I ain't taking out no bullets till I go home. May's gonna stay here on the pull out couch, to help watch the kids. I'ma go home and feed m'dog. Let Tracey get a nice hot bath and give'r something pretty to sleep in wit her kids—give'r your room. You," he said with a wink in Jerome's direction, "need to go get a good night's sleep with my future son-in-law."

Antoinette's mouth flew open and she looked

between the two men who both chuckled.

"Aw, now, Mr. Matt, that was between me and you. You done let the cat out the bag."

"You're getting engaged," Tracey whispered as a slow smile dawned on her face.

"He came over after work on his way home and those two had a long talk about the past," May piped in with delight. "We already knew. So, we'll be fine till tomorrow. Oh, yeah, and I called your other cousin, Patti. She's a saint—will watch Lauren while I'm at work. Called Adrienne, and told her too. Then Adrienne told us about Ness' mess over there—that's why Patti made sense to us, right Matt? We'll also be helping you watch her from now on."

Antoinette allowed the words to sink in. They'd be helping her with Lauren... from now on? It was ironic. Indeed she'd prayed for that type of local grandparent support, but she had mixed emotions about the way Vanessa had been removed from the family baby-sitting equation so abruptly, even though she had wanted to do so herself. Vanessa was still her sister-cousin, whom she loved very much—despite her cousin's lifestyle, and she wasn't quite sure of how to absorb the pronouncement. Yet, in a round-about-way, she could tell that this was a good thing, something designed to bring her immediate family together. May had indeed closed ranks for protection, motherly protection, and it shifted the relationship to more solid ground. Now, Antoinette knew that she'd be the one to have to back off to allow a new natural course to develop with its own eddies and pools.

"You've made all the calls, May," Antoinette began after a moment of hesitation, "so I guess you would know."

Antoinette looked at May deeply, and their gaze locked in an instant telepathic connection. May had taken the weight. It was something she'd needed to understand before May could be truly included within her mental inner circle; May would be there should she need to 'stand-down.' Another female of substance was going to be there to care for her child, to be 'the one,' so that the circle of life would not be broken if she died in the line of duty. Their brief exchange was an unspoken meeting of the minds that had not been there before. It was this silent promise that she finally felt she could count on, and it wholly brought May into the fold.

When Tracey nodded ever so slightly, Antoinette knew that a changing of the guard had officially occurred and been witnessed. All of the women's' shoulders relaxed imperceptibly, and they released their breaths slowly in unison.

"All I am is the thin black line of defense," her father chuckled in Jerome's direction, both appearing oblivious to the major event that had just happened before their eyes.

"But, Patti? Brian's cousin?" Antoinette had to sit, as the new family structure began to take root. She moved over to the sofa and flopped down. "Patti is a Saint, and I love her so, but... Vanessa has her ways..." she tried to defend. "Why on earth?"

"You know how much Patti loves Lauren, and it was time to let the peace-keeping forces on the Wellington side know that things had permanently changed—since they have," May said firmly, apparently refusing to be contradicted, and giving Jerome a nod of unspoken support.

May's voice was calm and had lost its once strident peal. Her statement was said in a way to make it clear to Antoinette that she was not breaking rank, but simply taking on her new elevated status to inner-circle.

"Plus," May went on, "Patti promised she would watch Lauren for the rest of the week so we could make sure Tracey was settled, and start moving things out of Pearline's. Vanessa has to get her act together before Lauren needs to go back into that environment."

Unprepared for the reference to Pearline, or

the casual way it had been delivered, all she could do was look at Jerome. Too many truths had collided in the same sentence.

"Naw, baby, he didn't tell us," her father said quietly, picking up on at least one unspoken cue to her distress. "Pearline told us Sunday after we got home. Said she was gonna let you know soon as she could catch up to you. Said you was the bearer of bad news for your Mom, and she didn't want you to have to worry about that for her. You know my sister. She's organized, don't leave nothin' for nobody to do. But, she lived a good life, and I'ma miss her crazy, superstitious ways."

"Oh, Toni..." Tracey's voice trailed off, "not Pearline?"

"It's all right, suga," her father said standing up slowly. "We all gittin' up there. A change a season, is all."

"I called all the family," May said quietly. Although she was obviously saddened, she also seemed pleased that she had been given a significant family role. "Pearline told me that you were fixing Easter dinner. You know what she said?"

"What?" Antoinette whispered. Her eyes filled and she looked down at her hands, which were tightly clasped, in her lap.

"She finally explained to me how things work in this family. I finally understand," May replied with a genuine smile. "It was never personal, just positional. She let me in. I never had family like this—so close."

"I know what you mean," Jerome said quietly, "it's something crazy, something outrageous, with a lot of unspoken ways, but something that you don't want to miss, May. I'm glad Pearline gave you her blessing—before everything happened. You know what I mean? That's why I gotta go up with Toni and the kids on Sunday, to let her know."

"Well, I'm glad y'all understand my sister. Hell, I never did know what she was talking about—dreams, and visions, and a pinch of the Lord snuck in-between," Matthew Reeves muttered as he put on his jacket and baseball cap. "Been tryin' to tell May that she was accepted all along. But, you know women. Some kinda psychic pronouncement gotta be made, I don't know what y'all call it."

"She told me," May said with her hand on her hip, "that the girls are the ones who keep the history. That Antoinette was the one for your side, just like Claudia was the one for your wife's side. Your wife's sister was the oldest, so her oldest daughter got all of the things passed from her favorite Aunt—not because the little bit of money mattered, but because she knew the stories that went with everything passed down. The sentimental pieces—like china, and pictures, and silver, recipes and cookbooks, and of course, the family Bible. Things that had history."

May's gaze flitted to each person in the room, seeming to request acceptance in the midst of her newfound confidence. "Now, our Antoinette is the oldest direct female on your side, Matt—and she knows all the stories. So, she becomes the hub, and all your wife's main stuff, her grandmother's stuff, and Pearline's stuff goes to her—because the child knows the stories. It's not about money, there's never much of that in our families, it's about relics that carry memory. That's why she's gotta start doing the meals, because she has a daughter," May added, looking at Jerome, "who has to learn at her side. Just like your oldest will be the one on your side for her mother. But, if all goes well, Patsy might also hold two family trees to help Lauren. See? It wasn't about keeping me out. I thought, well, never mind. It was about the order of things that I didn't understand," she sighed, "I was the oldest female on my side, so I expected to walk in and..."

"We got locked into a queen bee struggle," Antoinette said with a warm smile. "May, I'm sorry, but I've been groomed to take the baton since a little girl. It's something you know... I can't even explain it."

"Yeah," May said quietly, her gaze distant, "We're both queen bees. It's like everyone around you feeds you this royal jelly, and you just know, you're the one—the next in line. And, here, all this time, I thought you resented me because of your mother."

"May, my Mom had been gone for a long time, and my father had been so lonely, and he came back to life when you came into our family. It was never really about Mom. It was about your assumed authority over matters that had already been set in motion. It wasn't your turn, here."

"I know,' May said quietly. "I'm sorry, too, and I would get so angry at Matt sometimes..."

"But, you're still reigning queen bee on your side," Antoinette said with a chuckle, "you just can't rule both hives, hon."

May laughed and dropped her hand from her hip. "Okay, but at least let me bring the ham."

"Done," Antoinette laughed, "See, this can work."

Antoinette's father walked over to her and kissed her forehead, then gave Tracey a little peck on the cheek, and went to the kitchen doorway to give May a peck on her lips.

"This is too complicated for me," Mr. Reeves admitted with a yawn. "An' at one-fifteen in the mornin', I'm not trying to figure out all this queen bee mess. Would think this was the Royal Family, or somethin', and y'all was preparin' for a coronation. All we really talkin' about is, Easter dinner, and deciding who gets some old furniture, and old photos, which ain't nobody's choice, since m'sister done tol' y'all how it's gonna go." He walked away from May to give Jerome a big smile and a hearty handshake, "You sure you want in on this madness, brother? Wouldn't blame you if you changed your mind. All the women is bull-headed, superstitious, and—"

"—And beautiful," Jerome laughed as they gave each other a quick man-hug.

"Yeah..." the old man chuckled with pride as he opened the door. "They are that."

"Don't forget your gun, Daddy," Antoinette said as she stood, shaking her head the entire time. "Ummph, uhmph, uhmph."

"Oh, yeah. Cain't forget 'ol' faithful." Her father chuckled, pacing back to collect his weapon. "Well, y'all two might as well come on out wit me. Ain't like y'all in high school and gotta sneak it no more. I might be ol', but I ain't stupid."

Jerome just laughed as he held the door open for Antoinette. He glanced at Mr. Reeves with a sheepish expression when Antoinette didn't immediately stand up.

"See, now the girl's gonna try to act all dignified," Mr. Reeves whispered, and chuckled as his daughter cut him a sideways glance. "But, that's my chile, and she comes by her ways honest—runs in the family." Her father's wide grin mellowed and he looked away. "I owe you both an apology," he murmured. "Put my money on the wrong horse before. Wellington is good people; his folks are, too. But I didn't give you much of a chance, boy. Saw too much of myself in you, I guess."

A silent understanding hung in the chilly night air, but the warmth of her father's words wrapped around them like a protective cloak.

"Are you all going to be all right?" Antoinette finally asked May and Tracey, then walked over to the phone to leave an address and telephone number on the pad. Ignoring her father's gaze, she went into the bedroom to pull out a nightgown for Tracey, and took her time in finding a towel and wash cloth for all the guests that had descended upon her home. Finally returning to the kitchen she opened the refrigerator and gave May and Tracey instructions about what was under the foil wrapped platters in the freezer, and showed them three times where they could find breakfast cereal and snacks for all of the children.

Again, she ignored her father's knowing smirk as she unlocked the front door.

"Don't'chu need a bag, or somethin'," her father teased as they went left, "Or, do you all already have a set of clothes stashed at both apartments?"

"Aw, Mr. Reeves," Jerome chuckled, glancing at Antoinette as she looked ahead hiding a smile, "it ain't like that."

"Well, at y'all's age, it oughtta be," the older man flipped over his shoulder as he opened his car, "Y'all need to decide where y'all gonna live, too. Go on, and git."

*

"My Dad is such a trip—will embarrass you to death." She chuckled as Jerome opened the Bronco door for her. "I love him, but he can be so wild!"

"Yeah," Jerome added with newfound respect, "He's a real trip. Hindsight being twenty-twenty, I can appreciate where he was coming from, though. Even when he'd be in my face, I'd always liked him—just wanted him to like me back. But how could he, really? Toni, I swear the man had ESP—knew when I was hurtin' for ya. Those were the days that he'd take me through the wringer.

Will probably be the same way when it's my turn to look out for my girls."

"And I'ma do what my mother did," she said with a wide smile and a toss of her head.

"Which was?"

"I'm going to take it to the pillow, distract you, and get you to give them room to breathe."

He gave her a scowl that was mixed with a smile as they pulled up to the light. "Oh, no, woman. You ain't distractin' me—gettin' me to leave my post with your feminine wiles."

"Yes, I am." She laughed as he sped around the corner. "It's my job."

"To do what?" he said, becoming indignant. "It's my job to make sure my girls don't go astray."

"Astray?" Antoinette stared at him, then burst out with laughter. "Wait a minute. I was somebody's daughter too, you know."

"Yeah, but that was different."

"No it wasn't," she countered, still laughing. "And I hope my girls find somebody just like you."

"Heaven forbid," he said in a serious tone that amused her all the more.

"Isn't Patsy fourteen, like a half a year away from fifteen?"

"Yeah, it's comin' up on me fast, T. Maybe I should buy a gun?"

"Have you lost your mind?" she laughed harder. "Oh, no. I've got another one to live with all of my life. Jerome, that is so Neanderthal!"

"Well, if so, how come every father feels that way?"

All she could do is shake her head and try not to laugh harder. Regaining her composure, she touched his arm as he pulled into a space in front of his building. "Do you trust me?"

"Of course," he muttered, turning off the engine. "What's that got to do with anything?"

"Then, you'll want your girls to find someone who treats them the way you treated me in high school; somebody kind, and gentle, and supportive, and respectful, and nice."

"Yeah," he grumbled, looking out of the window, "but that's not all I did to you. Remember?"

"I remember that you loved me so, took me so gently the first time, and called me every night. I remember that you brought me ice cream, and took me to the movies, and we laughed, and laughed, and played, and danced. That's what the first time should be like, Jerome," she whispered softly. "Not traumatic, or forced, or under humiliation. Do you know how many women have their entire sexuality messed up because their first experiences were horrible, and what their parents told them about their own bodies was worse? You have to trust me on this, Jay. I learned from the best. That's what you should hope for them—the very best, because nature is inevitable."

He let his breath out in a rush and his shoulders dropped. Picking at the leather steering wheel encasement, he seemed to be considering her words as he tried to formulate his own.

"Baby," he said quietly, "I just don't want them to get in trouble, and have to get married. Can you understand that?"

"I do," she said honestly. "But, you know what? You have less trouble to worry about with girls, than boys."

"What?" His face held an expression of incredulous disbelief that made her smile.

"It's a secret, don't tell anybody, but you have more control over the girls."

"How so?" he stammered, looking at her hard for a definitive answer.

"Because," she said slowly, taking her time to let the concept sink in, "when you have girls, if the boy leaves, chances are you and I will be raising that baby."

"My point exactly," he said in a confident tone, then folded his arms over his chest.

"But, if you have a boy, that grandchild is left up to the fate of the girl and her family. Suppose your son picked a really whack-attack? The child would be in the crazy mother's custody, and we'd have no influence. Plus, your son might be forced to pay child support for twenty years of his life to a family that could use it for the lottery, drugs, or whatever. His life would be ruined. On the other hand, if your daughter hooked up with a bum... say a Scoop, then we'd be able to take her in, let her finish school, and raise that baby according to our combined dictates and values. We could manage visitations with the father, if he was shady, and she wouldn't have to pay him a cent. Her life would be her own. Girls are less trouble, and your child would have a fighting chance—giving your grandchild a fighting chance. Think about it."

"Damn, Toni... How do y'all always do it? Come up with stuff that makes so much sense, but that's so hard to swallow?"

She laughed and opened the car door for herself. "Because we're smarter, and wiser, and we listen better, and we watch the signs in detail. Y'all either kill it, eat it, or sleep with it. Neanderthal, like I said. You'll evolve. I'm patient."

Jerome stood on the curb and watched her go up the steps. Rifling in his jacket pocket, he leaned against his car, pulled out a cigarette and lit it. "You know," he said slowly, taking a drag and flinging away the match. "I'm going to like being married to you. I even have May's blessing, and she might have stirred up some mess on the Wellington side too," he chuckled, shaking his head. "Y'all sure do have a way of doing things. But, I think I like it."

"Oh, you think so." She chuckled and folded her arms as she leaned against his porch banister.

"Yup, only problem is, your Pop is right. We gotta find somewhere to live. And, baby, I just can't do it right now." He cast his gaze down to the pavement and kicked away a stone. "I don't know how long it will take to get back on my feet. I need a real lawyer. I need some extra cash, and whatever I make now's gotta go to the kids and Buddy's house, till things get straight. I don't have any more hours in a day to work, if I could," he said letting out his breath and the smoke along with it. "I'm not smart enough, I guess, to figure that out."

"I lost my job today," she said quietly, all the mirth dissipating from her voice. "Maybe it's a sign."

"Aw, T... Baby, this has been a day I could have skipped over. Guess you could have too. My pockets are turned out, honey. I can't help you this pay, not till—"

"I didn't tell you for that. I know you have bills

and stuff," she said gently, coming down the steps and putting her arm around his waist. She leaned her head on his shoulder and rubbed his back. "Hey, I'm broke, but I haven't burned a bridge. Here's what I'm gonna do. First thing in the morning, I'll call Darlene and Inez from my old job. I'll give them Valerie to place at The Arts Bank, since that's what she went to school for. Then I'll give them Tracey for a part-time job at Philadanco Dance Company. This will help my Executive Director show immediate placements for the agency... we'll finagle the paperwork to make it look like they were a part of my class... "

Antoinette's voice trailed off as her mind reflexively snapped into problem solving action. "Then," she continued, pushing herself away from him and walking in a circle. "That'll help Dar and Nez be able to possibly siphon some grant money into the agency so they can keep their jobs. Plus, Tracey and Val will get some childcare subsidy through the program, and they don't have the same issues as the women who'd be put off Welfare, since they aren't on it yet. It'll help their self esteem, give them a job history in their field—and in a field that they love. Gotta talk to Francis' Mom about this, and see Francis about all this Tracey business, and get over to the hospital to see Buddy and talk to Val. It'll take some of the pressure off him—and you, for that matter. Okay—"

"—Baby," he interrupted, "But what about you? What about us?"

"I'm getting to that," she said impatiently, "hold your horses. I'm trying to think of an angle. I have to settle my responsibilities first then I can move on. I give Linda Kravats two solid placements, she gives me a letter of recommendation as an outstanding trainer from a well respected agency—that makes me hot marketing property. My class is protected, her agency is protected, my girlfriend's save their jobs, and Tracey and Val can begin to re-start their lives. Therefore, Francis' situation, as sad as it is, won't be chaos." Antoinette paced away and looked up to the sky. "Yeah, that makes sense—right?" she muttered almost to the heavens. "Yeah."

"You're talking to the stars again, T. Haven't seen you do that in a long time. Did you know that's why I'd always look up at them and think of you? My crazy, far-out, baby—who talked to the stars. My grandmother used to do that. Said it helped her think."

"Yeah, well, I'm thinking, Jay," she whispered, almost annoyed at his verbal intrusion while she tried to fit pieces of the too-large jigsaw puzzle together. She could feel him watching her as she walked and looked at the sparkling lights of fire in the blue-black sky. Oddly, she could feel her personal power coming back and realigning itself. It was almost palpable as her fingertips tingled.

All she needed was a little time and just a few pieces to fall into place so that she could at least begin to see a common pattern. With a pattern, she felt confident that she could develop a solution and know where the edges were. Now all she had to do was pray and stay alert for the signs that would surely come. It always worked that way—pray for the signs, then be still and wait. That was always the hardest part for her. Waiting.

"Baby, let's go inside," he said quietly and threw his cigarette into the street. "No hanky-panky, just wanna hold you and wake up next to you in the morning. Truthfully, I'm beat, and you're so tired that you're running on adrenaline fumes—going in circles under the stars. Let it rest, and let it go. Sometimes we have to just accept the hand that's dealt. C'mon, before you wear a hole in the cement."

"Okay," she whispered, still looking up as he led her by the elbow up the front steps. "Maybe I'll just have to dream about it tonight?"

Chapter 12

He could hear her walking and fidgeting about in the distance as he tried to wrest his mind into consciousness. Peering at his clock radio, he rolled over and sat up, and wondered if she had ever really gone to sleep at all. Antoinette had mumbled and tossed and turned in his arms all night. Now, the sound of her voice came in crisp, clear, boot-camp-like commands. She was someone he had never seen.

Pulling his cigarettes off the nightstand, he lit one up, and watched her. She appeared more like a radio dispatcher, issuing directions, and in need of more than his single telephone line. The way she switched between what appeared to be a primary call, and an incoming call, was baffling. She could have used a headset and a full AT&T switchboard to handle the multiple, obviously top-priority, conversations. Who was this woman? he wondered, as she transformed into a high-powered executive right before his eyes. She wasn't a victim. She was in control. The snippets of serious news that she relayed were spoken without tears or emotion. She was handling things. He only wondered how she would handle him, now that this over-night change had occurred?

"Yeah, yeah, Dar. Two of them," Antoinette said with surety in her voice. "One, I haven't spoken to yet. I have to confer with her at the hospital this afternoon—but I'm sure she'll go for it. She has to. The other is ready for immediate placement. Yeah, give me Linda's home number. I'm going to cut a deal."

Antoinette paced away from the nightstand on her side of the bed and grabbed her purse as she kept talking. Flashes of Mr. Bullock, the jeweler, came into his mind. His baby was changing people's lives with a telephone call—several, in fact. It was eerie to watch her wield a level of power that he hadn't realized she ever had.

She turned and looked at him briefly, and mouthed the words, "Good morning, I love you," and blew him a kiss. With the cordless telephone in her hand, she walked away in her underwear towards the kitchen and returned with a mug of coffee. She brushed his forehead with a more solid kiss, and stood back as the phone line connected.

"Linda," she chimed in a salesman-like voice that startled him, "Good morning, it's Toni. I've got two bodies for you, doll. I know I'm a magician... no, we've been over that. Tell you what I'm gonna do, though—let Dar place one, and Inez place one before she leaves. I know she's leaving, but she's going somewhere that can help you—to the state level. Be nice to Inez, Linda. That's right... Uhmmm, hmmm. They fit the stats perfectly," Antoinette mewed. "Looks like your graduating class can be saved. Of course you owe me—no, my own non-profit will be a placement service for yours. Details, details—let's do that over lunch. Excellent. Yes, I also love a smart woman."

When Antoinette let out a little chuckle, and he wondered if it were real or false? Her business tone worried him. She played the game so well. Maybe too well.

"Right now, it'll only cost you a glowing letter of recommendation, and some contacts from your Rolodex." Antoinette laughed again, "Yes, I'm still a militant bitch, but I want the weak saved, the one's who have skills can be re-tooled. Inez knows what I'm talking about. Yeah. Now, was that hard? You said it yourself, we're cut from the same cloth. I have a catering organization that might be a good business linkage partner. Her contracts will be coming down in the health care arena. I'm working on that now. She can take in several client workers. Two months, tops... Tennis? How about next week?"

Antoinette pulled out her checkbook register and scribbled a date in the calendar section. "Marvelous," she crooned. "There's enough for everybody. One hand washes the other—you'll train them, I'll place them in my good paying apprenticeship program—you'll always have placements, I'll always have employees. You feed me, I'll guarantee stats for you. Right.. A subcontractor relationship to you. I love it too. It's an old-fashioned win-win."

The urge to urinate motivated him to get out of bed as Antoinette clicked over and took another call. He also wondered whether it was his need to get away from the cut-and-dried way she handled the calls that had made him get up. Her voice was so different from the soft timber he was used to hearing. There was no empathy in her tone, no kindness, strictly business. What had happened to his baby overnight?

Propelling himself down the hall, he entered the bathroom and shut the door—more to close off the sound of her grating conversations, than for privacy. He was glad that the deluge coming from his body muted Antoinette's voice. Was this what Brian had lived with? Jerome shuddered as he turned off his body faucet. This was not the image he'd envisioned, nor was it a woman that he could envision making love to. Instinct told him that this was the kind that ate her young. Hard reality met him in the mirror as he considered shaving his face.

He washed his hands and stared at the porcelain bowl. Where had she learned this? Adding water to lather up the soap in his shaving mug, he turned on the sink hot water full blast, and then the shower. He had to get out of there.

"Ms. LaMann... How are you?" Antoinette piped brightly, stepping into the bathroom with his mug in her hand. "Yes, I've been thinking about you too since our meeting in The Poconos, and I have a proposition for you. Tomorrow, at one o'clock? Consider it done," she said, issuing a wink in his direction that he ignored, "I have to make a few calls first... uh huh..." she purred. "How would a hundred thousand do? The standard—five percent up front as a retainer, ten percent upon delivery. Yes, I can guarantee it. Tomorrow, we'll go over your strategy. I know, I know—you were waiting for me to call, but I had other clients already in the cue. Well, thank you... I always make time for my best clients. Yes, I'll work it out," Antoinette added as she slipped beyond the bathroom door. "I know you'll love it."

Stunned, he couldn't even sip the reheated coffee that Antoinette had left for him. A hundred thousand dollars? From where? How? And he was worrying about getting credit for a ring that was a few grand. Last he'd heard, Antoinette was out of a job.

When she popped back into the bathroom, he kept his eyes focused on the razor as it slid down his throat.

"Good morning, baby," she said in a sexy voice, but the tone had lost all effect on him. "I love to watch a man shave," she murmured, sitting down on the toilet seat for a moment with the telephone in her hand. "My Dad used to use one of those," she added, watching him with a smile on her face.

"Shit!" he yelled as the phone rang and he nicked himself. A thick pink ooze of blood rose to the surface of his scraped skin and mixed with the foam on his face, and Antoinette casually tore off a piece of toilet paper and handed it to him.

"Here," she whispered, coming up behind him. "Be careful, baby. Can I answer this call?"

"Yeah, sure, " he muttered. "Do what'chu gotta do." Her tone had stirred him a little, and the effect that she had on him, irritated him no end. She was in control. She had turned into a brazenly sexy executive. He wondered if she used that same tone on her sales force, or clients, to get them to give into her wishes? He loved it, yet hated it at the same time—and the dilemma continued to affect his concentration.

"Well, that was strange," Antoinette said quietly, looking down at the telephone receiver in her hand. "Nobody was on the line, it disconnected. Probably a call that got hung up in call waiting?"

"Probably a bill collector," Jerome grumbled, pushing hard on the tissue over his wound. "Damn," he muttered, as his razor became a traitor, nicking him again.

"I'm hot today, baby!" she exclaimed, handing him another piece of toilet paper. "The old gray mare ain't what she used to be, but she's on a definite roll."

"Is this how you used to be, Antoinette?" he said sullenly, "All the time?"

"Yup," she said with a boom and chuckled, standing as she dialed, "used to slay dragons daily with one sword. I had a good blade, brother—I was a Ninja... Samurai... the best at Three Card Monte in the business, and could handle some thangs. It feels great to be back, you know?"

"I kinda liked the old Antoinette, myself," he grumbled, avoiding the cuts to his chin and throat as he worked.

"This is the old Antoinette," she laughed, then strode out of the room, talking to the new voice on the other end of the line.

Abandoning his shaving project, he jumped into the shower and tried to rinse the concern out of his body. This was not a warm, nurturing, mother-type—this was a businesswoman. This was not a damsel in distress—this was a wounded eagle that could now fly again, and she seemed to require fresh kill. Feeling that his domestic barnyard was at risk, he wondered what he'd taken in?

When he returned to his bedroom, Antoinette was already dressed. The fact that she was still on the telephone utterly annoyed him.

"Yeah, Cookie, I have a system, but I'm not hooked up to the Internet in the new place yet," she went on, ignoring his entry to the room. "Uh, huh, I need to get over there and pull some numbers to put 'em in a report for the LaMann job. Uh, huh—yeah, girl, we're cookin' with Crisco. Yeah, I'm back!" she exclaimed as she flopped down in a chair. "What's your Rolodex look like with the zoning commission? Oh, Cookie... you are so mean," she laughed giving the phone a series of little kissing noises. "Who do we know at the African American Chamber of Commerce that can help us leverage the banks? Good. Good. I've worked with him. Just make it happen."

He watched in awe as she circled the room and ran her fingers through her hair. The process was disorienting as she spoke like a Mafioso Godfather and hunted game like a panther.

"Call in every marker, Cook. This is for all of us—Trace, Val, Fran, Adrienne, me, and you. I'll need some arms twisted to push the paperwork through fast. Two months. Uh, huh, you're in good with the black press Excellent! Visible community support, and a heavy-influence board, is critical. The business property needs contractors? No problem," she smiled, looking at him for the first time since he'd entered the room. "I just don't want any b.s. from Licenses and Inspections. Handle it, and I'll get the money. Bet. No, I won't pay a hundred-eighty thousand for a building that's been on the market over a year. Right, right. No more than one-fifty tops. The owner will have to negotiate. We have to put Mack and Roundtree on this. Yeah, they're the best African American CPA firm in Philly. They'll get the paperwork done, and keep us honest."

"It's done," she piped, standing and rushing over to give him a big kiss.

He opened his arms for her by rote, and returned her affection without enthusiasm. "Do you mind clueing me in on what's going on?" he said evenly, staring at her hard and trying to find the woman he loved.

Her eyes held a quality of excitement that he couldn't fathom. Her body was electrified by some unknown power source. She frightened him.

"Baby—if the pieces fall right, if the stars line up and conjunct properly, if a little Divine Providence works—we're over the top. I had resources that I wasn't using. Pearline was right—your good name does count for something!" she said in an excited voice. "Listen," she boomed cheerfully, walking away from his embrace. "I don't have time this morning—will fill you in as the dominoes fall. So, do me a favor. Go over to my unit and get the key from Tracey. I'll take Tracey and her crew with me to Francis' and drop her off there, and May can drop off Lauren at Patti's. The children will be in the way and we've got too much to do. I have to then change into battle fatigues, my suit, and then hit the Community Development Project."

The children will be in the way? New horror

zigzagged through his mind. This was not his Toni. This person seemed possibly worse than Karen.

"Who?" he stammered, watching her whirlwind of motion until he became dizzy.

"The Community Development Project. I need to secure a contract there and see if they have loan money available to start my firm. I also need their support to start a business within the Empowerment Zone, or just outside of it. They have excellent resources so, I need to form an alliance with them in West Philadelphia. I also need to add finishing touches to my business plan—the one that's been collecting dust on my system—then go to Cookie's to draft a boilerplate proposal for LaMann before tomorrow. Maybe..." she murmured as though going within her own thoughts.

"I can save time and dust off one of my old proposals and plug in her numbers... What file would that be in?" she ruminated, mentally drifting even further away from him. "After that," she said in another sudden sonic boom, returning her attention to him in a manner that was totally disorienting, "I'm set."

Before he could speak, or process anything that she'd said, Antoinette was back to walking in circles.

"Jerome, I need to pick up some flowers—no, you pick up some flowers and leave them in my unit, I won't have time. Then I'll swing by... No. Pick up two bunches, one for Val and one for Pearline. I'll give you the money. Then I need to make a hospital run and stop up to Pearline's. I'm going to look at the property that Cookie told me about tonight. After that, I need to catch up with my sister to get her home for Easter. Okay, okay, focus, Toni," she muttered to herself as she snatched up her purse. "Meet me at Francis' Mom's no later than four with Tracey's stuff. We can go over the property together tonight—to see if it'll work. Or maybe I'll just meet you at the place instead of at Francis's Mom's house—I'll call you and let you know. You can get contractors—buddies from your job, right?"

"Well, I guess—"

"Good. Make it happen. I need an electrician, a plumber, and a serious carpenter for renovations. I'll need five grand down to hold it—earnest money—and will pay the contractors as I go for supplies. Tell them to give me a good price. LaMann's retainer will give me my earnest money, it's a gamble from there."

He just stared at her.

"After you move Tracey, between four and five, go over to the pizza shop," she yelled down the hall as she raced to get her coat.

"For what!" he bellowed behind her, his nerves finding a break-even point within her madness, "Pizza?"

"Don't be silly," she said out of breath, slipping on her coat as she returned to the bedroom. "Ask them if they can tell you where to buy used industrial ovens and sinks at a good price. If you talk to the owner right, she might be willing to personally walk you in to her suppliers. Don't do it over the phone, you have to do it in person. Tell her you're setting up a school, so she won't fear competition. That reminds me, I have to pick up a 501c3 non-profit kit down at Sixth and Arch—The Federal Building. Do you know where that is?"

"I think so, but, baby—"

"—Good. I'll write it down. Get a kit, and leave it for me while I'm at Francis.' I'll take it with me to Cookie's for the CPA," she commanded as she scribbled down a note and tossed it on the bed. "What are you standing around in a towel for, man? Get moving, we have work to do."

"Wait a minute, Antoinette," he said slowly, sitting down on the bed to let her know he would not be moved. Too many questions swirled in his mind at once, and he didn't like the commanding officer tone she used with him. "You've got some grand scheme cookin' in that big brain of yours, and I don't know what it is, how you're going to pull it off, how much it's gonna cost—"

"—It won't cost you anything, but time and sweat equity—"

"—But—"

"—Look," she said impatiently, "I have to get too much done to step through the basics with you right now."

"Is this how you operated when you were in corporate?" he asked in a severe tone, watching her carefully for the correct response, a response that he hadn't clarified in his own mind yet.

"Do you think they paid me six figures to stand around with my finger up my nose, Jerome? How do you think I landed multi-million dollar contracts? By crying and wringing my hands and saying 'mother may I,' 'pretty please?' I had a national sales force!" she bellowed, "I had to get the numbers and go to come-to-Jesus meetings—every Monday morning, with Region-by-Region results. Get with the program. I'm used to commanding troops, and when I tell you 'this is not a drill,' then it's not a goddamned drill. Now move it. We don't have time for some man-woman doo doo this morning."

His Toni used to make over a hundred thousand dollars a year.... God help him...

"I don't know, Toni... Everything is moving so fast. It's just that—"

"—You wanted to get married right?"

"Yeah, but—"

"—You were the one in a rush, right? Already went to my family, right?"

"—Yeah... it's just that—"

"—Then we've got to get our house in order, handle our business, and secure a fort, right?"

"—Yeah, honey, but—"

"—Do you trust me?" she sighed, clearly growing more impatient.

"That's not the poin—"

"—Good. Then get a move on," she said curtly, walking into the other room as she dialed the phone. "Oh, damn!" she yelled, coming back and standing before him. "I need you to take me to my car. Let's go, Jerome. I don't have time for you to cogitate and dilly-dally. Here, call your office," she demanded, clicking off her call and handing him the phone, "Tell them you'll be out for the day. It's seven thirty-five. You can't mess up your job, until this is finalized—if ever. That's where she'll probably garnish your wages, if she's hostile. She cannot touch my business—understood? Let's move out."

He accepted the telephone from her with belligerence, and turned away from her as she gave him hand signals to dress and talk at the same time. Her pacing, and her impatient walking about, got on his nerves. His life was being reordered without his consent. He wasn't going to let any woman take him there again. No matter how much he loved her.

"Listen," he said as soon as he clicked off the call. "We need to talk—"

"—Save it, Jerome," she said through her teeth, eyeing him defiantly, "We. Do. Not. Have. Time—for any macho-passive-resistant bull this morning. Here," she said in a harsh voice, tossing his clothes at him. "You've already showered and shaved soldier. Now move out."

He pulled on his clothes with indignation and brushed past her to get his jacket and cap. Who the hell did she think she was?

"I'm not your lackey, Antoinette!" he fumed, returning to the hall with his keys where she waited impatiently. "I have a right to—"

"—Listen," she said, now clearly seething with impatience. "We have a nine-eleven emergency on our hands, a funding hemorrhage, but, a perfect opportunity—with all the new Avenue of the Arts money coming into the system for improved tourism in the city, not to mention what's happening with the health care industry, and the Welfare push to create jobs, and an economic recovery with federal money down coming to help distressed businesses and commercial corridors. It's perfect. I saw it last night. We need a home and a revenue stream—"

"What?" he said waving his hands for her to stop, and cutting off her confusing tumble of words. She was talking too fast, connecting too many layers of the system. She spoke with acronyms that he didn't understand. Tossed out dollar figures that were incomprehensible. "I don't under—"

"—Listen!" she said as she threw up her arms and turned around in a circle of exasperation. "I am going to look at a property, ASAP," she said at a patronizingly slow pace.

"I got that much," he muttered, becoming angry and offended. "I understand real estate."

"Good. Because, I have to ensure that we have funds available to cover the construction, pay the mortgage, and operating cash flow for year one—at least," she said picking up her verbal pace again, and soaring with after-burner thrust as she gained sudden momentum right before his eyes. " It has to be big enough to handle five children, have a bedroom in there for us, and an office for me to work out of. That's a five, maybe six bed-room unit—with a living room and kitchen on the fourth floor—possibly a separate entrance. All the construction work will come off our taxes—if it houses a business in it. Four stories, not counting the basement—is what Cookie said. I'm starting a business that can produce enough revenue to pay the mortgage and cover business expenses.

"Meanwhile, it will provide a short-term placement opportunity for those who need work. Artists, like Val, can hang their work on consignment. That's my decoration strategy. Tracey... I'll find something for her to do... maybe even add a little gift shop, like the way The White Dog Cafe is set up. Yeah, that way we can inventory it with consignment handcraft goods from the students—the store gets a cut, the students make money. Yeah," she said, thinking and beginning to pace in the hall again. "That'll work."

"Wait a minute—"

"—I have to promote it, though," she went on, as though oblivious to his confusion. "One of the girls can help me manage the joint part-time—Trace, she's an organizer, and hostess, par excellant! Plus, her job is shaky, at best and is wearing her out. Must find something for Vanessa, my cousin, in this mix. She needs cash for her brood, so she can stop depending on crazy men. My sister can help me promote it. I need Adrienne's focus to give it a young, funky, eclectic feel. Multi-ethnic, urban, chic. Yeah. It can be like a restaurant school, dessert-coffee-art-house, with a built in retail gift shop for the preservation of cottage-industry arts. I can create a grant structure with a non-profit and for-profit arm. We could add a bookstore.... offer apprenticeship, mentoring, after-training center—fed by, and not competing with, other area programs, bolstered by a partnership with LaMann. Cooperative economics, sort of a Kujichakalia vibe. Maybe I can weave in a co-op element to help with funding, we'll see? Anyway, we'll live upstairs on the third and fourth floors, and take up that whole space. That okay with you?

"I guess," he stammered, feeling his life slip away from his grasp.

"Okay, good. I'm gonna work with Cookie to make all the paperwork and transactions click like a well-oiled engine. I'm calling in all my markers from the past, all my favors out there in the world to finance this sucker. Meanwhile, I've gotta make sure that my inner circle is well provided for. I've got to draw up a will, too. Hearing about Francis really made me think about that reality, especially now that we're blending families, and all. Now, are you satisfied?"

Antoinette crossed her arms over her chest. Her confidence and authority were like nothing he'd ever seen in a woman. It was both frightening and electrifying.

"You got a problem with that, Jerome? Tell me now before I turn Philadelphia up-side-down this morning," she said with a direct gaze. "What's your problem?" she pressed on when he took a millisecond too long to answer her. "If you can't deal with a woman shakin' and movin,' you better tell me now, because otherwise, we can call it a day right here at the door. This, is who I used to be."

He could only stare at her. She obviously meant business, but it was their relationship that he was unsure of. She had spoken clearly, and her judgment didn't seem impaired by the normal female histrionics that he'd been used to with Karen. She had broken down his issues in black and white male logical terms, developed an overnight solution, and had slapped him in the face with it in the morning. She'd also challenged him to step up to the bar, and act. Her tone suggested that she'd view him as a punk, if he didn't. Yet, his pride felt like he'd be one if he simply followed her lead versus his own, without input. He hated cold-light-of-day-discussions like this.

Trapped in a deadlock of wills, they just stared at each other for what felt like endless moments. Although he understood her intentions to be admirable, once she'd clarified them, she didn't seem to be in the least bit moved by the fact that their relationship could end abruptly in the hallway. Her only question seemed to be, did he want in on the deal—or not? The more important question was, could he live with that?

"It's just that... I'm—"

"—Last night you said you didn't have the money. Neither did I, Jerome. You said we needed a place to house all these children between us—"

"—Yeah, Toni, but—"

"—Then you can't sit around feeling sorry for yourself, you have to act decisively, man. Look," she said, turning to go down the steps, "I'm going to do this whether you want in, or not. This has always been my dream," she said flatly, walking down the stairs as she spoke. "I'm not waiting around like a victim anymore, for somebody to save me. You can't—no offense. You're still married, and I won't have your name on anything until your property is settled. I'll give you the name of a good, African American attorney from my Rolodex. I'll barter for your first visit, he owes me—and I'm sure I can get him to give you a reasonable pay-as- you-go-rate, versus a retainer relationship. That much I'll do. Handle your business, Jerome. The baton has been passed to me, and I have to secure the fort—with, or without a man. Either work with me, but don't ever work against me. I won't allow it. Been there. This time, I'm on a mission. You need to get on one too—and stop using excuses about what people won't let you do, or have made you do. Handle your business, Jerome. That's not my job, and I don't have time for it."

Her comment cut him to the quick. She had done what he'd never expected—used his personal confessions, their private conversations about his vulnerabilities, to make her point. This was a gash possibly beyond repair, and she wasn't even looking at him as she'd sliced into his Achilles' Heel to deliver her ultimatum.

Fuming with hurt and rage, he walked down the stairs and opened the door for her without a word. There were no words for this transgression. He'd run her errands—only because she obviously needed help to pull off her insanity, and he'd keep his commitment to move Tracey. Their friend Tracey needed his help, and had nothing to do with what Antoinette had just done, he reasoned. But, after that, he'd have to decide whether or not he could live with this new incarnation of woman before him.

He was a bachelor. She wasn't his wife.

Chapter 13

As he pulled his car into an available space at the corner of Forty-Fourth and Baltimore, he could see Antoinette pacing and angrily gesturing to the real estate agent. The commotion going on in front of, what he assumed to be Antoinette's nightmare of a dream building made him wonder why he'd agreed to even show up. Again, a hundred thoughts competed within his mind for answers. Maybe this whole thing was just a bad idea.

Still surly from the way she had handled him so abruptly that morning, and duly aggravated from the endless list of chores she'd given him, Jerome took a last drag on a Marlboro and crushed it out in the ashtray.

He sat for a moment before turning off his ignition. The sight of Antoinette complaining, and fussing, and walking about in a circle as she spoke, completely stripped his nervous system of any remaining tolerance. Who the hell did she think she was, anyway? Not to mention, she was standing in front of a veritable fortress. Jerome eyed the property carefully before exiting the car. He let each facet of the huge, twelve-inch, stone masonry façade remind him that they had a lot to talk about. He refused to be impressed by the height of the structure, and he would not be moved by its regal three tier hand-lain brick steps. No. He had to deal with this woman.

Approaching both women with his back straight and gaze steady, he climbed the front stairs to the building and stared at Antoinette hard.

"I'm glad you're finally here," she said with impunity. "Ms. Lipinsky, this is my General Contractor, Mr. Henderson."

Fury stopped the words in his throat. For a moment he couldn't even say hello, and opted to nod instead. Oh, so now he'd been demoted in front of some white woman from fiancé to General Contractor? He got the picture—he'd been dissed by her before, cool. What a difference a damned day made. Antoinette hadn't even kissed him hello, or thanked him for all of his efforts. All she had done was cut her eyes at him, then curtly spun on her heels, and had began walking around the perimeter of her wanna-be fortress. Some 'thank you.' Oh, yeah, they had to talk about this!

"Mr. Henderson, nice to meet you," the agent said calmly, yet her eyes pleaded for his support as she shook his hand. "I've been trying to tell Mrs. Wellington that, while this building is in need of some repair, it is otherwise a gem of a building—"

"A gem? A gem! Look at the cracks beginning around the foundation line. Over here—"

"—But, Ant—" His words fell on the brick landing as Antoinette shot a menacing, do not speak until spoken to, glance. He would deal with Mrs. Wellington.

"I want to see the heat source, the roof, and do a total walk through again— alone, with my contractor," Antoinette snapped. "From merely the outside, I can see why it's been on the market for over a year. It's a money pit! Almost an insult to the landscape of this block—and speaking of landscapes, look at this," Antoinette raged, kicking away broken bottles as she crossed the lawn. "With a drug park across the street creating security issues? I'm definitely insulted by the price you quoted. Never... Who could blame the owner for wanting to sell?"

Jerome stared at Antoinette until his ears began to ring, his gaze dodging the pitiful glances for help that the Realtor issued. "Whatever the lady says," he muttered with a shrug. "She runs the show. I'm only hired help."

Antoinette tossed the keys in Jerome's direction without a comment. In a reflex fueled by anger, he caught them with so much force as his hand clasped around the metal that his palm almost bled from the impact.

"I'll drop the keys in your night slot, and leave you a determination message on your voice-mail. It's almost dark, and getting late. I have several meetings in the morning, and need to view this property while there's a little light left.

"The electric is on," the Realtor said in an urgent tone, "But, you already know that from when we went through it earlier," she added with a nervous laugh. "The owner wants to sell, and will make it as convenient as possible for you to make a decision, one way or the other—so take as long as you need."

"Thank you for your time," Antoinette said crisply, walking up the stairs without looking back as she dismissed the agent with a non-verbal twist of her watch. "I'll be in touch within a day, or so."

Jerome took his time opening the door, and Antoinette folded her arms as she patted her foot on the top step. Her actions grated him. Out of habit, he allowed her to go through the door first into the eerie dark space—then wondered if he'd done so partly to avoid snatching her by the neck, or whether it was an attempt to give himself distance. It didn't matter anyway, he decided quickly. He knew the drill. They'd have a big argument, break up, then that part of his life would be over, again. That's pretty much the way his luck ran with women.

Once inside, he brushed past her and spun around, only to be met with a confusing, excited, wide grin on her face.

"Wait a minute, wait a minute," she giggled, peeping through the window like a small child, "wait till she's really gone."

Antoinette's new incarnation was disorienting, and as the Realtor's car pulled away from the curb, he listened to the interior silence to be sure that they were alone. This was going to be a big one, and didn't require spectators. The things he'd needed to say had been building up all day and had become volcanic. When Antoinette laughed and turned away from the window, he folded his arms, leveled his gaze at her, and stood firmly—legs apart. This was battle, if not war. He'd show her who was Samurai!

"Listen, godammit!" he declared. "I never want—"

"It's beautiful!" she laughed running at him full speed and filling his arms. "Look at it, Jay," she squealed, pushing her mouth to his so passionately that his knees buckled. "Oh, my God! Look!" she yelled, creating an echo through the building, "C'mon, c'mon," she yelled again, urging him through the structure by his sleeve, and flipping on lights as she raced along. "Look, baby, leaded-beveled glass windows," she exclaimed, pulling him by both arms and turning him to face the grand, sun-room bay window that opened out to Clark Park. Antoinette threw her head back and laughed, then broke away from him and did a little jig before him. Running at full tilt, she slid across the floor in her pumps. "Baby! Hardwood, parquet, wood floors!' she screamed with her arms stretched out wide, then ran over to the wall and thumped on it. "Cherry blossoms in the yard—mature azalea hedges!"

"I thought you hated the landscaping?" he grumbled dryly, drawing a breath to keep his temper in check.

"Ah, ha! Theater," she laughed and waved her hand, dismissing the subject. "Do you know what this is? Do you know what it is, huh, huh, huh!" she laughed and threw her head back, "it's a fireplace flu! A chimney—right in the middle of the damned living room, going up to the bedrooms on two, three, and the attic floor—four! Some complete idiot covered it over with dry wall! Baby, baby, baby—we hit pay dirt!"

"Listen," he said evenly, refusing to smile at her over-enthusiasm, "Eight foot windows are non-standards and create an insulation nightmare, eighteen-foot ceilings will be a bitch to paint. It'll cost a mint just to heat this joint, and—"

"—Did you see the foyer? Did you see it?" she screamed with merriment, doing another jig as she dragged him back toward it. "Hand. Laid. Tile. Stained. Glass. Windows. We, are in a cathedral!"

He refused to admit that he was impressed, or that her cheerfulness was rubbing him raw—perhaps even wearing him down.

"Look at this dining room," she whispered, covering her mouth after she had spoken. "Hand-carved moldings. They painted over them, and don't know what they are! Oh, God," she whispered again, crossing her breast and closing her eyes. "Thank you, Jesus," she murmured, then spun around on him again, "Yes!" she shouted,

"Look," she said as the breath rushed from her body and tears filled her eyes, "Oh, Jesus. Oak, floor-to-ceiling, built-in shelves," she murmured with her eyes closed. "Delicate interior wood ginger-breading over every arch that leads to it. Can you see it, our art center, close your eyes, Jay, and let this house talk to you." Antoinette covered her face with her hands, and just as he thought she was about to weep, she let out a loud whoop that startled him. "Come here," she laughed like a madwoman. "Feel the wall."

Begrudgingly, he moved to the archway that divided the living room from the dining room and tapped on it without enthusiasm.

"Yeah, so what?" he grumbled. "It's hollow. Probably just a false separation wall to—"

"Wanna know why? Huh, huh, huh, do ya?" she giggled.

"Not particul—"

"Stand back," she said with a comically serious expression. "Viola!" she screamed, flinging together two enormous oak doors that collided with a thud. "Recessed doors..." she whispered. "Come closely," she whispered again like an international spy. "This house was built in the early eighteen hundreds. Know how you can tell?"

He didn't answer immediately, but allowed his hands to trace behind hers on the perfect wood finish. His fingers followed the carefully defined grooves that had been cut by artisans and began to tingle with repressed excitement. "They don't do this kind of work any more, I'll grant you that," he said stoically, then pulled his hands away. He had to remember that he'd been offended, and was angry at her.

"Look at the mechanicals, the brass fixtures," she said triumphantly, pushing in a brass button which pooped out a small handle. "Yup, they don't make 'em like this anymore."

"No, they don't," he whispered in awe as his hands were drawn back to the fixture. Allowing his gaze to travel to the intricate metallurgy work on the handle, he could only shake his head with amazement.

"The brass almost looks like an Oriental rug, doesn't it—with all the details in-laid?" she cooed to the fixture, squatting and running her hands over it again. "Every doorknob in here, Jay, is either wood, crystal, or brass. Every lock inside the house has a skeleton key, with a before-the-turn-of-the-century brass lock and detailed plate just like this one. And they painted over it! They don't know what it is," she squealed in hushed satisfaction. "They don't know!"

"You have got to be kidding me?" he said quietly, finding no escape from his complete awe.

"My God, Antoinette, what have you found?"

"We sit back from a beautiful Park!" she declared in a hard whisper. "There are three operational floors—five, if you count the basement and the attic. This is a million-dollar property in disguise—and they don't even know it. Why?" she asked with indignation. "Simply because it sits in West Philly. Slum landlords abandoned her, and cut her up, and sold her to the highest student bidder for apartments. This, " she whispered through her teeth, as she spun away from him and opened her arms, "was a criminal act, and requires justice."

Spinning around to face him again with tears in her eyes, she took a deep breath and bellowed with rage, "It was no less than a tragedy!" Suddenly becoming quiet, her eyes shimmered with desperation. "The old man that owns this, is willing to let her rot for a song—a hundred and eighty grand, Jay, just so he can get away from 'the urban element,'" she whispered, making little quote marks in the air with her fingers, "just like the seventies, he's running away to hide in the 'so-called safe suburbs,' and he's desperate enough to sell fast and leave this treasure behind—to rot! I won't stand for it. I grew up in this neighborhood. We gotta save her. It's our job! Plus, I got him down to under one-fifty!" She spun around and covered her mouth with her hands and laughed.

Before he could respond, Antoinette paced away from him and ran her palm down the wall as she walked. "She's got mahogany chair rail through the entire structure that separates hand-done, stucco plaster designs on the top half, and some sort of leather-like, hand-tooled, wall covering that runs the length on the bottom of every wall. Irreplaceable. They don't even make it anymore," she exclaimed waving her arms abruptly as he followed her quick start-stop pace. "Ceilings with fresco-plastering underneath layers of bullshit paint! Freakin' claw foot, stand alone, porcelain tubs—and turn-of-the-century pedestal sinks with brass faucets on every floor. Jay, do you hear me?" she bellowed, pacing down the hall so fast that he could barely admire one treasure before she pointed out the next.

"She?" he yelled behind Antoinette while trying to keep up with her.

"Yes. She..." Antoinette yelled back as she raced ahead of him. "The old girl still has life in her. Places keep a trace of energy, and this house speaks to me. That's it," she piped over her shoulder quickly, "We're buying her, and we are saving her. She's too majestic for this! Look, follow me into the kitchen, then tell me what the hell you see."

Without much choice, he nearly ran again to keep up with her, and they almost collided when she spun around unexpectedly to face him.

"Look at her hard," Antoinette said folding her arms while pure appreciation transformed her expression.

Almost afraid to disappoint Antoinette with his assessment, he tried to carefully form the words while staying true to reality; the property would need a team of workhorses to convert it to its original splendor.

"The refrigerator looks about near fifteen years old, T. No lie. The stove looks like a piece of shit, Toni—seriously. The linoleum has got to go, and—"

"Are you blind?" she snapped, appearing practically hang-jawed as she stood before him.

Warding off her challenging stare, he began again slowly. "There are cracks in the ceiling, and some old monstrosity in the corner, that has to go out—looks like it weighs a ton. Maybe you can get scrap metal—"

"Are you out of your black mind?" she whispered as though he'd slapped her face.

His gaze darted around the room and landed back on Antoinette. He scavenged his brain as she seemed to wait for another response, and yet, dared him with her eyes to speak ill of her house again.

"Come. Here!" she said curtly, in a tone that he expected she had probably used on Lauren before. "Squat," she commanded before the eight-foot long blackened iron object that took up a considerable amount of wall space. When he did so, she squatted next to him and rubbed a small plate on the front of it. "Read it to me," she directed, sounding more like a schoolteacher than a fiancée. "Then weep."

"Toni, come on... what?" he shrugged, becoming annoyed again by her tone. "Okay. It's old. Says, eighteen something..."

"This," she said standing, "is a FIRE. Burning. Wood. Stove. Perfectly cast, and in mint condition. Its flu runs up the wall four stories out to the second chimney on the roof, and additional fireplaces can outlet to it—just like the one in the living room. It terminates in the basement past this stove. Are you hearing me? You can't find the parts for this baby anymore, and, it alone is worth several thousand dollars!"

He stood up, walked to the far side of the room, and leaned on the double porcelain sink. "Jesus H. Christ..." he whispered, battling for composure. "Jesus..."

"And, all His company in Heaven, Jerome."

Antoinette turned her attention to one set of six foot by eight-foot wood cabinets, and flung open the doors. "Oak, with brass hinges and interlocks," she said like a car demonstration salesperson, then pointed to a door. "Tell me where that leads?"

"I don't know... The basement?" he murmured with full respect for her assessments.

"It's a back staircase," she sputtered in a harsh whisper. "At the top of the steps, in what used to be a drawing room, is a dumb-waiter. The whole back half of this mansion was for servants quarters. That's why there's an extra two-room area, built-in armoire, and bathroom down here on one. We have to buy this—if for no other reason, than for poetic justice."

"Justice, Toni? We're not buying a property to make money, now we're buying it for justice?" He let out a weary sigh and shook his head as she stood before him with her arms folded.

"The women in my family used to clean in houses like this—and, people in our ancestry were slaves in houses like this. They'll bring us good luck—all those ghosts... you know." She smiled. "They want us here. The house speaks."

"Toni... Baby..."

"For real, Jay."

He tried hard not to laugh when she sucked

her teeth, becoming peevish, but he couldn't resist teasing her about her eclectic beliefs. "What about the ghosts of the master's of the house. I'd rattle some chains if I thought my mansion had been turned over to the children of my servants. Have you thought about that? Hmmmmm? Could be haunted?"

"No problem," she scoffed with a wave of her hand. "Having it blessed by two ministers before we move in, for insurance. Plus, the bad ghosts don't get to come back, only the good ones. The way I figure it is, for perfect punishment, they'd have to sit by and watch all the good ghosts help out a young, struggling couple—in what used to be their house."

"What if you're wrong, and we get chased out of here—like, Tales from The Crypt?" he smiled as he needled her. "Or, Amityville Horror? Maybe that's why it was on the market for so long?"

She hesitated for a moment, then banished the brief flicker of fear he'd seen in her eyes. "Then... then... I'll tell my mother on them... she's got connections with The Man Upstairs... a watts-line to The President," she flipped, looking more and more like a school-age child as she spoke. "And... well... I'll tell Pearline to take it to her prayer group. So, there. No problem."

He swallowed down a chuckle and nodded.

"Pretty big house to be in all by yourself, at night... I hope you're sure about this?" He watched her peep around the room and he couldn't contain his smile. It was like teasing his sister when they were younger.

"Come with me," she commanded, brushing past him and moving swiftly down the long hallway to the front stairs. "The brass heat-vent coverings must have been added later in the century, when the heating system was converted," she said casually.

Some of her enthusiasm had seemed to wane as she walked ahead of him. He looked down as she pointed toward the floor at the coverings before she bound up the steps, and he was beginning to feel sorry that he had teased her about the possibility of ghosts.

Almost ashamed of his original assessment of the property, he took the stairs by two to keep up with her. When they arrived at the top landing, he drew an audible breath. He stood in disbelief before double, glass-paned, French doors that held immaculate, hand-blown, stained-glass windows that were housed within hand-carved gingerbread work. Antoinette had been right. It was an artisan's paradise, and it had been butchered and slaughtered for cheap student rents. No, the ghosts would probably haunt them if they didn't buy it, he thought, but he just hoped ghosts and angels had influence at the bank.

Antoinette opened both doors with a singular graceful motion, and swept into the room. Without facing him, she pointed at a soot-covered, marble-edged fireplace and mantle. "Your master bedroom, sir," she denoted in a contrived British accent, then roared with laughter as she spun back around to face him, "or, would you prefer to retire on level three?"

"This is... there are no words, Toni..."

"Down the hall, and on the other side of the staircase, there are four more big rooms like this—but only one shared bathroom for this level. These must have been the cheap rooms. Thank, God, the landlord only put deadbolts on each door and didn't tear out the original locks. Pity, though," she whispered to the door, touching it like a mother gently rubs a child's boo boo. "We'll have to add some wood where they hacked her door to put in the modern locks. We can save the original doors, even though it'll leave a small scar after we stain them."

"Yeah," he murmured with appreciation. "We can save 'em... But, Toni," he said looking at her with newfound disbelief, did you say—these were the cheap rooms?"

"Yeah," she laughed, "Let me show you the

penthouse suites!" Racing from the room, she bound towards the second staircase and he followed her in hot pursuit. When they'd reached the landing, she began flinging open doors like a rampaging banshee.

"Count 'em, Jay! A two bedroom apartment, with full bath, kitchen, and living room," she panted out of breath. "The four girls can go in here. Then," she laughed, running away from him with a short burst of speed down the hall, and ducking into another apartment, "Knock out this wall in the one bedroom unit—to open up and adjoin the living rooms, put the boy in there," she noted with a wave of her hand. Swiftly moving back into the hall before he could react, she flounced past the large shared bathroom to an enormous studio unit that contained a tiny kitchenette.

"We can put in a laundry room. Just build a false wall around it for me, Jay, and we've got a bedroom, with a fireplace, right next to what can be my office—and it's far enough away from the kid's rooms—and, with the bathroom in-between, and back steps between us and the kids—that they won't hear the bed squeak on those warm, summer nights," she laughed as she snuggled into his chest. "Tell me you can see it, honey," she said with her face up-turned to his, then shut her eyes. "Tell me I'm not dreaming," she whispered passionately, "But, baby, there's more!"

Before he could lower his mouth to hers for a kiss, she broke free of his embrace and dashed away down the steps. He wanted her in that moment, just as much as he wanted to holler at her, so he opted to slowly follow her down three flights to the basement. He needed the time and the space differential to compose himself. The sound of Antoinette's heels clicking quickly a level ahead of him at every turn, helped considerably. However, he would still talk to her about all of her offenses, he affirmed mentally. Every, last one of them.

"Check it out, Jay," she yelled up the steps, walking around in a circle until he finally descended the basement stairs. Full length—"

"With a dirt floor, damp walls, and an oil tank. Oil, Toni."

"Yeah... dirt floors, crumbly walls... but no oil. Gas."

"What is that monstrosity in the corner, then?"

"Oh, yeah, that..."

"Yeah, that," he said evenly, walking toward the enormous oil unit. "Probably takes two thousand bucks to fill 'er up in the winter—and with all these giant windows in here, a full tank will probably only last a month. The utilities in here will cost more than the mortgage, T. You're the business woman—think about it."

"No, no, no," she sighed and paced past him. "Behind there. New hot water tanks, gas. See. Remember, I was in insurance sales, and they trained me to look for stuff—that's how I could tell this was a gem!"

Not to be defeated by the fact that the oil tank had been disconnected, or the fact that the property had been converted to a cheaper energy source, he inspected the gas units for himself.

"Where's the fuse box?" he said in a sudden rush of authority. "See, along the foundation line," he noted as he walked, "there could also be structural problems."

"The box is on the wall over here," she muttered, seeming to lose a little steam as she walked. "There is one teeny-weenie, little, problem," she said more cheerfully, blocking his access to the box. "Not a big one. Look at the length of this basement. Runs the full house, Jay," she added in a sing-song voice. "I see shelves, classroom and space. We have enough exits—that I am glad the landlord added, plus fire escapes on every level, which means we'd pass code. That door which leads to the street, could be made handicap-accessible—and we can build a ramp to the side door on the first floor and stay in code—"

"And, just as I suspected, when we walked through the entire house," he said in a low, building rumble that ended in an explosion, "half of the freakin' house is tube and knob wiring from the early nineteen hundreds!" Pacing away from her, he began to walk in a circle in the middle of the dirt floor. "How can you say we, when it's you?"

"Well—"

"No, you said it this morning—you're doing this, with or without me!"

"Where's your vision, Jay?"

Her casual tone, and her assumption of his time, went through him like an electric current.

"Vision?" he yelled, striding back towards her, "You know what I see, Toni?" he bellowed with his arms opened wide, leaning in her face, "I see a fifteen thousand dollar wiring job—alone. You see brass fixtures. I see possible plumbing problems on every level. You see stained glass and gingerbread. I see custom masonry work that requires skilled labor. You see a quaint old stove—I see three thousand dollars worth of chimney re-sleeving work, before you attempt to light it and burn the house down. You see a church and cathedral ceilings, and I see under-paid men going up on extension ladders who'll need Ben-Gay, for their aching muscles, when the have to scrape that lead paint off—"

"Lead paint," she gasped and covered her mouth, "the children—"

"Yes. Lead paint, Antoinette. And a crew that needs face masks and special permits, woman! You see claw-foot tubs, I see cracked, half and quarter-inch tiles that will have a man on his hands and knees for three days per bathroom!" He paced away from her and ignored her stricken expression. "You see hardwood floors, chandeliers, and candelabras, and have probably envisioned some kinda baby grand piano from the Victorian era!" he continued, ranting toward the ceiling and addressing The Almighty. "God, help me—she sees classrooms and shelves, and I see a potential foundation problem, insurance and security liability problems, a pest control problem—with these damned dirt floors, and at least five thousand dollars worth of cement to be poured for the floor, and her licensed, State-required-for-business, Americans with Disabilities Act, access ramps... not to mention the retrofitting for the handicapped bathroom fixtures."

Antoinette stood mute in front of him, and at the moment, he didn't care that he'd shocked or frightened her with his outburst. What he'd said was the truth, and he still had a lot more to say. This time, she'd have to just listen, instead of talk.

It was his turn, now—and, to his way of thinking, his fury had been justified. Before she could think of a reply, he decided to press on.

"And," he said firmly, reaching into his jacket pocket for his smokes—then stopping for a moment before he retrieved them. He looked at her hard, even though admittedly, the pause was purely for effect. She'd wanted theater, so, he'd give her theater, if it would help make his point to sink into her brain! Lighting the cigarette angrily with a deep drag, he slowly let the smoke out through his nose.

"All, 'honey-has-to-do,'" he mocked in a bad approximation of her voice, "is make it happen." Jerome took another drag then let his voice thunder within the basement like an earthquake, "For a mere, hundred-and-eighty thousand dollars!"

"Okay," she said calmly, perhaps too calmly. "Maybe that's why it has been on the market for over a year. You win. I'm done. I tried," she whispered, walking toward the steps. "I just saw the cup as half-full, as opposed to half-empty."

"Wait a minute. I'm not done, so don't dismiss me like you did that Realtor," he seethed through another puff. "I am not your hired help, and I have just begun to read you."

He watched her as she tossed her head, thrust her chin up, and moved toward a dusty shelf to sit down.

"What have I been doing all day?" he asked quietly, holding her in his gaze.

"Running a lot of errands," she said softly, "and you moved Tracey after I spoke to Francis' Mom, and I didn't say, thank you..."

"No. That's what you saw. What I did was, risk getting in trouble at work—that's number one, because I wasn't sick, but was out in the street all day where any of my crew, or supervisor, could've been cruisin'. Start there. For two, I didn't move Tracey—I risked my got-damned life!"

"What!"

The shock on her face made him even angrier. She obviously had no clue. Women never did.

"Antoinette—I had to sit outside in my car, case Scoop's house like a thief, wait till I saw my boy slip out of dodge to go to his job, go into another man's house with a key—and risk being shot if he doubled back for some reason. I risked the cops nabbin' me for B & E, which is why I called Cooper first. That way, at least when they brought me in all bloodied from gettin' my ass kicked in some paddy-wagon, one of their own might recognize me—and would know the deal—if I did get picked up. See, women don't even think of these realities," he warned, "And, oh, by the way—risking getting picked up, could put a real top-spin on the divorce, my custody rights. Girl, I was so mad at you, because I was thinking we were going into her house together today. Going in alone, without Tracey, was not on my agenda."

"Jay, I'm so sorry—"

"—I'm not done!"

Antoinette blinked her eyes and looked down. Amazingly, she seemed so different, and he wondered how many various personalities he was dealing with inside of the one luscious body that sat contrite in front of him? He took a long drag on his cigarette, and made her wait, to let her transgressions sink in. The wait was also necessary to help him keep his priorities in focus as her innocent, child-like expression began to have an annoying affect on his judgment.

"Then," he said with more control, "you talk to me like a dog—just plain ignore me in my own apartment. Tell me that was right? And you order me to pick up flowers—like I was the FTD florist, or your secretary, or somethin.' You could've asked me nicer than you did."

"Oh... Jay... I'm—"

"—I am not finished," he snapped with military precision. "I'll let you know when I am. Not a peep, until I'm done."

He waited almost a minute before saying a word—to test her, finishing his cigarette in the process and lighting another. He threw the completed butt on the dirt floor and glowered at her, daring her to say a word with his eyes. When she didn't challenge him, he relaxed and paced in a slow circle under the exposed basement light bulb that swung overhead.

"Now, after I run around all day for you and your girls, you have the nerve to call me your contractor—in front of some white woman. Antoinette, that was the last straw that broke the camel's back," he sputtered with renewed, but quiet rage, "and then you expect me to be all happy about spending money I don't have? Now—you can talk to me. Make me understand that shit."

He folded his arms and leaned against the adjacent damp wall with a cigarette dangling from his mouth. He stared at her hard through the puffs of smoke that billowed up from his deep inhales and exhales, hoping to make himself look more formidable as he completed his basement interrogation.

Chapter 14

He waited and watched her. To his surprise, she stood calmly, brushed off her skirt and addressed him with a slow, sad smile. This was not the way he'd planned it. She was supposed to fly into a fit. The conversation wasn't supposed to get far beyond his opening. But, Toni looked rational, quite calm, and had even sighed with what he could only imagine to be resignation. He could feel his heart pounding an exit out of his chest. She was breaking it off, he could tell. She said she'd do it with him or without him. God, he loved this woman, wanted to be with her—but he was no punk. He could never respect himself if he let her just walk over him at this juncture. He'd been there, seen it, and done that. Never again, he told himself. Ever.

"First of all," she said softly, "I am so sorry. You're right. I had no reason to speak to you that way at the apartment. It was wrong. I could have asked you nicely. That's the least anybody can do, is be courteous," she added, sucking her teeth, and shaking her head as though in deep thought. "I don't know what came over me. I saw you moving slow and assumed you were going to be against everything, just because I thought it up first. So, I got snippy. I'm sorry. And, I didn't think about the risk at Tracey's. God, Jay, me and May didn't even think... I'm sorry."

He took a drag on his cigarette, and let the smoke out as he formulated a response. She wasn't fighting fair. She was using admission of guilt, an apology, and a soft tone of voice. He wanted to holler, yell, create some drama—but, nooooo, she was being nice—which required facing the issues, and she had him pegged. He looked away from her wide-eyed expression toward the fuse box. So what if he hadn't liked the fact that she'd come up with an overnight solution, first? That was immaterial, he told himself.

"Yeah, well..." he muttered, saying really nothing, "let's squash this morning."

"No," she said quietly, "I want to talk about it."

He let out his breath in a rush and shook his head. "What about? This morning is over."

"It leads to this basement," she went on placidly.

"What?" Jerome pushed himself away from the wall and walked over to the fuses and checked them again.

"Because," she whispered gently, "I had a Brian flashback, and assumed you wouldn't be supportive because I had come up with a way to raise quick capital through sales."

"I'm not Brian," he fumed.

"I know. That's why I had no right to even go there. But, it happens sometimes—force of habit."

He considered her words for a moment, then looked at the floor. "Yeah... happened to me a couple of times this morning... and this evening."

"I know it had too," she chuckled as he took a drag from his Marlboro. "Might happen again, too. We're both Vet's."

"Well..." he muttered, "as long as you don't sleep with a Bowie knife under your pillow—might get a flashback and cut me, woman."

"No," she laughed softly, "I'm not that bad. I've been stateside for a while now, de-programmed a lot. Flashbacks are temporary, but I agree that an honest apology is mandatory. For real, Jay. I'm sorry."

"I didn't like the way you handled people on the phones today either, girl. It was just..."

"It was just sales," she murmured, walking over to him to give him a peck. "I can't be no punk, not when you're asking people for a lot of money," she said, gazing at him cheerfully, then strolling to the other side of the room. "Can't blink. Can't stutter. Gotta put some sizzle on your steak. It's an old sales axiom. Like A-1 Sauce, that's all I was doing with the Realtor, couldn't show her my hand. Anyway, you were the one who taught me. Didn't learn street-heart from no business school—can't get that outta no text book, Jay, pullleeeze."

"Me?" Totally perplexed, yet finding her compliment fulfilling, he turned around and gave her a wink. "How?"

"How?" she exclaimed, catching him off-guard and forcing him to laugh at himself. "You used to be the best at Three-Card-Monte on the Broad Street subway. Where's your heart, brother? You gonna let these people tell you what you can, or can not do—in your own community? Pullleeeze," she said as though shocked and walked away. "I didn't have time to argue with you this morning. Wasn't about me caveman, you woman. We're partners. That's how I view it—since you're all about tellin' me how you see thangs," she teased as she strutted around the room. "We had a mission, captain, and only one plane flyin'. Your back is legally up against the wall for the moment, mine ain't," she said with a snap of her fingers, " So, I went up in the air, took Philly by storm for a good cause. Is that a problem?"

"No..." he admitted, "but it would have been nice if you'da at least asked me first."

"I did too ask you," she chuckled, "in a telling you sort of way."

"You told me, woman," he chuckled, "you did not ask me."

"Well... particulars. Anyway, I was settin' up a way to rob 'em blind, and give back to those who need it. I do not feel guilty about them. Do you?"

"Not even."

In a mercurial change of temperament that he was oddly becoming fond of, she turned around and beamed at him. "'Member how you used to hustle up extra cash to take me on a date or have you gotten so staid, in your old age," she teased, "that you can't remember?" Antoinette bent over, bounced her body to an invisible subway motion, and mimed having a subway seat in front of her—laughing as she shuffled an imaginary deck of cards and moved her hands rapidly. "Where's the queen? Red queen. Where's the queen? Black? Ace, king, jack. Find me a pretty face, only queens please. Here's your queen, bam. There's my queen, bap. My name's Red—I'm red. Your queen's black—like you. Pull mine you win, pull yours ya lose. Find her fast jack, or I take ya money back! Gotta play to win—yeah, yeah," she laughed, encouraging him to join the song with her eyes.

"Gotta win ta keep playin'—yeah, yeah," he joined in, laughing hard as he suddenly recalled his old money-making ditty, "Gotta play the max, gotta max the play—fives, tens, twenties—no punks here today!"

"Right!" she exclaimed.

"Girl, I used to take all their money, and beat everybody's ass on the base!"

"Know you did, 'cause you were one wild, gamblin' fool," she laughed.

"Never lost. Well, after a while my luck ran out, and had to give it up," he said still smiling, but becoming sad at the memory.

"Yeah, well, I'm not trying to marry a gambler," she said warmly, "but, you have to take a little risk. Gotta play the max, sometimes. Didn't you tell me that?"

"A little risk?" he chuckled, and threw his head back as a solid belly laugh overtook him. He loved the way she interweaved the past with the present and the future. "Antoinette, if you pull this off, this will be the best Three Card Monte I have ever seen! How much you got in the bank, be honest, girl?"

"Twenty three dollars and seventeen cents. Why, boy?" she said with mock indignation as she folded her arms over her breasts and cocked her head to the side. "And?"

He stared at her for a moment then howled with laughter. Striding away from her, he spun around, did a double take when he looked at her, and began laughing all over again.

"Well, then, that makes a difference. I stand corrected. You're flush, baby. Only got about twenty-five dollars less than me," he roared, wiping his eyes as he sat down on a broken shelf. "Heaven help me."

"There is a famous quote, I think it was Henry Ford, or somebody who said, 'I may not have any money right now, but as long as I know people with money, I'll never go broke.' It was something to that effect. Anyway, I rest my case. I know folks with program budgets, and where all the money is buried within the city and state from my old profession, and from my interactions with my girls, who all work for non-profits. I'm excellent at writing proposals. So..."

"You got brass balls, Antoinette. Damn."

"That's just because I'm a Leo, and you're a Taurus," she said as she squinched her face to hold back a bright smile that came out despite her efforts. "You play a dollar or two on the lottery each week—easy access in a deli, no complicated directions, with low risk, low return, and expecting on a couple of thousand dollars. Maybe you might even spend a hundred bucks in Atlantic City—if you still go down there like we used to when it first became a casino town. Who knows? But your low risk ventures don't pay-off big, and you spend more on that low risk than you think you do."

He could not respond to her comment about Atlantic City. In that moment, it hit him, maybe he had been thinking of Antoinette down there all along? Maybe that's what had freaked Karen out? But, in his heart and soul, he couldn't remember thinking that way, really. Damn, how did women know these things?

"You're confusing the issues," he said calmly, trying to smile and shake the eerie feeling that had crept over him.

"Whereas," she continued cheerfully, ignoring his comment, "I play The Publisher's Clearing House Sweepstakes, once a year for the cost of a stamp—thirty two cents. To be fair, I'll even throw in the cost of a magazine—one that I was gonna buy anyway, but ordered to help my sweepstake along, plus I get that subscription at a lower price. True, it's a little more complicated to fill out the entry form and find all the sticker puzzles, than just buying a lottery ticket. But the pay-off is a phenomenal ten million big ones. The only time I play the state lottery is when it goes over ten million and is worth a huge payout, and I only bet one dollar one time, that's it. You're the Taurus, safe and dependable. I'm the Leo, grand and adventurous. Both are loyal, and a good compliment, I think. So, it's a cosmic difference of opinion, that's all, honey."

"What?" He could not believe his ears.

"I do things on a slightly grander scale; you do things with a much more methodical approach," she continued, justifying the indefensible notion that they could actually obtain the property. "Neither is right or wrong, just different world views—but both are complimentary. One must be both methodical to get the details right, and visionary, to ensure that a high goal is set for achievement."

Again, he stared at her for a moment as a new wave of laughter forced him to hold his head in his hands. "She says it's only a cosmic difference of opinion! Oh, so, I see now—my mistake. It's in the stars. We are astrologically destined, and the ghosts even agree. Oh, the bank is clearly wrong. The Realtor must be mad, and this is my woman. Nooooo. She's not crazy!"

They both laughed and she plopped down next to him on the steps, fighting against the giggles.

"Jay..." She chuckled, becoming more serious as she leaned her head on his shoulder. "Honey, it'll take a miracle for all these details to fall into place. You are right about that, and I respect your opinion. There's a lot of work that needs to be done in here. It'll cost a mint. I just got to dreamin,' and hopin', and I felt my old edge coming back. Plus, I wanted so bad to have a way to house me, you, and the kids. You should have seen Tracey's face when I told her I might have a creative, fulfilling job for her, something to make her feel good about herself. I went to see Francis at her Mom's today between all that running around, and she's bad off, honey."

Antoinette's voice trailed off, and he wrapped his arm about her shoulder. "Camille and Mrs. Johnson both looked so frightened, yet, when that child's Aunt Tracey came in, with her wild gang—life just breathed itself back into that house. It took ten years off that old lady's heart, Jay. And Val cried in my arms like a baby when I saw her and Buddy. I told him about you working for him for a while, and told her about the job thing, too. All I have to do is land a few contracts."

He could feel her voice tremble through her shoulders as it made it's way up her back and out of her throat. Why had he judged her wrong? he wondered. She loved them all, and had gone on a mission of mercy. He knew her well enough to know that she wasn't going to let him, or anyone else, get in her way. She hadn't changed; her family, her circle came first, and now he was a part of that intimate, complex tapestry. That had always been his Toni, so why had he ever doubted that about her? Yes, she was a Leo, and like a mother lion, she had bared fangs and claws this morning in protection of her family. He knew that as her soft form molded to his.

"It was like something inside of me broke when I saw everybody. But it wasn't my spirit this time, it was my fear. This was so important, and it could help so many people that, I simply wasn't afraid to do whatever it took to make it happen. Please don't be angry at me for trying."

"Oh, baby," he whispered, kissing her cheek, "This house is grand. It's fabulous. I guess I just initially hated the fact that you'd have to be the one to get it, is all," he admitted quietly. "I kept feeling like it would be your house, not mine. This time, I wanted a home with somebody, not just a house, and I wanted somewhere that I could claim some peace and space for myself. I never had that where I was before. Plus, there's still a lot of issues. We don't know if all the kids will like me, or you. We don't know how we're gonna furnish it, even if we got it. I could do the work, but that'll take a while... and the risk, baby. Think of the risk."

"No. You think about it," she murmured as he continued stroking her. "I've already met the kids, they're wonderful. In a few days, they'll know who I am—the oldest will, even if we try to hide it. Kids know. They aren't dumb. They're closer to their instincts than adults, sometimes. Your oldest may be the only one we have to convince. The younger ones are still little enough to give back as much love as we give them without questions, or resentment."

"Yeah, and we'll all freeze to death because we won't be able to afford heat, and we'll sleep in the one room that our combined furniture will fill up," he chuckled sadly. "C'mon, baby. Even if the kids love us both..."

"If we turn this into a funky art deco joint, my students will give me consignment art to cover this gallery space of walls that we have—see a gallery, Jay," she countered softly. "Where's your vision?"

"Oh, Toni," he murmured as hope became the marrow in his bones.

"We can pick through the trash," she pleaded, "and get tables and chairs, and paint each one a different bright color—like mini murals—even let the kids paint them, so we have child art all around us. We'll use wildflowers and spring water bottles on the tables—it's cheap, but looks so Manyunk, South Street, art-funk, you know?

If half of the property is dedicated to a non-profit classroom space—this basement, which can double for extra restaurant seating at night, and the other half goes to the restaurant—floor one and two, it will work. We can get student chefs to bring in their daily specialties, thereby eliminating my need to fully stock the kitchen with food that will only spoil if we have a light turn out in the beginning phase. Plus, having a hot menu item that runs out, will be a marketing ploy. People hate to think they've missed something so good because everybody else got there first. And I won't have to constantly cook if I share the space with students. It's a win-win proposition for everybody, Jay. The community wins by having a local, viable business. The students win, by having a place to learn, show, and market their creations. The artists win by having a place to show and sell their work. And nobody we love has to be on

Welfare, or jobless, as long as this business is run right."

She had begun clicking off her points on her fingers as she spoke, and she continued, increasing in passion as she went on. "The agencies win, by having a place to send people for jobs. The State and City wins, because they might get some folks off the Welfare rolls, and they've increased their tax base with a new business addition. We win, because we have somewhere to live, and we can make money at working hard to do what we love. Me and my girls can crunch the numbers and promote the joint, and I'll have family work the registers and books. Everybody gets to do, or be a part of, something good—this is the new model. Corporations are dead and dying—it's the trend. People have to work together, and stop being greedy. Hell, even the corporations are consolidating these days."

"And, what will I do, honey? Think about it real hard. I'm a man, and I have to feel useful, or else—"

"—Useful? Oh, Jay!" she exclaimed, turning to him to kiss him gently. "Baby..." she whispered as she closed her eyes and he kissed her eyelids. "Do you think I could turn this dream into a reality without you? There's no way this can happen without your building vision, your technical expertise! That's why I've been trying to get you to really see this house—because I know what you can do, when you're into it. Is that what's wrong?"

"I don't have a nickel in this dime, T... can't put a penny to it, right now."

"It was never about the money," she whispered.

"It's always about the money, in the end," he said quietly, turning away and standing. "I can't allow a woman to buy a house—not one like this," he murmured as his gaze swept the expanse of the structure, "not one that I'd live in. And I'd have to draw up a prenuptial agreement to protect you from Karen when I married you, since Pennsylvania is a joint property state. I have been thinking, Toni. I may not be as smart as you in business, but I do know the basics. You don't have to school me on that."

She stood slowly, and took him by the hand. "It does get down to the money, in the end. That you're right about, I suppose. And, yes, you have to protect this joint venture with a prenuptial—and I have to will it back to you in the event of my demise."

"You don't have to do that. You're not going to die." He turned away from her, hating the thought of how it sounded. He didn't want to talk about wills, or prenuptial agreements, or legal papers of any kind any more. He just wanted to love her, raise a family with her, and grow old with her. Why was that so hard, he wondered, when it was such a simple dream?

"How much would it take for you to convert this house—in man hours—with a crew, a crew working at a reduced rate, on a your-word-as-your-bond relationship? And, how much would it take for a security guard, plus a community coordinator to work with male students?"

Her question made his shoulders sag. She was gonna try to beat the odds, when the odds were against her. He loved her too much to let her put it all on red. Life was not a casino. "I know where you're going, T, but—"

"—No," she said firmly, holding his hand tighter. "Give me a number. We're too old for games, too old for allowing passion to sweep us away, and this is too big a project. I'm not gambling. I'm serious. As an entrepreneur, there are risks—but they should be well researched, calculated risks. Managed risks. My credit is already shot, so you aren't hurting me. A few contracts will pay off my debt load and make me bankable again. This is America, remember—where everything is negotiable, and capitalism drives the system. We just have to work it, Jay."

He considered her words with the utmost seriousness and gazed around the property. This was indeed a contractor's paradise, and he knew his hands could turn it into whatever she'd envisioned. The one thing he did know was real estate, and properties, and how to use his hands. She was right about America, too. He'd seen developers go near bankrupt and be back on a construction site in no time. But he also knew what it would cost to convert the building.

"You said that you'd do it with, or without me," he murmured, looking away from her direct, penetrating gaze.

"The Three Card Monte, yes. Placing my girlfriends, yes. Taking care of my financial business, yes. Getting back on a roll, definitely. But, I can just as easily work out of May's unit too. Doing this, and making space for five children alone—that was a bluff, said in the heat of the moment, only 'cause you were movin' slow and pissin' me off with your Taurean stubbornness. But, I'm not trying to do a family alone."

Her comment made him chuckle, but he still didn't trust himself enough to look at her.

"Give me a rough, General Contractor's estimate," she insisted quietly, "a real number that I could take to a Realtor."

"Thirty to fifty thousand to get it top notch,

and paying a third of the going rate," he said without blinking as he finally looked at her. "That's not nearly what they'll charge you in the real world, honey."

"And, what will you charge me?"

He was taken aback. "Nothin', baby. Jesus," he exclaimed, walking away from her. "My boys, Joey Petrullo, and Julio Gonzales—from work, need a little cash. We gotta buy supplies. However, a lot can fall off the back of the truck, like really nice marble, fixtures, and stuff. What we do have to order, can go in when the Sup puts in for supplies. That way, you'll get everything wholesale. I do have a lot of building trade and supply contacts, now that you mention it. Joey might be able to get me a better price than the lady at the pizza shop, too, for ovens, and stuff. I already spoke to her, and she gave me a few names and estimates. I don't know. Maybe fifteen, tops—to do what you want to do."

"Pay as we go?" she asked without a smile.

"Yeah... we could do that."

"If it was not through friends, what would all of that cost?"

"I don't know," he shrugged. "I'd have to do a room by room estimate."

"Give it a guess. Just first blanche calculations. Somewhere in the six digits?"

"Probably. Especially if I get that Italian marble, and those bathroom fixtures, maybe real stainless steel commercial ovens and freezers for my baby. My boys and I do the hotels, a lot. Can get stuff at crazy prices—or like I said, some things fall off the trucks in the business."

"So, you just sunk over a hundred thousand into an investment property for both of us. If I do the one half of it through getting contracts and a mortgage, and you do the other half from the renovations, how is it that I did any of this alone?"

His gaze roved over her face, drinking in the sparkling quality of her eyes. "I always wanted something to invest in, something that would last and that I could be proud of. I saw this brother who built a business with his wife," he murmured, but neglecting to tell her about the jeweler in order not to spoil her surprise. "They worked as a team. They had something to show for all the years together. When I walked out of his shop, I knew that I could fly and wanted that for me, you, and the kids. At first, I thought I was dreaming."

Antoinette nodded and walked over to him slowly.

"We are coming back from the ashes with nothing," she countered quietly. "What can they take? We don't have anything. That's the glory in it this time out. So, if we can't make the mortgage, we sell this old beaut for three times what we bought her for. That's what they did manage to teach me in an MBA program, it's called capitalism, which is why your sweat-equity portion, making this place a showcase, is critical. It's the best insurance policy against bankruptcy. You fix it up, if we go belly up, we sell. And, we don't just sell some dilapidated old apartment building, we sell a business, at possibly five to eight times the investment. Now, if the business fails before we sell, the non-profit side of our paper-tent just might provide a temporary safety net and, vice versa. If it all goes kaput, where's the risk? We don't own any property, Jay, and I'll never leverage anything, or collateralize anything, but my consulting accounts receivable. I learned that mistake in my first marriage when we got strung out in high-credit card bills and just consuming."

"Toni, I learned an awful lot in my first marriage too."

"Then are we partners?"

She'd moved in toward him and wrapped her arms around him. His mouth found hers, and the kiss he delivered was one of tender reverence. It all made so much sense, and it had all come to her mysteriously in the night, through her zany, inexplicable dreams. Yet, she shared her dreams with him, included him, and had made room for his. His kiss deepened, and her mouth gently probed his, telling him without words that she'd meant to share her live, her dreams, her tomorrows with him. This was the Toni he knew and loved... the woman, no longer a girl, who made his dreams come true.

Chapter 15

Emotionally spent from his basement surrender, he had followed Antoinette to his apartment. This time he allowed her car to lead his—just as he'd followed her up the steps, then into the building, and to his inside entrance without resistance. What was next, and what was he going to do with his life? Maybe she was right. Time was marching on, and he'd never dreamed of being in construction. It was always a means to an end, not an end to the means. In a matter of moments he'd become an entrepreneur, an investor, had something to hope for beyond his wildest imagination. She'd given him the gift of hope that he could not fathom to measure.

Jerome managed each set of locks for her, opening doors for her to pass through first, and he followed her gentle, but insistent lead. She'd said let go and let God. Tonight, it dawned on him that he had to—because he had no choice. Let someone else help with their plan.

And as she removed his hat and coat, then discarded her own, and took his face between her hands, surrender never felt so good. It was not defeat, as he'd once imagined it to be—but rather a certain calm. Release of his control within Antoinette's arms brought him to a sudden level of relaxation. Stress vanished. It was as though in that instant, he'd finally let go and allowed the cosmos to rule the flow of energy within him.

"It's gonna be all right," she whispered, healing any remaining doubts with her breath, her touch, her scent in the dark hallway inside his unit.

But, her hands soon became lightening rods that siphoned renewed hope in the form of surging energy through his nervous system, then through his pores, making his skin burn for the sensation again each time she touched a new vortex of it. Tranquility gave way to a purer form of tension. And, yet, he let her lead, knowing that she had found a place of peace that remained wilderness to him, but that she was willing to share.

"I love you so much, Antoinette," he murmured against the softness of her hairline. "Are you sure you still want me in this condition—to marry me, with all the obstacles that still stand in our way?"

"I love you, too," she whispered into his mouth, pulling back slightly to look into his eyes in the moonlight. "You have no idea how much you mean to me? There are no words, and there simply are no conditions."

As her unconditional love saturated him, for the first time in his life he knew what feeling safe meant—having one's dreams held sacred within another's heart. For this woman to have seen him in all his youthful glory, yet also in all of his mature confusion, and to still look up to him with admiration and desire flickering in her eyes. Oh, yes. This was the one. This was the other half of his wholeness.

A deep burn conquered the reply to her that was forming in his mind, and he could only communicate to her now through immediate, searing touch. His hands found the nape of her neck, and brought her to him forcefully, while his mouth spoke the silent language of Eros heat against hers.

He could feel her body yield in a deep sway that his caught, and his palm found the small of her back to press her spine towards him more.

Something fragile within him snapped when she melted against him and his mouth sought her neck, biting down on the delicate flesh near it while his hands worked feverishly to remove her suit. She whimpered when he bit her, and it drove him harder to get her out of the suit.

Helping him, she matched his pace to assist in stripping away his clothes—both of them leaving a trail of articles adrift in the hall, as they became a swiftly moving rapid. Their bodies danced, swirled, and lapped against the walls on the way to the bedroom in white-water urgency. Polarized at moments, they'd separate into eddies of coming together, kissing hard, breaking away, falling against the corridor walls, dropping a piece of clothing, coming together on a hard breathed moan, whimpering from want as they parted again to wrest away another layer of fabric. Entering his bedroom naked, this time when they came together, they ended the aching river dance in a slow fall to the mattress.

Blanketing her, his knee parted her legs only to slide against a searing wetness. The contact of his skin against her desire-slicked inner thighs uncoiled a serpent of immediate want within him. The molten sensation shot through the length of his vertebrae and released a hard shudder. Just knowing that she wanted him that much, that badly...

Her head was tilted back, her eyes were shut tight, and her lush body formed a high-voltage arc beneath him. Her knees had opened in a wide V of invitation as he held himself up on his hands, trembling forearms braced—trying to make himself reach into the drawer before her legs wrapped around him and pulled him into her raging river.

Ample cinnamon breasts with dark-coffee-colored, hard nipples heaved as his woman took in short pants of air. Looking down at her, only inches beneath him, he found his breath matching hers, with pants for clarity, pants for common-sense, as he lowered his face to the velvety surface of her skin, nuzzling, licking, nipping at the small coffee-beans that rose and fell on her moans.

This was the woman that should have borne his babies. Her body called him and threatened him not to resist. This is the woman whose belly should have imploded with life from his planted seed. Hot liquid memory filled his shaft. This was the stomach that he should have kissed and whispered to. His mouth suckled her breasts then his lips planted a series of kisses against her abdomen. One hand slipped under the small of her back, while the other trembled as it held his full weight. She peered at him breathing hard then her eyes went to half slits. He could tell that she knew it, too. Oh, God, yes. This was the only woman. She had become still waters that ran so deep within him, and had called him from his own depths.

His attention to her soft mounds charted the eminent course. Soft calves wrapped around his waist, and his shoulders were drawn in by a gentle tug, and he felt himself sinking into a hot, pulsing whirlpool, drowning, being sucked deeper the more he fought against her tide and the delirium-producing spasms within it.

"Oh, God, Toni... I can't stop this time..."

And, just as suddenly, he felt a shift that created a vacuum—and just as nature abhors a vacuum, so too his body abhorred the shift in temperature. Then came a shift in his weight. The withdrawal collided with his desire so hard that he almost convulsed as a deep spasm gripped him, making him shut his eyes tight and clench the edge of the headboard for support.

"Let me drive," she whispered. "You're in no condition and the road is wet."

In some distant part of his mind, he heard her request. She was right. Five kids... No, more babies. Time had elapsed. He found himself on his back, and he heard paper tear. She was right—friends don't let friends drive drunk, and he was intoxicated on love. He wasn't sober. Tomorrow would bring blinding reality. But, dear God, he wanted her without latex.

That's as much as he could process. Tears ran from the corners of his eyes. As though knowing how conflicted he was, her lips kissed his forehead while her luscious breasts brushed against his mouth, and her fingers deftly rolled a layer of reality down over him, and she straddled him fast, like he needed her to, so he could sink again into her warmth. He reached for her as she leaned back, and her head nearly met her spine, then she arched hard and cried out. Delicate fingers laced into his, forcing his abdomen and thighs to become steel cable that pulled and released him according to her specifications.

His hands were massive against her own, and she glimpsed at his white knuckles that she used for her leverage as she moved. Seesawing against him hard, she thanked him with her body... thanking him for making her feel capable, making her feel this beautiful again. Loving strokes echoed the truth that permeated any latex barrier between them—they were one. There was trust.

Power surged through her as the expression on his face transformed from sheer pleasure to hovering-near-the-edge-agony. His eyes rolled backward under their lids, and he began gasping in air through his mouth. The sight of his ecstasy, knowing that she had taken him to such abandon, decimated her, and she altered her rhythm to keep them both balanced at the edge of their certain fall.

But, his deep, agony-filled groan traveled through his body into hers, up through her womb to reside in her lower-belly. The sensation immediately stripped a gear within her and she lost control. Releasing his hands, her body lurched forward and her nails dug into his chest to avoid the head-on collision. His shoulders lifted from the sweat-dampened blanket, and his arms became steel girding around her waist. The impact of his upward thrusts made her pull his head to her breasts, while the frenzied pace fused a sob of pleasure with the moan of his name.

It was as though hearing his name had pierced his heart. A deep seizure, emanated from her passionate, staccato chant and claimed him. He immediately convulsed hard against her, feeling her lap against him with wave after wave of spasmodic releases, undulating, whimpering—still calling him by name. Exquisite, aching, release ripped through him, causing one convulsion to overlap and drown into the next as his body jerked, and his hands clutched her hair, and her voice with his name branded into it burned the inner shaft of his ear.

Her nails raked his shoulder blades and she held onto him tight, swept away by a repetitive pleasure that eclipsed all reason. Never in her life... not twenty years before, nor since. Wave after wave of sonic level after-shocks crashed against her, forcing her to gulp air through her mouth. The sensations riveted her eyes shut tight, and it was all she could do to try to keep from drooling as the grand mal-like ecstasy ruined her, reset her biological clock, and made her bear down hard as though her womb needed his seed to live. This was the man that should have been the father of her child...

Her uninhibited hunger caused a hydraulic reaction in him. Unable to stop his movements against her, he held her by the waist and buried his face into the flesh of her shoulder. Not since he was a teenager had a woman made him feel like this. Not since Antoinette, nor before her. Not since he'd found her again. Blinding pleasure fired through his system fast and hard as it ricocheted through hers—joining hers, blending with hers, their cries a unison wail that ended in dazed struggles for air.

Consciousness returned to him in slow advances of awareness. She was sitting on his lap straddling him, and he was sitting up holding her against him as she wept into his shoulder. And her tears of profound pleasure made him want to sob, for never in his life had it been like this.

Stroking her back, kissing her face, petting her hair, he gently led her to lie against him. Pulling the sides of the blankets up to cover them, both too exhausted to move, they fell asleep, linked body inside of body, hands and legs intertwined, unafraid to drown in their still waters that ran deep.

Jerome let his fingers carefully admire the small, white leather box within his pocket as he drove. Despite all of his former protests against her crazy scheme, he had to admit Antoinette had a plan. He chuckled to himself as he thought back on their argument, and how she'd calmly met every one of his points with her own exotic counterpoints. She'd challenged his commitment to the community, and told him that black people had to make their own jobs, and ultimately she'd been the one to pull his work buddies into this madness as she showed them a contractor's paradise. They were even stealing fixtures and plumbing and supplies for her from their contracting sites! Damn. He understood why they'd once paid her so well to talk and convince. She was good at it. After all, she'd even convinced him that he had worth.

Feeling invincible, he'd waited like a big kid for Friday to come, and now felt the same rush that Christmas Eve used to bring. He'd done it. Actually pulled it off. He turned the small case containing Antoinette's engagement ring over and over between his fingers, manipulating it like worry-beads. Although he hadn't had a chance to go home and stash it first, he reasoned that he could put it away after he picked up the kids. All he had to do was drop his usual dough on Karen, collect his children, and he could start his life.

He rolled his neck and worked his shoulders as he waited for the light to turn green. A few more minutes and he'd be gunning up Johnson Street towards his old home. In just moments, he'd get to see all of the smiling faces that he adored, and maybe, in a couple of hours, he could coax Antoinette away from her obsession of building her non-profit restaurant art center. He had so much to tell her, so much to show her, things that their short conversations during the week didn't allow. Anticipation idled within him like his Bronco engine. Turning up the volume on the radio, he flipped to the mind-altering music that his daughter's loved. Even the rap music made him smile. For some reason, although he should have been tired as a dog after putting in serious hours for his friend, he felt renewed, electrified. It felt fantastic to be back to his old self. He'd have to show Antoinette when he saw her.

Double parking in front of the house, he clicked on his flashers, and walked swiftly to the door. He didn't even have to ring. Patsy had spotted him and had run out to fill his arms before he'd hit the steps.

"Daddy!" she screamed with delight, almost knocking him down. "I'll get the bags, gimme your keys."

"Okay, okay." He laughed. "Hold your horses? Where's the fire?"

His daughter's face drooped, and she pulled him down so that she could whisper in his ear. "The fire's in the house, Daddy. Listen to what I'm saying. Let me get the bags now. You give me the keys. Talk to Mom from the steps. No matter what, don't go inside."

He stared at his daughter and nodded. Whatever was wrong was written all over the child's face, and he could tell by her urgent tone that there was a serious element of risk.

"No matter what happens, you're taking us with you for the whole weekend, right? Promise, Daddy?"

Her pleading voice was like that of a fugitive, and her eyes darted around like a frightened doe. Every now and then the child would go still, squeeze his arm, listen, then relax. The sight of her terror nearly drove him insane with rage. Why did his child have to speak to him like armed guards might accost her at any moment? Her fear made him feel so helpless, and he could tell that she was making him pledge to break her out of some sort of prison camp—but he didn't know the terms of her arrest, or where the other children had been hidden. He didn't even know his full rights. He'd never thought to ask about them when he briefly met with his attorney, and had never assumed it would come to this. However, he wasn't about to leave any of them behind. When tears began to fill Patsy's eyes, it did something to him. He'd have to die trying. These were his children too!

"Yeah, baby. Whatever come what may," he said sternly, "go get yall's stuff—

quietly, then you and the little ones get in the car. I just have to leave your mother her money."

Patsy nodded, and ducked into the house while he waited and smoked a cigarette, then crept out with four plastic bags. Something was definitely wrong. The children had luggage. She peeped around, then made a run for his Bronco, and he noted how she shut the door gently without a sound after she'd stashed the clothes.

"Where are they?" he whispered, controlling his fury for the sake of his child.

"In their rooms crying cause she told them they couldn't go tonight. She's on the phone in the basement doing laundry—talking to her girlfriend, Aunt Shirleen—so we can't hear her."

"Go get your brother and sisters, and put them in the car before she gets off the phone, baby. Hurry. I can't go in the house with you."

He stood on the steps helplessly as his daughter went back inside. It was like watching a child do gun-running behind enemy lines during a war. Survival instinct snapped into gear, and he ran down the street to Miss Hattie's house—base camp within hostile terrain.

"Miss Hattie! Miss Hattie! Open up, quick, please! It's Jerome," he hollered as he banged. From down the street he watched his oldest daughter look twice, sneak the two youngest across to the car, then run back for the baby which she half carried, half dropped, as she thrust him into the vehicle. He motioned to Patsy to drop the automatic locks and watched his secret agent-child follow orders.

"Miss Hattie," he panted again as he heard the elderly woman move inside her home. "Please,

Miss Hattie, open up." Adrenaline spikes staggered his words as the old woman appeared at the door, "My kids," he panicked, losing his ability to string the words together for a second, "she might not let me have my kids tonight. Don't know what happened, who she been talkin' to, but 'posed to have 'em all weekend!" His words sputtered out as his heart pounded within his ears. Desperation took his breath, yet he continued to form the words sloppily to try to make the older woman understand. "Patsy tol' me—but if the police come, I need a witness that I didn't hit Karen, rape her, push her, cuss her—just peaceably came like I'm supposed to—to get my kids."

"C'mon, boy," Miss Hattie said, not even bothering to put on her shoes. She marched ahead of him down the block with her slippers, robe, and night scarf on like a five star general. "Don' make no sense! Now, you got her money tonight? What you give her every week?" Miss Hattie inquired as she held out her hand without judgment. "An' bet'chu ain't missed no payments, neither."

"Yeah, right here," he said, pulling out a wad of cash as he caught his breath. "My attorney said I didn't have to till we went to settlement, but I'm not trying to cause no static. Jus' wanna see my kids for awhile, is all. Didn't even really talk about this part, yet, 'cause hasn't been no trouble so far."

"Check, or money order, baby," the older woman said with disgust as she waved away his fist of bills. "Don' be givin' no evil woman no cash—hear? Keep her straight an' honest when y'all gits front'a da judge. Lawyer tol' you that, I know. Got a check on you?"

"Yeah," he whispered, putting his money back into his jeans pocket and fishing past the ring in his breast pocket. His lawyer had told him that, but this was a peace offering of sorts, against his lawyer's wishes. Before this moment, he'd been happy, and wanted to try to be nice, have a civil moment to apologize about the things he was coming to understand. He'd never be that stupid again.

Writing out the check, he handed it to Ms. Hattie, who glimpsed it then looked up at him.

"You can't keep this up, boy. Dis what'chu do evr'y coupla weeks?"

"Gotta get my kids, Ms. Hattie. C'mon, please, can't cha give it to her for me?"

"Much as I hate to give that heifer a penny, I will. But it's blood money, ya hear, and way too much, wit what'chu already don' lef' 'er. Hmmmph!"

Jerome just nodded, and kissed the old woman on her forehead. "Thanks, Mom Hattie. I gotta get outta—"

"Where the hell do you think you're going!"

Jerome stood still and stared at Karen as she appeared in the doorway with the cordless phone.

"Miss Hattie, this ain't none of your bizness—so go on home!"

"Jus' thought I'd come down da street to make sure wasn't no trouble, so's I could tell the police exac'ly what I saw, ifn' dey come. But all dat don' seem necessary, do it?"

He held his breath as Karen's gaze narrowed on him and the old woman who body-shielded him with her arms folded over her sagging breasts.

"You're not taking my children anywhere to be in no bitch's company, okay," Karen raged quietly through her teeth, "I heard her voice on the telephone! So bring my babies back in this goddamned house. Now."

"You the one who put 'im out," Miss Hattie said calmly, "he ain't on no drugs, ain't no freak molester, ain't hit'cha, and pay you good money. Dey his too—ain't dey?"

"This ain't your bizness, old woman. And, yeah, they're all his, but—"

"—Den, go live yo' life, go git yo some, an' leave Jerome be."

"How dare you!" Karen screamed, "I'll call the

cops on the both of you! Get off my steps, you old biddy!"

"Don't'chu want your check first?" Ms. Hattie said with an angry smile, producing the check for Karen. "The boy ain't stupid no more, won't be no cash free-ride to lie to the judge 'bout him not payin' you 'nough—I'ma witness. Plus, I stays up late too, you know. Call da police, so's I can tell 'em who I see comin' by at night when da kids be at dey gran'parents." Ms. Hattie took back the check and folded her arms over her chest in the unspoken declaration of senior citizen authority; she would not be moved. "Hear tell, da boy's livin' in a nice, clean, apartment—done fixed it up his-self, an' kids need dere Daddy, if he a good one like Jerome. Go 'head, call da cops. I'll be right here waitin' fer 'em, if you dat crazy."

"I've seen his place," Karen seethed in Jerome's direction, "Me and Shirleen saw it Monday, and your next door neighbor, who's my friend, told us everything we needed to know! He's keeping late hours—"

"Yeah, working for my boy, Buddy, who had a damned heart attack!" Jerome yelled across Miss Hattie's line of defense. "Did you know Buddy almost died in my arms, huh, K—and I'm working to keep the lights on in the man's house—plus working to keep the lights on in yours?"

Karen paused for a moment, and placed her hand on her hip. "I heard her voice on your phone," she snapped, "And I don't have to—"

"You don' have to do nothin' but, mind yo bizness—his bizness ain't yourn no mo!"

"Get off my property, you old bat, and mind your bizness. I'm talking to my husband, not you, you—"

"Hey, don't you speak to Miss Hattie like that!" Jerome bellowed, almost crossing past Miss Hattie till she grabbed his arm.

"Don't be foolish, boy," the older woman cautioned. "Now, yo' just flare down, go git in your car, and leave witout no incidents. She don' bother me." Turning to face Karen, the older woman brandished the check. "Take it, and go spend it up on da lottery, like ya do evr'y day, 'stead of workin' for a living while all dem babies be in school! You call the judge, or police, hear—den Jerome's lawyer kin call me to see how much money go to the kids, and how much go to yo' personal vices—like vodka. I knows da ol' man at da licka sto'—cleans my church. Call 'em, hear?" she threatened, as Karen snatched the check away from her, "an' I be waiting on the curb for 'em to come. Try me."

The front door slammed so hard the the glass panes within it nearly shattered. Jerome moved to the older woman's side, and hugged her with all his might. "Thank you, Jesus, Miss Hattie," he whispered against the moist dark skin. "I'ma have to get a support order to get 'em again next time..."

"Go on, son. It'a be all right. Do what'chu gotta do. Feed 'em, den take your babies to a real home. I'll look out on dis end, and I'ma pray."

*

"Daddy," Pasty said quietly, as she waited at the pizza shop counter with him, "Why does she treat you like that?"

His nerves popped and frayed under his skin as the child's question connected to his mind. Jittery from the altercation at the door with Karen, and fearful of arriving at his apartment only to find the police, he could only shrug. Looking over at his other children, who were battling over potato chips and soda at a nearby table, he shook his head and rolled his shoulders.

"Things happen between grown folks sometimes, sweetheart. I dunno."

His daughter's eyes searched his face, and she touched his arm lightly. "You look so sad and tired all the time. I wish there was somebody that made you happy."

Jerome swallowed hard and swept Patsy into his arms. "You make me happy, love-bug," he whispered, "go on, now. Y'all sit together, and keep the little ones from gettin' in trouble. Maybe we'll get some movies. Go visiting a little. I'll bring the pizza over to the table, when it's ready. Gotta make a phone call to check on Uncle Buddy."

His daughter slowly removed herself from his embrace, as though afraid that he might vanish the moment they stopped touching. His heart broke with her sad smile as she left him to plop down beside the younger children. Exiting the store, he watched his brood through the window, focusing on his Pasty as she looked down and picked at the chipped tabletop. He could barely dial Buddy's number as his vision blurred the keypad on the pay phone, and he wiped at his face angrily while he waited for the call to connect.

"Hey, Val," he said slowly, "got somethin' for you an' the kids. Be around in 'bout a half hour, after the kids finish eating. How's my man?"

"Jerome, thanks so much," she murmured through the line. "C'mon by. Buddy's comin' along."

"All right, honey. See you soon. Take care, kiss the kids for me."

"Ain't you stoppin' in?"

"Naw... I'ma try to catch up with Toni. Don't need to go home, till things cool off a little."

"What happened?"

Valerie's question gouged a hole in his lungs.

"Talk to you 'bout it later, honey. Don't worry. Everything's fine. Just gonna put an envelope in your door—cash. I'll put some more in next week. It's only five-sixty—"

"—Five hundred and sixty dollars, Jerome.... in one week? You must have been working like a slave for Miles! Jesus, you gotta keep some of that—"

"—Gotta sleep at night, Val. Buddy, and me and you go way back. Okay. Just put it up safe, and I'll send you some more when I make it next week. Gotta run. Bye, honey."

He stood outside the pizza shop and pulled out his cigarettes. He needed some time away from pressing children's questions, and their jarring requests for more this, or that. His nervous system couldn't handle it at the moment, and he felt like he would nearly jump out of his skin when a homeless man tapped him for some change. Dropping a dollar into the vagrant's blackened palm, Jerome turned back toward the phone and took a heavy drag from his Marlboro.

His mind scattered thoughts in random order throughout his brain. He counted his change twice and leaned against the metal phone stand to finish his smoke. How did his life get this messed up? How did this crazy drama just jump off and change direction within a matter of minutes? How was he going to tell Antoinette that he was possibly on the run from the cops, with four tired children in his possession—kids who'd just been traumatized by a bitter argument between their parents in the street? This wasn't anything close to her world. Her child was probably home, safe, well fed with a balanced meal, and happy. His children were eating pizza, and chips, and fighting over portions. Her ex-husband probably came in, chatted pleasantly, then left. His ex-wife had thrown a literal fit, was holding his children for ransom money, and had probably called the police when she'd slammed the front door.

Jerome pushed himself away from the post, and looked at the telephone, fingering the ring in his pocket as the numbers on the telephone began to blur again. He was out of his league, no matter what Antoinette said, or believed. He couldn't marry his Toni in this condition.

Chapter 16

"So, you kiss Mom Johnson good night for me, and we'll both say a prayer for Francis, I know..." Antoinette murmured into the receiver to Tracey as she sat down Lauren's dinner. "You okay? He checked on you... Officer Cooper? I'm glad he's a presence. Scoop hasn't been by, has he? Good. Uh, huh... I've talked to Val, and Buddy's coming along nicely. Yeah, it'll be awhile, if ever. No, he can't pull those hours any more."

Antoinette dished up some mashed potatoes, gravy, carrots and peas, then plopped a biscuit on her plate to go with the pot-roast, and sighed, wondering if her pure gamble of a business plan would work.

Feeling relaxed, she listened to Tracey's virulent, but comical rebuttal about their friend Val's new lease on life, then cut in with her own point of view after tasting a dripping piece of pot-roast from the hot pan. She marched to the table, and giggled, then looked at Lauren's wide-eyed expression. It was good to have her old friend back, and even better to have Val back and to be working in a new venture with Cookie, regardless of their sometimes diametric opposition to each other. "Listen, gotta run. Teeny ears. Yeah, it's me and Lauren's ladies night. Gonna watch Beethoven together. Again.

I love that big, dumb dog—"

"Beethoven's not dumb, Mommy. He knows everyt'ing!" Lauren corrected.

"My mistake," Antoinette chuckled as she stroked the top of Lauren's hair, then went back to her conversation, picking up where she'd left off with Tracey, "...got a bunch of other Disney's. Yeah, I missed my little bird all week. Gotta run."

"Mommy, I wanna say bye!" Lauren exclaimed as she turned her gravied face up to Antoinette.

"Okay," she laughed, "Let Mommy wipe your hands," she added, snatching a rag off her shoulder and trying to wipe her daughter's sticky fingers before handing Lauren the phone, "Say 'bye-bye' to Aunt Tracey, then let me tell her bye-bye.

Don't hang up—we gotta tell her we love her."

"Bye-bye, Aunt T'acey," Lauren said and then laughed, getting a chinful of mashed potatoes on the phone despite her mother's attempt to swab her face. Lauren wriggled away and blurted out, "Love you—here Mommy, say love you to Aunt T'acy," before Antoinette could save the phone from gravy.

Holding the receiver between two fingers, and away from her face, Antoinette laughed into the phone. "Girl, gonna mess up my perm with gravy and mashed potatoes. Yes, I did get my hair done. Yeah, tomorrow, gonna take 'em to the museum. Of course I'm nervous—"

"—The museum! I love the museum, Mommy."

"Yes, suga-lump, we'll go tomorrow, okay—finish your dinner," she chuckled looking at Lauren, then turning back to Tracey on the phone, "I'll call you tomorrow after little ears are asleep. I love you too. Bye, sweetie."

Antoinette hung up the cordless telephone and walked over to the television to insert the video for Lauren. Using the remote to pass by the coming attractions, she sat down and watched Lauren's expression of sheer delight. This was the way it was supposed to be, she thought, looking at her plump, happy child, then wondered what Jerome had cooked up to have fun with his children during their first evening in his apartment. He was such a hoot when they were younger, no doubt it would be something totally zany.

When the phone rang again, she didn't answer it immediately. This was Lauren's time. But something in her gut pulled her to it anyway. She reminded herself that there were a lot of pending issues with clients, Pearline was sick, and she hadn't really talked to her sister since she'd gone back to LA. She looked at Lauren again, who was totally immersed in the movie, then got up to answer the phone.

"Hello?"

"It's me, Jerome... I need to talk to you."

His tone immediately stopped the flow of anticipation that rushed through her when she heard his voice. Antoinette became very still, and she listened to the traffic sounds behind him.

"What's the matter?" she asked quietly. "Where are you?"

"On Penn's campus at a pizza place. Need to go over to Val's to take her some money... then, I thought maybe me, you, and the kids could rent a movie."

"You don't sound right, Jay, and why did you go all the way down there, instead of around to Royal Pizza?"

"Needed some distance from the apartment...

kids... they need a place to just get comfortable and chill out for a while. Never mind, we didn't plan it—it's a hassle for you. I don't know if we can go tomorrow... my pockets are lighter than expected... I don't know Toni."

She let her mind work on the puzzle for a moment, then walked deep into the kitchen to respond to him. "Just answer me yes, or no, so the kids don't think you're talking about them. Okay?

"Okay."

"You can't go back there tonight, can you?"

"No."

"Something kicked off when you tried to pick them up?"

"Yes."

"She threatened to call the police?"

"Yes."

"You don't have a custody order yet, do you?"

"No."

"You're afraid the police might be there, when you get to the apartment."

"Yes," he whispered, sounding like his voice would break at any moment. "I just wanted to spend some time with them, T."

"Let them finish eating, and bring them here for dessert. Park your car in Buddy's garage, I'm sure Val won't mind—if you explain. Then walk back around here. Don't worry about movies, I've got plenty."

"But, my locusts will eat you out of house and home. You can't—"

"Went to the market already. Me and Lauren are eating pot-roast, as we speak, okay. I've got a brand new, half-gallon of ice cream in the fridge, made a scratch butter pound cake, bought microwave popcorn a-go-go, and plenty of snacks, fruit, juice and Kool-Aide mix, even have pancake mix, eggs, bacon, milk, and cereal. Ruby LaMann said yes, and gave me a check, and my severance check from the agency came—so, I went nuts at Pathmark. Now, let's have a good weekend."

"I love you, baby. Thank you," he murmured. "Be there in a few."

"I love you, too. No thanks needed. Bye."

Antoinette held the telephone in her hands, then walked over to her daughter. "How would you like some company to watch the movie with us?"

"Kids?" Lauren exclaimed, giving Antoinette only cursory attention as the television captivated her again within moments.

"Lots of kids... remember the kids at the flea market?"

"Uh, uh," Lauren shrugged, still watching the movie.

Antoinette's mind barreled through various options—prayer being one of them. "Remember the girls who could jump rope who came to your school? The big girls?" she attempted again urgently, but tried to sound casual.

Lauren's eyes opened wide, and she giggled. "The girls you jumped rope with?"

"Yeah, you remember, baby. Right?"

"Yup. They're gonna come here to play?" Lauren laughed and wiggled.

"Yeah, honey... So, Mommy's gonna go clean up, then we'll all watch movies together."

"Can they sleep in my room?"

Antoinette paused and stared at her daughter, and said another little prayer inwardly before she answered. She had no idea of what psychological condition these children would be in when they arrived—or what would happen once they stayed a while. So, she hedged with a Mommy-can't-promise-but-hope, answer.

"If their Daddy says they can stay. But if not, no tears, because we'll be going to the museum—me and you, tomorrow."

"Can't they go to the museum, too?" Lauren grilled, seeming unsure about why her mother had begun to pull back a little.

"We'll see, suga-lump. I don't know what he already has planned for them."

She brushed Lauren's forehead with a kiss as on-screen puppies stole her daughter's attention again. Maybe it was for the best that Lauren stay oblivious, she told herself. Antoinette's eyes darted around the condo as her mind tried to do spatial analysis. How was she going to fit them all in—and preserve the appropriate distance from Jerome?

Moving to the bedroom, she worked fast to provide a clean space, knowing how she felt about Lauren's first overnight away from her... away with her father, and a competitive threat. She ripped her week-old sheets from the bed and ran to the linen closet, returning with a newly laundered set. She'd be prepared, just in case, she told herself, her mind going over and over the basics. These children weren't hers. They wouldn't trust her yet, and unlike Lauren, they would probably react at a basic level of resistance. Her sheets didn't have their Mommy's smell... that space was a place where children jumped in to feel safe. Men didn't think about these things.

Racing against some non-specific element of time, she went to Lauren's room and changed her bed as well. It was precautionary, even though she felt sure that the children could deal better with that room than her own. She stood in the middle of the floor and tried to guess sizes that went with ages. A big tee shirt could suffice as pajamas for the girls... and even the boy. Making a snap decision, she found four of her smaller summer tee's from an era gone by, then put them onto the top of the closed dryer—along with five sets of clean towels.

"Jerome..." she whispered, and asked herself what in the world could she do with him? Moving back to her room, she found a pair of clean sweats, then scavenged her dresser for socks to fit the children. Even though her socks would be too big, it would keep their feet warm. It was imperative that they got a good night's sleep in a non-hostile environment. It was imperative that they could feel warm, and safe, and clean. She'd do laundry and they could wear what they came with to the museum. Toothbrushes and combs! Those unplanned for toiletry items would be missing, she was sure. Okay, then, he could make a run to the store once they were settled.

When the doorbell chimed, Lauren arrived to the door first, happily laughing and wiggling about as 'her company' stood on the landing. Gently bumping her daughter out of the way with her hip, Antoinette managed the locks and stared at the huddle of children on the landing apron. Taking a deep breath, she pasted on an exuberant smile.

"Hi, everybody," she chimed, "C'mon in."

"We got videos! Beethoven!" Lauren yelled, "C'mon."

Not one child moved. They just stared at her, then glanced back to their father.

"Would y'all go on in the house," Jerome commanded, "and speak to Mrs. Wellington on your way in!"

Appalled by his handling of them, Antoinette could only step aside as they slowly moved into her living room. These were his children, and she didn't want to cross his line of authority. But these were also children who were probably terrified. They didn't know who she was, where she came from, or what she meant to their father. If the kids hadn't been there, she would have read one Jerome Henderson. Yet, at the same time, she could tell that his bark came from the need to get them safely stowed inside. Fear did funny things to people...

"Well," Antoinette said as calmly as she could, "are you all ready for some dessert?"

Even Lauren had picked up something uncomfortable, and she'd taken a position between her mother's legs with her thumb in her mouth. The oldest said 'Hi', in a voice so tiny, so quiet, that Antoinette had to strain to hear it. The boy had his thumb in his mouth, and was clinging to Jerome's leg. The two middle girls hung back, just beyond his elbows. It was as though they were all waiting.

"Well? Ain't y'all gonna speak?" Jerome said testily, "I taught y'all better than that!"

Fire shot from her expression to his, and he looked at her in confusion. He had to shut up, and stop the man-in-control-tone. "C'mon... we can jump double-dutch tomorrow... and nothing in here is so new that you can't sit down and have ice cream," Antoinette said gently.

"You were at the flea market," Patsy said with a shy smile. "You were gonna play with us... but, we got in trouble."

"Yeah," Antoinette said brightly, "and you're not going to get in trouble while you're here. Right Dad?" she said casting a hard gaze at Jerome.

"If they cut up..." he trailed off, accepting her eye-laser warning. "No. They won't get in trouble for being kids here."

"That's, right," Antoinette said quietly, "and you must be Kitty and Darlene?"

The two girls giggled and hid their faces against their father's jacket. "You were the one who was singing, I Been Told, and you worked the food table at the fair," Kitty said brightly.

"Yup," Antoinette laughed. "Know why they put me on the food table?" She waited for the kids to ask why with their eyes and then leaned into them real close, "Because I can bake a mean butter pound cake from scratch. Want some warmed up in the microwave, with some ice cream on it... and we can all watch a movie on the sofa together?"

Four sets of children's eyes turned to Jerome for permission, but the boy still troubled her. He hadn't come out from hiding between his father's legs.

"Yeah, y'all can have some ice cream. But, don't be spillin' it on Ms. Wellington's furniture. You don't know how they can be Antoinette," he said in a grumpy voice which seemed to transform the children into stone again.

"Listen, Jerome, that's what they make carpet cleaner for—okay? They're kids, for Christ's sake. Let 'em alone. Lauren's almost five, and she drops stuff all the time. My house ain't no museum. C'mon y'all, your Daddy's tired and ready to pick a fight with everybody. Let's get some cake while he parks his car."

She waved him away with a flip of her wrist, and acted as though she was casually on her way to the kitchen, watching their body language the entire time from the corner of her eye.

"I want chocolate," Lauren yelled and grabbed Darlene's hand.

"Me too," Kitty giggled and followed her immediately.

"Do you have strawberry, or vanilla?" Patsy whispered.

"Hey, don't be getting choosy—"

"Yes, I bought Neapolitan, all three flavors in one box. Can you dish it out for the little ones, while I see what's wrong with Christopher? Go ahead, you can't break anything." Antoinette said cheerfully as she cut Jerome off by doubling back to place her arm over the child's shoulder. It was an unconscious thing, but she'd almost body-blocked Patsy from her own father.

"For real? You don't mind?" Patsy whispered appearing amazed that Antoinette had invited her into the kitchen, but not like a guest.

"The cake is on the counter, and I trust you to cut the portions right, so everybody will get some. Go 'head, baby. Use the knife I laid out—you're old enough to manage."

"Wow..." Patsy murmured as she walked away to join the others. "We never get to do this by ourselves..."

Antoinette closed her eyes briefly to fight off a flashback. It was a monster that she'd kept under control from an era gone by. But the oldest child's eyes had made it resurface, had made her want to nearly kill in order to protect the helpless. She waited until she heard giggles and shouts for fair portions, then she turned on Jerome. "Go park the car man, and walk around the block until your temper is straight," she added in a tight whisper, "And don't come back in here to turn that attitude against these children," she warned. "Ever again."

She ignored the dumbfounded expression on Jerome's face, to kneel before him and try to detach the tiny barnacle that clung to his knees. Not cake, not ice cream, not movies, or the promise of fun had made the small boy loosen his grip on Jerome's leg, or his own thumb, which had stayed cemented into his mouth from the moment they'd walked in the door.

"I bet you want to be with Daddy... and don't want him to leave you for even a second, huh? And you don't want him to go away, and just leave you with some lady you don't know," she murmured from her knees, stroking the child's head.

Two big tears brimmed, fell, and rolled down Christopher's cheeks, as he shook his head adamantly no.

"Listen, I'm double parked with my blinkers on, boy. I'll be right back. Don't be such a bab—"

"—Patience, man," she hissed through her teeth as she glanced up quickly. "The child's scared, aren't you?" she said more gently, returning her gaze to the wide brown eyes full of tears. She let her breath out heavily, and let herself fall back to sit cross-legged on the floor before the small boy. "Your Daddy is too," she whispered, "and so am I... a lot of adults were yelling today, huh?"

The child nodded his head yes, and she ignored Jerome's look of shock.

"Well, me myself, loud voices make me scared too."

Christopher blinked and sucked his thumb harder.

"So, tell you what," Antoinette hedged, "why don't we sit right here on the floor and eat our ice cream by the front door. Let's leave it unlocked, so we can tell that Daddy's coming back after he parks his car. We don't want him to get a ticket, and your big sister can bring you ice cream to eat right here till he gets back. Will you help me not to be scared of the loud voices?"

She waited and prayed and held her breath as the child eased his grip from Jerome's leg.

"I like choc'late," the tiny voice said over a thumb, and eased over to her, steadily eyeing his father and Antoinette as he made his way to her lap.

"Tell him you'll be right back, Daddy,"

Antoinette said in a soft voice, "Give the child your word, and leave the door cracked open when you go."

Jerome stared at her and his gaze went gentle as he squatted before Christopher. "I'ma leave the door open, okay, Buddy? I'll only be a minute, and Pasty will get you some chocolate ice cream to go with some cake. Ms. Wellington won't move from this spot till I get back. Deal, man? Slap me five on the promise," he said standing, and receiving a tentative male handshake from his son. "Be back in a minute, Miss Toni," he whispered, "Thanks a lot."

"No, problem," she murmured back as the child climbed into her lap and laid his head against her breast. She closed her eyes and stroked the small head against her, calling softly for Pasty to bring the child ice cream while Jerome headed out the door. She could only imagine what these children had seen as she rocked and talked softly and prayed hard with her mind.

"Can we put on a movie?" Pasty said brightly, skipping over to Antoinette and handing her a dish for Christopher.

"Sure, take a paper towel with you, and you guys can eat on the coffee table. Drop your jackets on my bed, and grab the throw—can't watch no movies without a blanket," she chuckled.

"From your room?" Patsy whispered in disbelief.

"From my room," Antoinette affirmed. "That's why they make laundry detergent. Go, on. Scoot. Go put something good on, take your shoes off, and visit for a while."

"Sure!" Pasty laughed, ushering the other kids behind her like a mother hen.

Antoinette watched her from a distant place in her mind, and remembered. Their laughter rang out and she could hear them dropping coats and shoes, and investigating around the new place with ease. Their father was gone. No one was going to yell, or scream, or bark out commands. No woman was going to throw a hissey-fit about them looking at a piece of furniture wrong, or sitting wrong, or getting a drip of food on fine upholstery. She watched from memory as Christopher took the first spoonful of ice cream, and looked up nervously to see whether or not it was okay to enjoy it. "It's good, isn't it, baby?" she whispered, then watched a full smile open up on the boy's face.

By the time Jerome had returned, she couldn't feel her legs. But she'd vowed not to move until he graced the doorsill. And, even though Christopher had finally joined the others on the couch—unable to resist the movie or his sister's merriment, he still peeped back over to Antoinette from time to time to ensure that she'd keep her promise. It was a matter of principle. She had promised to guard the door.

"What'are you still doing here on the floor?" Jerome muttered with confusion as he crossed the threshold and locked the door behind himself.

"Made the boy a promise," she grunted, standing and shaking out her legs with a bit of effort.

"They look like they're having fun... whad'dya do to to 'em?"

"Gave them space to investigate, without loud voices, without jumping on their cases for every little infraction, and without invading their personal space, until they invited me in."

Antoinette could feel herself becoming weary as she spoke. Crossing past Jerome, she went into the kitchen and began covering her uneaten plate, and putting away food. "Did you eat?" she grumbled, pulling down a clean plate before he could respond.

"I'm cool." Jerome eyed her and reached for a cigarette.

"Not in here around the kids. Lauren has asthma. Did you eat?"

"No," he said cautiously. "I let the kids eat. I wasn't hungry at the time."

"Sounds like it was a real Malox moment up in

Mount Airy—you ready to eat now?"

"Yeah, Toni, it was—"

"—Something to discuss once they've gone to bed," she said firmly, dishing up his plate hard. "Not in front of the children," she whispered, "Ever!" Antoinette turned and looked at him hard, and held the plate in mid-air. "No loud angry voices in my house—you follow. That's my only ground rule."

He accepted the plate from her and picked at it slowly. "Pot roast is good, Antoinette."

"Thank you," she murmured stoically, then cut him a piece of cake and poured him a glass of soda. "Take off your jacket and hat. Then go eat your dinner, and cake on the sofa with your children. Leave me in the kitchen for a while."

"What?"

"You heard me." She turned away from him and held onto the edge of the sink for control as he got up and moved into the living room. Ghosts from the past waved in and out of her mind, haunting it as she cleaned up the dirty dishes with inexplicable fervor. She'd seen this before, knew these frightened children. She had been one herself.

"I told you not to set that glass on the edge when you took a sip!" Jerome bellowed from the other room. "Damn, Patsy, how could you be so stupid!"

A chord snapped within Antoinette's brain, and tears filled her eyes as she heard the child's yelp. Then she flew.

"Stop. Nobody move!" Antoinette said firmly as she stood before the coffee table with her arms folded. "These are just things, Jerome. Replaceable things. Nobody in here is stupid. Nobody is dumb. No child under the sun is bad, or evil, or clumsy..." her voice broke as a near sob took her breath. "The only thing that will make me angry, really angry, is if any of you call each other horrible names. Not here," she warned through her teeth, while gathering up Christopher into her arms. "What—over a glass of spilled soda? He's four, and tired, and so is Lauren. I'll clean it up, but don't holler at these children like that, Jerome. Not in here. Especially Patsy!"

She paced away from their muted expressions with Christopher in her arms, and tore off a paper towel when they'd reached the kitchen and handed it to the child.

"C'mon, honey. Things happen. Accidents happen. Let's clean it up and we'll try to be more careful next time, is all. Daddies get tired, too. And sometimes they get cranky, too, when they've had a bad day," she whispered, walking back into the living room and setting him down. "Now, I'm gonna show you how to wipe it up, then where the trash is. And, if something else spills, you can show the big girls how to do it. Okay?"

Christopher nodded, and five little sets of hands helped clear away the mess. Jerome stood and took his plate to the kitchen, placed it on the counter, and fished in his jacket. "Look y'all... I need to go down on the landing for a cigarette. Wind the movie back to where we went passed, and me and Miss Toni will be in, in a minute." Without looking back, he slipped out the door.

Antoinette let out a deep sigh as she kissed Christopher's cheek, and gave Lauren a little wink. "It's all right, " she murmured with a smile, then looked at Patsy, Darlene, and Kitty. "Your Dad is just tired. He's stressed, but we've been friends a long time. You didn't do anything bad. So, go ahead and watch the movie. In fact, I even have some microwave popcorn in the cabinet. I'll show you guys some pictures later."

"Microwave popcorn?" Kitty giggled. "Are you sure it's all right?"

"Yup. Put it on three minutes and thirty seconds—that way, it won't scorch. Patsy, there's a plastic bowl under the sink—help them so they don't get a steam burn. I'll be back."

Antoinette drew herself up and walked out the front door with her head held high. Jerome hadn't even bothered to turn around when she'd joined him on the landing.

They stood together side-by-side for a few moments as he puffed on his cigarette and she contemplated the stars.

"We have different parenting styles, Toni," he began quietly, "and you undermined my authority in front of my children. I didn't like it, and can't go for that."

She stood calmly next to him, the sudden rush of protective adrenaline having dissipated considerably. "If I didn't know you, and saw you in a supermarket, calling your kid stupid, I would have spoke on it. Don't ever call a child names, Jerome. What the hell were you two doing up there to them in Mount Airy? Somebody oughtta have slapped the both of you."

He spun on her and looked at her hard.

"That's right," she continued in a low voice. "Both you and her were wrong if you did that to 'em. Not the hell in my home. I've never called Lauren stupid—your own fucking father did that to you, I know the damage. Don't test me, Jay. I'm serious." The startled expression on his face told her that her words were beginning to sink in.

"Hey... we were just kids when we started having 'em, T—"

"If you are going to parent with me, I won't

have it. They were traumatized when they walked in here. And just because you're mad at Karen, or whatever, don't you bring that mess to my door. No. That's what I will not excuse. My baby didn't grow up with screaming and yelling. I won't have it around here. It's like cancer, Jay. Goddamned cancer!"

He took a long drag on his cigarette and turned away from her as he blew out the smoke. "It is like cancer," he murmured after a moment. "It gets into your bones, and you can't cut it out. Creeps into your mind like an octopus, then runs through every cell in your body. You know, I didn't even know how to sit and watch a movie with my own children—me and Karen couldn't. She'd always go lock herself in her room with some vodka and get on the telephone, and I'd go work on the basement with a flask nearby. We didn't sit with 'em much, or eat at the table together much... was the same thing I saw, more or less, growing up. Everybody went to a neutral corner. There's a lot I have to learn."

"C'mon," she said gently, touching his shoulder with her hand, "Let's peel off some of your personal lead paint, finish our dinners, and watch a movie with the kids."

She held the door open for him to move through it first, and noted how the children seemed to hold a breath as they entered.

"Okay, you guys, make some room and pile up," Antoinette piped, "Let the movie fest begin!"

Chapter 17

Patsy yawned and laid her head on her father's shoulder. Darlene and Kitty blinked so slowly that it made Antoinette chuckle. Christopher had become a fetal ball in his father's lap, and Lauren had sprawled across hers like it was a king-sized bed.

"You guys ready to cry uncle yet?" Antoinette chuckled as the credits for the last movie came up.

"We can hang," Patsy yawned again, "we're not tired."

"Well, I am," Antoinette said with a stretch around Lauren's limp body, "and the two little one's are gone."

"Do we have to go home?" Kitty yawned, "can't we watch one more?"

"Tell you what," Antoinette said carefully, standing with effort as she gathered up Lauren. "How 'bout if you guys go climb in my bed to rest your eyes—you, Darlene, and Patsy. Maybe I might join you? Your Dad can stretch out on the sofa with the blankets, just to rest awhile before he has to drive. He can squeeze Christopher in with Lauren, since they're so little. I might even have some big tee shirts around, and some clean towels, so you can wash your faces and get comfortable."

She cast a glance in Jerome's direction, and receiving his nod of approval; she motioned with her head for the bigger girls to follow her.

"You have a pretty room," Patsy said quietly as she gathered up the towels and laundry that Antoinette showed her. "You sure you don't mind?"

"No, baby. You all get comfortable."

"But, the living room's a mess..."

"I'll pull it together this time—next time you can help."

Antoinette left the bigger children in her room, and hauled Lauren to her own bed. Dumping her load carefully, she kissed the sweaty curls, and checked Lauren's rump. "Don't you pee pee," she chuckled with a kiss to the unconscious form, "you've got a visitor."

Jerome appeared in the doorway, and she helped him pull off Christopher's clothes and get a tee shirt over his head.

"Tuck him in tight," she whispered, "I'll collect the girls' laundry, and throw in a load. There's some of my big-butt sweats on the dryer that you can put on."

"Good night," she murmured as she kissed each child that created a lump in her bed. "I'ma wash your clothes, and they'll be on the dryer in the morning."

Patsy stared at her for a moment, then shut her eyes. "Thanks a lot, Miss Toni, for making my Dad happy. He's so much nicer when he's happy. That's all he needed."

"We all are, baby," Antoinette whispered back as she turned off the light.

Antoinette stood in the hallway and considered the child's words, then flung in a load of laundry before she moved into the living room where Jerome sat, donning her sweat pants and shirt. Immediate fatigue hit her, and she flopped down beside him and let out a sigh.

"T, baby, " he said brushing her mouth with a kiss, "it really is going to be all right, isn't it?"

"Yeah, I hope so, Jerome. But, you can't let

them go through this again. Get your papers in order. Let them call their mother in the morning."

"I can't call Karen—"

"—It's parental courtesy, and I don't care what the attorney says, you offer her the opportunity to come by your apartment, with whomever she wants, so that she can see where her babies will be. It's mother-to-mother protocol. It's about a trust factor."

He rubbed his face with both palms and yawned. "That's the problem, Toni... we never established trust going in. I'm as much at fault for that as she is."

"Then listen," she insisted, standing slowly to collect the remnants of the food-movie fest, "establish it now. Even under strained terms... for the children. Stop the war, eat crow, do whatever you must, but atone."

"Atone?" he said quietly, standing to help her clear away the mess and following her into the kitchen. "I did that when I stood with over a million brothers down in DC in front of The White House—and I had to go through hell-fire and brimstone at home to do that. I take care of my kids, work hard—like they said we should—give to my community by trying to clean up the drug houses, Town Watch. We all atoned. We marched, every one of us. I pay child support.

What do you mean at—"

"—And I believe the good ministers and speakers said to do it where it counts—at home, Jerome. You did it for me, after twenty years. You simply told the truth and apologized. Period. So, after giving you four beautiful children, under whatever circumstances, you can give her that much. Atone, apologize, admit whatever you did to make this woman angry. Even though you feel you had grounds. Say, you're sorry, for the part you played in this drama. Even if she never accepts it, you can sleep at night, and maybe, just maybe, she won't feel so bitter. Isn't that all any of us want? To get an open, validating apology for what wrongs we think someone committed. I know you slept with someone else on her—it's the only thing that could've caused this much rage."

She watched him stand before her in the kitchen entrance, then look away.

"Before I married her... she was pregnant, when it happened... after that..."

"It's not important to me," Antoinette murmured, clicking off the light and moving past him. "What's important now is that you learn from the damage, and get it out of your system." She stopped and looked at him in the shadows that bounced from the low light of the living room. "I'm not the type to stay and fight viciously, Jerome.

In that regard, I'm a punk. If it happens here, I'll run for cover. Handle your business. Call Cooper and let him know what happened, then call your attorney. Tomorrow, I intend to take the children to the museum with you. I'm not about to run and hide in my own town, or be party to an abduction—ever again. It goes against the code of motherhood. Tell that woman where her babies are, man, and let her hear their voices. Put them on the damned phone so she can let it rest."

They stood before each other as silence engulfed them. He touched her cheek and then removed his hand.

"Good night, Toni. See you in the morning."

"Yeah, baby..." she whispered. "Tomorrow. Call her."

❋

She awakened to the smell of bacon and eggs, and she sat up quickly as she became aware of the emptiness of her bed. Pulling on her robe, she didn't bother to hunt for her slippers, but followed the sounds of the television and children squabbling.

"I don't want a burnt one," Lauren complained, casting aspersion on a dark brown pancake.

"Hey, sleepy-head. Want a flap jack?" Jerome

called out to her, "Better get a move on so we can go to the museum."

"I want more syrup," Christopher fussed, "Kitty won't give me any!"

"Pass the syrup to your brother, would'ya please, and stop foolin' around."

"He had it first, already," Kitty protested.

"I need some butter, c'mon Patsy—stop hogging the butter," Darlene yelled. "Dag!"

"I don't want a burnt one!" Lauren insisted. "Mommy, mine's brown!"

"Well, give it to me," Jerome fussed back, "and take one off your Mom's plate. I'll pour another one for her."

"Can you guys stop hogging the orange juice?" Patsy fussed, "you all are so greedy!"

"I want syrup!" Christopher hollered, making his voice screech above the cacophony of female voices at the table.

Antoinette wrapped her arms around her waist and chuckled with amazement as she watched Jerome manage like a short order cook. He really can do this, she thought, and a whole lot better than she could. Never in her life had she had to deal with this order of magnitude... what would she do in the restaurant?

"You need some help?" she said tentatively, glancing around her kitchen, which had become a disaster zone.

"Naw, just get your clothes on, grab a bite, then we're movin' out. We hit the museum, then the park, we'll figure out where to eat later."

She watched him maneuver over tiny hands that competed for bacon, spilled juice, as he slapped fingers away from the meat tray with a spatula. Voices collided and made her ears ring, and laughter permeated his barks of military orders. He could do it, she giggled to herself. The man could actually do it. A new level of respect for him entered her soul. This was what she knew was within him—the beauty that resided underneath all the scars his own family had created.

Almost afraid to jump into the fray, she did a military 'stand down' and let Jerome negotiate the terms of her kitchen space. She'd never turned over her kitchen to any woman, and the last thing she'd expected to do was turn it over to a man. Giggling to herself, Antoinette ran into the bathroom to quickly shower and dress. Through the water and the door, she could hear the blare of the children's voices, mixed in with Saturday cartoons. The sound did something to her inside, warming her, softening her fears, and lowering her resistance with love.

*

"I don't know how you do this," she huffed, trying to keep pace with Jerome as the walked along the Valley Green path.

"Gotta wear'em out, get 'em in the fresh air—that's the only way you'll survive, Toni. Gotta be physically fit to handle a brood like this," he laughed as the children ran ahead of them. "By the time the sugar they had at the museum wears off, after they climb a few hills and get dirty, then we get them by Pearline's," he panted, "Then, we feed 'em again at a pizza shop, they'll fall out for the night," he laughed, "and maybe... just maybe... I can get next to my baby."

"You have got to be kidding me," she laughed through deep breaths, "First of all, I'll pass out half-way up this hill," she said looking at the steps the kids had run up without effort. "And, Lord knows, I don't know how you had the energy to make them all," she said with a grunt as he helped her under her arm.

"Be surprised what you can do when you have no choice—started in a one bedroom, girl."

"What?" she laughed, "I don't want to even hear about it."

"Have to be real quiet," he teased, "or you'd never get none."

Antoinette stopped and looked at him before

she howled with laughter. "I ain't giving you nothin'—with five kids in an apartment. That's raggedy, Jay. Don't tell me no more!"

"That was youth," he laughed, going up a flight of stone steps before her. "C'mon, girl. Gonna take you all to my secret spot."

"Can't we just look out at it from here? Plus, I don't think the little ones ought to climb so high."

Antoinette stopped and cast her gaze up the massive hill toward the stone Indian statue that she could barely make out through the newly budding foliage. Another season had indeed gone by, bringing with it the eminent promise that life would indeed go on. She wrapped that comforting reality around her like a blanket, and closed her eyes briefly as she took in a deep breath to smell nature's fragrant promise. The simplicity of God's peace held her in awe for a moment. Then she opened her eyes again to pay homage to the little green buds on every surface, which had fought so hard to stay alive and come out after the winter. "Why is that you never took me here?" she said, yielding to his lead, having become mellow.

"C'mon... I never took anybody here—it was my space."

"Okay... okay..." she conceded in good humor, following him up the windy, treacherous path as the children laughed and ran ahead of them.

When she finally got to the top, her ears were ringing and she had to gulp in air through her mouth.

The space opened to a massive stone monument that looked over the North-end of the Henry Avenue Park entrance. The majestic view held her still, and she tried to imagine the peaceful solitude that it could bring to one's soul where there were no children's inquisitive voices surrounding it.

"This is beautiful, Jerome. My God. Who is it?" she whispered, running her hand over the exquisitely aged stone figure.

"It's Chief Tedyuscung. Legend has it that he sat on this hill and died in 1763, during a snow storm. I used to come up here to think. Somebody told me he froze to death looking for his wife who'd been lost in a blizzard. He couldn't go on without her, and just stayed here, in this crouched position—like they carved him, calling for her. That's how they found him," he whispered. "He couldn't leave her, Toni, could never get her out of his mind. I needed to come up here to ask a question that your eyes answered for me."

"I'm hungry," Kitty interrupted.

"Me too," Darlene yelled from her precarious position at the edge of the monument.

"Y'all are always hungry," Patsy grumbled, and sucked her teeth. "We just got up here. Dad, tell 'em to shut up!"

Antoinette's eyes darted away from Jerome's and she called for the two youngest to come away from the edge of certain death.

"I have something I want to talk to you about, later, baby. Let's go see Pearline, and feed these kids," he whispered, squeezing her hand and scooping Lauren up with a free arm. "C'mon, littl'Buddy," he murmured to Christopher who looked up at Lauren indignantly as he placed her on his back. "You're a big boy now, and you can make it down without Daddy's help."

⁂

The scent of garlic and cheese steaks made their stomach's rumble as they entered the brightly lit campus restaurant. The day had been tiring but exhilarating, and yet also tinged with the sadness of the approaching changes in the family.

"Pearline looks pretty bad, Toni," Jerome murmured, casting a glance at the children who fought and giggled at the adjacent free standing tables that had been joined together to accommodate their lively brood. "I'm glad she got to see the kids, and us standing side by side again."

"Yeah," Antoinette whispered, then looked

down at her slice of pizza. "Won't be long. Another season's passed."

"But, we were lucky to have had her this long. Think about Francis, how her Mom and kid must feel, and her boyfriend. She broke up with him, just so he wouldn't be left with Camille and have to settle her business. Val told me that much. Francis didn't even give him a choice, that's how much she loved him. He was younger than her, and didn't have any kids—so, she left him in Atlanta. Don't love me that hard, Toni, to ever make that kind of decision for me, baby. Whatever happens, I'm there."

"I know, Jay. That's why this project is so important. I just want to give the kids a safe place."

"Well, it's gonna happen. If I can just keep my nosy neighbor outta my business. Do you know," he whispered confidentially, leaning in towards her, "that the woman has been clocking me? Karen came by my apartment on the sly after she heard your voice, with her girl, Shirleen, in tow. Apparently, we were already gone, but our neighbor wasn't—"

"—That's who was on the phone?" Antoinette whispered in awe. "Maybe that's why I was in such a rush, and couldn't explain why?"

"Maybe. You've always had this uncanny gut

hunch about things—almost like second sight radar. Either way, the woman told her everything, probably down to the bed squeaks. Karen went off—that's what happened the other day. But like you always say, everything happens for the best. It was just time, I suppose, to bring everything out in the open and finally deal with it. Sweeping it under the rug just prolongs the inevitable, and time is short. We both know that. So, they saw us."

"No...." Antoinette said quietly. Then almost as an afterthought, she murmured, "This is history repeating itself, Jay. This is what happened in Dover—Karen must be freaking out."

"Listen," he whispered, sitting up straighter in the booth, "I was in my own apartment, minding my own business, and continuing with my own life. I'm not going to hide you, Antoinette. Remember, you told me that, too."

He watched her face, and she'd become distant. Her gaze swept the restaurant like it was a minefield. He could almost see the hairs stand up on the back of her neck and arms. Guilt ran through him. Why was she so suddenly afraid? They weren't doing anything wrong?

"Listen," he said more firmly, "I don't want you—"

Antoinette abruptly shot out of the seat and

cut off his words with her sudden action. Her eyes narrowed on a subject over his shoulder, and he spun around to see the object of her glare.

"Get away from my son!" she bellowed, in a tone he'd never heard. "I'll kill you!"

Before he could clear the booth, Antoinette had created a body shield between herself and the double table of children.

"That's right—I'm talking to you!"

Flanking her immediately, he stared at a drunk who'd taken a seat just behind the children, previously out of his line of vision. "What's the matter, baby?" Jerome whispered, trying to find out what had caused her to go instantaneously ballistic.

"I ain't messin' wit no children," the drunk laughed, winking at Patsy, "just talking to the boy. What's your name, son?"

"I'll kick his natural ass, Jerome. Heaven help me," she screamed, snatching Jerome's forty-ounce beer bottle and brandishing it like a weapon.

The whole restaurant had gone still, and he noticed from the corner of his eye that eight African men had stood up as well.

"My damned children can't eat in peace, for this lecherous bastard touching my boy—trying to get to my oldest daughter! I'll kill 'im!"

When the drunk stood, Jerome came in front of Antoinette, almost pushing her out of the way. She repositioned herself quickly to his left, as though instinctively avoiding his swing arm, both boxing in the offender as they stared him down.

"Touch my kids, and you die. Right through this plate glass window. Put my beer down, baby," he instructed Antoinette firmly. "Don't waste it on this trash."

"That's right," one at the table of men who stood, chimed in. "Got no bizness trying to talk to dat young girl in 'er moder and fader face. Who you tink you is? Put 'im out! We seen 'im, da lady don' lie... touches children. Bad sort."

The drunk stood before him defiantly, obviously too out of it to understand that he'd awakened a mother and father bear. Jerome's senses were on full alert as Antoinette practically growled low in her throat. It was as though he were seeing her with a new inner vision as she became some unknown female creature; fangs were visible, her ears laid back, her hair bristled, and he knew without looking at her directly that she was prepared to attack at the slightest provocation. The stupid man before him only weaved and laughed. Antoinette would tear out his windpipe as a mother, he was sure, if the fool breathed too hard.

"Talk to whoever I want to, ain't against the law," the drunk chuckled, reaching into his breast pocket.

Before he could react, Antoinette had rushed him with a chair, and pinned him against the booth between the legs of it. "Move, and you die," she whispered and clamped her hand around his throat.

Jerome lunged with his foot against the seat, and tried to pry Antoinette away from the offender as her full body weight against the rim of the chair crushed the wind from the drunk's lungs.

"Let him go, T—he might have AIDS."

She stared down into the drunkard's stunned, bleary eyes, and slowly removed her hands from around his filthy neck. But, it was clear from the fire in her glare that she wouldn't lift her body weight from the chair. Only when the old Italian proprietor came over to the fracas, cocked the hammer on a gun, and put it against the drunk's temple did she move.

"Time to go, Buddy. Not in my store where decent people come," the proprietor said calmly. "Let him up, folks. I'll take it from here in the parking lot. Pizza's on the house—lady, you can wash your hands in the manager's bathroom. I hate this scum-bag."

Almost too pumped to move, they both withdrew themselves from the chair reluctantly and went over to the children, squeezing all of them tight between their embrace.

"Nothing's gone happen to y'all, while we're here. I promise," Jerome whispered into their hair. "Nothing. T, go wash your hands, baby—they're all right, I'll watch 'em, and keep 'em safe with me."

Chapter 18

It had taken them all several moments to calm down enough to eat. She and Jerome had lost their appetites, even though the children seemed to quickly recover. For them, it had been an exciting adventure—one where their Dad was the hero and Miss Toni was the heroine. For the adults, it had simply sent stomach acid through their systems.

All the way out of the restaurant, and on the ride home, the children recounted their version of the events. Jerome and Antoinette sat silent, realizing just how much danger they had narrowly missed, and understanding how temporal life and safety for a family truly was.

When they finally reached his apartment, five eager youngsters barreled through the opened door. Amid the squeals of the children's delight, he watched Antoinette carefully as she smiled, tried to look calm, and nodded when they showed her their room.

He had to respect her ability to keep a straight face as Patsy took her through the apartment she'd already seen, without as much as a hint of recognition. They'd obviously taught her to keep a poker face well in her previous jobs, he thought, as Antoinette indulged the children with so much apparently on her mind.

"Okay, okay, you guys," he chuckled, waving the children away from them. "We're gonna go talk in the kitchen, and you can play the games I left for you in your room—quietly, with no fights. Hear?"

"May I use your telephone?" Antoinette asked calmly, and receiving his nod, she motioned for him to follow her into his bedroom.

"Sure" he murmured while standing beside her while she dialed.

"Pearline has to put this on the prayer line."

He didn't answer her, and stood by Antoinette's side as he watched her connect to the call, speak in quiet parables, then hang up.

Leaving the bedroom, Antoinette walked ahead

of him to the kitchen and sat down. There was something in the duality of her nature that had always disturbed him. It was in the way Antoinette only exposed glimpses of herself to each person. Yet, those slivers of her were so deep, that most times, even those people closest to her believed they'd seen all of her shape-shifting dimensions. That's why, despite her fiery nature, she reminded him of water, still waters, in that regard. Powerful, subtle, and evaporating, rushing, always able to mold to the object that dared contain her, and able to wear down mountains to mere sand.

"We have to hold hands and pray, Jerome," she said quietly when he joined her. "I want to take the kids by the property tomorrow, and get their pure energy attached to the house. If something bad is going to happen, then we have to pray that something good comes from it. This is the way Pearline taught me to view bad luck—not just as a trial, but as an opportunity in disguise. It's how you chase away dark with light."

"You and Pearline sound like my martial arts instructor, finding opportunity in the middle of every crisis."

"We've been through a lot of crisis lately, Jay," she murmured in a distant voice. "Wouldn't it be so much better in the world if we could all view our struggles as opportunities in disguise? That's the only thing, at some points, keeping me sane."

"I hear you, but tell me you are not that superstitious to want to take the children by the house, Toni?" he chuckled, taking her hands within his own. "We shouldn't get their hopes up, till we know for sure."

"Under normal circumstances, I'd agree. But, I feel a bad wind blowing, Jay. That restaurant incident spells chaos coming. We need to pray for protection, cast a bright light around them, you and me. Call on your mother, your grandmother, my mother as ancestors in Heaven to help the angels. Let's go back as far as we can, remembering all those that loved us, to keep this little family in the light."

"Ain't nothing wrong with a little prayer," he murmured. "I prayed that you would come back. I prayed that you would still love me, and, I prayed to my mother and grandmother to watch over the children when I left. All I wanted was to see them make it through the transition I had to make with their mother—without trauma. I didn't even bother to pray for myself. Then, I prayed that they would love you, and you'd love them too. When we all got to your house, and piled up on the sofa under a blanket—I knew. They were home. Funny, but Mr. Miles, that nice old man who let me stay with him for a few weeks while I got myself together, used to try to get me to pray—but while I was angry, I couldn't. Now, I understand why he demanded it."

"Prayer really does work, Jerome. Ask me how I know," Antoinette whispered.

"When you went after that bum, and almost ripped his throat out... and called Christopher your son, and told him to back off your daughter, Patsy—the last doubt in my mind was answered, girl. That's what I had to ask The Chief in the park... would this work? Did we stand a chance? You didn't even think about it, or stutter," Jerome murmured, shaking his head in amazement. "It was like they were your own. You even went up against me, for them."

He squeezed her hands and looked into her wide-brown eyes as tears began to form in them.

"Children belong to everybody, Jay. They're a gift to be shared and equally cared for. When I was little," she whispered, casting her gaze down to the table, "my cousin, Ness, lost her mother, and nobody cared for her sisters and brothers collectively—but my Mom. Her older sister tried, but she was almost a baby herself—no other Aunts really stepped in, and that wasn't Pearline's side of the family. Ness became my sister, even though we were cousins. Yet, my mother had limited resources, and her arms weren't wide enough to reach over to another household where drunken men came, grown people battled like animals—and called each other and the children filthy, horrible names... and grown people touched children. I saw so much, and not one of those children made it through. That's why poverty terrifies me so. I have to die trying—to keep that from ours."

He could only stare at her, as another complex layer of her soul was revealed before him. Tears streamed down her face, and she didn't bother to wipe them away. His fingers trembled as they went to the wet traces on her cheeks to follow the rivers that led to her soul.

"Antoinette... you never told me..." he whispered. "Your parent's home was so peaceful, so loving..."

"Yes," she murmured thickly, "it was 'the safe house' in the family," she sniffed, motioning with her fingers, "the place where adults stood guard and made a haven through sacrifice. But, there were times when I went to stay with my cousins, times when no lucid adult was around, because Ness' sister worked so hard so many hours just to keep the lights on, and the wolf from their door. Times when I would sit cringed in a corner and watch my sister-cousin Ness beaten, or touched.

Times when I was called stupid, or fat, or clumsy. Times when I was warned not to tell, and when my cousin begged me with her eyes to make them stop. But I was younger than her, and afraid, and because I didn't want my Daddy killed, or to risk his life by telling him something that would call him to arms, I never told."

"Oh, baby..." His heart fractured and he pulled her face to his and nestled her cheek.

"I can't," she whispered hard, "hear a child called names. I can't, Jay. And, whatever Ness needs, I'm there for her—even if I disagree with some of the things that go on in her house. Like Adrienne, she's my sister, whatever come what may. Ness is also my sister-cousin. So, I love and worry about Ness' kids like they were my own, and love and worry about my sister like she was my own child. I have them to consider, when I do anything. Me and Cookie share that. We came from humble beginnings, but can't just leave everybody behind. And I can't hear a child spoken to in a certain way, it does something to me inside."

"I know, baby... Shhhh."

"I can't," she persisted through a quiet sob, "sit witness to a child's terror, ever again... that's what that man in Allantro Pizza did to our children... right in our faces..."

"Baby, I was gonna—"

She pressed her fingertips to his mouth and drew back to look at him through her sparkling wet eyes, and the quiet shimmer of desperation halted any words he was prepared to utter.

"A man tried me, when I was Kitty's age. He smelled like liquor, was so massive... so dirty... so heavy... in a basement, because my oldest cousin had to work, and he was a supposed friend of the family."

"Baby..." Jerome's voice caught in his throat and he swallowed hard and clasped her hand.

"I screamed and bit him, and fought him tooth and nail—and, luckily, he was so drunk that he fell and I won because I ran. I was eleven and I flipped-out on him, and picked up a lamp and clocked him good. When he fell back, I escaped. But, it never left me—the reality that I didn't have to get away."

He could only stare at her as the scene in the pizza parlor came back into his mind.

"And all of my cousins, under that roof, were vulnerable because of poverty. No one had planned for their existence, no one had decided to work hard to ensure their safety. Only the women came to the rescue, with their crumbs of bread."

He was speechless, and her eyes blazed with a smoky fury in them when she looked at him hard then looked away.

"That's why I drive myself to the brink, and beyond. That's why May probably resented me and Adrienne, at first, because we were jeopardizing all that she'd built and worked hard for to protect her children. Just like my mother made provisions for her own children when she was alive. When I dropped into May's world, she had just married my father, and I was using her resources that were supposed to be put up for a rainy day for her kids—and she knew that my father hadn't planned, and couldn't really help, no matter how much he loved her or she loved him."

He was about to speak, but thought better of it. Just watching the expression on her face told him to let her get this out of her system.

Antoinette pressed her fingers to her lips for a moment as though choosing her words very carefully and forbidding them to seep out until she'd made a selection, and then pulled her hand away.

"That's why I want a fortress against the world." Her voice was a mere whisper, and her gaze traveled past him to a distant, unknown point. "That's why I have to lose this weight, and you have to stop smoking, because we have to live a long time—because, nobody will raise them like us if we're gone. Nobody came behind my mother and took her place. She left such a hole, such an empty space behind her. That's why I can't have it any other way, because poverty, baby, puts children at risk to the sick elements that attract to it. I tried to explain this to Brian, when he'd go out, mess up money, and wouldn't come home. I was afraid, Jay." Her gaze returned to his and she looked at him hard. "I was terrified of having my household lapse into what I'd seen as a kid. I've never seen a man plan, or execute, as well as a woman—not even my own father."

Again, her gaze had traveled away from his, and her voice had become far-off as she'd spoken. Within her eyes shone a brand of determination that told him if he failed to support her, she'd leave him. It wasn't personal, it was business. Family business. Women's business. Something that went to the core, which had withstood the tests of time. She'd given him the privilege of seeing the source of her personal depths. But, understanding that meant he'd have to accept knowing that she wouldn't let a man, love of a man, or anyone get in the way of creating some semblance of security. It was an awe-inspiring revelation, one so simple, but so real. She'd survive with or without him, and make the business fly with or without him. He finally understood the route of her current that ran beneath her surface.

He looked down at her hands and spread them

between his palms. Her tone had not been accusatory, just plain. "I judged you wrong, girl. I didn't know. But I could tell something had snapped, like a flashback, when you went for that man in the restaurant. Even before that, Toni, you'd get this weird look on your face, and even spun on me like a tiger when it had to do with the kids, or money. I wasn't about the money. You kept telling me that but I couldn't understand what you were really saying. It was about safety, security all along, wasn't it, baby?"

"Yeah," she whispered, finally wiping her face and letting out a deep sigh. "Pray with me, Jay? Pray that we'll always be able to find a silver lining in whatever negativity gets sent our way. We gotta live long enough to see 'em grown."

He held her hands, and let the silence engulf them, praying with all his might with her that they'd always be protected, always find a haven, and never, ever, would their children be hurt.

"Listen," he said after a long while, "I can't promise you a lifetime without problems. That's the way of the world. All I can do is try my best, Toni. Will you take my best, for now, as long as it improves as we go along?"

"Yes," she murmured, and gave him a sad half smile. "But you'd better get a short chain for me, I can be dangerous when crossed. I'm on a mission."

Chuckling he stood up, and kissed the top of her head. "Wait right here for me, honey. I have something for you."

Chapter 19

His heart beat so hard within his chest, that he could barely breathe as he made his way down the hall to grab his jacket. Oddly, he felt that what he'd thought he'd sacrificed so hard to give her wasn't nearly enough to compare to what she was giving him. He paused for a moment before collecting the garment, wondering if any man truly gave a woman what she truly deserved? Even Karen.

Women gave life and true security, legacy. Men gave material things that were easily replaceable. What was so hard about that? The question drew him to all the men he knew, and he shook the vague feeling of helplessness as he snatched up the jacket. Running back toward Antoinette where she waited in the kitchen, he fished in his pocket and produced the tiny white box that he'd carried next to his heart for two days.

"It was the best I could do," he said, going down on one knee before her when he returned to the kitchen table. "I'll try to plan better. I'll try to be better, and I'd give my life to protect you and these babies," he said quietly, placing his head in her lap. "Just trust me, is all I ask. And know that somehow, I'll be able to contribute, be able to give you enough to make this dream happen—even if all the contracts don't pan out. I'm going to pray on that too, Toni. Some days, you look so tired, baby, and have been fighting this by yourself for so long."

He could feel her fingers roaming through his hair like a gentle breeze, and he looked up to see her eyes shimmering with new tears as she bent forward to take his mouth.

"I have loved you for so long. Trusted you from the beginning with my heart and soul. All I ever wanted was a little help. Yes, Jay... this is beautiful..."

"Oooooh!" Darlene giggled from the doorway, causing him to bang his head against the table with start.

"Y'all kissin'...." Kitty laughed, covering her

mouth.

"Tell them who I am, Jay," Antoinette said quietly. "If they've—"

"You're the lady from the picture in Daddy's high school book," Patsy exclaimed with a wide grin. "But, y'all had big afro's before, right?"

"You were in my military trunk in the basement!" he hollered, feeling totally violated. Jerome stood, folded his arms over his chest, and glared at Patsy.

"I had the key, Mom didn't—so, don't worry," Patsy giggled as Christopher climbed into Antoinette's lap. "I hid it from her, 'cause she goes through everybody's stuff. That was yours, personal, and the only safe place in the house to keep my diary. That's why I went in there—cross my heart."

"Can I see?" the small boy who'd consumed her lap giggled with mischief, reaching for the ring box quickly without permission—only to have it snatched up by Lauren.

"No, lemme see!" Lauren hollered back. "I saw it first."

"Well, can y'all all stand back, and give the woman some breathin' room, so I can at least put it on her finger?" Jerome laughed, relieved that she'd have him. "Dag, gimme some elbow room to do it right!"

"Do it like in the movies, Daddy," Kitty swooned and fell against the door molding. "Romantic-like."

"Is it all right that I put this on?" Antoinette said quietly, gazing at the faces that stood eagerly around the table, then focusing specifically on Patsy.

"Yeah... you make Daddy happy," the eldest girl murmured softly, "and you care about us. Can't fake that funk about that, you know. 'Sides, Mom's always angry. All she does is scream and yell and hit us. It wasn't just Daddy, it was her," she added in nearly a whisper, then looked down. "It's nice to be somewhere people don't fight or always say mean things. Can we live with you guys, one day? Can't fake the funk. She never wanted us, 'specially me."

Intuitively, Antoinette knew in that moment, it was not about competing with the mother they knew and loved—no matter how they felt about their mother at present. It was about allowing them enough space to come to terms with the slow acceptance that, although their father had moved out, there would always be a safe haven for them in the world. All that truly mattered was reassuring them that someone, somewhere, would forever have their back, reinforcing that there was someone who loved them that they could count on.

Antoinette cast her gaze in Patsy's direction, firmly holding the child's line of vision within her own in a silent entreaty. It was her first attempt at woman-to-woman telepathy with the young girl, something they had to begin to establish if they'd ever become inner-circle friends. Yet, she also wondered how she'd be able to make a child understand what took many adults a lifetime to comprehend? How did one communicate that, while the two families had come together under blended duress, replacing what had been was never the objective—nor was it a contest?

She focused her mind to covey that their mother would always be their mother—the queen bee of their hive, with Antoinette as a supportive extended family member. It would be a position that she'd hold with honor, she mentally promised, as the child's eyes gave her a scant glimmer of understanding. Yes, she told Patsy in a quiet thought, one day Lauren will also face this dilemma as well... of loving two queen bees. And, she could only hope that Brian's choice would be as understanding of the order of things by not trying to replace or compete with her and Lauren's water under the bridge.

Connecting to Jerome's eldest daughter was so fundamental in this tiny sliver of time, for she too was the eldest, and the holder of collective history for their family.

"Your mother loves you," Antoinette whispered into the silence that had enveloped the small kitchen, extending her arms around Christopher's wriggling form for Patsy to fill them. When the woman-child came to her, Antoinette nuzzled her hair. "Baby... she just doesn't love herself, yet... and I hope one day you can live with us, more. But, I don't know if she'll ever let you totally come here. What mother would?"

"What'chu gonna tell Mom, though? She's gonna be mad," Patsy said with a deep sigh, as she withdrew from the embrace with reluctance and flopped into a kitchen chair. "She'll never let us come over, after this, and I wanna be in the wedding... Pleeease?"

"I'ma tell your mother the truth," Jerome said quietly, tipping his daughter's chin with his finger and staring into her eyes. "And, I'm going to try to reason with her, apologize for any hurts on my part... and take it to the judge if that doesn't work. You'll always be mine—no matter who says what, and Toni's too. We fought a bum today, right? Think we scared of some judge? We may not get to have you all of the time, but I can guarantee you some of the time, for now."

A brilliant smile came out on Patsy's face, and

he kissed his daughter before turning back to Antoinette.

"Okay, drum roll please," he said with a laugh, carefully retrieving the ring and dropping down on his knee again. As he took Antoinette's hand, he looked in her eyes, repeating the silent prayer that had drawn him to her in the first place. "Will you marry me?"

"Absolutely," she murmured, and kissed him lightly in front of the children.

He wanted to deepen it, to find a quiet place to call their own, however, he held himself in check. This was a shared decision, a joint family venture—as Antoinette had called it, and he had to turn her lose before he forgot that there were children in the apartment.

"Can we all spend the night here?" Darlene whined, "Lauren, too?"

"Pleeeeaaaase..." Lauren echoed.

"Yeah," Kitty and Patsy chimed in.

He looked at Antoinette, but she looked away with a smile that told him 'not yet.'

"How about if Lauren stays tonight.... but, I'd better go," she whispered, as though reading his mind.

"Yay!" Lauren squealed, "Can Patsy do my hair like hers?"

"Yup, and I'll be over bright and early to bring

her some clothes—okay?"

"C'mon, y'all. Dag. Let Daddy walk Miss Toni to the door by hisself, so he can kiss her again. Y'all so noooosey!" Patsy huffed with authority, snagging little bodies by clothing parts in her grip as they tried to wriggle away.

He stared at Antoinette and realized what she'd just told him without words. She'd trust him with her baby, the most precious possession she had. Despite the fears he'd uncovered, despite all that had happened, even despite Lauren's asthma, she trusted that he wouldn't smoke in the house, or harm her child in any way. She'd conferred the deepest honor upon him; the genuine respect and dignity that went with solid-as-a-rock trust.

A series of "Get off a me's," and "she's touchin' me's," followed them down the hall as they ran and laughed, making a break toward privacy in the hall. Cornering Antoinette in the vestibule of the building, he pulled her close, and kissed her hard.

"You have no idea how badly I want you right now," he whispered, wondering if the kids would stay behind the apartment door for more than five minutes. "It's been a week...."

"Twenty years..." she murmured, burning his ear with her breath as she melted into his body.

"When?" he whispered quickly, glancing back up the stairs to the apartment door.

"Monday... on your lunch hour," she breathed huskily through a laugh. "I feel it too, but not with everybody in this tiny apartment."

"I know," he panted, feeling like he was going to explode, "Damn, I can't take it..."

"Come on, Jay," she giggled and scooted away from him as the apartment door opened.

"Kinda blows the groove, don't it," he laughed, opening the outside door and watching her descend the landing. "Call me when you get in the house," he yelled, "It's just a coupla blocks, but—call me. Hear?"

She blew him a kiss and giggled as she ran down the steps. In that moment, twenty years vanished before his eyes.

⁂

"Good morning, sleepy-head," he crooned into the receiver as the line connected.

"Hi, baby..." she murmured sleepily, "we must have been crazy staying up on the phone till one-thirty."

"The only reason I got off then was because the two little one's jumped in bed with me. Couldn't keep listening to the sound of your voice with them climbing all over me," he laughed.

"Yeah, sort of blows the groove, doesn't it," she giggled, then yawned. "Well, everybody, okay?"

"They're eating cereal now," he yawned back. "These hours are catching up to me, Toni, but I was thinking, maybe you were right. Let's show 'em the house."

"Are you serious?"

"Yeah, baby, why not? Pearline said it was gonna happen. And if they flipped over my apartment, I can just imagine how they'll run through that joint. Then we can let 'em blow off at that steam and run in the park across the street. How 'bout it?"

"I have to bring you some clothes for Lauren—"

"—Patsy already dressed her, gave her one of Darlene's extra outfits that was in the Bronco in a plastic bag. C'mon, baby... you go get the keys, and we'll hang out in the park till you meet us. Whaduya say?"

Antoinette allowed the bright sun to warm her, and she twisted her hand in the rays of it, casting brilliant sparkles around the room. "Yeah..." she murmured, listening through the phone to the gaggle of children's voices in the background, "it's such a pretty day. I'll be ready in a half hour, is that okay?"

"I miss you, baby," he whispered, "Don't take too long. I love you."

⁂

"Okay, what's going on?" he yelled as all the kids piled in the back seat.

"I'm doing Lauren's hair," Patsy protested.

"We wanna sit in the hatch-back part and look out the window. Dag," Kitty exclaimed. "We're just going around the corner!"

"Watch your tone, young lady," he warned as his two middle children tumbled over the back into the hatch space. "Look, get some seat belts on, all of you—Okay?"

"Yeah... yeah..." Patsy muttered, and he shot her the evil-eye. "Gimme a minute, I just have to put a coupla beanie-balls on the end of Lauren's braids... Dag..."

"Get the belt on, Patsy," he hollered over the seat. "When will you all listen, without a whole lotta lip?"

"All right, but I can't do Lauren's hair right."

"Where's we goin' Dad?" Christopher whined, "I'm hungry."

"You just ate, boy," Jerome said shaking his head, finding a new appreciation for the energy it took to watch children alone. "Look, we're gonna spin around the corner, go see something cool, then hit the park. That's all I'ma tell you. We'll wait for Miss Toni outside."

Rap music blasted from his radio on the over-rule vote the children had cast, and he yawned as he slowed to wait for the light to turn green at the corner. A week's worth of over-time, and a life-time of pressure that had suddenly lifted, made him drowsy. He yawned, checked his watch, and proceeded down Baltimore as the light turned green.

Jerome rubbed his face for a moment and stopped suddenly. His peripheral vision caught the flicker of silver metal in the sunlight. Adrenaline snapped his senses into focus and he immediately willed his brain to connect his foot to the break. The sound of locked gears, and an end-less screech, made him turn to see his eldest child leaning over Lauren without a seat beat. Almost in slow motion, he saw Patsy hold on, then heard her scream first as an impact slammed against their world.

In an instant, glass shattered and his neck snapped. Terror gripped his breath as a second impact spun them out of control and his shoulder felt like it had separated from it's seam. Children cried and screamed in the distance, and his body floated on a sea of black. Gasoline fumes filled his nostrils. Then it all went still. Until he heard his mother's voice scream his name.

A salty hot substance stung his eyes, and his right arm hung limp at his side. Pain stabbed his body from every direction. A large oak had claimed the front of his car, and a slow moving white apparition felt like it touched his face. Billows of smoke blanched his lungs. He could hear people yelling... his children crying. Moving through the delirium and agony, he staggered out of the car, falling and holding onto it for support as he forced the back door open. Christopher toppled into his arms, and he snatched his son before he hit the ground by the front of his jacket.

Pasty tumbled out next, screaming and holding her leg, and he hurriedly pushed her away from the vehicle with a body slam, as he tossed Christopher to the grass. Snatching his keys from the ignition, he opened the back hatch, which no longer had glass in it, and grabbed both of his daughters by their clothing, dumping them into the street. Black plumes began at the bottom of the car, and he fought against the smoke, to free Lauren. Heat scorched his left side and raced up his pant leg. Her little body was caught by the seat beat, and the smell of gasoline drove panic though his soul. Her eyes rolled back in her head as she struggled for breath, and he sobbed openly for God to lend him a hand. The bones in his shoulder ground out their sounds of resistance, yet he finally managed to untangle her legs and slip the convulsing child against his breast.

He wept and puffed shallow breaths over her little face as flames engulfed his vehicle. The sounds of approaching sirens nearly made him pass out—when, the child didn't respond to his prayers.

*

Singing as she drove, Antoinette opened up her windpipes to belt out Sunday morning gospel at full pitch. She didn't care if other drivers looked at her funny. It was a gorgeous day—all except for the inordinate traffic blocking her access to Baltimore Avenue. Swerving around the annoying delay, she went down the back streets of Pine, then forty-fifth, only to find Baltimore blocked from both entry points. Nearly ready to lose her religion, she pulled over and parked. She would just have to walk down, she told herself. The trolleys always created a hassle, and construction crews were always doing ill-timed work.

But, the sight of flashing red lights adjacent to the park, made her stop. She could smell smoke as she got out of her car and made her way down the street. Oddly, the sirens had started again.

Half running, half walking, she made her way through the crowd that had gathered, and stared at the silver BMW that was wedged and against what looked like a blackened Jeep that had become a part of a tree. Her gaze ripped through the throng and landed on a section of glass on the ground. It contained a blue and white union bumper sticker...

Shrieking wildly, she pushed her way through to the fire engines, and grabbed the closest uniformed person within her grasp. "My babies! My babies!" she screamed hysterically. "Where are they?"

"We got the mother over here, Captain," the uniform that she held intoned.

"Move out a car!" a distant voice yelled, "Take her in a squad car to University of Pennsylvania Emergency—radio ahead, they're gonna need ta have psychiatric ready to medicate her, when she sees 'em."

She never saw the ride over to the hospital. Everything was a blur of sensations. Her eyes remained closed and her palms covered her face. The policeman's words rolled off of her brain, as she pleaded to The Lord and tried to barter with Him for salvation. Between calls to Jesus, she screamed for her mother, and rocked—banging on the door to open. Out of her mind with a mother's panic, she begged the officer to let her run, rather than wait for traffic that only whirred by at fifty miles per hour.

Two orderlies fought against her struggles as they brought her to her bloodied children. The sight of them each tucked in a bed, whimpering, bandaged, buckled her knees and she went down—blackness covered her eyes.

It took a few moments to orient herself and stand, as the ones who held her under her arms put an acidic, violent smell beneath her nose. Vomiting once, she stood with their aide, and looked at the human destruction before her. Tears wouldn't even come as she took her breath in and let it out in small sips. She could feel a tiny feminine hand at her back while she looked on in horror with her hand covering her mouth.

"The boy has a concussion, but he'll be all right, Mrs. Wellington," a familiar female voice said. "He's banged up a little, and has a few cuts. The two girls in the back were cut, and had to get stitches in their knees—but no internal or facial damage, no broken bones. The eldest child has a fractured leg, and had to have her knee sewn up.

But, the littlest one, she didn't get cut, it was the severe asthma attack that we had to get regulated."

Antoinette couldn't move as she watched Lauren struggle for breath under a respirator. Her mind could only count the lives that had been spared. It became a mantra that she repeated over and over in her brain. "Jerome..." she whispered, floating and speaking almost as though outside her own body.

"They're all gonna make it, Mrs. Wellington.... thanks to their father. He's in pretty bad shape, though; a dislocated shoulder, bad case of whiplash, a concussion, two broken ribs, and a third degree burn on his left leg from going into the blaze for the last baby. But, this little one wouldn't have made it if he hadn't. However, we still need to do some more tests on him for any signs of internal bleeding. Needs an MRI."

Antoinette walked over to each child and slowly touched their brows, kissing past the wounds as she bent to anoint them with her tears. "I have to call my parents," she choked, "and their other parents. Please, can I use you phone?"

Following the nurse's lead, Antoinette allowed herself to be guided to a telephone, and fought her mind to remember the number. "May," she whispered, then broke down. "All my babies are in the hospital...." she wailed, "Help me, Father," she cried between May's lucid requests for information. "Call Brian... tell Adrienne, Cookie... call everybody. The kids were in a car accident, and Jerome is almost dead!"

"I have Mr. Henderson's wallet here," the nurse interrupted calmly, but piercing through her hysteria by a tight grip as she spoke. "That rich S.O.B. who blew the light, and hit your husband and kids, was a damned University medical student, and he had cocaine in his system. Students! The University will try to protect him. But you didn't hear it from me—call your attorney, Mrs. Wellington," she said with fire in her blue eyes. "Pull yourself together, and make the call. Nobody's gonna die on my shift!" The nurse squeezed her arm again, as though to ensure that the information had sunk in. It was a telepathic message, sent from woman to woman.

The nurse's words dug a hole in her brain, and she squeezed the tough hands that just moments ago held her around the arms.

"First," Antoinette murmured, "I have to call his father's house... to get a number... and then, call his wife."

*

May ran at her, and swallowed her into her arms, and her father circled them both as they all exchanged a wet embrace.

"Go check on Jerome," her father whispered, "I'll be up to see that boy in a minute. I'm watchin' over my gran'babies—don'chu worry, honey..."

"We're right here," May whispered angrily. "We ain't going nowhere. Something good has to come of all this... there's no reason... My children," May broke off as a sob stole her voice, "this could have been mine, or anyone's... they're halfway around the country, and this could have been mine... Why...?"

"Go on, baby," her father whispered and pulling May into his arms. "We'll stand watch."

She kissed May's crumbled face again, and touched her father's cheek. Reluctantly, she left her children under her mother's watchful care, and moved to pass the rows of curtains that separated Jerome from their children. She stood in the doorway, and held her breath, watching him fight for air as white coats worked on his broken body.

Moving to his side, she whispered softly, "Karen is on her way, with your father and Sissey—"

"The kids... Baby, I tried!" he wept as uniformed workers pushed against his shoulder, "Lauren... Christopher—they didn't move!" he yelled hysterically. "My other one's—all bloody," he sobbed as pain contorted his face. "You trusted me with her, Toni... Dear God, you trusted me!"

His agony moved her hand to his chest. "They're all alive, baby," she whispered. "You got 'em all out alive."

The waiting room filled with family and inner circle, and as each received the story, she touched their faces and held them briefly as they wept. There were no words that she could give them... no comfort from the bottom of her well. Their solace came from silent touching as each laid their hands upon the other. Mr. Miles' old face seemed so much older. Jerome's union brethren from work breathed hard and turned away. Val dissolved into tears and held onto Tracey, then wept openly in May's arms. Cookie stood by her side, and held May's hand like a child. Her father paced like a caged animal, then accepted a hug from Cooper. Co-workers and friends spilled into the lobby in grieving waves, and she composed herself in their midst until she saw Brian's face.

The gathering receded around him, to allow

him through to Antoinette. He passed them with tears rolling down his face, scooped her up in his arms, then wept like a baby against her face, pulling at her hair and her clothes.

"We coulda lost her, Nette," he croaked. "Our baby coulda been gone because of that fool! Did you see my baby, lying under a bubble? If it wasn't for Jerome, she'd a burned like a rag doll," he sobbed as she rocked him. "I have to thank him, Nette. God was good enough to let my baby live. All this other stuff doesn't matter."

"No, it doesn't," she whispered, as her eye caught the glimpse of a shy figure who wept silently by the door. "Tell her it's okay," Antoinette murmured, motioning to Brian's girlfriend. "It ain't about us, it's about the kids. She's family now, too."

"Thanks," he said heavily, then pulled himself away. "Crystal," he motioned in the pretty woman's direction. "You can go up and see Lauren, too... Nette says it's okay."

The gathering nodded an assent in unison, as they permitted the couple to pass through. May squeezed Antoinette's hand, and petted her back as Brian's form disappeared around the corner.

"I called your sister," May said quietly. "She'll be home tonight. We'll tell Pearline in person. Even though she's sick, we'll need her prayers."

But Antoinette went still when she saw the frightened woman whom she'd called come through the door. Flanked by Jerome's father, and sister, and two girlfriends, Karen's gaze picked her out of the human sea immediately, and defied her to speak. Ignoring the tension in her massive army of family, Antoinette crossed enemy lines and spoke to the rightfully hostile parties.

"They're working on them now... He was not drunk. A medical student hit him blindside. The children will be all right. Only two of you can go up at a time."

Karen did not respond, but picked a lieutenant to follow her, leaving one angry girlfriend, a sister-in-law, and her father-in-law behind.

Walking up to Mr. Henderson senior, Matt Reeves extended his hand. "We go way back—connected by these kids, me and you. I'm only sorry to see you again, under the circumstance. But, your boy saved my granddaughter," he said quietly. "Almost lost his arm and got burned up in the process. You've got one hell of a son."

Jerome's father swallowed hard and looked down as he accepted Mr. Reeves' hand. His sister, Sissey, took one look at Antoinette, and barreled into her arms.

"Lady... I didn't know it was you... Jerome didn't tell us who he was seeing, didn't tell us it was you—family," Jerome's sister whimpered against Antoinette's hair. "Sister-in-law, what are we going to do?"

"Pray," Antoinette said quietly, emotion filling her again as Jerome's sister clung to her embrace.

"I told, Rev, and he's got everybody sending up light now, from the pews," Sissey murmured. "He said it was history repeating itself... the way you came back... said dark was trying to steal your joy."

"Your son, and your brother, worked for me," Mr. Miles chimed in, coming into the smaller circle of Hendersons holding Reeves. "Covered his friend too, when 'is friend had a heart attack. You almos' los' dat boy... Couldn't be prouder of a young man, testimony goes to da way you raised 'im, Sir."

Antoinette watched as Jerome's father lowered his eyes and turned away. Sissey, pulled herself away from the embrace, and touched her father's arm. Her eyes searched his face, and pleaded without words. "Let it go, Daddy," she whispered. "It's time to let it go. We almost lost him."

"I'ma go up an' see how he's doin'," his father said in a low, garbled voice. Turning to Mr. Reeves and Mr. Miles, he fell silent for a moment, as though afraid to ask what his heart needed to know. "My grandbabies 'live? Gonna make it?"

"Yeah," Antoinette whispered. "But, first, Sir... please go check on your son."

Jerome stared at the tall brother who sat quietly in a chair beside him and forced his mouth to speak. "Brian, man... I'm sorry... I tried to get her out as quick as I could. My arm gave out, and she went into a convulsion... the car came out of nowhere..."

His gaze riveted between Karen who hovered at the doorway, and the worried father who sat next to him. "Jerome... you saved my daughter... just.... take care of my ex-wife. From what May told me on the phone, if Nette had been with you, she would have died on impact."

"I almost made Patsy sit in that seat..." Jerome whispered, looking in his wife's direction. "Coulda lost either one of 'em, by the flip of a coin..."

"I owe you, man," Brian said quietly and stood. "Look, somebody else is waiting for you. I'm going back to see if Nette or the family needs anything. My Mom is pretty shook up. My folks'll be driving down from Connecticut in the morning. Call me, if you or Nette need anything, hear?"

"Yeah, man. Thanks. Funny how things work... never thought I'd be shaking your hand."

Brian chuckled and threw his coat over his arm and looked at Karen, then at Jerome. "Kinda puts everything in perspective—doesn't it? Wonder what Pearline would say about this?"

"She'd have a parable for it, I'm sure," Jerome chuckled through a cough. "Thanks, man... for lettin' me share your little girl's, life," he said becoming serious. "I'm not trying to take your place... just to fill in some of the gaps. You'll always be her Daddy, and from what Toni tells me, you're a pretty good one, too, brother. I'll try my best to be good to her, too," he added, and then looked at Karen, "just like she is to ours."

"Antoinette said that about me?" Brian whispered, stopping his retreat to the door and staring at Jerome hard for a second before looking away.

"Yeah, man. She only speaks well of you, and defends your name in front of people, too. 'Specially in front of Lauren. Said you were her friend."

"I am," Brian murmured through a thick swallow, then moved away again. "She was my best friend."

He watched Karen's expression as Brian disappeared through the door. She took her time to find a place to position herself in the room near his bed. There was no tension in her pace, just a methodical movement that contained deep thought and certain fatigue—perhaps it was resignation.

She said nothing immediately, but her stricken expression told him that the war was over. It was in the way she simply laid her hand on his chest, then closed her eyes as the tears fell.

"I know," he murmured, as his father's form filled the door. "I love you too, and I'm sorry, baby... for all of it."

She nodded and withdrew her hand, clutching her purse to her stomach as though for support. "I'll check on the kids," she whispered. "Then Lauren. Hope that little girl will be all right, too. Take care of yourself, Jay. I'ma leave the signed papers with your sister. I'm sorry."

Heaviness filled his chest as he watched the last vestige of his old life peel away with Karen's exit from the room. Part of his soul wanted to run behind her and hug her, the other half of him knew that it was time to let her go. Jerome's father allowed his gaze to rove over his bandage's, then suddenly, the old man sat down heavily beside him, drew a deep breath, and wept quietly in his hands. He could only console the one who'd given him life with a silent prayer for peace, and tell the reborn truth on an exhausted whisper that he murmured from his whole heart for them both to hear.

"I love you, Dad. All the past is forgiven, and forgotten. All that matters is, we were given a gift. The future. We're alive. It'll be all right."

Epilogue

New Years Eve.... Almost One Year Later

"Renaissance House is rockin' tonight! Where is Mrs. Henderson?" Jerome yelled as he pushed through the crowded establishment with a magnum of champagne over his head. "Hey Joey, A—you seen my wife?"

"No, bro," Joey laughed, brushing Adrienne's mouth with a kiss, "try downstairs, or hail her on the intercoms. That's why we put 'em in for you."

"Tol' ya to read da directions, man," Julio laughed and slapped Jerome on the back as he refilled his wife's glass. "Hey, Mama, dis guy is more stubborn dan me!"

"See how your son treats me, Mrs. Gonzales," Jerome laughed as he passed the elderly woman's table and filled her glass with champagne, then kissed her cheek. "And, he's supposed to be my homeboy. My tight. Forget c'hall," he laughed, looking in his partners' direction and waving away Julio and Joey's protests with his hand.

"Give me and Wendell some of that too, would you, Rome?" Cookie laughed as she raised her empty glass in Jerome's direction. "Last time I saw her, she was on the phone to North Carolina with Inez, giving her some advice about how to push up her due date. I told Toni that Inez was gonna have that baby when she was ready! Even her Rev couldn't pray it out."

"Then, maybe we need two ministers on the case for Inez," his sister chuckled, squeezing her husband's hand across their table.

"Don't get her started, Rev. Y'all know my wife," Jerome laughed as a wave of kids rushed up the steps, "Go find your mother," he yelled behind them over the din of seventies music. "Tell her it's almost midnight, and y'all come down here, too! Family's got to ring-in the New Year together, for good luck."

"Yo, man!" Julio hollered through the throng as another gang of multi-aged children ran between the Maitre D's podium and Jerome. "Coop! Thought you and Trace would be stuck in the house with all them kids," he laughed.

"You know we would, if we couldn't bring 'em here. Mom Johnson went to Aruba—can you get to that? Said she'd paid her babysittin' dues, and we can't blame her," Officer Cooper chuckled. "Hey, man," he yelled, slapping Jerome five as he handed him a bottle. "Got this for you, and this for Antoinette."

Tracey's new boyfriend produced a puppy from under his jacket, and handed the squirming infant animal over to Jerome as the men around the nearby table doubled over with laughter.

"Toni's gonna kill you, Cooper! Buddy, tell that fool she ain't goin' for no dog messin' up her hardwoods," Julio roared. "A damned Rot puppy—what possessed you, man? Tell me? Did Tracey put you up to this?"

"Oh, hell no!" Buddy roared, shaking his head and taking a deep swig of his sparkling apple cider. "Nope. No way, not today."

"T, ain't going for no dog, Coop," Jerome chuckled, trying to give back the dog to his friend.

"She's been in my business from day one, Reds," Cooper laughed, "called me, Tracey's Rotweiler, so, this is a joke she will definitely understand."

"She ain't gonna understand something that'll eventually eat fifty pounds of dog food a week. Val, our girl is gonna flip," Cookie whooped, "Toni! They plottin' on you, gurrrrl!"

"Give it back, Jay," Valerie laughed as she took a sip of champagne. "Give that fool his dog back, and stay out of trouble with my girl. And, I don't want my kids gettin' any funny ideas, either. A dog? Pulleeeese!" Standing and pacing towards the stairs, Val laughed and yelled up the steps, "Whatever the question is, y'all, the answer is no!"

"If you wanna find your wife, Jay," Adrienne chuckled, "give the kids the puppy, then listen for her scream." She turned toward two of Antoinette's former co-workers, searching their faces for support. "Iola, Dar, would you kill the man, or what?"

Antoinette's cousin, Vanessa, threw her head back with laughter, as Patti giggled into her hands.

"My cousin ain't goin' for it, Jay, and I'ma send my teenagers over to your house to play with it! Ain't no dog comin' in my house. I'm almost done with anything that eats and poops and messes up furniture!"

"I heard that!" Patti giggled, wiping her eyes, "You are in big trouble, boy."

"Yup, ain't no lie," Dar laughed, slapping five with the others at her table. "You're in troooouble! How you gonna have a dog in her gourmet soul-food kitchen, or scaring people when they order their specialty teas?"

"Or barking when a serious poet gets up on stage—or, worse, when that little, bitty, thing transforms into a wolf and starts howling at the moon?" Adrienne nearly screamed with laughter.

"All I know is," Antoinette's student intern, Tianisha, roared, "it better stay out of Miz Toni and Darelette's kitchen. Y'all, Miz Toni's gonna have a bird! I'm going to tell the rest of the girls workin' this shift to take cover," she giggled and flounced out of the room down the hall. "Miss Tooooonaaaay! Fayletta.... Rashina... Jerome done lost his mind! Kishaaaaa!"

Hitting the intercom, Jerome laughed hard and called the children down. When they all assembled in a thunderous procession, he handed over the dog amid shrieks and high-pitched squeals of ecstasy.

"Ooooh, a puppy!" they cried out in unison. "Can we keep it?"

"Yeah, Dad!"

"This is so cool," Patsy blared, then ran away leading the pack of innumerable children, "I'ma ask Mom T."

"Go find your Mom," he yelled behind them, "ask her can you keep it. Tell her Uncle Cooper was the one who brought it—not me."

Jerome covered his head as Adrienne and May pelted him with balled up napkins amid whoops and jeers from his male compatriots.

"See how you do my sister, boy! Ooooh, I'ma

tell her," Adrienne laughed, "I'm gonna dime you out—good! Joey," she giggled, turning to her escort, "see how yall do!"

"I'm not in it," her guest chuckled, "But, it is the man's house, so—"

"—Matt, Mr. Miles, tell this fool he done lost his mind!" May shrieked as she doubled over with the giggles. "A dog, Jerome? Lord, have mercy!"

"My name's Bennet, and I ain't in it," Mr. Miles laughed, and clinked a tumbler with Matt Reeves, and Mr. Henderson senior.

"See, my son-in-law done los' his nat'ral mind. Toni's got a temper like a fire-cracker. Wait til she see that dog peeing and pooping on these floors."

A loud scream from the kitchen brought another gale of riotous laughter to the dining rooms. Ducking for cover, Jerome ran past wide-eyed patrons who joined in the fun by giving him little slaps on the back as he dodged Toni's slaps between the tables.

"Save me," he laughed as he darted through the room. "Don't let her get me! It's just a baby dog. Where's your religion, woman?"

"No-I-don't-care-what-y'all-say—NO!" she laughed, trying to whack Jerome with a spoon as she ignored the crowd, and tucked the frightened puppy more securely under her arm.

"C'mon, Mom," a chorus of voices exploded

behind her.

"Call him Beethoven," Lauren squealed as the children joined the fray. "Pleeeaaase."

"Who brought it in here?" Antoinette laughed, as she set upon Cooper, who stood and ran away with Jerome. "I'ma get you too, Cooper! I was trying to put more black eye peas on, send up a prayer to Pearline and Francis before the clock struck, and y'all come in my kitchen with a dog? I'm putting everybody out, and callin' Licenses and Inspections!" she laughed becoming winded and falling into Jerome's arms with giggles.

"Hurry up woman, and kiss me quick—before you forget how much you love me!" Jerome teased, pulling her svelte form against him hard to nuzzle her neck while petting the whimpering pup. "Aw... he's just a little guy. Look at him, T," he persisted, taking the puppy away from her as the children all ran to his side. "Here, y'all take this dog upstairs and find him a box—put some newspaper in it. He's a nice dog."

Giving Antoinette a wink and chuckling as she scowled then laughed, he picked up the house-phone near the podium when it rang. But, from his peripheral vision he noticed that all the children, except Patsy, had run up the stairs. She waited and fidgeted and lowered her eyes. He became suspicious.

All his mirth dissipated as a young male voice connected to his senses, and a strange phobia descended upon him. Yet, oddly, Antoinette wrapped her arms around her waist, and waited with an expectant grin that he'd come to learn meant trouble.

"Do you know what time it is, boy?" Jerome bellowed, which only seemed to make the crowd laugh harder.

"It's your turn now, son. Leave that contender for the throne be," Mr. Reeves yelled across the room with a laugh. "I'ma love watchin' this!"

"Tol' dat boy, it ain't as easy as it looks," Henderson senior chuckled. "Now, he'll see."

"Gimme the phone, Jerome" Antoinette giggled, as she motioned for Pasty who appeared from behind a cove looking mortified. "Take this up in your room, and don't stay on too long, hear?"

"What?" Jerome looked at Antoinette as though she'd lost her mind when his oldest daughter bolted up the steps, taking them by threes.

"Guess we do need a Rot now... and we can take this discussion to the pillow— later," Antoinette murmured with triumph as the crowd erupted again. "He's such a nice boy. I always liked him."

"Oh, no," Jerome groaned, then chuckled reluctantly. "Kiss me quick, woman, before I forget how much I love you."

"Ease up on Patsy, and I'll make sure you remember," she whispered in his ear and warming him considerably, "Just like old times..."

INDIGO

Winter & Spring 2002

June

Still Waters Run Deep	*Leslie Esdaile*	*$9.95*
Indigo After Dark Vol. V		*$14.95*
Ebony Butterfly	*Delilah Dawson*	

OTHER INDIGO TITLES

A Dangerous Deception	*J.M. Jeffries*	*$8.*
A Dangerous Love	*J.M. Jeffries*	*$8.*
After The Vows (Summer Anthology)	*Leslie Esdaile*	*$10.*
	T.T. Henderson	
	Jacquelin Thomas	
Again My Love	*Kayla Perrin*	*$10.*
A Lighter Shade of Brown	*Vicki Andrews*	*$8.*
All I Ask	*Barbara Keaton*	*$8.*
A Love to Cherish	*Beverly Clark*	*$8.*
Ambrosia	*T.T. Henderson*	*$8.*
And Then Came You	*Dorothy Love*	*$8.*
Best of Friends	*Natalie Dunbar*	*$8.*
Bound by Love	*Beverly Clark*	*$8*
Breeze	*Robin Hampton*	*$10*

Cajun Heat	*Charlene Berry*	**$8.95**
Careless Whispers	*Rochelle Alers*	**$8.95**
Caught in a Trap	*Andree Michele*	**$8.95**
Chances	*Pamela Leigh Starr*	**$8.95**
Dark Embrace	*Crystal Wilson Harris*	**$8.95**
Dark Storm Rising	*Chinelu Moore*	**$10.95**
Eve's Prescription	*Edwinna Martin Arnold*	**$8.95**
Everlastin' Love	*Gay G. Gunn*	**$8.95**
Gentle Yearning	*Rochelle Alers*	**$10.95**
Glory of Love	*Sinclair LeBeau*	**$10.95**
Illusions	*Pamela Leigh Starr*	**$8.95**
Indiscretions	*Donna Hill*	**$8.95**
Interlude	*Donna Hill*	**$8.95**
Intimate Intentions	*Angie Daniels*	**$8.95**
Kiss or Keep	*Debra Phillips*	**$8.95**
Love Always	*Mildred E. Riley*	**$10.95**
Love Unveiled	*Gloria Green*	**$10.95**
Love's Deception	*Charlene Berry*	**$10.95**
Mae's Promise	*Melody Walcott*	**$8.95**
Midnight Clear (Anthology)	*Leslie Esdaile*	**$10.95**
	Gwynne Forster	
	Carmen Green	
	Monica Jackson	
Midnight Magic	*Gwynne Forster*	**$8.95**
Midnight Peril	*Vicki Andrews*	**$10.95**
Naked Soul	*Gwynne Forster*	**$8.95**
No Regrets	*Mildred E. Riley*	**$8.95**
Nowhere to Run	*Gay G. Gunn*	**$10.95**
assion	*T.T. Henderson*	**$10.95**

Love Spectrum Romance

Romance across the culture lines

Forbidden Quest	Dar Tomlinson	$10.95
Designer Passion	Dar Tomlinson	$8.95
Fate	Pamela Leigh Starr	$8.95
Against the Wind	Gwynne Forster	$8.95
From The Ashes	Kathleen Suzanne Jeanne Summerix	$8.95
Heartbeat	Stephanie Bedwell-Grime	$8.95
My Buffalo Soldier	Barbara B. K. Reeves	$8.95
Meant to Be	Jeanne Sumerix	$8.95
A Risk of Rain	Dar Tomlinson	$8.95

Indigo After Dark

erotica beyond sensuous

Indigo After Dark Vol. I		$10.95
In Between the Night	Angelique	
Midnight Erotic Fantasies	Nia Dixon	
Indigo After Dark Vol. II		$10.95
The Forbidden Art of Desire	Cole Riley	
Erotic Short Stories	Dolores Bundy	
Indigo After Dark Vol. III		$10.95
Impulse	Montana Blue	
Pant	Coco Morena	

ORDER FORM

Mail to: Genesis Press, Inc.
315 3rd Avenue North
Columbus, MS 39701

Name ____

Address ____

City/State _______________________ Zip ______________________

Telephone ____

Ship to (if different from above)

Name ____

Address ____

City/State _______________________ Zip ______________________

Telephone ____

Qty	Author	Title	Price	Total

Use this order form, or call
1-888-INDIGO-1

Total for books ____________________
Shipping and handling:
$3 first book, $1 each additional book ____________________
Total S & H ____________________
Total amount enclosed ____________________
MS residents add 7% sales tax

ORDER FORM

Mail to: Genesis Press, Inc.
315 3rd Avenue North
Columbus, MS 39701

Name ______________________________

Address ______________________________

City/State ______________ Zip ______________

Telephone ______________________________

Ship to (if different from above)

Name ______________________________

Address ______________________________

City/State ______________ Zip ______________

Telephone ______________________________

Qty	Author	Title	Price	Total

Use this order form, or call
1-888-INDIGO-1

Total for books ______________
Shipping and handling:
$3 first book, $1 each additional book ______________
Total S & H ______________
Total amount enclosed ______________
MS residents add 7% sales tax

Visit www.genesis-press.com for latest releases and excerpts from upcoming Indigo stories.

ORDER FORM

Mail to: Genesis Press, Inc.
315 3rd Avenue North
Columbus, MS 39701

Name ____________________

Address ____________________

City/State ____________ Zip ____________

Telephone ____________________

Ship to (if different from above)

Name ____________________

Address ____________________

City/State ____________ Zip ____________

Telephone ____________________

Qty	Author	Title	Price	Total

Use this order form, or
call
1-888-INDIGO-1

ORDER FORM

Mail to: Genesis Press, Inc.
315 3rd Avenue North
Columbus, MS 39701

Name ______________________________

Address ______________________________

City/State ______________ Zip ______________

Telephone ______________________________

Ship to (if different from above)

Name ______________________________

Address ______________________________

City/State ______________ Zip ______________

Telephone ______________________________

Qty	Author	Title	Price	Total

Use this order form, or call 1-888-INDIGO-1

Total for books ______________

Shipping and handling:
$3 first book, $1 each additional book ______________

Total S & H ______________

Total amount enclosed ______________

MS residents add 7% sales tax

Visit www.genesis-press.com for latest releases and excerpts from upcoming Indigo stories.